ALL
FOR
LOVE

Also by Pat Booth

PAT BOOTH

ALL FOR LOVE

CROWN PUBLISHERS, INC., NEW YORK

Published by Crown Publishers, Inc., 201 East 50th Street,
New York, New York 10022. Member of the Crown Publishing
Group.

Random House, Inc. New York, Toronto, London, Sydney,
Auckland

CROWN is a trademark of Crown Publishers, Inc.

Manufactured in the United States of America

Library of Congress Cataloging-in-Publication Data

Booth, Pat.
    All for love / Pat Booth. — 1st ed.
        p.   cm.
        I. Title.
    PS3552.O646L68   1993
    813'.54—dc20   93-9890
                                        CIP

ISBN 0-517-58416-6

10 9 8 7 6 5 4 3 2 1

First Edition

For Betty A. Prashker and Garth Wood—with love.

"Although I had grown more accustomed to the unexpected by that time, I was still very surprised when I wrote, 'This is a course in miracles . . .' That was my introduction to the Voice. It made no sound, but seemed to be giving me a kind of rapid, inner dictation which I took down in a shorthand notebook. The writing was never automatic. It could be interrupted at any time and later picked up again. It made me very uncomfortable, but it never occurred to me to stop. It seemed to be a special assignment I had somehow, somewhere agreed to complete."

—Dr. Helen Shucman, professor of medical psychology, Columbia University, College of Physicians and Surgeons, New York City.

A Course in Miracles was first published in June 1976. It has sold more than a million copies.

ALL
FOR
LOVE

1

SHE MET him on a plane. Tari was window and she saw him first. The Miami-bound flight out of New York was late, and she was tired, but there was still the excitement of wondering who would sit next to her. The second she saw him she knew he would be a prize. Then he saw her, too. Their eyes locked, left, locked again. Both were thinking the same thought. Tari looked down, but her lap was unremarkable. The stranger peered at the plastic ceiling, but seemed to discover no great secrets there. He moved forward, looking at his boarding card. It would be close, thought Tari. So near yet so far, perhaps, a looking but not a speaking seat. Again their eyes met, as he waited patiently. The woman in front was taking her time with the overhead storage.

Tari glanced at the two empty seats next to her. Her magazine was on one of them. She picked it up as she might a banana skin on a road, and stuck it in the pocket in front of her. Chance needed all the help it could get, even though she knew that the seat allocation was already history. He had arrived. He looked up at the number. He looked down at her.

"Hi," he said.

"Hello." Her tone was purposefully casual. She was denying what they both knew. But she smiled as she spoke.

"This is mine," he said, dropping a bag into the aisle seat. He stood half in and half out of the walkway. Four eyes stared balefully at the vacant center seat as if it were an accident waiting to happen.

Having laid claim to his seat, he now set about owning it. He swung his bag into the overhead and sat down. His shoulders shifted in the loose leather jacket. Tari watched him out of the corner of her eye. He was dark like a Brando biker, with slicked-back hair and a craggy, vaguely familiar face that bent the word attractive to the breaking point. His nose was simply broken—no other way to describe it—and his brown eyes were big and inquisitive. They moved fast for their size, like a couple of quick boxers round a small ring. He looked as if he ought to be dirty, but Tari could see that in fact he was scrupulously clean. His long fingers and nails hardly would have needed gloves in an operating theater.

He turned toward her.

"I hope this seat stays empty," he said.

She hoped so too, but didn't say so.

"It's a pretty full flight," she said.

"But not a long one." He managed to make that sound disappointing. They lapsed into silence. Contact had been made, but not commitment. When the shoe salesman from Nebraska separated them with 200 pounds of blubber, the regrets could be kept to a minimum. But he looked while he could. The girl was fascinating. No model agency would have taken her on, because somehow looks were not her point, although she *was* beautiful. He tried to put it together. Her hair was mouse brown, cut in a bob. It surrounded a sharply intelligent face that was, at the same time, ethereal, radiating a serenity that was at war with the sensuality of a huge but perfectly shaped mouth. Her body was only half-visible. Long-ish legs raced away under the seat in front, covered by clinging blue jeans. Her upper part was tented beneath an outsize sweater. A blue denim jacket lay in her lap.

She was watching the passengers. They were still boarding,

but the aisle was thinning out. Who would be the unwelcome filling for the sandwich? One by one they threatened the empty seat, consulting boarding cards, scanning seat numbers anxiously. Some were playing the same game that Tari and the stranger had played, hope merging into despair as promising moments came and went. Others just wanted to find a seat, any seat, as the irrational fear of rejection hovered around the edges of their travel paranoia.

Suddenly, the aisle was empty. It was over. They were alone on the crowded plane.

"That was lucky," he said. His voice was deep, his tone confident. He didn't mind this at all. There was no hint of a come-on, but of course it was one. It was in the telling, the body language, both. Some men could talk to women they didn't know. Others couldn't. It was one of the many vital things they didn't teach you in school.

"I'm Tarleton," said Tari. "Tarleton Jones. Friends call me Tari." she added. She put out her hand to him, taking control. She was always an equal, often more, never less. He took it, surprised by her response but not unsettled by it. His grip was firm, but appropriate. "Neat name," he said.

"I chose it myself," she replied. Her jaw set slightly. "I felt I was allowed to, because I'm adopted."

His eyes widened. He hadn't meant to pry into her life. Now he knew perhaps the most intimate and important fact about this girl. But that was cool. He dealt in deep ends. So, apparently, did she.

"I'm Rickey . . ."

The flight attendant interrupted him. "Oh, Mr. Cage, I'm sorry . . ." she gushed as she approached. She knelt down beside him, a brown hand on his armrest, a full breast not far away. "The captain is going to come back later and apologize himself, but in the meantime he asked me to say how very sorry we all are, and of course there'll be a free round-trip ticket to anywhere we fly . . ."

The flight attendant's eyes were open wide. Her face was equal parts feigned sorrow and barely disguised lust.

"Do me a favor, will you, and tell the captain to stay behind the wheel while he's driving this thing." Rickey Cage smiled a lazy smile as he spoke, but there was a cutting edge to his words. The message was unmistakable. *Can the bullshit. The damage is done.* The flight attendant heard him. She stood up, smoothing her skirt, and there was a tiny flush of rejection high on her cheeks. "Well, anyway, if there's anything we can get you, anything at all, you just let us know, Mr. Cage. I'm a great fan, we all are . . ." He raised his hand for her silence, and got it.

He turned to Tari.

"Can she get you anything?" he said.

"An autograph book?" Tari laughed as she spoke. Rickey Cage! It was almost unbelievable that she hadn't recognized him. Like her, he had been born in New York. Then he'd moved to Hollywood and hit it big in the movies. Tari had followed his meteoric rise to fame, and she was aware of his extracurricular activities, too. He liked to take tip-top cover girls on search-and-destroy missions to the hot clubs on the Strip, like Bar One and Roxbury. He liked to ride Harleys, and to flatten photographers in the small hours of the morning. He'd been a fighter before becoming an actor, which was how he'd got the famous nose, and he moved between the gilded tables of haute cafe society and the scuz of the dirty boulevard with chameleonlike poise. Now she'd drawn him in a flight lottery. That was a good one from God. Tari smiled. She wasn't the kind of person to be impressed by any old movie star. In fact, she believed that acting wasn't really a proper job for a grown-up, but Rickey Cage was motoring. He was an original, and he always had been. The only difference was that the world had finally woken up to the fact. But why the hell was he sitting in coach?

The flight attendant withdrew amid the confusion caused by the subtle Cage rebuke.

"They bumped you from first class?" said Tari.

"But I made a soft landing," drawled Rickey. He half-turned toward her so that she could see him head-on, and his eyes drilled into her. His mouth was softening at the corners but still hard as nails in the middle. God, he was attractive. God, did he know it.

"I'd have thought they'd have found somebody else to

bump," said Tari, ignoring his "soft landing" come-on. She smiled so that her words wouldn't be too discouraging.

"Nah, it happens all the time. Some jerk with ego problems has a girlfriend who doesn't know illusion from reality, and he zaps me to get even. It's no big deal. I wasn't born first-class."

"I guess it's nice to get a free round-trip ticket," said Tari.

"From what I hear, the shitty airline won't be around long enough to honor it."

A silence descended. Across the aisle a mother and daughter had slipped into famous-person-recognition mode. There was whispering, a giggle, hands hovered over mouths.

Tari looked out of the window. The plane was taxiing toward takeoff. She checked her seat belt, and double-checked her emotions. She had a couple of hours alone with Rickey Cage. The stranger on her plane was the most interesting, raunchiest, happening movie star in the country, and already the guy was making the moves he was supposed to make.

"Cabin crew, take your seats for takeoff."

The plane was poised like a phallic rocket for blast-off into the unknown. Tari could feel the floor vibrating beneath her feet as the engines roared. She stole a look at him. He was stretched out, eyes closed, but his hands were relaxed on the armrests. Fear of flying was apparently not a Cage problem. What would be? All those kamikaze girls? The fights the *Enquirer* wrote about? Booze, pills, worse? He hadn't shown any downside yet. He had been old-world courteous to her, and he had paid Tari the ultimate compliment of putting down an attractive and obviously interested woman in her presence. And then there had been the moment when their eyes had first met, long before his fame had complicated the equation. The thought occurred to Tari quite suddenly. It was nearly ten o'clock. At some stage before landing in Miami, she and Rickey Cage might well be sleeping within inches of each other. As the plane thrust forward, and her body shook with the energy of the engines, Tarleton Jones was rather looking forward to that.

The plane pushed into the sky. The engines lost their manic roar.

"What takes you to Miami?" As he spoke, Rickey opened his eyes as if it were a slow dawn, lazily, almost sleepily. He turned his head toward Tari, stretching as he did so. He seemed deeply relaxed, not a care in the world . . . except, just possibly, her.

Tari took a "long story" breath. There were so many reasons, and some of them she was still trying to understand. Her move to Miami would, with hindsight, be forced to "make sense" in the way that all things were in life. Right now it was safer to keep it simple.

"I'm going there to live. I've been down on and off for a couple of months. New York tidying up is just about over."

"Where in Miami?"

"South Beach. I've got an apartment on the Intracoastal. Do you know about South Beach?"

"Yeah, I know about South Beach. In fact I've just invested in a club there. On Fourteenth Street. I've rented a place on South Pointe. I'm doing the same as you."

He smiled. He had paid her a subtle compliment. He was copying her—not the other way around.

"But when you're in the movies, don't you have to be in Hollywood?"

"Not anymore. I gotta fax and a telephone number. I've even got an agent, but I'm not taking his calls right now."

He was cocky, but it was part of his act. He was poking fun at his own self-confidence. It came out as playful and charming. He might have a big head, but carefully selected people would be allowed to kick it about like a football. Tari was flattered to feel that she was already one of those.

She tried to visualize Fourteenth Street. She vaguely remembered a boarded-up storefront next to the launderette. Would that be the Cage club?

"What sort of a club is it going to be?" Even as she asked the question, Tari realized that what she wanted to know more about was not his club, but Rickey Cage. But the one would help illuminate the other.

"Sort of minimalistic . . . a spit-on-the-floor place where the food wins no prizes but doesn't cheat you. Pool, loud music, a hangout bar for bikers, geriatrics, drunks, billionaire designers, and the sort of losers Lou Reed sings about."

She laughed. "And you behind the bar? That should keep the place full."

"Me under it."

"I'm beginning to understand how you get your press."

He didn't like that very much. She could see the cloud scud across his face.

"It's not PR." He turned to face her fully. His eyes were serious. "I want to do some living. Hang out. Relax."

"Well, South Beach is the place to get down. It's amazing the difference in attitude from New York. People are loose, polite, nonjudgmental. Nobody's that desperate to get anything together. It's living for the moment, not worrying. I guess that's one of the reasons I'm going there—and the weather, and the brightness. I'm fed up with being cold and gray!"

"What do you do that you can just get up and go? You an heiress, or something?"

Tari laughed. "I wish! No, I was doing a business administration degree at New York University and working part-time as a waitress in a Wall Street bar. The customers used to tell me what to buy and I bought some stock options. I made some money, not much, but enough to buy a small apartment. I was turning into a neat little capitalist, and then I sort of looked at what I was becoming, and didn't like it."

"A Reagan materialist in the kinder, gentler America."

His smile wasn't mocking. He liked her. She could see that. He was intrigued by the way she thought, about the deeper things, the things that should mean something, but seldom did.

"Yeah, in a way . . . that was the future . . . the grabbing, grasping thing. Forever scrambling up the ladder with your foot in the face of the guy or girl below. Where's the payoff in that? Their animosity? Your nastiness? Every time I won something on the calls and the puts I kept thinking about the fact that there was someone out there who lost . . . maybe his son's college tuition, his wife's operation, the car he needed to get to work. What good did I do? Made the market more efficient? Oiled the wheels of capitalism? Punished inefficiency and rewarded success? I couldn't get to believing all that. I bought an apartment, and I've just dropped thirty percent on the resale, which pisses me off. So, frankly, fuck capitalism."

"So what are you doing now?"

"I got a place in med school. I had all the right science scores, and I'd done pretty well in the business program, so I transferred."

"But how can you move to Miami?"

"You can swap schools halfway through the course. I get credited for the rotations I've done already in New York. I just start up again at the Florida State Medical College, and in a couple of years I'm an M.D. I got on real well with the dean in New York and he was friends with the guy at the med school down there. So that was that."

For a while he was silent, digesting the information.

"Jesus," he said at last, his smile merging with an expression of feigned disgust. "I run a mile when I see a sick person."

"You'd have enjoyed the year cutting up corpses." She laughed to show she wasn't shocked by his up-front attitude toward the sick. Cage had a tough-guy image to maintain. It was money in his bank. But his remark hinted that he was trying to impress her.

He threw up his hands in mock horror.

"How do you *do* that? How do people allow their bodies to be used for that stuff?"

"Oh, they leave their bodies to medical research thinking that they'll be used to discover a cure for cancer or something. Then they get chopped up by students who steal their fingers to play gruesome tricks on each other in the dorm."

"You're putting me on." Rickey was looking at her in a different way. She wasn't fazed by him. She was totally natural.

"Well, *I* don't do that! They're not really like you'd imagine dead bodies. I mean ... they're all brown and gray and impersonal. On the operating table, when they're alive, they're sort of bright colors, more like real people. The worst part is the formaldehyde they stick into the vascular system as a preservative. It makes my eyes run, and it's real greasy when you're dissecting."

He laughed. She was funny. Completely open. Totally real. Ninety-nine out of a hundred girls would have started right in on *his* career. "I loved your movie," or "I loathed it." "What's Jodie Summerfield *really* like?" "Gee, my girlfriend isn't going to *believe* I sat next to Rickey Cage on a plane." In return he would then have to *be* "Rickey Cage." With this girl there was the tantalizing, and also marginally unsettling, possibility that he could be himself.

"What sort of a doctor are you planning to be?"

"A pediatrician or a shrink. I haven't decided yet. Kids or crazies, anyway."

"You should be in L.A., not Miami. Everyone's crazy in L.A. Everyone's a kid."

"Is that why you're moving to Miami . . . to get away from the crazy kids?"

"Yeah, from all those furious, self-obsessed people. From the 'star' thing." He laughed contemptuously.

"Don't you just hate that word 'star'?" He ran his hands up and down his body in a gesture of contempt. "I mean this . . . is a star? People forget what real stars are—great lumps of rock, hurtling through space and going nowhere fast. The best that a genuine star can hope for is to vanish up its own black hole in a cloud of cosmic shit."

He smiled at her out of the corner of his eyes, to take some of the bitterness out of his tone.

Tari laughed out loud. "That's funny."

"Oh, yeah, I do comedy, too."

The "too" was a veiled reference to the other things Rickey Cage did, the ones he was well-known for. He half-turned to watch her reaction.

She watched him watch her. He was so incredibly relaxed. That in itself was charming. He lay back in the seat as if it had been made for him, and he was talking to her as if he had known her for years, not minutes. Was that what people paid for at the box office? Or was the bad-boy image the vital ingredient in the mix? Perhaps it was both, a filling of danger sandwiched between twin layers of charm. She liked him a lot, that instant liking that happened in books more often than in life. It was a gut thing, the melding of auras, the conversation in body language, the secret harmony in the thousands of subterranean messages that people exchanged. He was easier than hell to like, and she knew that he would not be hard to love . . . a love that could only be sweet pain. She smiled inside as she realized just how far she had to go in her analysis of Mr. Richard Cage, antistar, midnight tabloid rambler, and dinner companion at twenty thousand feet over the Carolinas.

For a second or two they were silent. It was a "who-goes-first" moment. She sensed he wanted to move to the next stage, where casual repartee merged with more serious getting to know you. She had been here before with men, actually with boys. Part of her wanted a shortcut to intimacy, another part a more sedate and careful exploration. But speed was of the essence. Two hours and change could waste fast, and yet she didn't lead, sensing that he might be uncomfortable with that. He would have to be allowed his maleness, this one. It was a part of him she liked. And yet she knew that the caveman exterior was, if not an act, then at least a kind of a cul-de-sac in the understanding of Rickey Cage. He looked mondo macho, but he liked women, loved them really. She could see it shining in his eyes.

"What's it like, being adopted?" he said at last. "I mean . . . like is it a big deal?"

Their thoughts had been in parallel. Adoption was heavy-duty emotional intercourse. She would have to let her inside out. He wanted that. And she was pleased he did.

"It sort of is and isn't." She cocked her head to one side as she wrestled with her age-old question. "I mean, sometimes I think it's just an intellectual problem. You know, my real parents, the ones I know, are alive and well and living in Queens. Then, out there, somewhere, are the ones with all the genetic information, and maybe they ought to be tracked down and debriefed so that I can feed the information into my brain and use it in living my life. I mean, did they have diabetes, were they tall, were they short, fat? Those things are like a *neatness* problem. You know, it's untidy not to know that stuff. Then, other times, I feel it's really an emotional problem about all sorts of terrifying irrational things like why was I so unlovable that I got dumped, what sort of emotional cripples would get rid of their babies, and do those traits get passed on, too. It's mostly about Mother, I guess. I want to meet her so I can give her a hard time, and to see if she *looks* like me, that's maybe the strongest and silliest thing I want. I guess, overall, the thing is that I sort of feel adoption *ought* to be a problem. I'd be pretty strange if I genuinely had no interest in finding my 'real' parents . . . wouldn't I? Maybe not."

"Sounds like it's 'unfinished business.' "

She laughed. "That's *exactly* what it is. Did I say that? I must

have. It's unfinished business that you don't know how important it is. Probably it should be left unfinished, but the
obsessional bit inside keeps picking away at it until you feel
that the line of least resistance is to get it out of the way. Maybe
if I found my real parents I could just forget them, but I don't
think so, somehow, do you?''

"Forgetting parents, real or otherwise, is a trick not many
manage," said Rickey with a short laugh. "I've tried hard
enough."

It was the window of opportunity into him. He'd opened it
on purpose.

"Unhappy childhood?" She dove happily into the gloom.
She had just done adoption, and it had felt like a million
dollars as his tough-guy face had softened in sympathy. He had
leaned in closer to her physical private space as he had roamed
freely in her spiritual one. Now they would "do" his childhood,
and she would empathize and they would touch at far deeper
levels than flesh. Did the light in his eye suggest he recognized
that, too? Were words ever what they pretended to be?

"Unhappy is middle-class kids left with a baby-sitter and
getting fobbed off with toys and cable TV. Mine was more . . .
like torment, I mean getting pushed around, booze everywhere, nothing to eat 'cept crap, and always too hot, too cold,
an' lice an' fleas and roaches that were a helluva lot nicer than
the people."

He shifted in his seat as if the creepy-crawlies were still on his
skin when really they were beneath it. His face twisted in a
discomfort that said he'd painted a rosy picture of his childhood.

"Your father drank, and beat you?"

"I guess somebody had to do it." Rickey laughed, finding
the tough tone with difficulty. Then he let it slip. "Yes, he beat
me and you know what, he used to laugh when he did it. Like
it was some sort of a grown-ups' joke. That hurt most of all. I
can still hear the sound of that laughter. I mean, if he'd been
mad at me because of the drink, or just been plain mean,
somehow it could have mattered less, but . . . but . . . he beat up
on me and it was like a . . . the funniest thing . . . I mean . . . I
mean . . .''

Tari touched him. She reached out and she touched his

hand. He didn't withdraw it, but he clenched it hard and her fingers rested on his tense knuckles.

"That's the cruelest thing I've ever heard."

The pressure of her fingers on his hand said the rest.

He smiled the lazy gunfighter smile, but tears were glistening in his eyes. Whatever happened at high noon, in the quiet night this one would know how to cry.

"But you know, the thing about jokes is they can backfire," he said suddenly. "One thing I learned from my old man is that sometimes the nastiest sound in the whole world is laughter. One thing he learned from me is that the hardest thing of all is to swallow your own teeth."

She didn't reply, but her mind was full of what would have been Rickey Cage's revenge. He'd been a boxer. He reeked of danger. The fights were folklore. One humid afternoon as a drunken father Cage poured himself out of the Tic Toc Saloon and headed home to laugh while he tortured his son, he would have overlooked one fact. That his child had become a man. What would Rickey have used? His fists? A baseball bat? A dirty hammer from his father's workbox? Tari shuddered at the thought of the terrible justice, and at the wickedness that had caused it.

"You left home after that?"

"Yeah, I left home. Went to Hollywood. Hustled, bustled, and here I am, bumped from first class an' with a consolation prize that makes it better than worthwhile."

It was over, their brief encounter with each other's dark places. They were back in the real world of banter and small talk. But they were no longer strangers. As if to emphasize the change, there was a distraction.

The flight attendant, without her cart, was hovering in the aisle. As part of the promised favored treatment, Rickey Cage was going to get his drink before the tourist-class losers. But there was a wary look in the still star-struck eyes. She had been censured once before for giving Cage preferential treatment over the good-looking nobody he was presumably trying to pull. She wouldn't make the same mistake again.

"Can I get you a drink?" she said coolly to Tari, while stealing a "Didn't I do well?" look at Rickey.

"Tomato juice, please."

"Bloody Mary with Absolut if you've got it. I'll have a couple of shots."

Was that defiance in his voice? He looked at Tari as if expecting some "medical" comment on his alcohol intake. He waited in vain.

"Helps me sleep," he drawled at last.

"Isn't it funny, how on planes you get to sleep with total strangers?" said Tari suddenly.

His eyes opened wide. From anyone else, anywhere else, that would have been an invitation. From this girl, high in the sky, it wasn't. It couldn't be . . . could it? Despite his wider eyes, he could see no answer on her face.

$\mathcal{2}$

"I'M VERY strong," said Tari, "but sometimes I'm not very happy."

She laughed as she spoke. Then suddenly, she wondered what was funny. Her arms were folded across her lap. A stethoscope poked out past her fingers. Unhappy, but laughing. Strong, but her body language all buttoned-up. She reached for the plastic cup and sipped her coffee. All around her, the cavernous canteen buzzed with the neurotic hum of hurried conversation. You could all but see the ulcers growing as the busy young doctors tried to talk and eat in half the time it took to swallow and digest. You could tell the students from the interns. They were the ones taking time between mouthfuls. They smiled. They laughed. Their expressions were devoid of the tormented exhaustion that blanketed the faces of the real doctors. And they had suntans, because they had free time that could actually be used for something other than sleeping. In contrast, the genuine medics shone like slugs in the neon glow, their pasty, glistening faces merging queasily with the white of their jackets. Tari glanced quickly at a bearded doctor at the next table. His eyes were hooded from lack of sleep, black-rimmed and bleary. With one hand he poured coffee into himself as if it were gas for an empty auto. With the other, shaking, he held a computer printout of lab results before unfocused eyes. When it came to measuring out the contents of the syringe, would the decimal point be in the right place? Tari hoped so.

"Calling Dr. Sassovitz. Calling Dr. Sassovitz," said the P.A. system soothingly.

Mary Allard watched her. She had just flown "Unhappiness is a weakness" as a philosophical trial balloon. Now, she had her best friend's reply.

"I don't think of you as being unhappy," said Mary.

"Well, 'happy' is sort of a silly word, isn't it?" said Tari. "Kinda ditzy. I guess what I mean is discontented, like life isn't what it should be. It ought to be more . . ."

Tari sighed. There wasn't time for this before the psychology lecture. Shit, words and feelings just weren't the same thing. It was why relationships were shot to hell.

"Yeah, I know what you mean. 'Happy' is like what a child is when Santa comes across with the doll. Connotations of simplicity, maybe idiocy. But that's all the world wants. That's what we're all after."

Tari put down the cup. She sunk her chin onto her hand. It was a "what-did-she-really-want" moment. She took a deep breath. The topic needed air. Her brown eyes seemed to stare through Mary.

"I don't think people want to be happy. Not first and foremost, I mean. They want to be rich. It's crazy, but I really believe it's true. They actually want to be incredibly rich. Obscenely rich."

"That's nonsense, Tari. Everyone knows money isn't where it's at anymore. Maybe it was true in the eighties, but not even then. Anyone with an ounce of intelligence knows that money isn't what it's all about. You're always going on about it yourself. I mean, you could have been a businesswoman and you traded it in for this. God knows why." Mary waved her hand around the room. It was not a room about money. So what, there were millionaires-to-be scattered about. Right now, most of the newly qualified physicians looked as though they needed a pint of blood.

Tari shook her head from side to side. "No, Mary, you don't get what I'm saying. Okay, if you had people answer a multiple-choice question in some exam about what they wanted, for sure they wouldn't tick money and material things, 'cause they know it's like the 'wrong answer.' Anyone with half a brain knows that 'money doesn't buy happiness ...' " Tari flicked two fingers into the air to put quotes around the phrase. "But actually in the guts, where the real deals get done, people sincerely want to be rich. They feel the loot is like the hard part, and when it's taken care of, the rest will follow.... You know, being loved, being respected, liking yourself and all the *really meaningful* stuff."

"Tell that to a kid on the cancer ward."

"I'm talking grown-ups, Mary," scolded Tari. "And I'm not talking right and wrong, I'm talking reality. It's all part of life's great fuck-up, that in the end all the energy goes toward trying to get the wrong stuff."

"Instead of the right stuff, which is ... dah, dah!" Mary swung her hands around like a conductress bringing the orchestra to a crescendo.

"Love," said Tari simply.

"Love, not as in 'sex.' " Mary smiled wickedly. "Love, not as in 'Rickey Cage.' "

She couldn't resist the reference to Tari's jackpot plane ride from New York.

Tari blushed, but she wasn't going to be distracted.

"Love as in love," said Tari. She was serious. "It's another rotten word, but I can feel it, in here." She tapped her heart.

Her eyes were wide with the intensity of her effort to communicate.

"If you have so much love, why discontented?"

"Maybe we should take it to the psych lecture. We'll be late."

But Mary waited for Tari to stand up. Mary might be the logician, but she wasn't the prime mover. Tari might be unhappy despite her chestful of love, but she was also strong.

"Yeah," said Tari, still lost in thought. She surfaced slowly from the morass of metaphysics. "Is this the IQ lecture?"

"Yup. Dr. Donovan. Nature/nurture, doubtless. Genes versus environment and no firm conclusion. Sometimes I think this whole course is an exercise in 'on-the-one-hand-this' and 'on-the-other-hand-that.' "

Tari laughed. She stood up, drawing Mary with her as if she were magnetic.

They threaded through the tables carrying their trays toward the trash-disposal bin. The doctors looked up at Tari as she passed, neither too tired nor too busy to notice her. She smiled back at them, taking them in. They wore short coats of standard issue, but there was room for the expression of individuality. The more raffish sported brightly colored stethoscopes of red and blue, draped casually over their shoulders rather than hanging from their necks. Some were spartan in their simplicity, pockets empty, jackets well-pressed. The side pockets of others exploded with medical paraphernalia—otoscopes, blood-pressure cuffs, manuals and research papers, patella hammers; their breast pockets rigid with tongue depressors, flashlights, pens, pins with colored tips, tuning forks, and other more exotic tools of neurological examination. There were tidy doctors and scruffy ones, and their shoes foretold their future. The shiny Bass Weejuns tasseled loafers would make megabucks in country-club medicine. The scuffed thick-soled Hush Puppies would cure the poor for peanuts in the small hospitals of a big city. Tari strode past good doctors, bad doctors, and ones in between, but right now all had one thing in common. They were slaves to their beepers and to the silken-voiced dominatrix that controlled them.

"Calling Dr. McBride. That's Dr. McBride. Calling Dr. McBride please . . ."

They dumped the tray detritus and pushed through the swing doors of the canteen. All around them other students on the psychiatry rotation were being sucked into the corridor by the unseen pied piper of the class schedule. They joked as they clattered along the aseptic corridor, its pastel colors totally failing to hide the fact that this was a hospital where people were dying and hurting. The seminar room, too, had sacrificed comfort and homeliness for clinical efficiency. It was a brightly lit, windowless room, aggressively air-conditioned. Chairs that would be good for the back and bad for the butt were arranged in a deep semicircle around a central chair. This throne equivalent, raised on a small dais, was Dr. Donovan's chair. Sheila Donovan was already sitting in it, sharp as an ice pick and as warm, looking down her nose at the roomful of medical students she would condescend to "teach."

Tari and Mary sat down. Tari pulled a notebook out of her shoulder bag and adjusted it on the platform that stuck out from the armrest of the chair. How many pages of notes had she written over the last five years, a novel's worth, a couple of textbooks, more? She scrawled "IQ Tests" across the top of the page, sat back, and waited. The hum of conversation quieted.

"Assuming that there is a measurable quantity of it in this room," sniffed Sheila Donovan in a bored voice, "I propose to start by testing at random the 'intelligence' of various students."

The previous quiet now became a silence.

"Obviously, I can't give the entire test to each of you," said Donovan, "but I will select one or more questions and see how you get on trying to answer them."

Tari looked around her. The room was quite suddenly charged with anxiety. Medical students were notoriously competitive. As a class there were few groups who cared more about their intelligence, and whether or not they were perceived by their peers as possessing it. Now, publicly, they were going to be put to the test. Next to her, Mary took a deep breath.

"Mr. Dorkins, in the front row there, can we start with you?"

Dorkins shifted uncomfortably in his seat. A sickly smile was on his face.

"Let's keep it simple at first, shall we?" said Sheila Donovan, well aware that by lowering expectations she was setting her victim up for a harder fall.

"Okay. You are in a forest, and you're lost. The trees are so thick above your head, you can't see the sky. How do you get out of there?"

You could all but hear the whirring of the minds. Those not in the spotlight had a hundred brilliant answers. Dorkins, however, had lost the power of thought. The words roamed around in his empty mind. They might well have been uttered in Swahili. A forest. A way out. Escape. Shit, what he wanted to do was get out of the lecture room. Screw the forest. Okay. Think. What about making notches on the trees with a penknife. That way he'd avoid going around in circles, or at least recognize it when he had.

"Am I allowed a pocketknife?" asked Dorkins in a small voice.

"Answer the question," rasped Dr. Donovan.

Tari could feel the boy's pain. It cut into her heart. It was hers as much as it was his.

"What are you going to do with a knife, Dorkins?" said some wag in a loud stage whisper. "Cut down the fucking trees?"

The ripple of laughter spread through the audience. Dr. Donovan allowed herself a glacial smile. Dorkins's face was already a sunset at sea.

Tari could feel the panic inside him. His angst was expanding like a balloon in *her* chest, and she wanted more than anything else to remove it. Already, she was furious with the sadistic teacher. All was not as it seemed. What was posing as an interesting way to teach an academic topic was in fact a subtle form of psychological torture. Dorkins was on the rack, and yet it was impossible for him to complain without seeming a fool, a wimp, or both.

"I guess," said Dorkins in a tiny voice, "I could look for the tracks I'd made getting in there, and kinda retrace my steps on the way out."

"Yo, Tonto," said someone into the silence that followed.

The Donovan smile said that this had not been a particularly intelligent response.

"I think, on the whole, Mr. Dorkins, it might be a good idea for you to steer clear of forests in the future," said Dr. Donovan with the sting of an asp.

"What I think," said Tari in a loud voice, "is that this whole question-and-answer thing is an invasion of privacy, and an impoliteness, and I think it ought to be canned."

Dr. Donovan's head shot back.

"Oh, *do* you . . . oh, you do, do you . . . Ms. . . . ." she peered toward Tari through thick glasses.

"Jones. Tari Jones."

"What possible objection could you have, Ms. Jones, to answering the sort of question you will be asking your future patients—*if* you ever get to have such things—to firm up diagnoses in diseases as far apart as Alzheimer's and schizophrenia, lead poisoning, and academic underachievement disorder? Are you telling me that you would expect them to answer questions you are not prepared to answer yourself?"

"Those questions would be asked of my patient in a private situation," said Tari calmly. "My intelligence, or the relative lack of it, is my own private and privileged information. I have the right not to have it measured in front of my colleagues and friends. It's intrusive, anxiety-provoking, and, I think, a little cruel."

"My, my, what an incredibly *sensitive* soul you are, Ms. Jones."

Sarcasm dripped from the Donovan lips.

"You make 'sensitive' sound like a pejorative term," said Tari evenly. "I always thought it was *in*sensitivity we should guard against, Dr. Donovan, especially, perhaps, in the field of psychology."

Donovan was angry now, but there was something about the Jones girl, some quality that simply could not be ignored or overridden.

"Well, well, your 'objections' are noted. We will leave the fascinating mystery of *your* 'intelligence' unexplored in deference to your insecurities, Ms. Jones. And now, if you'll excuse the rest of us, we will continue with our little exercise."

"It may be that we don't want to continue with the little exercise," said Tari. "Let's vote on it."

The red was expanding from the center of Sheila Donovan's cheeks.

"Oh, and so we have a democracy here now, do we?"

"Some of the best countries are democracies," said Tari. "Sensitive democracies," she added.

That was more than enough for Dr. Donovan. She was livid. She shot to her feet.

"Either I will teach this class the way I want to teach it, or I will not teach it at all," she snarled. "And I shall speak to Professor Hodges about your insubordination, Ms. Jones. You may not care about your education, but I'm sure your 'friends' do. They will not thank you if there is a question on this topic in the exam.''

She spun around and clattered from the room.

They turned to look at her, impressed, not very surprised, not totally sure of their feelings for the leader in their midst.

Some joker broke the silence.

"How do we get out of a seminar room if we can't see the sky, Tari?''

"If you've got an ounce of intelligence, you follow me, Bozo,'' laughed Tari, making for the exit.

And they all did.

3

HE LOOKED shattered. His face was pale. He shifted in his seat, and his terrified eyes kept hurrying away from hers. His fingers drummed on the table and his tongue licked dry lips.

Tari sat across the table from him. Nobody had told her what to say. They had just told her to go in there and be supportive, be kind, and provide the right information. That had seemed like enough. Finding things to say had never been her problem. It was now.

"You do realize, don't you," said Tari, "that although you are HIV-positive and you have antibodies to the virus in your blood, you do *not* have AIDS."

He stammered as he spoke.

"But it means I'll get it, doesn't it? I ... I ... I ... mean that's certain, isn't it?"

The truth. Tell the truth, they had said. It was the great American way. Everyone had the right to know anything and everything. It was part of being free, free to feel pain, free to stare into the jaws of death, free to experience despair.

She stared around the room for inspiration. There wasn't any. It could have been a solitary-confinement cell. The window revealed the tent of blue that prisoners called the sky, but it was double-glazed, and it didn't open. Its function was to keep the real air out and the fake air in. The picture on the wall was art by computer. The plastic-topped table was bolted to the floor. The paper ficus plant was redeemed only by an atmospheric coating of genuine dust. How many tragedies had these white walls heard? How many tears had mops wiped from the green nonslip linoleum of the floor? Only voices from lonely graves could tell. For the room had been sucked dry of its history and scrubbed clean of contaminated feeling. This terrible drama was playing in a place that was nowhere.

Tari took a deep breath.

"At the moment, the best guess is that nearly everyone who is positive will get AIDS . . . one day. But not for years. Maybe many, many years. And during that time it's entirely possible they'll find a cure. There have been all sorts of encouraging research findings. . . ."

"How many years, on average?"

He spat the words out through a throat that sounded as if it were being strangled.

"Eight," said Tari. "From the time of infection. But that's only an average. It could be longer."

"Or less." There were tears in his eyes. He was her age, maybe even younger, and although he had committed no crime, he had been sentenced to die.

She shied away from his response. "And if you do develop AIDS, when you do . . . then you can live for years after that. There are all sorts of new treatments in development."

He twisted his head from side to side. He was hardly listening to her. It was too soon. He was in shock.

"Is there any chance of a mistake?" It was a plea.

Tari looked down at the test results, praying herself for a miracle she knew she wouldn't find. The positive ELISA test had been confirmed by the Western Blot. The CD 4 lymphocyte numbers were way down. It was certain.

"I'm sorry," she said. "No."

She felt the wrench at her heart. Why had nobody told her

how impossibly difficult this was going to be? AIDS counseling was a new part of the psych curriculum, but several of the others had already done it. Mary had done it *yesterday,* for heaven's sake, and last night they'd caught a movie. All she'd said was that it had been "tough." But this wasn't tough. This was impossible. Worse than the cancer ward, worse than oncology, worse than anything.

He began to cry soundlessly, the tears rolling down his cheeks.

"I just don't know how I can tell my mom," he whispered. "She doesn't know I'm gay."

Tari took a deep breath. There was a mist in front of her own eyes.

What was it about AIDS that made it such an evil illness? Why was it even more hideous than childhood leukemia and leprosy? It was the slowness of it. The suspended sentence hung like a Damoclean sword over the heads of the young and the hopeful. These victims were formed. They weren't children, and they were more than adolescents. They had reached the springboard of life. Their own personal dreams were on the table. They were full of innocence and optimism, and then their futures were brutally murdered and they were left alone amidst the ruins to exist, but never again to live. And how had it happened? Through the desire for intimacy, for another's warmth. Their bodies were on fire with the lust of the young, and their only sins were impatience and the confidence that they were untouchables, bound only for great things and better times. Tari felt those feelings. They were part of the drama of life, of the early acts, when hearts, not heads, ruled, and now the play was a tragedy because of the virus the Lord had made. She shuddered. The Lord had created the virus that would wreck this boy's immune system. He had dreamed it up. He had designed its cunning programs. He had invented the mechanisms that allowed it to creep into the cells of the body and subvert them to its wicked purpose. The good Lord had set the eight-year limit, laid down the irrevocable death penalty, and invented the oh-so-original method of spread.

She fought against the doubt. Throughout her Catholic

childhood, she had learned the folly of questioning the mystery of God's purpose. Blind faith was the answer. Oh yes, theologians, but what should the boy who would die say to his mother? That was her question. Would some priest please stand and answer it? A boy who loved the mother who had borne him, could not bear to tell her that he would die. The world had taught him shame and he was as afraid of the hurt in his mother's eyes as he was of the grave's cold. Where was the value in this? Where the wisdom? Where the *hell* did this fit in with the power and the glory of an Almighty God?

"You don't have to tell her, not yet. I mean, you're healthy, you're all right. You just have antibodies to the virus. Look at Magic Johnson. Don't you wish you could shoot hoops like him? He's positive, but he's healthy."

He hardly heard her. He looked out of the window at a palm tree that poked at the powder blue sky. High cirrus clouds sat like pocket handkerchiefs in the clear heavens. At the edge of the panorama, the buildings, shimmering in the sunlight, were edged by the aquamarine frame of the sea. In a day that Miami was paradise, this suffering boy was plumbing the depths of his personal hell.

He spoke at last in a faraway voice.

"I love her so much," he whispered. "So much. I always have. My father went away . . . years ago . . . and it's been just us, against the world." He stopped, as the tears started again. He swallowed hard and Tari saw his neck dart up and down with the effort of containing his sorrow. "I mean . . . I don't want to leave her. And I don't want her to know about me. I just don't want her to know that part. Not my mom . . ."

Tari stood up. She walked around the table and she took the boy who could be her brother in her arms. And she held him. He dissolved against her. All the wetness in his body flowed from his eyes, and the room was full of the sound of his sobbing as Tari rocked him like the baby he had become.

"It's okay, it's okay," she whispered. She tried to force her strength into him, but she knew that there was no shortcut through the pain. She simply had to show him she cared. There was never much else.

Slowly, he responded to the warmth of her. The sharp,

shuddering intakes of breath receded. He uncoiled in her arms.

"I'm sorry," he said. "I shouldn't lay this on you."

"It's what I'm here for."

Tari's own words reverberated in her mind. At one level, they were a platitude. At another, they were a revelation. There was the weird sense that she had said something profound, not so much to the boy as to herself. This *was* what she was here for.

She looked down at the boy. His shoulders were sagging with despair. His face was stricken. His sorrow was in danger of acquiring its own momentum. Tari felt it strongly. There was a time for sadness, and a time for controlling it.

"I'm going to die," said the boy, and his tears started to come again. Her sympathy had felt so good. He wanted more of it, more of her.

Tari felt the fight within her. She had to put some inside him.

"Yes, you are. But listen, aren't we all going to get ill and die one day? I am. You are. We all are. Marianne Williamson said it—we're all leaving from the goddamn station, it's just that some of us are catching the five-thirty, some the eight o'clock, and some the later trains."

It was shock therapy. Was tough love, love? Yes, it was. Her heart said so.

He was looking at her strangely. He had expected to be allowed to wallow in some more gloom, now he was picked up short by this girl's attitude.

Her voice was quieter, more kindly, when she continued. Her words were no longer the slap across the face that had been intended to cut through his defeatism.

"You know, Jim, what I'm going to say sounds really weird, but it's true, I promise you. A terrible thing has happened to you. That's for sure. But you know, if you take up the right attitude toward it, you can make it work for you. You can. I know it sounds crazy. You can describe this thing as a sentence to die, or you can think of it as the beginning of your life. Some people, maybe most people, take life for granted. They stumble through it, grumbling and worrying, and when it's all over they've never really *lived*. Haven't you heard people who have been really close to death say how much that experience taught them about the value of life? Afterward, they really appreciated being alive, just smelling the roses and looking at nature and enjoying loved ones. They spent more time with their children, and they were less materialistic, more spiritual, concentrating on the important and valuable things in their lives. You've got maybe ten wonderful years, and the fact that you're HIV-positive can help you extract the maximum from living every minute of every hour of every day. Life isn't about quantity, it's about quality, like everything else. You just have to choose your attitude. If you choose right, you win. If you choose wrong, you lose. Nothing has to be. It's up to you."

Her reward was a watery smile across the table.

"It puts a whole new slant on winning the lottery if getting AIDS is lucky."

Tari smiled. "You remember that saying—'The harder I work the luckier I get.' Well, let me tell you, it's bullshit. The really lucky person is the one who feels lucky. It comes from within, that feeling, not from the outside. Bad things can happen to us, but if we feel lucky, we are. Good things can happen, but if we don't feel lucky, we're not. The trouble with us is we waste all our time slaving to make good things happen and bad things go away, and no time at all on getting our basic attitudes right. What's money, power, success, and fame, if we don't feel great about them? Similarly, what's poverty, disease, obscurity, and death if we don't feel bad about them? They're all meaningless. Only our attitude counts."

"How do I get my attitude right?" He was listening.

"You keep screwing your thoughts back to all the advantages you have, and away from all the perceived disadvantages. Learn to love and appreciate the food you have, the warmth of the sun on your back, the incredible, wonderful city you live in. You must force yourself toward happiness, and lose yourself in the love of others, and you must pray to God to help you. And I will pray to God to help you, and he will. I promise he will."

She leaned across the table. Fire was in her eyes. God had been at the beginning of this, and God would be at the end. How could she instill in this boy the confidence trick of faith?

On her desk were the lists of the organizations that could help him—Positive Link, AIDS Anonymous, the hot lines, the help lines, the treatment centers. But whether they knew it or not, all were the agents of God.

And so was she. Tari didn't hesitate. She walked back to the desk and scribbled her telephone number on a notepad. Tearing it off, she handed it to him.

"Listen, Jim, whenever it gets too hard to deal with and you need someone to talk to, call me, okay?"

It was against all the rules, except the most important rule book of all. The one Tari Jones kept in her heart.

4

TARI COULD never decide about tuna. There was whether to or not, because of the dolphin thing, and porpoises getting caught in the fishermen's nets. That had been partially resolved, but then there was water or oil; Star Kist or Bumble Bee; big white bits or mashed brown stuff; and of course, the question of how much to buy. It lasted, was always useful, but how much cash did you want to tie up in stored tuna? Her hand dithered at the decision. Then she smiled. What would Rickey Cage do? That had become her game lately, after the extraordinary airplane journey they had shared. Well, Rickey wouldn't be trolling the aisles in the Washington Supermarket in the first place, would he? He'd have a gofer to shop for him . . . big, red, juicy steaks, Kellogg's corn flakes, and bottles of booze with handles. Her smile deepened at the memory of him. They had caught the movie, munched on the airline fodder, and drunk white wine as if it had been a date. They had talked and laughed and unconsciously copied each other's body language in the way that people did when they really liked each other. Each had been astounded how little the one's fame and the other's lack of it had mattered. When dinner was over and some of the passengers had begun to drop off to sleep, they had stopped talking but stayed together, warm in a glow of instant attraction, high on the realization that this only happened once or twice in a lifetime.

He had seemed to doze, and she had flicked through the flight magazine, unable to concentrate on its literary Muzak, and she had watched his breathing deepen, his posture slacken as he drifted into light sleep. The famous face had softened, and she had plundered it visually in the dim light. Who was he? What did he want? He was so self-confident. It almost had to be an act. Did the Rhett Butler machismo paper over all sorts of creepy-crawlies in the deeper parts of his psyche? Or was what you saw what you would get for as long as it mattered? Then, as she had watched, his head had rolled toward her and his body had followed it, slumping in sleep across the empty seat that separated them. Closer, she had even been able to smell him, the faintest hint of a lemony cologne mixed with masculine smells that were not quite sweat, but tantalizingly earthy. Shamelessly, she had filled her nostrils with him, and her heart, until she too had begun to feel sleepy. She hadn't resisted it, although there was a part of her that wanted to savor every second of this. But sleep meant dreams, and reality had a way of disappointing, so she had let herself go.

Waking was when it had happened. They had surfaced together, in the religious light of the airplane, and they were as good as in each other's arms. Her head was on his shoulder, his cheek covered by her hair. Her left arm, numb, was crunched beneath her and her other hand, cruelly unable to feel, was lying in his lap. His right leg was against her left one. His hand lay on her thigh. Neither had spoken as wakefulness had revealed its surprise, and each had wanted to pretend to be half-asleep to prolong the moment. Then he had moved. Quite simply, he had taken her head between both his hands and tenderly, as if taking the sacrament in church, he had turned her face up to his and he had kissed her.

"Tuna," said Tari, trying to return from the memory. She was only partially successful. "Tuna," she said again.

She grabbed three cans at random and threw them clattering into the empty cart. She wandered on past diet soups to salty ones. God, shopping was a pain, especially when she had to compute the cost of everything and balance it against the cash limit in her pocket. Rickey Cage wouldn't have to worry about money. On the gofer's day off, he'd cruise the aisles like a minesweeper, gathering tins to him—baked beans, six-packs of Bud, no-nonsense minestrone soups. Tari giggled as her thoughts tumbled on, because of course, what she was really thinking about was the taste of him. His lips had lain on hers, and his breath had filtered through them, washing her face with his intimacy—his lungs to her lungs, molecules shared, *All I need is the air that you breathe.* His gentleness had amazed her almost as much as the very fact of their kiss. His hands had been strong on her cheeks, but somehow the touch had been light, the command there, but force absent. There had been no single area of her that had not wanted it, and yet there was a sense in which she knew she would not have been allowed to resist. Delicious coercion had merged wonderfully with the incredible strength of her desire, and his mouth had opened on her acceptance, and his tongue had invaded her. She shuddered at the memory. Leaning against the cart, she closed her eyes to prolong it.

She wandered wistfully on past TV dinners and cold meats, through dairy, toward cereals. The three cans of tuna stared accusingly up at her from the silver mesh of the cart. *This is Miami, not Moscow,* they seemed to be saying. *Even if you don't want it, for God's sake, buy it.*

She stopped. Okay, cereals were a good place to stock up. No cooking, filled you up, didn't break the bank. A hundred choices mocked her. Did she want to cure the cancer she didn't have, send her blood sugar through the roof, or score some plastic toys that she could give away on the children's ward? It didn't seem to be about food or eating. Instead it was all about fun and/or survival. Some advertised the fact that they were noisy, others appealed blatantly to the consumer's sense of color, a few took the line that they were basically not food, but medicine.

What would Rickey choose? Oh, something very straight-up,

like puffed wheat or Special K—conservative, hold the frills
and the cheap tricks. She frowned. The thought of the kiss had
merged with another memory. At the airport, when she had
walked beside him through the arrival gate, Jodie Summerfield
had been waiting. The megamodel had run straight up to
Rickey and wiped Tari's symbolic kiss from his lips with the
lush redness of her own. He had introduced them, as unfazed
by the encounter as by anything else, and had stood back to
watch her cope. Jodie Summerfield's disinterested eyes had
zipped through Tari's brain like an X ray, unseeing, uncaring.
Tari had muttered something like "Hi," but the supermodel
had already been rapping on to Rickey. The Harley was
apparently downstairs, and they'd finished the new paint job,
and wasn't it cool they could go for a ride because the
production company that was handling her shoot had sent
some guy with a van who could do the luggage, and Rickey
must have missed his bike in freezing New York, and they could
catch a late dinner at The Strand and then go home and gee,
shit . . . it was so great to see him again and wasn't she going to
show him just how great it was. He had allowed her to bear him
away, but he had looked over his shoulder as he had left and
he had smiled a funny smile at Tari as he had mouthed
"good-bye."

She had seen them from afar in the baggage hall as Rickey
had picked out his body-bag canvas luggage for the driver,
Summerfield draped over him like a patriotic flag. They had
made quite a couple and quite a stir even in the baggage hall
at the Miami airport, where you had to be Iglesias or Estefan to
get a second look from the South American tourists. Tari had
already gotten used to it on an intellectual level. She had met
the woman-killer in the night, lusted after him, and he'd
seemed to return the compliment, but you couldn't ask too
much of luck. So she had stood there and tried to be detached
as she'd watched the lovers, but inside, her hormones had
boiled in a stew that was already equal parts lust and jealousy.

She reached for the corn flakes. The hand clasped on her
elbow from behind. Another snaked around her waist. A head
buried into the back of hers. Shit! The alarm bells crashed in
her brain. She was being attacked. She opened her mouth and

let out a sharp cry in the sparsely populated store. At the same
time she ducked down, and then shot up, banging her head
back against the face of her attacker. She thrust down on her
feet, and suddenly she was going backward, carrying her
unknown assailant with her. She kept going, aware that it was
only feet to the other side of the aisle, and that in the
confusion and the delay she'd won for herself, help would
come. *Dear God, let him not have a knife,* she prayed. Joined at the
hip like Siamese twins, Tari and the would-be rapist crashed
into the display behind them. A man-made mountain of dog
food provided no adequate barrier to their backward momentum. She knew they would fall, and fall they did, crashing in a
tin fountain, rolling, head over heels, limbs entwined in the
collapsed pyramid of pet fodder.

"Oh *fuck*," howled her assailant, and that was the moment
that Tari Jones realized that all was not as it seemed.

She turned around, her hand guarding her face to shield
against a blow. Rickey Cage's amazed face stared back at her
through the pile of Gravy Train.

"Rickey!"

"Shit, Tari, you zapped me."

"What are you *doing*?"

"I'm shopping for the fucking dog I don't have."

"Hell, I'm sorry. I . . . I thought . . ."

But he was already beginning to smile.

"I was a rapist. Listen, lady, my PR doesn't read like this."
He held out a hand to her, and they helped each other up.

A couple of Hispanic employees and a curious customer
came around the edge of the aisle at a fast walk.

Rickey held up a hand.

"It's okay. It's cool. I slipped. She slipped. We're sorry."

All three knew who he was, and that he was right. It was okay.
He was cool. He was the movie-star dude. The head clerk said,
"No problema. It happens. I'll come clear it up later." Then
the trio beat a retreat.

"What were you trying to *do* to me?" said Tari, still laughing,
once the audience had gone.

He took one small step forward.

"This," he said.

He took her in his arms. They were around her like rope. His body was plastered against her, squeezing the breath from her body in the tightness of the embrace.

"Hey," she gasped. But his lips closed on hers, and this time there was no thought of resisting him. So what if they were in public? Public was where they did this. On planes. In supermarkets. Wherever. This was not like the first time. There was no gentleness now. There was the fury of thwarted passion. His. Hers. It was a week since he had ridden off into the steamy Miami night on a blood red Harley with Jodie plastered to his back like Scotch tape. It was a week of dreams that didn't turn out as they had on the plane. It was seven days of might-have-beens and missed chances, and nerve-racking what-ifs. Now, there was only one reason for the kiss to end, and that was this—to find out if Rickey Cage and Tari Jones had met at midnight next to the dog food by chance or by choice. But that could wait.

She kissed him back, and they ground together as if trying to set the fire that was already ablaze. His lips consumed her, but she fought him inch for inch. Their mouths were open, wet and slippery with lust, slick with saliva. Against the Muzak she could hear the shameless noise they were making. They moaned in the clash of teeth. They groaned with excitement as their tongues slid together. The stubble of his beard rasped against her skin, damp already with his moisture. In his jeans she could feel his hardness pushed up against her, and she thrust back at him, loving it, wanting it, rubbing against him with her soft heat. She pushed her thigh between his straining legs, and her miniskirt rucked up to show brown skin. She tightened her gluteals and jammed her pelvis against him, and all the time she licked at the mouth that loved her.

Her eyes were open wide, with the next-door emotions of lust and fear. Any moment they would be found. But embarrassment paled beside the awful notion that they would be stopped. A shopper reconnoitered the mouth of the aisle, hesitated, then withdrew. She put her hands on his chest to push him away. Not here. Not now. Somewhere else. Soon. But he ignored her half-hearted plea. He was drinking her. Her mouth was flowing like a river into his. She was soaked with instant sweat. Between her legs, where her velvet core was separated from his pulsing hardness by a thin wall of denim, she was already awash with the juice of lust. She wound her fingers into his hair, binding him near, and with her left hand she reached down and rubbed him, marveling at his fierce contours and wanting the hot skin to touch and to love.

He leaned back from her, watching her, his expression tender, his lips moist with the wetness of hers.

"We're going to be lovers," he whispered.

5

THE CROWD was crammed against the marble walls of the NBC building, and it hummed like a bumblebee caught in a window. A red rope kept the people plastered against two sides of the cavernous upper-floor reception area, and they sipped on coffee and breakfast doughnuts as they waited. At the head of the line was a lectern. A uniformed usher, splattered with scrambled-egg gold braid, stood sternly beside it. Occasionally, the elevator regurgitated more people for the tail of the lengthening snake. Marcus Douglas was among them.

He didn't look like one of the crowd. He was tall, almost gaunt in appearance, and his face was a saint's face . . . calm, strong, and devoid of lines, despite the forty-odd years it had been forming expressions. There was no gray in his hair, no weakness around his sensitive mouth, and no nonsense at all in his purposeful stride. Only his eyes said "danger." They were deep-set in his face, and they sparkled with a fierce intelligence as he walked.

He did not join the end of the line. He moved along it, sizing up the people who would be his audience. A woman recognized him. She nudged her friend, and said, quite loudly, "That's him." He turned toward her and smiled.

"We loved your book," she said.

"Thanks," he said. He slowed down, giving her a chance to say more. He didn't stop in case she had no more to say.

The woman had achieved all her objectives. Fame had been stroked. Attention had been gained. The brand-name author had spoken to her. More might be risky in terms of intellectual poverty revealed. The crowd around her caught on fast to the presence of the star. Whispers hissed from mouth to ear. "Priest," murmured someone. "Psychiatrist," muttered another. "Good-looking to be celibate," was the sotto voce comment of a third.

Marcus's smile lingered, but he didn't. He walked to the head of the line, keeping pace with a ripple of recognition that moved along the crowd . . . sometimes just behind him, at others a little ahead.

"I'm Dr. Marcus Douglas," he said to the usher. "I'm here for the 'Donahue' show."

The military surrogate clicked to attention.

"Ah, yes, sir, good," he said, and he picked up a telephone.

"Ms. DiMaggio, Dr. Douglas is here." He put down the telephone. "Ms. DiMaggio will be right out to get you, sir."

Marcus waited. The people at the front of the line, a few feet away from him, had hit punctuality pay dirt.

"Good luck, Doctor," said a stocky woman of fifty with a girlish laugh.

Marcus's polite reply was swallowed up in the drama of the DiMaggio arrival. The assistant producer burst through the swing doors that the usher guarded. Her words sprayed about like spit. "Thank God you're not too early. Professor Hodges has been here for *hours* and she's driving us all *mad*. Did you fly up from Florida? God, what a great *tan*! Are priests *allowed* to lie in the sun? Ha! Ha! You know what I mean . . . I mean, one never thinks of priests enjoying themselves . . . like sunbathing . . ."

The glacial Douglas eyes froze her stream of nervous consciousness. He didn't have to speak.

"Sorry. Too much coffee. God, what a day . . ." bubbled the girl, pushing Marcus through the doors ahead of her. "Listen, when the researcher spoke to you yesterday, apparently you said that most alcohol-treatment programs were 'rip-offs.' That's really far-out coming from a psychiatrist. Will you say that on the air? We want you to, if that's what you believe."

"I certainly won't say anything I don't believe to be true," said Marcus grimly.

"Of course not. It's just that Phil feels this whole show is elitist, and it was my idea, and I don't think it is. Phil feels that shrinks yakking on to each other is last year. And I say yes, but once in a while won't hurt."

"So the more outrageous one can be, the better it is for Phil's ratings?"

"Well, it's just that Professor Hodges is rather buttoned-up. It's a plus she's a woman, but she isn't exactly Roseanne."

Marcus wondered if he had ever disliked anyone so intensely in such a short time.

"Raunchy jokes are hardly a psychiatrist's stock in trade," he said with all the scorn and sarcasm he could muster. They were passing the empty set now, on the way to the hospitality room. At last Marcus felt the welcome sensation of butterflies in the stomach. It was essential to be mildly nervous on TV. It lifted energy, dilated the pupils, and gave one vital "attack." Out there in the couch-potato fields, people had to be kept awake.

"No, but at least your book is controversial. I read the digest. What was all that about it being a wise choice to take heroin if you live in a ghetto? I mean, that's dynamite from a shrink who doubles as a priest. If you say something like that on camera, Phil will just die . . . I mean, he'd love it."

"What I *said* was that avoiding drugs makes perfect sense if you have a comfortable present, and/or expectations of a reasonable future. When people are without hope, they take their pleasure where they can get it. If we all knew the world would end next week, the struggle to escape reality would become a stampede. It would be totally understandable to try to maximize pleasure in the here and now. The terminally ill often become addicted to the painkillers their doctors pre-scribe. It's not thought to be bad, because they have no future.

In practical terms, many unfortunates in society have no future. I hardly think your one-liner does justice to those sorts of thoughts.''

"You will keep it *simple,* won't you?'' said Ms. DiMaggio, riding roughshod over the subtlety of the Douglas sentiments.

Marcus smiled grimly. He'd been in the writing game long enough to know the media. He did a major book tour every three or four years. TV especially dealt in short sound bites, and catered to shorter attention spans. An "in-depth" discussion of a book seldom got past a recital of the juicier chapter headings.

The door to the "greenroom" where they stacked the program guests was not green. It was gray. Ms. DiMaggio threw open the door and ushered Marcus Douglas in.

It was done up like the VIP room of a second-class airline. The sofas and armchairs were covered with man-made materials in a herringbone pattern. Bright cushions in garish, clashing colors were scattered about on them. A synthetic-fiber carpet, the only touch of green, was not supposed to get dirty, but had managed it nonetheless. Neon strip lighting cast an aggressive glow on the proceedings. Along one wall, a table held an assortment of tired pastries and a machine that made coffee. There were piles of polystyrene cups, a bowl of paper-wrapped sweeteners, a dish of plastic "creamers," a glass of white "stirrers." Everything seemed destined to exacerbate anxiety, including the large soundless TV in the corner, which played the tail end of Gumbel/Couric as a reminder that the trial by tube was soon to begin.

Professor Hodges sat on the edge of a chair in the corner. She looked up from a copy of the *American Journal of Psychiatry.* A wintry smile of welcome creased the mean features of her face. She stood up reluctantly, putting down her magazine.

"Ah," she said. "There you are." The *at last* hung in the air.

"You two know each other, I think, don't you?'' blustered Ms. DiMaggio.

Professor Hodges seemed reluctant to admit to it.

"Yes, of course," said Marcus. "We live in the same small town. How are you, Professor?'' He walked forward, extending his hand.

"Miami? A small town?" Veronica Hodges shook Marcus's hand as if she had learned he had leprosy. A thin laugh coated her words, like the buffer around aspirin. It was her mission in life to make awkward moments more nerve-racking. The field of psychiatry had provided ample opportunity to indulge her ambition.

Marcus took his hand back. He was enough of a professional to know that the greenroom was where television debates were won or lost. Dominance established here would carry through to the show.

He turned to the assistant producer.

"Professor Hodges has been kind enough to invite me to contribute to the student teaching program in her department," he said. "She's even been kind enough to give me the use of an office."

"Is it?" said the professor dismissively. "Yes, my younger colleagues, the trendy ones, were very keen to have Dr. Douglas," she explained to Ms. DiMaggio. "You know how it is. The young do so *love* provocative ideas."

"Yes," said Douglas. "And now that you've done a 'Donahue,' you'll probably find a few people turning up to *your* lectures."

"Well, I can see you two have lots of things to discuss. Save some for the show, won't you?" said the assistant producer, satisfied that greenroom tension was rising toward desirable levels. "So I'll just run along and persuade Phil that we were right to hold off on transsexual teachers. I'll be back about five minutes from airtime to take you in to the studio. Oh, and Phil will be along to give you his spiel before the show. Makeup will want you in a minute or two, Dr. Douglas."

"I don't want any makeup."

"You'll shine under the lights. It's hot in there."

"I don't shine."

"Okay, that's your call. We can always touch you up in the breaks. But I advise makeup. You know . . . never let them see you sweat! Makes you look untrustworthy."

Marcus Douglas's voice was razor-sharp when he spoke.

"My secretary told me the other day that this would be the two hundred fifty-seventh television show that I've done in the last five years. In none of them have I ever worn makeup."

Professor Hodges laughed appreciatively.

Marcus turned his back on both of them. He walked to the end of the room and poured himself a cup of coffee.

Ms. DiMaggio was effectively dismissed. "Okay, well, see you later," she said as she retreated.

"Helpful girl," said Professor Hodges.

"God loves her," said Marcus in disagreement. "One should try to remember that."

An uneasy silence descended. In the corner Katie Couric, smiling broadly, was clearly sticking it to some senator, who squirmed uncomfortably in his seat.

Douglas watched Veronica Hodges over the rim of his coffee cup. She was seriously second-rate, yet she was a woman and she sat in the chair of psychiatry at one of the biggest medical schools in the country. She must have done something right. What could it have been? He knew a bit about her, nearly all of it secondhand. She was famous for her sly aggression, and for the time and enthusiasm she devoted to medical politics and fund-raising. Perhaps that had been enough. Certainly, her original contributions to psychiatry were nonexistent. He had read a paper she had once published in the *Archives of General Psychiatry,* a journal that printed the more tedious and less original articles. It had set a new standard for dull mediocrity.

"I gather," said Hodges in a thin, speculative tone, "that the topic of the debate is the status of alcoholism as a disease. I must confess I haven't read your book, but I'm told you take the view that it is not an illness."

Marcus smiled. He wasn't going to be drawn into this game.

"In my experience, it's better to save the discussion for the show," he said. She had already made a bad greenroom mistake. She had admitted to not reading his book. It had been an attempt to patronize him, but, on camera, he would use her own remark against her.

"Yes, of course. You spend so much of your time on TV, don't you? And writing, and all those other things. It's a wonder you have any time at all for your patients."

"That's true. Not many psychiatrists do a lot of writing. Of course, a few of the ones who made a significant difference did . . . Freud, Jung, Adler. I expect Sigmund would have done quite a bit of TV in his time, if they'd had it in those days."

Her eyes narrowed. "A significant difference." She would never make that. And it infuriated her. Her strength, her slavish determination to go by the textbook, was also her terminal weakness. It was men like Douglas—brilliant, uncompromising, and unafraid—who spotlit the inadequacy in her. For that they must be punished, and if possible, ridiculed, so that the safe hands of this world, the Veronicas, could plod on in the secrecy of their respectable mediocrity.

Only one thing mattered now. Douglas must be humbled in public and before his peers, and she must be the instrument of his humiliation. Back in Miami, the faculty, her faculty, would be watching. And her students. And her patients . . . all the people in the world whose opinions mattered to her. She had to win, to win big and be seen to win. The adrenaline surged inside her. She *would* win, because she had right on her side. In the *Diagnostic and Statistical Manual* of the American Psychiatric Association in which diseases were codified, it said that alcoholism was a disease. This truth was repeated in all the textbooks. In the multiple-choice questions in the exams, the right answer to the question "Is alcoholism a disease?" was yes. Therefore it followed, as the night the day, that it *was* a disease. The profession could not be wrong, straitjackets, lobotomies, and electricity-for-all notwithstanding.

The door opened suddenly. The man who stood there was a familiar relative. He was taller than the TVs in which he lived, jabbing his finger into the air as he painted people's faces with his portable mike.

He hurried in.

"Hello. I'm Phil Donahue. Thanks for coming."

They shook hands, but it was the host who did the talking.

"Look, I just like to make a few things clear to the guests who come on this show, and the first thing is this. You are not the stars on this show, right? The stars on this show are the people in the audience and the folks at home. This is their show . . . not yours, not mine. You are here to react to their questions and concerns."

He paused for dissent, clearly expecting none. The practiced flow of words signaled that this was his standard preshow greenroom pitch. Marcus wondered whether he canned it for Elizabeth Taylor and other serious stellar guests. Almost certainly. Lowly psychiatrists did not command respect. They came somewhere between used-car salesmen and certified public accountants in the great American pecking order, and priests didn't come a whole lot higher. One other thing, thought Marcus. The speech so far had contained one mighty terminological inexactitude. It was clear as the overhead neon that in reality Donahue recognized only one star within a million miles of his network time slot . . . and that was himself.

"The other thing I like to say is this. You are going to have to fight for every word of airtime. If you hold back, you're lost. You won't get heard. And that'll mean you won't sell so many books." He laughed as he spoke to defuse the bracing tone of his remarks.

"So I'll just say 'good luck' and see you out there."

He was gone, mission half accomplished. Veronica Hodges was now a whiter shade of pale.

When showtime came, things moved fast. The dreadful DiMaggio hurried them along the corridor and thrust them onto the stage. The high semicircle of the audience confronted them. It was not unlike the arena in ancient Rome, thought Marcus. They were gladiators preparing to shed their psychic blood for the fun of the crowd, the gray-haired emperor, and the electronic masses. *We who are about to die salute you, Phil. We will risk the wounds of ridicule and intellectual humiliation, and dice with the death of career oblivion for network ratings and the chance to sell more books.* He smiled beneath the super-hot lights. Because he knew that every penny of his royalties would go to the church of his God. This was not his Andy Warhol fifteen minutes. This was his work on earth. This was his chance to feed the hungry in distant lands, and to protect the needy here at home. If he was good today and the housewives in the hinterland flocked to the malls to buy his book, then children that otherwise would have died would live. The royalty on a single hardback would feed a child for a week. His was a sacred mission dressed in the rags of cheap publicity. He knew that. The audience didn't. And he didn't care. He turned to look at

Veronica Hodges in the chair beside him. That the children might live, she must be sacrificed. And Marcus smiled, because it was a rare occasion in life when a moral duty doubled as a pleasure.

The red light was on. They were seconds from the air. Then it was green, and Donahue was off and running. He held high a copy of Marcus's book, and his analysis of it painted a broad brushstroke picture of its message.

"I have here a book, *The Pursuit of Happiness,* in which a psychiatrist—a very famous, very well-known psychiatrist—maintains that alcoholism is not a disease . . . that alcoholics are not ill and that physicians have absolutely nothing to offer them in terms of treatment. Dr. Marcus Douglas is not only a psychiatrist, he is also a Roman Catholic priest. He maintains that those who abuse alcohol choose freely to do so. He says that they are not compelled toward this behavior by any disease process, and that they are responsible for their actions. Now you've all heard the ads on television and everywhere else for treatment centers that specialize in treating alcoholism. Well . . . get this . . . Dr. Douglas maintains that these treatments don't work, and that the people who offer them do so under false pretenses. Wow! Is this going to give some people indigestion out there . . . that's a few Maalox moments for sure. . . . Get in here, Dr. Douglas. Have I summarized your position correctly?"

Marcus leaned forward.

"Forty years ago alcoholism was not considered to be a disease. Today it is. What scientific breakthrough has occurred to change everyone's mind? The answer, quite simply, is none. No new scientific evidence has been discovered. The only thing that has changed is people's attitudes. The only change has been a change in fashion. Everywhere the concept of disease expands remorselessly at the expense of the concept of responsibility. We are all patients now, in this diseasing of America. There are two basic reasons for this widening of the disease category. Firstly, by allowing ourselves to become patients we escape blame for our inadequate actions and join in the general retreat from responsibility. Secondly, by pretending to be able to treat all these new diseases, the medical profession colludes with us in our illness excuses, getting richer and more powerful in the process."

"Any alcoholics here?" said Donahue. A forest of hands sprang up. "Would you mind sharing your experiences with us, sir?" The microphone disappeared up the nostrils of a tall, fat man at the back.

"I just want to say that I'm an alcoholic, and I haven't had a drink for six months and five days. If I had one drink, I know I wouldn't be able to stop."

Donahue's owl-like face twisted into an expression of appropriate sympathy.

"And you believe you have a disease?"

"Yes, I do. My doctor told me that. Everybody knows it's a disease."

"How did your doctor treat it?"

"He sent me to a clinic that specializes in the treatment of the illness."

"And it worked for you?"

"Yes, it did. I couldn't have done it on my own."

The thin, reedy voice of Professor Hodges jumped into the dialogue.

"I agree with that man," she said.

"The reason she agrees is because she is professor of psychiatry at the Florida State Medical College," said Donahue with a laugh. "Okay, Professor, let's hear it from you. If you agree with this gentleman, then you have to be saying that Dr. Douglas is talking rubbish. You say disease. He says it's a weakness. Come on, psychiatrists. Let's get it on."

"Yes, it's a disease," said Hodges. "It's in the *Diagnostic and Statistical Manual* of the American Psychiatric Association. That's the official book in which diseases are categorized."

"It's sad," said Marcus, his voice full of scorn, "to hear a professor of psychiatry at one of our most prestigious schools producing such a slavish and unoriginal reason for the disease status of alcoholism. The professor's argument is pathetically circular. It's a disease because it's in the book. It's in the book because it's a disease. Let me remind you that a few short years ago, homosexuality was a disease in the D.S.M. Now it's no longer thought to be a disease. What happened to change the supposedly 'scientific' minds of the psychiatrists? Fashion changed them. That's all. And what other gems does this 'bible' contain? Well, 'tobacco-misuse disorder,' for one. That reels about a third of the population into the professor's illness category. And what about 'academic underachievement disorder,' the shrinks' version of 'Johnny can do better.' A few million hours at a hundred bucks a throw there, I dare say, for the professor and her well-heeled psychiatric fellow travelers. Then there is the famous disease of 'specific work inhibition,' the 'illness' that was once called laziness. So now the stupid, the lazy, and the smokers all have illnesses to excuse their behavior or condition. And have you heard what they're up to now? What's the next new disease, hot from the press? Rapism. The desire of a man to rape women. The psychiatrists have been trying desperately to get that included in the book by which the good professor here sets so much store. Luckily, pressure from vigilant women's groups has put that on the back burner for now. The scientists caved in for political reasons. Thank the Lord. At least 'I was ill' won't be a defense in rape trials for a year or two more. The trouble with people like the professor is they spend all their time listening to their colleagues and not enough time thinking for themselves. If Professor Hodges had been around before the Civil War, I fear she would have been one of the majority of doctors who believed in the validity of a very widespread 'disease.' The desire of slaves to escape and be free was thought to be a form of illness. I know the professor sees the ridiculousness of that now. But I have to wonder what she would have felt about it then.''

He turned toward the professor for the last bit, and shot his sarcasm into her at short range. She was totally unprepared for the onslaught. Her face registered the hit first. Twin patches of red exploded in the middle of her cheeks. Her mouth dropped open in shock. Her mind tried to compute the damage. Unoriginal. Her stomach churned. Her mouth was blown dry. The parts of her face that weren't red were white. A cloud of confusion fuzzed her brain, but thoughts pierced through. Out there, they were listening to this . . . her students, her peers, her inferiors, even her patients . . . all were hearing the ghastly truth that Veronica Hodges's whole life had been an exercise in denying. This brilliant, famous man, who had rocked the profession with his ideas, had nailed her to the wall on national television. He had recognized her as second-rate. He had blown her deepest, darkest secret. As long as she lived she would never recover from this ghastly moment.

There was silence in the studio. They were waiting for her. They wanted her cunning comeback. The women especially were rooting for her. She had to defend herself. Better, she must counterattack. But her mind was empty of everything but panic. Words were what she wanted, but words had gone.

"Well, what do you say to that?" urged Donahue. "Oh, boy, it sounds as if psychiatrists have rows too. They're just like the rest of us after all." The audience tittered, but they were still waiting.

"I think," she stuttered, "I think that what you have just said is incredibly unkind."

What! The bomb of her reply stunned the audience. Immediately, she knew she had made a terrible mistake. She had taken it personally. The break in her voice said so. So did the mist in her eyes. She was no longer the professional professor. She was a woman for whom the kitchen had just gotten too hot, and during the preparation of the soup.

Marcus Douglas knew he had won. His adversary would hardly utter a word for the rest of the show. But already he was feeling compassion for this bullying woman whose bullying ways had met their Waterloo.

"I am sorry if you feel I have been unkind," he said in a kindly tone. "But we are discussing vital issues here. A vast industry has been created to profit from the plight of weak people who want to be excused of responsibility for their weakness. Billions of dollars are wasted on 'treatments' whose effect is unproven. These 'cures' are sold as if they are scientifically valid. But there is no good evidence of their validity. That is confidence trickery by a profession that should not stoop to collude with people whose natural interest is in avoiding blame. If my words were harsh, they were harsh in a good cause."

Veronica Hodges just looked at him. She was spent. She had

no fight left. He had crushed the nuts that had taken her to the top of her profession. But she was still alive in there. There were thoughts of a kind, and feelings. Inside Veronica Hodges was hatred. It bubbled and simmered in a sauce of vicious violence. Eternity was too short for the revenge she would wreak on Dr. Marcus Douglas. Somehow she would get through this hour. She would stutter and stammer and be silent while the TV virtuoso won the argument that she should have won. Then it would be over, and the future would begin. She had no plans for her retribution. For now, it was distilling. Later, much later, she would find a use for the venom that squirted like a fountain within her. And Marcus Douglas would live to regret the day he had humiliated her.

6

"HE'S JUST a young guy like anyone else . . ."
tried Tari, dangling her feet over the table
on which she sat, and sipping at a plastic cup
of coffee. The two psychiatric nurses and the psychiatry
resident exchanged smiles. They sat around the table on which
Tari was the centerpiece, and they weren't buying the fact that
Rickey Cage was just a regular guy.

"Only more attractive, famous, richer . . ." said the less pretty
nurse longingly. She couldn't believe that Tarleton Jones, a
lowly medical student, had actually met Rickey Cage on a plane
and was now going *out* with him. Okay, so she was a neat girl and
really cute, but a star like Cage, a *student,* on a plane!

"What I can't understand is how they bumped him from first
class. I mean, an airline would be crazy to do that. It just
doesn't make sense." The older nurse had been a looker, tall
and thin with an aerobicized body, but her mouth was mean
and her eyes were cold. Somehow she seemed to insinuate that
Tari's story had holes in it, although there was no denying the
picture of Cage and Tari in the *Globe*.

"Rickey says that kind of thing happens all the time. Some guys are just longing to dump on famous people, especially ones like Rickey who are sort of sex symbols." She couldn't stop the blush. It exploded onto her cheeks like twin red suns rising.

"The airline guy probably had all sorts of unresolved oedipal problems, you know, hatred and mistrust of males at war with a latent homosexuality. Cage would be emotional dynamite to a man like that. He was probably lucky to get bumped, not strangled."

Seagram, the psych resident, had his eyes on a lucrative psychotherapy practice. His tongue rolled around the psychobabble with practiced ease.

"Maybe the guy was just a jerk!" Tari's explanation had the virtue of both simplicity and sincerity. Rickey was special. Despite his machismo, he needed protecting. She looked at her watch. It was ten P.M. Rickey had promised to pick her up at eleven. He was coming on his Harley, and already she was dying to see him. But she would have to slip away and meet him in the lot. She didn't want this little panel of medicos alternately drooling over him and dissecting him . . . and neither would he. An hour to go. It had been a quiet night on call for the emergency room. A couple of suicidal "gestures"—one who'd swallowed fifteen five-milligram Valium, a drug that couldn't kill you if it tried, and one who'd nicked her wrist with a razor, making a cut so small you could hardly see it. Otherwise, there had been a heroin withdrawal, puking everywhere and trying to get a shot of very nearly anything; and a homeless person wondering if he could exchange some nebulous "voices" for a cool bed for the night. Last and least had been an earnest young man on time warp from the sixties with a pamphlet about the evils of psychiatry and its role as the agent of a repressive and reactionary "state."

Tari had been the duty medical student on psych call for the emergency room since lunchtime, and she had had enough. The bright lights of the hospital bore down on her, the smell of antiseptic was strong in her nostrils, and the unyielding rigidity of the institution was tying up her thoughts. It would be great to get out on Washington Avenue on the Harley, and feel the wind in her hair, the warmth of Rickey's back against her chest. And then there would be the dark, boozy smell of a hot club, where life was unpredictable and weird things happened. She smiled at the paradox. Here on emergency call at the South Beach Hospital, it was as exciting as church on a slow day. In the roped-off VIP area of the Van Dome, however, anything could happen. Not for the first time, Tari realized how much her safe, sensible life had changed since meeting Rickey. There was contrast now, black against white and grays in between, and she felt the thrill of being alive course through her.

The telephone banged into her reverie.

The doctor picked it up.

He listened for a minute or two, then said, "Okay, fine, yeah, we'll be right down."

He looked pleased as he put down the phone.

"Catatonic schizophrenic. The cops picked him up on the causeway. Haven't seen one for ages. Break open the Haldol, boys and girls. It's party time."

Tari picked up on the excitement immediately. Schizophrenics were two a penny, the common cold of psychiatry. One in one hundred people would have a schizophrenic illness in a seventy-five-year lifetime. True catatonia, however, was as rare as hens' teeth. She jumped off the table. The others stood up.

"Okay, Ms. Jones," said the resident. "This is the exam. What are we expecting?"

He wasn't technically a teacher, but he liked to play the role and most of the medical students humored him, especially the keen ones like Tari.

"Somebody who is speechless, possibly unable to move, taking up strange positions that have incredible significance for him, but are totally weird to anyone else."

"If we're lucky, that's what we'll get. More likely it'll be some mute guy slumped in a heap, and the trick will be to differentiate it from some designer-drug OD or a catatonic depression. Anyway, we'll sort it out. It'll be more fun than we've had all day."

His enthusiasm was contagious. Even the two nurses, steeped in déjà vu, looked energized for the encounter with genuine madness.

They took the elevator from the second-floor psychiatry department to the ground-floor emergency room. The two nurses opened the ER doors. A remarkable sight unfolded. Two paramedics stood on either side of a man of about twenty-five who to all intents and purposes was a statue cast in stone. He was unkempt, bearded, and his vacant eyes stared into space. His right hand was stretched way above his head as if he were reaching for the ceiling. The index finger was rigid, the thumb cocked back. His three remaining fingers folded over in what appeared to be a child's imitation of a gun. His other arm stuck straight forward, pointing with the elbow, but the fist was curled back in a tight ball and was crammed against his chest. His legs were wide apart, as if he were trying to secure his balance on the deck of a boat on a rough sea. He stood in his bizarre position, unsupported. He didn't blink, but he breathed heavily, his chest rising and falling in the only sign that he was alive.

"Good Lord," said Tari.

"What's the story?" said Seagram to the admitting doctor, who sat at a desk in the corner.

"The cops found him on the MacArthur Causeway. Nobody knows who he is or where he comes from, but from the smell of him and from the clothes, he looks like he's a homeless schizo."

"Okay, no history," said Seagram to himself. He stood close to the man.

"Can you tell me your name, sir?" There was no flicker in the man's seemingly unseeing eyes. He appeared not to know that he was being spoken to.

"Does he have waxy inflexibility?" said Tari.

"Help yourself," said the doctor, standing back.

Very gently, she leaned forward and took hold of the fist of the man's left hand. She pulled. The fist moved away from his chest. She let go. It stayed where she had left it, several inches from his chest wall. Now she prized open a finger from his fist, then another. The man's body seemed to be made of medium-tensile wax. However she arranged his limbs, they stayed in the new positions. It wasn't difficult to move them, but it took a certain amount of force.

Seagram tried the same thing. A smile lit up his face.

"Absolutely classic," he murmured. "You could wait a couple of years before you see another quite like this."

"What's going on?"

"He's probably absolutely terrified, and hearing voices that tell him to take up this position. Maybe he believes that in some magic way this position will protect him from some horrors in his private delusional system. You know, the CIA or the Mafia or the Martians won't be able to harm him as long as he stays put."

"Will he remember this when he gets better?" said Tari.

"Yes, but he'll be embarrassed about it. He won't want to discuss it. And that's *if* he gets better. The fact that he's homeless probably means his chances of getting better are poor. Anyway, we'll fill him full of major tranquilizers and see what happens. I don't think there's any problem at all about the diagnosis."

"No consent?" said the more experienced nurse.

"Nobody to give it, and he can't. It's okay, we're acting in good faith, and he's not the type to sue. He may look pretty funny, but he's got a private hell going on in there. Haloperidol is what he needs."

"No insurance," tried the nurse again, eyeing the filthy clothes with disdain. She would be the one to have to take them off.

"Superb teaching material," countered the doctor. "Go ahead and get his vital signs, will you? I'll listen to his chest and check him over and then we'll start him off on, oh . . . say one hundred milligrams. Haldol intramuscular, and see how we go. We can get some blood for a drug screen later."

"You need us anymore?" said one of the paramedics.

"No, no problem. He's ours now. Thanks for thinking of us."

They disappeared from view, pleased to be excused from further contact with the lunatic. The admitting doctor, too, got up. The buck had passed. The psychiatrists had taken over. He could get some coffee in the canteen.

Dr. Seagram turned once more to the patient. "Can you please put down your hand, sir?"

To everyone's surprise, the hand began, slowly, to descend.

"Automatic obedience," said the doctor quietly. "Sometimes you see that." Again he addressed the patient. "Please go and lie on the bed."

Now, for the first time the man's eyes moved, and then, lizardlike, his head. His eyes flicked to the bed, to the bedside table, back to the doctor. There was light behind the staring eyes. He was warming up, as he prepared to obey the instruction.

Tari stood back. Quite suddenly, creepy fingers were crawling all over her spine. The premonition was total. Everything was proceeding smoothly, but she knew with complete certainty that something terrible was going to happen.

And it did. The bearded man was a blur of speed. He opened his mouth as he moved, and a terrible roar of rage and excitement exploded from him. In a single bound he leaped for the bedside table and swept up the scissors that lay there. He swung around and he faced them, the madness flowing from his eyes, and his hand was high again, holding the big scissors like a dagger.

"Don't torture me! Don't torture me, you bastards, you bastards!" he screamed.

It was they who were now rooted to the spot. They stood there, mouths open, eyes staring as they tried to take in what had happened.

"Put down the scissors," said the doctor in a small voice.

Tari felt the adrenaline fountain within her. The sweat broke out on her lip. It wasn't going to be all right. Somehow she knew it.

And it wasn't.

The man flew like a dart toward the doctor's words. He grabbed him by the throat and the doctor staggered backward under the momentum of the assault. "You fucking bastard," he screamed, and he stuck the scissors in the doctor's eye.

"Oooooooh!" moaned Seagram. He pushed up a hand to his skewered eye, feeling in disbelief the shaft of the scissors buried deep in his orbital fossa. Six inches of cold steel had slid past his eyeball, slipped through the canal that contained his optic nerve, and sliced through the thin layer of bone that housed it. Now the point of the scissors was lodged deep in the bit of his brain where his emotions lived. A trickle of blood oozed through his splayed fingers. He stood there, locked in the terrible embrace of the schizophrenic. Apart from the blood, his face and the hand that was clasped against it were as white as the coat he wore.

From behind Tari the screams of the two nurses played from two voice boxes in Sensurround.

But the madman hadn't finished. Oh, no, he hadn't. One hand was behind the doctor's neck. The other was still on the shaft of the scissors, and the twin blades, closed together, were buried in the cerebral cortex of the doctor.

The crazy eyes swiveled from side to side, and then opened wide as he whispered. . . .

"Slay the devil . . . slay the devil. . . ."

His thumb was in one hole of the scissors' handle. His forefinger was in the other. Now he opened the scissors, twisting them as he did so. In the brain of the doctor, they opened. In the brain of the doctor, they turned. That way and this, in the gray matter of the doctor's brain, the steel moved.

Tari could see the anatomy book in the eye of her mind. She could see the crude frontal leucotomy as it was performed. She could see in her imagination the mashed tissue of the emotional center of the man who a few minutes before had been a human being, but who now, if he lived, would never feel again. His love would be lost in the destruction of the cells that experienced it. His hate would be muted, his sympathy drained, his moods were being obliterated by the scissors of the maniac, and the milliseconds ticked as she stood and watched.

But then something strange happened in the soul of Tarleton Jones. In the carnage, in the terror, in the middle of the danger, she was still. She was becalmed on a glassy sea of tranquility, and all around her the room was charged with a wonderful excitement. It was a moment of total significance. It felt as if, at that very moment, she were being born. She was new with knowledge. She was transfixed with belief. A magic voice inside her spoke, soft but firm in its certainty.

"You are my daughter," it said. "You will bring love to the world."

And then she spoke, not aware of where her words came from, aware only of their absolute power.

"In the name of God, stop," she said. "In the name of my father, stop now."

7

MARCUS RAN. The sound of his feet boomed back from the walls. The nurse trailed behind him, tears tearing down her cheeks. They thundered down the stairs. In the corridor, at the bottom, Marcus pushed at a cart, sending it crashing away from his path. The hot lights of the hospital glared down. Through the chaos in his mind he was dimly aware of the ludicrously calm voice on the intercom.

"Security to ER immediately, please. Crash team to emergency room, please. . . ."

Way behind him he half-heard the disjointed sounds of general alarm. A woman's voice was loud, but controlled in her determination not to appear hysterical amid the cool science of the hospital.

"What's happening? Marcus, are you on crash? Shit, is there an arrest in the ER?"

At the foot of the stairs, Marcus gathered his thoughts. He had been getting ready to leave his second-floor office, pushing lecture notes into his briefcase. The terrified nurse had thrown open his door without knocking. She had blabbered the news through gusts of panic. A crazy had stuck scissors in a doctor's eye. There were people down there. A girl student. Another nurse. They were going to be butchered. Was he a doctor? He had to do something.

The swing doors to the inside entrance to ER were closed. Bright lights and silence oozed through the opaque glass. What would he find? Blood? Everywhere? The butcher's shop of a schizophrenic rampage? The thought of danger didn't exist. He worried only that he wouldn't know what to do in the horror that lurked behind the doors. He braced his shoulder for the impact. The tip of his shoulder hit the right-hand door. He burst through it. His wide-open eyes swiveled to compute the information. On either side the curtained cubicles stretched ahead. The room was empty. He stopped. Behind him he heard the nurse's whimper of fear. All around was the grave's stillness. The quiet was unholy. Behind any one of the closed curtains lurked a psycho's scissors, already caked with blood. He remembered the strength of the paranoid. They were far more than a match for one man. He remembered well wrestling them down with the paramedics in the early days in the Phipps Clinic at Johns Hopkins, where he'd done his psych residency. But right now there was nobody but him, and the terrified nurse. There was no syringeful of quieters, no straitjacket, nothing except the quickness of his mind and the strength in his bare hands.

He took a deep breath into his oxygen-starved lungs, aware of the lactic-acid pain in his trembling legs. He reached for the edge of the nearest curtain. He drew it back. Nothing stared back at him. The neat bed, the blood pressure cuff on the wall, the bedside chair would have passed a Marine Corps inspection. He moved on, to another curtain, another empty space, and then he heard the sound.

It was farther down the cubicle corridor, near to the end, where the interview rooms merged with the nurses' station, the doctors' offices, and the reception area. It was a small sound but it made the blood in Marcus Douglas's veins run cold and fast as a mountain stream.

It was the growl of a maddened animal, low and throaty. It

was the sound of a half-dead dog on a road, menacing the helping hand, crazed by the fury of its pain. There was no intelligence to it. There was only its pure power, its total terror.

He walked fast, trying to be quiet, desperate to be fast. Then he saw it and his mouth dropped open, not to speak, but to register his shock.

A still life from hell was what he saw. The bearded man was locked in an immobile dance of death with the doctor. The neon flashed from the handles of the scissors. Bright blood oozed from the whitened finger that gripped them. Beside them stood the girl, calm, quiet, and even in the horror, Marcus was struck by the extraordinary expression on her face. Her eyes were on fire with the brightest light. Her expression was ecstatic, absolutely astounding in its incongruity. She stood next to death and yet joy burst from her. It was inescapable, joy, bliss, and . . . for want of a better word . . . love. He forced his thoughts to move on, amazed that he had even found time to notice the girl's bizarre attitude toward her terrible peril. Obviously, she was in shock. Good. Stillness with the mad made sense. Marcus stopped. He could hear his heart. The doctor was badly wounded, slumped unconscious in the bearded man's embrace. The other nurse was on the floor, trying to come out of her faint, reaching drunkenly for the legs of a chair. The scissors were deeply embedded in the doctor's brain. Marcus could tell that from the angle and their size. Any movement at all could be fatal.

What should he say? What words would reach this man whose mind he couldn't know? His whole appearance said "schizo," the beard, the staring eyes, his thinness, the filth on his clothes. Marcus's heart sank. You couldn't reason with schizophrenics. You couldn't talk to them. Drugs were the only way to influence them and drugs took time. But there was no time.

He was suddenly aware of the sound of the silence. It was total. It was pregnant with dread. And Marcus Douglas didn't know what the hell to do.

Tari tried to understand the extraordinary feeling that gripped her. The room was on fire with light, the actors in the insane drama frozen in place as time stood still. It was as if the world had stopped turning. Outside, the traffic would be motionless, teacups poised at open mouths, thoughts hanging in the thinnest air, blocked in the middle of suddenly inactive neurons. Only she could still move and think. In a world that had died for a second or two, she alone lived. There was a power in her that filled her up with wonder. There was a glory around her, wrapping her in a shroud of mightiness. She could feel love exploding in star bursts in her rediscovered soul. Her voice was low when she spoke, but it was absolutely commanding.

"Lay him down," she whispered. "Lay him down gently, and let go of the scissors."

She held up her hand like the conductor of an orchestra, and the madman obeyed her in time to the slowness of her descending limb. No father with a sick child in his arms had ever been as gentle. The bleeding doctor was laid to the floor and his attacker let go of the scissors, using his freed hand to cradle the wounded head against the hardness of the linoleum.

"Stand back," said Tari. He did so, the lion now lamblike.

Marcus Douglas stared in amazement. What was happening? The girl with the extraordinary expression was totally in control. He could feel it in his gut. It wasn't just what he had seen. He tried to make sense of it. Had this been an example of catatonic excitement, the rare textbook occurrence when a catatonic schizophrenic burst from his stupor into a period of frantic and unpredictable action? If so, perhaps this was an example of automatic obedience, the girl's command an incredibly lucky shot in the dark that had hit home in the wounded mind. Whatever. The danger was still intense. He was free to move at last. The feeling of suspended animation that had gripped him now loosened. Behind him he was aware of the glass doors to the ER crashing open. Two orderlies and a large security guard preceded a mass of white coats. It was the cardiac-arrest team, with the arrest gurney. Marcus thanked God for their arrival as he prayed they would not be needed.

His words shot out.

"Hold that patient, quickly. *Everybody.*" He sprang into action, rushing at the bewildered lunatic and pinioning his arms in a bear hug. The two orderlies and the security guard ran to help and in seconds the schizophrenic was wrapped in a web of arms. "Somebody get a straitjacket. Quick. And some chlorpromazine—at least a thousand milligrams. Get it into him through his trousers, upper outer buttock quadrant, screw prepping the area. For God's sake, nobody let go."

The physician from the arrest team knelt by the wounded doctor. His hand was on his pulse, his eyes were on the pupil of the intact eye.

"Roaring tachycardia. Somebody get a cuff on him. Rita, get intensive care on the phone. Tell them to get a theater open, and we need the duty neurosurgeon and whoever's the ophthalmic guy on. We'll need a brain scan. Nobody touch him, okay? Don't *touch* him. These scissors are in deep. If they hit the midbrain, he's had it."

The schizophrenic was still as a statue in the muscular embrace. In seconds, his arms were being fed into a straitjacket, a needle was disappearing through the bacteria-riddled pants, and intramuscular phenothiazine was coursing into his blood. His threat was over. But his damage had been done. Marcus stood back.

"Lock him up. Two male nurses in the room with him, all night, okay? Twenty-four-hour specialing until further notice. And get the duty attending psychiatrist on the phone. I'll speak to him, but he'll have to get over here right away. Have them beep him if he's out."

Now Marcus knelt down across from the physician who was the leader of the arrest team. The wounded doctor was beginning to move, his feet making scratching movements on the floor. Douglas and the physician, in reflex action, bent across the prostrate psychiatrist. He must be kept still. The scissors were adrift in his brain. If they touched the breathing center, or the control neurons that regulated the heartbeat, there would be no saving him. Their faces were inches apart across the chest of the man who was so very nearly a corpse.

"What do you think?" rasped Douglas.

"I don't know. From the angle, it could have zapped the circle of Willis. If his cerebral artery's gone, so is he. The blood pressure will tell us if his intracranial pressure's through the roof. The good pupil isn't dilated. The first thing is to get him sedated to stop movement."

"Diamorph and IV Valium?" Douglas was asking. This was a medical emergency, or rather a surgical one. It was the physician's call.

"Diamorph'll lower the blood pressure if he has a bleed, and it will help sedate him. It's important to keep the goddamn scissors still."

"I agree," said Marcus. "The best-case scenario is he loses the eye and a slice of his frontal lobe."

Tari's voice was absolutely certain.

"He will see," she said.

In the normal way, at a time like this, the comments of the girl who was the medical student would have been background noise. But they weren't. Marcus looked up at her. She stood over them, and he was drawn into her eyes. They were serene, as they had been before, but now he remembered again that it had been *her* words that had stopped the maniac in his tracks. That was a coincidence, of course. Most probably. Probably. He tried to ignore her, and to concentrate on the business of saving life, but he couldn't.

"He will see," she repeated. "His eye is safe. His cortex is intact."

"Somebody look after that girl," said the physician. She was clearly in shock. Her whole demeanor said so.

"How do you know?" asked Marcus Douglas. He almost bit his tongue off, seeing the suddenly incredulous expression of the physician. The girl was talking rubbish. The eyeball was obliterated, the retina and the optic nerve would be paste, the frontal lobe of the cerebral cortex would be gray cream cheese. She was a clinical student. That meant she'd passed her anatomy course. She was talking shit from shock, and he, the famed psychiatrist, was dignifying her babble by asking her how she knew. But he had to ask. Something mysterious had made him.

She looked straight into him, past his eyes, past his mind and into his essence, and she said—

"My father has told me so."

Tari herself didn't quite know what she meant. She was two people, held together by a force field of incredible happiness. One was recognizably Tari; brave, fierce Tari who stood no nonsense and dreamed few dreams. That Tari knew what the doctors on the floor knew. But now there was another Tari, soaring above, around and beyond the old one, and this Tari possessed ultimate knowledge and ultimate power. The world had receded. It was no longer a place of reality and illusion; of fact and fiction; right and wrong. It had become a wondrous place of infinite possibility where only purity existed, beyond pain and feeling, beyond the pathetic irrelevance of life and death. The old Tari fell back in awe at the presence of the new one, even as she tried to make sense of her.

Something was happening to her. It could be the shock of what she had seen . . . a headlong denial of intolerable reality and a flight to a fantasy whose clever trick was to appear more real than the flesh-and-blood world she had left. But it didn't feel like that. It felt mystic. It felt religious. It was to do with God and all the love within her. It was as if all the threads of her life had come together in an instant of magic, and nothing would be the same again. She knew the meaning of everything now. The meaning was this experience, this feeling that no words had been invented to describe. She was aglow, on fire, her fingers buzzing with vital energy. She was calm, still at her core, more perfectly at peace than she had ever been, and the place that had been her mind was an infinity of tender loving. On the faces of those around her, she could see the irrelevant expressions of concern and fear. She could peer into their minds and know their hurt, their anger and frustration as they struggled to be alive in the make-believe world of Tari past. And she flew above them as she loved them, and she only wanted them to know the certainty she now knew and the endless, wonderful joy that was hers and could be theirs.

"Somebody look after that girl," repeated the physician quickly, his words a rebuke to the celebrity shrink who couldn't recognize simple shock when he saw it.

A nurse took Tari's hand, and it was the old Tari's hand that she held. Tari shook herself free.

"It's okay," she said. "I'm okay."

The emergency was on the move, passing her by, and she was content to let it move away from her. They fixed a frame around the doctor's head and neck as they tranquilized him.

They lifted him with supreme care onto the gurney, and soon he was being borne away through the swing doors through which Marcus Douglas had so recently burst.

He remained behind. So did Tari. The schizophrenic was being led away by two male nurses to the locked ward.

"Dr. Adams is coming," said a nurse from the telephone. "He was seeing a patient in the hospital. He should be here any minute."

"Is he the attending psychiatrist?" said Douglas.

"Yes."

Marcus felt the burden lifting. Everything had been done. The maniac was a threat no longer, and the unfortunate doctor whom he had attacked was under the surgeons now. Soon the neuro would be scrubbing up as his intern showed him the brain scan. The eye surgeon would be in if for no better reason than to throw out the trash. There would be Burr holes in the skull for the bleeding if that was a problem and the poor guy would probably live . . . a life of some sort, in a room somewhere, with a mother who loved him, his once-brilliant future cut to pieces by a pair of simple scissors in the hands of a man with a diseased brain.

He sat down on a chair. His brow glistened with sweat. His mouth was dry.

"What the hell happened?" he said.

He spoke to Tari, and once again, as he watched her, he felt the sharp interest within him. She probably wouldn't be able to tell him. It was a silly question to ask, and medically, not very sensible, given her state of mind. For the second time, he wished he could have had his question back.

Tari's reply was brisk. "He was a catatonic schizophrenic. He came in stuporous, waxy inflexibility, automatic obedience. . . . Then quite suddenly he went into catatonic excitement before we could get any Haldol into him. . . . He was going to lie down and have his blood pressure taken and then he picked up the scissors and attacked Dr. Seagram. There was absolutely no warning. . . ."

Once again, she had surprised him. She made total sense.

"He stuck the scissors into the doctor's eye, but then he stopped . . ."

Marcus looked at her quizzically. There was a funny feeling in his stomach. He was going to ask another question. "What made him stop?" he said.

"I did," said Tari. She looked straight at him. There was no boasting in her tone. No false modesty. It was a statement of fact.

"You did?"

"God did."

"God did." Douglas repeated her statement slowly. He was a priest, but he was also a psychiatrist. When people attributed actions to God, the remark always needed sorting out.

"You are very religious? You see God as present in everything?"

"God is in me. He told the man to stop. I told the man to stop. He stopped."

She looked perplexed as she spoke.

"Sit down," he said, gesturing to the chair beside him. Suddenly he was worried. This might not be shock. This might not be a religious medical student who took God seriously. This might be something else.

"Are you feeling sort of . . . strange?" he asked her.

Tari nodded. It was true. Bliss was strange. Fulfillment was strange. The dull pain of life had left her, and it felt bizarre, wonderfully weird, but now, with these questions, the old Tari was creeping back. It was not the same Tari. It was a Tari baptized by an otherworldly experience that simultaneously made no sense and yet made all the sense of the universe.

"What exactly did you say to the schizophrenic?" said Marcus. For the first time he saw her as a woman. He saw the fierce, intelligent brown eyes; the no-nonsense mouth around the white, even teeth; the jutting, just-too-prominent jaw. She was tall, with very good legs beneath the short black skirt . . . and she looked remarkably vulnerable and absolutely all-powerful at one and the same time.

For a second she paused. Was she trying to remember? Was she wondering whether or not to tell him the truth?

"I said, 'In the name of my father, stop.' " She paused. "I think that's what I said," she added.

" 'In the name of the Father, stop,' " prompted Marcus.

"No. 'In the name of *my* father, stop.' "

"*My* father?"

"Yes."

"That's what you said a minute or two ago. Something about your father knowing the eye would be okay, and there would be no brain damage."

"Yes." There was defiance in her voice. Douglas had the feeling that it sounded as strange to her as it did to him.

He cocked his head to one side. He was slipping into the role of inquisitor, but who was asking the questions? Was it the psychiatrist? Or was it the priest? Or, far more disturbing, was it ... the man?

"Some of us believe that God is in all of us, and of course in the Christian religions we tend to pray to our Father ... I suppose that's what you meant."

"I'm not quite sure what I meant. I'm more sure of what I felt."

Now she looked frankly confused. Inside, she was. The brand-new Tari was moving away from her, ethereal now, less tangible, less accessible. But a string of light attached her old self to the new. It was a string that might get longer or shorter, but it was a string that would never break. That she knew.

"I think I've had some sort of religious experience," she said suddenly. Marcus noticed that her hand was trembling.

Instinctively, he reached out to touch it. She did not withdraw. His own hand tingled with electricity as he did so, a burst of static that made him pull back.

"You shocked me," he laughed. She smiled.

"Sorry."

"That's okay." He swallowed hard. He shifted in his chair. It was late. They had all been through a terrible experience. But he felt out of his depth, he, Marcus Douglas, who, it was joked in the Vatican, was the only man in Christendom who made the pope nervous.

"Are you a very remarkable person?" he asked suddenly.

She laughed openly and her face relaxed. It was a wonderful sight. Her smile was a sunrise.

"No, I'm just Tarleton Jones. I'm just me," she said. Just plain, ordinary Tarleton Jones, medical student. That was how she described herself. That was what she was. Yet, possibly she had saved a man's life. She had done so in the name of a father who just happened to go by the name of God, and when Marcus Douglas had touched her hand she had shocked him. Oh, and she had talked some nonsense about anatomy, too.

He called out across the ward to a bustling crowd of new nurses spewing into the ER by both the hospital emergency procedure and the grapevine.

"Could I get a pot of tea, do you think?" he asked. "The English swear by it," he said to Tari.

"I'd like that."

He didn't want to ask the next question, because he didn't want the wrong answer, but the shrink in him had to know.

"When you had what you call your . . . religious experience, did you have the sensation that the world had changed, I mean, like things had a special significance? The feeling that events were charged, kind of especially meaningful?"

Tari nodded.

"And then did you feel that you had a special power, that you were in some way chosen for some task?"

"You're asking if I had a primary delusion."

"Ah," said Douglas. The adjective *clever* now applied to Tari, to add to *remarkable, religious . . . beautiful.* But possibly, just possibly, from the psychological point of view, she was not very well.

"So you know all about autochthonous delusions?" he said.

"Yes, I do. Out of the blue a person has a strange experience that is particularly meaningful to him . . . to her . . . and . . . she feels that the experience represents some sort of a turning point in her life . . ."

She petered out. It was what had happened to her.

"And it often takes place in the setting of a strange mood in which there's a sense of mystery and importance that's called the delusional atmosphere . . ." she continued.

He was peering deep into her eyes.

"Is that what you felt?"

"Yes, it was a little like that."

"And did you suddenly have a strong belief in something?"

She shook her head. "I know what you're getting at. If it was primary delusion, it's the most important Schneiderian first rank symptom of schizophrenia. But I'm not ill. I'm not, really.''

She smiled a suddenly rather desperate smile.

"What did you believe? What do you believe, Tarleton?''

He had to know. He had to ask.

Her pause was an age. She was going to cover it up. She was embarrassed by what she believed because she realized he would think it ridiculous, or worse, crazy. Relief flooded through Douglas. She had insight. Schizophrenics never did. They believed in their delusions, especially primary delusions, with a bizarre and irrational strength. The schizophrenic's delusion was by definition a totally false belief held with extreme force in the face of all evidence to the contrary. It was unshakable. It was held with extraordinary conviction. And it was totally inappropriate to the individual's culture and intellectual background. This girl had had some sort of experience and wondered if something might or might not be true. She didn't know it for sure, otherwise she wouldn't be so reticent about repeating it.

"You're a priest, aren't you . . . I mean, as well.''

"You've heard about me.''

"We all have. I'm coming . . . I was coming to your lecture tomorrow. . . .''

"What did you believe, Tarleton?''

"Can you believe something totally that part of you knows is ridiculous?''

"I am a priest, Tarleton.'' He smiled gently. "I've had a lifetime of practice.''

It seemed to make up her mind.

"I believed,'' she paused. She took a deep breath. "I believe that I'm the daughter of God.''

Once again there was defiance on her face.

"Did one particular thing make you think so, one tiny thing?''

"As in an autochthonous delusion, like when some totally unrelated perception leads to an unshakable conviction?''

"I think you know that's what I'm asking.''

He was holding his breath. He didn't want her to be crazy.

But the jury was out. A primary delusion was a rare and beautiful symptom in psychiatry. Against the background of a delusional atmosphere a crazy conclusion is drawn. The example he liked to use in lectures was this. "A man is walking down the street. Suddenly he feels everything is strange. Then a passing car hoots its horn and instantly, as a result of the hooting of the horn, the man realizes that he has been sent to rule the world." So far, a key element in Tari's description was missing. The hooting-of-the-horn element was absent.

"There wasn't an unrelated perception," she said.

He breathed again. No schizophrenic could have given that measured, considered reply.

"There is a sense, of course, that we are all the children of God," he said, offering her a safe pass back to the world of reassuring normality.

"But Jesus more so than others," said Tari. She had not taken his metaphorical helping hand.

"More so, yes." Marcus felt the doubts begin again. What was she really saying? That she had a special relationship with God? That she could use his powers in the world? That she could predict the future, work miracles? One thing was already certain. Tari Jones was perhaps the most fascinating person that he had ever met, and that was before the telephone rang.

A nurse picked it up.

"It's for you, Dr. Douglas."

"Marcus Douglas," he said into the mouthpiece.

"Dr. Douglas, this is Arnott. I'm the professor of neurosurgery, and I've just taken the scissors out of this doctor's eye." He spoke fast, urgently. "He's going to be fine."

But Marcus knew not to reply. The good news had been given, but the real news hadn't been given at all. He could sense it in the professor's excited tones. He·could feel it in the pit of his stomach, and yes, as he looked at her sitting beside him he could see it in Tarleton Jones's eyes.

"But the amazing thing is this—mind-boggling thing, actually—we've done computerized axial tomography of the guy's brain, and a very careful electromagnetic nuclear resonancy study and there is zero evidence—I mean, literally zero evidence—of cerebral-cortex damage in the frontal lobes or anywhere else. The scissors went in and they came out and they simply didn't leave a hole. I mean, in all my years . . . I've never seen anything like it. Listen, Douglas, there was no brain tissue on the scissor blades . . . I mean, what does it mean?"

"Bone fragments on the CAT scan?" said Douglas, his stomach a fast-descending elevator.

"No damage to the skull base. Totally intact. I have had three guys look at it and I'm grabbing every doctor I can find. They all agree."

"And the eye?" Marcus Douglas's face was red. In his lifetime he hadn't experienced this.

"He's conscious and he's seeing through it," said the surgeon, his voice thick with awe. "Heidelberger can see an intact retina. There's no damage to the optic nerve. It's as if the scissors weren't made of anything at all, and yet I've just cut a thick piece of cardboard with them. I mean, I have, just now."

"I'm coming up," said Marcus. He put down the telephone. His hand was shaking.

"I think there has been a miracle," he said.

8

"**G**OD, TARI, I don't know how you can *eat* after that thing. I mean, it would have grossed me out, really. Shit, weren't you just *freaked* . . . ?"

Tari dangled the piece of pizza over her mouth, hoping the bits wouldn't fall off. It was late, but never too late for food. She grabbed at it with her mouth, capturing it. She spoke through crunching toppings.

"But Mary, it was so weird. It was as if I was totally in control of the whole thing. Nothing mattered because I could make it stop, and anything that happened I could make not happen. It sounds crazy, but it wasn't just a feeling. I knew it. It was for sure."

"But that's not normal, Tari," Mary looked at Tari carefully as she demolished the slice. She looked as normal as ever. More so. She was just a girl at an open-air food counter, eating junk, and talking with her mouth full.

"I know it's not normal, Mo, but it's what happened. I'm just trying to tell it like it was. I mean, I tried to explain it to Dr.

Douglas, and he thought I was suffering a primary delusion, which is absolutely diagnostic of schizophrenia. But I'm not crazy. I'm incredibly sane. Look at me.''

She laughed and waved the slice to show how sane she was. Mary laughed too. It was just the facts that were strange. The feelings were totally okay.

''Douglas thought you were schizo?''

''He was sort of suspicious, you know, checking me out for it. But of course I knew what his questions meant. I don't blame him. If you'd just told me what I've told you, I'd worry. But the guy's eye, and his brain, that's what it's all about. It has to have been some kind of miracle . . . and I made it happen. I knew it would happen, like I know there's pepperoni in this pizza. I knew it that strongly.''

''There has to be some explanation. Perhaps you all just thought the scissors went into his eye, you know . . . the excitement and the shock. It had to have been total chaos in there . . .''

''The neurosurgeon had them on his X ray. There was an operating room full of cool-as-cucumber interns and nurses. They pulled the scissors out of his brain, Mo. His brain, for God's sake.''

Mary shook her head. There had to be an explanation. There always was. She tried again.

''Okay, let's imagine, by some incredible chance, the scissors slipped along the side of the eyeball, then they slid along the *side* of the optic canal without damaging the optic nerve. Then they sort of parted the brain like the electrodes do when they're doing one of those stereotactic leucotomies. . . . I guess it could have happened that way.''

''Right on, except that the scissors had to break through bone to get into the skull, and they're at least six millimeters wide, not like brain probes, which are needle-thin. There just isn't room for them in the optic canal. The nerve would have been pulped even if it wasn't skewered.''

Tari swallowed a mouthful of pizza and wiped her chin with the back of her hand. She was incredibly hungry, and elated, too. Whatever had happened was good, not bad. There was no question about it.

"Okay, okay, so what do *you* think happened? You're not crazy, and there's no possible scientific explanation for what happened. So what does that add up to?"

Tari paused. She looked at her friend.

"I think there was a miracle," she said at last. "I mean a real one, like in the Bible."

"Lazarus-from-the-dead type miracle? Water into wine?"

Mary wasn't joking.

"Yes."

Tari put down the slice of pizza on her plate. She had tried to confront this several times since Dr. Douglas had given her a lift home. Now, with her best friend giving her total concentration, she tried again. Miracles were things that God did. Her Roman Catholic upbringing had taught her that much, if not much else, about religion. But when miracles happened through the intervention of people, that meant those people were very special people indeed. They were saints. She shook her head at the notion. If she had made a miracle happen, then she was very, very close to God, but that was ridiculous. She was just Tarleton Jones, medical student, adopted daughter of Tom and Frances Bennett. As a child, Tari had gone through the right religious motions of baptism, CCD classes, and first communion, but she had sleepwalked through it all. The moment she had learned to think for herself it had been the objections to religion that had impressed her rational, scientific mind—the problem of why an all-powerful God would dream up evil, disease, murdered babies. And how could you know about a God who was by definition incapable of being experienced? Faith was a giant leap in the dark. And you couldn't deduce God from anything because any such deduction would always be capable of a different interpretation. In the end, belief in God was a choice. It could neither be proved nor disproved. So for Tari, remarks about "God" had been like remarks about fate or destiny, without ultimate meaning. "God loves us," the priests would say. But when Tari looked around she could see precious little evidence of his love. Had God loved the little children that he had allowed to troop off to the gas chamber? In what spirit of love and affection had he thought up the AIDS virus, leprosy,

leukemia? Genocide, nuclear weapons, depression, the priva-
tions of old age, the pain of childbirth were all the products of
God's boundless love. With friends like him, Tari had often
thought, one didn't need enemies.

Now, it was different. She had experienced God firsthand.
But had she? Wasn't it more accurate to say she had had a
strange experience? Dr. Douglas, a priest and a psychiatrist,
had insinuated that she had been deluded. Mary, her best
friend, had wondered if her strange feeling had been the
product of shock. Why couldn't they be right? Maybe she was
crazy, or hyperimpressionable. That would be the sensible
conclusion, wouldn't it? How many people had had a genuine
encounter with God? For every St. Paul, there were a thousand
nuts and fruits and flakes scattered across the slippery surface
of America. But she *knew*. *She* knew. Nothing else mattered. In
the hospital, this very evening, she had heard God speak to
her. It had been his voice. It had not been a thought of a voice.
It had been an actual sound, deep and resonant and full of the
mightiest love. He had said, "You are my daughter. You will
bring love to the world." Then, full of his power, she had
ordered the schizophrenic to cease his murderous attack, and
for no other reason he had obeyed. She had reached inside the
twisted mind, and spoken to the sane soul of the tortured man,
and he had become quiet and at peace. Then, later, there had
been a miracle, and she had predicted it. That was fact. There
was no surer, more certain form of knowledge.

Tari reached for the piece of pizza, aware of the incongruity.
It was after midnight, but the snack bar off Ocean was still
two-deep with people who couldn't bear to go to bed. Refugees
from sleep, they milled about her, unaware of her predicament
in the balmy heat of the night. But in the middle of the
insomniac throng, the voice of God still reverberated in Tari's
mind.

"What exactly did the voice say?" asked Mary. There was an
accusatory tone in her voice, the detective searching for
inconsistencies in the suspect's story.

Tari didn't resent it. She wanted to go over it again and
again. It was too big for her alone. In a way it would actually be
simpler if she was ill. Then some chemical could simply
blockade the dopamine receptors in the overactive area of her

cortex, and the whole business would go away. She smiled ruefully, because it was ridiculous. She had insight. She was looking at every side of this. The crazy didn't doubt their delusions, but she could entertain doubt. Or could she? What had happened had happened. It could not be denied. She actually believed the unreasonable. The tennis ball of argument crossed and recrossed the net in her mind.

"It said . . . he said . . . 'You are my daughter. You will bring love to the world.' "

"If God said that," said Mary forcefully, "that means you are Jesus' sister." It was a shock tactic. Tari with her mouth full, in her blue jeans and V-necked sweatshirt, did not look like the sister of Jesus.

"Or it could have meant . . . he could have meant that I was his daughter in the way that all human beings are the children of God."

"But then he said that you would bring love to the world. You, not anyone else."

"That could have meant that all humans have love to give," said Tari. Her tone lacked conviction. Mary picked up on it.

"What do you think the voice meant . . . in your heart of hearts?" said Mary.

Tari took a deep breath. There were all sorts of different ways to put friendship to the test. This was one of the more unusual.

"I think he meant that I was his daughter, as in 'only daughter.' And I think he meant that I would bring love to the world as in "only me.' " She felt the red flush break out all over her cheeks. It was the truth. It was what she felt. But she was acutely aware of the implications of her belief.

"Should I be on my knees?" said Mary. It wasn't intended as an unkind remark, but there was an edge to her tone.

"Oh, Mary, don't. I'm as confused as you. I mean, that's what I feel. I can't lie to you, of all people. I'm not bullshitting. I'm not on anything. You know that. And I don't feel crazy. I feel calm, not shocked. I don't feel dissociated, or derealized, or depersonalized. I just feel that I'm struggling with a great big wonderful thing that I don't understand right now. But I know I will understand it. One day I will. You'll see."

Mary reached out to touch her friend. "Oh, Tari, it's a mess.

I'm worried for you. I mean, you look perfectly sane, but you're saying all these weird things. I mean, don't you remember last month when you threw up after you pigged out on that cheap wine that the photographer brought back after that night in the Loft? You fucked his brains out, don't you remember, and then passed out in a pile of puke. I mean, Tari, you're my best friend, but you steal my makeup all the time, and my moisturizer, and you leave the bathroom like shit when you're late for lectures. I mean, I can't sort of see you as the daughter of God. You like the Black Crowes and Nirvana, you do grass sometimes, and you can be a real bitch, I mean a *real* bitch, although I love you . . ."

"A bitch for God," said Tari.

It wasn't quite a joke.

"What!" said Mary, laughing.

Tari smiled slowly. "It's probably what God needs in the nineties. A bitch who can get things done, bring love to the world even if it has to be stuck down the world's throat."

"Thank God you can laugh about this. That makes me feel better." Mary gave her a squeeze.

"I sort of mean it, Mary," said Tari quietly. She did, but what did she mean? It was serious, but you could laugh about serious things. Sometimes it was the best thing to do about them. She had never felt more alive, but she had changed. She was simply no longer the person who had lived her past. In some specious present she had metamorphosed into a new creature, and her future would be vastly different.

"What about Rickey?" said Mary suddenly.

Tari felt the slap across the face that was the impact of his name. Rickey, ah yes, Rickey. He was a thread that ran slam bang through her past, her present, and her future. She had arranged to spend the evening with him, but she had called from the hospital to cancel their date without explaining why. Rickey was a test, all right. How would he fit into her brave new world? She was infatuated with him, in love, in passion. She was as far from God and as near to heaven as it was possible to be when she was in his arms. What would happen now? What could happen?

"I don't know about Rickey," said Tari, because she didn't.

"Can daughters of God have lovers?" Mary's question was shrewd.

Tari was silent.

"Darling, I think you're going to need help of some kind," said Mary. "Whatever's going down, I don't think you can handle this on your own."

Tari simply nodded. Mary was right. There was a vastness about the things that were happening to her that had simply swamped her. She felt huge, but alone, poised on the edge of an eternal adventure.

"Dr. Douglas said he would really like to talk to me some more about what happened. He was kind. I liked him."

"What does he look like?" said Mary. "As good as on the talk shows?"

"Sort of better," said Tari Jones in a faraway voice.

9

THE SOFT, sultry breeze was coming in from the ocean. It curled around the high balcony of Tari's apartment, and crept in from the side at her, sly and sexy as the city itself. She looked up from the psychiatry textbook and her eyes slid across the milky aquamarine waterway to Star Island and the cruise ships in the cut. They stood there in line like great white nuns at an altar, full of mystery and the promise of fun with strangers on distant oceans. Beyond was downtown, a light show at night, but now gleaming like new-minted money in the sunglow of late afternoon. In the Jacuzzi, ten floors below her tiny penthouse apartment, a muscled boy was doing calisthenics. A model lay sunbathing poolside in a thong bikini. A harder, tougher girl, with quads like ropes, washed one of the express cruisers in the condo's boat dock. From somewhere, Rod Stewart's "Broken Arrow" summed up visual memories of the stunning video— his wife, Rachel Hunter, swinging across the water by the witness tree a billion miles from the chapter on schizophrenia that Tari had been reading.

Mary called from inside. "It's Rickey Cage on the tele-phone," she laughed. "Shall I tell him to get lost?"

"Mary!" said Tari, leaping up and vowing for the hundredth time to buy a cordless telephone. "I'm coming," she yelled unnecessarily. She took the telephone from her friend and slumped down in an outsize armchair.

"Hello?" she asked.

"Hi, Tarleton Jones, this is Rickey Cage. The guy you stand up." His laugh was late-night hoarse.

"Listen, I'm sorry about that, Rickey. Something really weird happened at the hospital. I've got to talk to you about it."

"As far as I'm concerned, *only* weird things happen in hospitals. I'm not sure my stomach would be able to handle it. Anyway, can I see you?"

"For sure, like when?"

"Like this evening. A drink at . . . say The Whiskey, maybe dinner at Milano. Then we could catch Tara Solomon's karaoke thing after the drag cabaret at Lido. Later it's death by dancing at Van Dome. I need the exercise."

"Oh, that sounds great, Rickey. If we cut the whole evening short, I should be able to make my ward round by nine o'clock tomorrow morning."

"You're only young once, sweetheart."

"But if you insist, you can feel young forever."

"Sounds profound, but then I'm from L.A., where they think intellectuals are people who read the future from crystal balls."

"And I'm from New York, where they think an intellectual is someone who talks balls about the future after drinking too much Cristal."

"Listen, sweetheart, in Florida, an intellectual is anyone who can spell it. Anyway, this nonintellectual will pick up that nonintellectual around ten on his Harley. You provide the looks and the brains, and I'll provide the helmet to hold them together. Have we dealt?"

Tari had the words ready. Yes. Yes. Yes. Then she remem-bered. *Shit! The test.* It was immediately after the ward round, and the night that Rickey had planned would wipe tomorrow off the face of the map.

"Oh, Rickey, I'm sorry. I'm really sorry. But I can't go out tonight. I've got a big test tomorrow, and I have to study. And, more important, I have to get some sleep. If I spend all night dancing and drinking, I'll be a basket case in the morning."

There was a long pause. It was clear that Rickey Cage was not used to being turned down, for a test . . . or anything else.

"Well," he said at last, with a rueful laugh. "I guess that serves me right for trying to date a girl who has homework."

"I'd love to do it another time," said Tari.

"Yeah, well, we will."

Again, there was a silence. She had given him the chance to offer another evening. But he didn't do that.

He just said, "I might be falling in love with you," and he put down the telephone before she could think of a reply.

Mary stood there, the demand for chapter and verse all over her face.

"He said," said Tari, cutting through to the bottom line, "that he might be falling in love with me."

"Might?"

"Might. If the trumpet hath an uncertain sound . . ."

She laughed with pleasure. Rickey Cage was playing games with her. But she was a tough little cookie who could match him all the way. It was fun that he was interested in her, fun and flattering 'cause he had great-looking girls on permanent kamikaze flyby overhead. In the back of her mind was his enigmatic Parthian shot in the supermarket, the one Mary didn't know about. "We're going to be lovers," made an interesting trailer for his "I might be falling in love with you." Was that how he talked to all his girls, throwing tidbits of romantic prediction to whet their appetites for the Cage seduction scenes? It was childish in a way, or maybe childlike, there being a difference. He was saying he was cool, that his lovemaking would be oh-so-casual, and full of patronizing progress reports like the card from school. "This girl shows promise, but must try harder for the straight A's I know she's capable of." Did it serve to straighten up his dates at the makeup table? Did it push them the extra half-mile in the clothes-closet selection process? Did it encourage them to go just that bit heavier on the Pat Booth "Miami" scent, which was par for the course of embryonic lovers these days?

"You going out with him?"

"Whiskey. Milano. Di Lido. Van Dome. And my test in the morning. No way."

"Yeah. You'd need a bed in intensive care after an evening like that, with Pepto-Bismol in the IV line."

"Well, at least it won't be bed with Rickey Cage," said Tari with a laugh.

"I don't think Cage does beds. Too sissy. Standing up in a parking lot, more like. With an audience that claps when he comes."

"Mary, that is soooo gross. He's not like that at all. He's a real gentleman." Tari smiled to show she wasn't cross, secretly stimulating Mary to greater heights. So far, sexual activity with Rickey had occurred on a plane and in a supermarket. Maybe Mary had a point.

"I'm sure he is. He'll probably say please before and thank-you afterward, and call you Tina when he gives you the bogus telephone number."

"Mary, one could be forgiven for thinking you've had one too many unhappy experiences with the opposite sex."

"Nonsense, sweetheart. Oh, by the way, do you know the name of that little piece of insensitive skin that's attached to a dick?"

"No. Is this a joke coming?"

"That, too. It's called a man."

"I *like* men, Mary."

"Well, I know you love everyone and all that stuff, but men . . . I mean, those little black socks that smell, and stubble, and shoulder-blade hair. And the way they laugh, and that horrible, hideous underwear. Sometimes I think a man dropping his pants is one of the most disgusting sights in the whole wide world. That sordid little piece of . . . gristle!"

"Mary, this sounds like a problem," scolded Tari, mock-serious. "I think we need a little therapy here so that you can reclaim your sexual birthright. I had no idea that Frank had had such a powerful effect . . . although it was unkind of him not to call."

"It's nothing to do with Frank," lied Mary. "He's just an *example* of maleness. A good example, mind you. Almost a definitive sample, come to think of it, but he's not why men make me want to puke. It's their naïveté, their predictability, their fear of sensitivity. Why can't they be soft, I mean *feel* soft and be sort of smooth and sweet-smelling, rounded and not all angles? I suppose what I'm saying is why the hell can't a man be more like a woman?"

"Uh-oh," said Tari, taking a step back and putting her hands defensively across her breasts in mock fear.

"Wait a minute, Tari, I'm not saying I'm gay . . . it's just that well, actually, the bottom line is I *would* rather fuck Julia Roberts than your famous Rickey or all the other gorillas we're supposed to want."

"She sure does have a cute giggle," said Tari speculatively. "But I'm not sure that all this is going to help with the psychiatry test tomorrow."

"Well, I'm sorry you missed out on your night with super-stud, dear. Hey, aren't all those Don Juan types supposed to be gay? You'd better see his paperwork before you ball him, and remember it's a month or two before you test positive. Just being realistic, Tari."

Mary added the last bit as she saw Tari's face cloud over. She had gone too far.

"Mary," said Tari, "it's okay to poke fun at Rickey. I don't mind that. It's a little mean, but it's okay. But *please* spare me the redneck gay-bashing, all right? You of all people ought to know AIDS isn't a gay disease. From here on in, the spread is hetero. Go test yourself. I heard you yelping the other night with Frank. Did you see his paperwork? I mean, really . . ."

Mary put up her hands in surrender. She knew she had gone too far. She'd hit Tari in her righteous indignation, and that was never a clever spot to zap her.

"Sorry. You're right. AIDS isn't a gay disease. And Rickey isn't gay. I was just warming up my anti-man charger. It feels good to give it a ride from time to time."

"That's okay, Mary. I'm a bit sensitized myself. I did AIDS counseling the other day, and it really got to me. This neat-looking guy was so young, and so completely devastated. And all he could think about was what to tell his mother. I mean, you're going to die a horrible death and all you're worried about is what people *think*? And maybe he's right. Maybe his mother *would* be horrified. Maybe she'd worry as much about the neighbors as her only son falling to pieces in front of her."

A big tear grew in Tari's eyes. It escaped, and rolled down her cheeks. It was Mary's turn to feel shame.

Tari was never far from moments like this. She cared passionately about both the bleeding crowd and the needing friend. She always had, from the time Mary had first met her in New York as a freshman in med school. Together they had made the decision to transfer to Miami, and Mary loved Tari in the way that Tari loved the world. It was the range of her. She wasn't hung up on holiness, a tiresome preacher at war with fun and frivolity. She was full of life, and lusty, sexual, actually incredibly so, and she could end a night and start a day with the stamina of the ultimate party animal. But running through her, like beautiful theme music in an uplifting movie, was her goodness. It was real, very far from theory, and it showed up in remarkable places at odd times. Like now. Suddenly, in the middle of the girl talk about the boys, Tari was all but weeping at the thought of a stranger's tragedy, and the silly world that had allowed it.

"You want some juice?" said Mary, subtly interrupting her friend's sadness.

"Yeah, thanks," said Tari.

Mary walked into the kitchen and opened the refrigerator. A plastic milk bottle was full of fresh pink grapefruit juice from the market on Washington. She filled a couple of glasses and the two friends sat down at the round table in the corner, sipping pensively on the delicious drink.

"To Florida," said Mary, raising her glass. "Hot, bright, and juicy."

"It is beautiful here, isn't it?" said Tari. "Aren't you glad we did it?"

"For sure. Half the money, twice the life. Everyone's waking up to it, and not just the rich mothers. It's like wiping the slate clean and everyone starting out equal. The recession doesn't seem to be here. Just lots of young people, low rents, cheap food. You don't even need clothes. You hardly need a car. I heard the other day that Barry Diller and David Geffen were buying property."

"Yeah, and Madonna, Stallone and his pal Gianni Versace,

Matt Dillon, Costner, Mickey Rourke—they've all either bought or are buying. And then there's Rickey . . . the one who just might be in love with me.'' She laughed the Tari laugh, infectious, an invitation to party. Her mood had moved on.

"Isn't he supposed to be an item with that model from L.A.—Jodie Summerfield, or something?''

"He sees her," said Tari.

"You think maybe he sees, but doesn't touch," said Mary slyly.

Tari wasn't to be bumped from her good mood.

"Knowing Rickey, he probably touches, but doesn't look.''

"Well, he'd better be nice to you, or I'll piss in the gas tank of his bike.''

"Are you that good a shot, Mary? I'm impressed. Been practicing?''

The two girls laughed then, still competitors, still sparring partners, but as good friends as the world allowed.

Tari stood up, finishing her drink.

"Listen, I'm going over to the hospital to see Peter Seagram. He's doing so well. I think just about every neuro in South Florida has given him the once-over, and they all agree something really strange happened.'' .

"Still your miracle?''

"For want of a better word," said Tari.

The room was full of flowers. Dr. Peter Seagram was sitting up in bed, looking out of the window over the bay. As Tari walked in, he turned to her and smiled.

"How are you feeling?''

"Still in shock. Otherwise better than a million dollars.''

Tari peered at his right eye. It was a little bloodshot. Otherwise it seemed fine. From the way he held his head and watched her, it was obvious he could see out of it. A copy of the *Miami Herald* lay on the bed.

"Not even an eye patch? Twenty-twenty vision?''

"Not even a headache. What the hell happened, Tari?'' There was more to his question than on the surface of the words.

"I don't think we'll ever know.''

"But you made him stop, didn't you? If he'd moved the

scissors, if he'd just wiggled them around, I'd have been a blind zombie from there on in. You made him stop. Could it have been automatic obedience cutting in? That's what I keep going back to. Somehow you found the words that worked. You saved my life . . . any meaningful life. Shit, thanks, Tari.''

He held out his hand to her, and she took it with his gratitude. Out across Government Cut, a speedboat turned on a wide circle. A flight of pelicans flew in close formation overhead. It was early evening and the low sun angled across the water. God was busy with his paint box on the bay.

"They took the guy up to Robert E. Lee Memorial. He's inaccessible, but quiet on Haldol. I can't believe how quickly it happened," said Tari.

"It was my fault. I wasn't ready for catatonic excitement. Too busy being the teacher . . ." He smiled sheepishly. Then he turned serious again. "Douglas was in here this morning, you know, the supershrink. He was asking all sorts of questions about you—what you said, how you behaved. I wasn't quite sure what he was getting at . . . something about you commanding the schizo to stop in the name of God. Is that what you said? I can't remember a thing except this thing sticking in my eye."

"I just said what came into my mind, and it worked. That's all I know."

"Well, I think you're going to be one hell of a psychiatrist. Knowing the right thing to say is the most important thing of all."

"What else did Douglas say?" said Tari. For some reason she wanted the conversation to turn back to him.

Seagram half-laughed. "He didn't seem very interested in me. It was more you. Were you a regular guy? Did you seem introverted? Did you show sort of mystical preoccupations? It was almost as if he was asking if you were a schizoid personality. I told him you were a borderline psychotic with severe narcissistic personality problems, and that you'd make one hell of a professor of psychiatry one day."

Tari laughed. "What did he say to that?"

"He said that maybe we'd all be surprised by what you turned out to be."

"What a funny thing for him to say."

"To tell you the truth, if he wasn't a priest and celibate and all that, I'd have said he was pretty interested in you . . . if you know what I mean."

"Oh, nonsense," said Tari. *But attractive nonsense,* she thought.

10

AT FIRST the cloud on the radar seemed no bigger than a man's hand, but by the end of the week the storm had a name. They called it Andrew. It had been quiet out there in the Atlantic and the Caribbean, and now there was this little tropical wave that became a depression, that turned into a storm, that was to become the most devastating hurricane ever to hit North America. Tari heard about it first on Wednesday evening, after class. She had her feet up on the sofa, and the weatherman said they were watching a relatively unimpressive system way out in the ocean due east of Miami. It was apparently no big deal, but on Thursday morning it was still coming, and the winds had picked up some speed, although it was hardly a hurricane yet. By Friday, South Florida's anxiety was up, and so was the force of the storm. Winds were pushing ninety miles an hour, and it was scurrying over the warm ocean, sucking strength from the sea. Now they talked of possible landfall sometime the following Tuesday. No sweat. No panic. It looked like a wimp of a storm. And there was still a ton of time for it to go somewhere else. It could wander up the coast to catch the Carolinas. It could slip south of Key West and curl up into the gulf to pillage Galveston, Corpus Christi, or coastal Louisiana. By Friday evening, there was a watch, but no talk of a hurricane warning and a general evacuation of the coastal areas. Nobody was seriously worried, because nobody was vibing in on the static ridge of high pressure over central Florida that would send Andrew crashing into southern Miami, not deviating in course, not moving one inch from the path of its due-eastward approach.

On Saturday morning, Tari watched the increased traffic on the Intracoastal Waterway as the more nervous boat captains sailed north to the safety of the Port St. Lucie River and the mangroves.

She called the medical school and they reassured her. Evacuation looked like only a remote possibility. They told her to stay in touch, however. If the patients had to be moved from Robert E. Lee Memorial, South Beach, and the other coastal hospitals, every pair of hands would be needed.

Tari put down the phone.

"Jeez, Mary, this could be it."

"Nah. It's going south. It'll miss the Keys."

"Anyway, the office wants us to stay close to the South Beach and be part of the hospital evacuation there. I guess out to the airport or something."

"Are you going to leave?" asked Mary.

"The beach? You'd better believe it. Aren't you?"

"I guess so." Mary couldn't get too excited. Outside, it was bright sunshine. She'd been looking forward to a weekend of sunbathing. And she was still a New Yorker. Nothing fazed them, except the very *small* things.

"Listen, nine out of ten hurricane deaths are caused by drowning. This place is zero feet above sea level. A twenty-foot surge tide would wipe South Beach off the map."

"But everyone says it's only a little hurricane," whined Mary. Her tan really needed some work.

Tari was quiet. She checked out the storm on TV. It was wound tight around its central hole on the Doppler, and Eleuthera and Bimini still separated it from the coast. But its course hadn't deviated one iota. Its winds were strengthening. It was picking up speed. Tari didn't like the look in its eye.

She glanced around her apartment. Would it be gone by next week? The wind wouldn't knock the building over. The worst case would be windows blown in, and her belongings blown out. The only thing she'd really miss would be her photographs. But all over the beach, all kinds of people would be in danger . . . the old people, the winos, the Mexicans whose cars weren't working and whose language problems would put them out of the information loop. The med school wanted her to help with the patients, but there would be a ton of people doing that. It would be overkill. Her heart beat faster.

"The hurricane center in Coral Gables has just reported further strengthening of Andrew," said the weatherman. "It continues on its course, due east toward Miami, and winds are now topping ninety miles an hour. So Andrew is a category-two storm. But it appears to be picking up speed. We are tracking it now at twelve miles an hour, which would give a possible landfall Monday night or early Tuesday morning. We repeat that a hurricane watch is in effect from Vero Beach south to Key West. Please stay tuned to this station. We will keep you posted on the latest developments. May we remind you of some tips for hurricane preparedness. Throw deck furniture into your swimming pool. Make sure you have a radio, batteries, a flashlight. Fill the bathtub full of water for drinking in case water supplies . . ."

"Mary! It's going to hit. I just felt it. Like, I *know* it." Tari jumped up. Her face was reddening.

"Oh, shit, not another premonition," wailed Mary. "Where is it going to hit, weatherwoman? Can you please make it be somewhere far away from here?"

"Close, very close. South. We've got to get down to the streets and help get people organized."

"Listen, there isn't even an evacuation yet. All you'll do is get people wound up, and rushing around and panicking unnecessarily. I mean, this is America. They'll tell us all what to do when it has to be done, and not before."

"Do what the hell you like," said Tari. "I'm telling you this thing is going to happen, and sooner than anyone thinks."

"Hurricane Andrew has increased its speed. The latest report has winds topping one hundred miles per hour," said the voice from the TV. "We have been told to stand by for the issuing of a hurricane warning. I repeat, we have heard that an evacuation order is imminent. It has not been issued yet, but please keep tuned to this station. . . ."

11

THE SMELL of urine melded unhappily with the lysine disinfectant. The room was dark and warm, cooled by fan, not air-conditioning. Faces around the walls peered suspiciously at Tari.

She turned to the woman beside her.

"Who's going to organize the evacuation? Where are they going to? How are they going to get there?"

"I don't know. I know nothing. They don't tell me nothing. I try to phone them. They don't answer. My van, it only hold six and I have twenty residents. Some of them can't walk. Some of them are incontinent. They don't understand. Oh, I don't know what to do. I just don't know." The woman was close to tears.

"Don't worry. It's going to be all right. I'm going to help. These people are all going to be safe. Trust me."

Tari looked around her and realized the cheapness of words. It looked suspiciously like a long-stay geriatric ward. Some of the faces were already skeletal. Sunken, hollow eyes, yellow from the jaundice of early liver failure, stared morosely into the gloom. Thin, arthritic fingers plucked pointlessly at woolen bed jackets that were matted with congealed food. Thick ankles, swollen with the edema of congestive cardiac disease, were crammed into filthy slippers. Beneath several of the chairs small pools of urine gathered on the dirty linoleum. It was the waiting room for heaven. It looked like the living room of hell.

"Who owns this place?" said Tari.

"Some people they live in Cincinnati," said the woman by her side.

It figured. Before South Beach had become trendy, senior citizens and crack dealers had lived here. A few old people's homes survived. This was one. Any minute now, Andrew willing, it would be sold to Euro-trash as a restaurant or nightclub. But right now it was a disaster waiting to happen. Out there, across the beach, Andrew's wall of water was building. It wouldn't take more than a few feet of flood to drown the inhabitants of this room. The owners of the old people's home up north clearly didn't give a damn.

Tari did. Most of the previous night she had hurried from door to door, trying to be of help. She had persuaded some old people to move, helped others pack, and made endless calls to the authorities to get directions to the inland shelters. She had finally fallen, exhausted, into bed in the small hours. When she woke on Sunday morning, it was to discover that Andrew had metamorphosed into a monster. The hurricane, packing winds of 145 miles per hour, was roaring through the Bahamas at nearly twenty miles an hour, and its course was as unswerving as a speeding bullet. Forget Tuesday. Sometime that very night, part or all of Miami was going to be flattened by a category-four hurricane. Tari had filled herself full of coffee and taken to the streets once again. Around ten o'clock, amid the chaos of a general evacuation, she had found this place. The supervisor, wringing her hands and talking to herself, had been rushing around on the veranda like a headless chicken. When Tari had stopped to ask what was wrong, the litany of complaints had poured out. The distraught woman was in charge of twenty elderly people, and she hadn't a clue what to do with them.

"Who deals with their medical problems?" said Tari. A

quick look was enough to tell her that most of these people should be in a hospital.

"Dr. Mendoza, he come a couple times a week."

"Are you a qualified nurse?"

"I work in a hospital in Guatemala once."

Great! thought Tari. She let her eyes do the walking, assessing the situation. The chair-bound inhabitants of this room had the medical problems and the advanced Alzheimer's. They presented most of the problems. The ones sitting quietly on the outside terrace would be easier to handle. The others, cruising about in the corridors, buzzing like flies on hot glass, seemed to possess most of their marbles. They would be prone to panic, indeed were panicked already. Some of them wouldn't want to leave. There were three groups: the sick, the passive, and the anxious.

"Have you got medical notes on these people?" said Tari.

"Yes, and Dr. Mendoza leave their medicine in the refrigerator, and I hand it out whenever."

"Where are the notes?" But Tari could see them already. They were stacked on a cart in the corner. She walked over and picked up a folder. Dr. Mendoza was not a talkative man on paper. A date was usually juxtaposed with a tick, and nothing else. That presumably permitted him to charge an "examination fee." Otherwise, information was scanty . . . CCF for congestive cardiac failure, AF for atrial fibrillation, SD for senile dementia. Most were on digoxin for their heart arrhythmias, and diuretics for the water retention caused by their heart failure. Quite a few were tranquilized with Amytal. There was a wheezing asthmatic, three catheterized patients trailing bags of urine, and one ancient lady on an IV line for what looked to Tari like severe dehydration. At the end of the room an old man moaned gently, clutching his stomach with both hands.

"What's that man's name?" said Tari.

"Mr. Abrahams."

Tari walked toward him. She knelt down to the level of his eyes.

"Are you all right, Mr. Abrahams?" she asked.

"Oooooooh," he moaned in answer.

Tari stood up. She leaned forward. "Do you mind if I take a

look at your tummy, sir?'' she said gently. He nodded his assent. She undid the cord of his pajamas. His belly was distended. She laid her hand flat on it and tapped briskly. The sound of her middle finger banging on the back of her other one was dull. The man had a full bladder. It was highly likely that he had urinary retention.

"Can you get me a bottle?" Tari spoke quickly to the supervisor.

She reached out for the hand of the ancient man. His fingers in hers were the texture of parchment. He turned his face up to hers. His eyes were milky with cataracts, wet and rheumy. His skin was covered with liver spots. His head shook gently with the tremors of Parkinson's disease.

"Do you mind my asking how old you are, Mr. Abrahams?" she asked. He seemed to hear her. A light went on in the old eyes.

He opened his mouth to speak, but on the first attempt no sound came out. He tried to wet dry lips with a dry tongue.

"Ninety-two," he rasped, collapsing back against his chair with the effort. A wintry smile creased his features. His age was all he had left to be proud of.

"That's wonderful." She smiled at him and squeezed his hand. "Listen, sir, I want you to try and urinate in a bottle. It may be that you can't, and if you can't, I want to put a tube into your bladder. It'll take away the pain, and it won't be too uncomfortable."

"Catheter," he murmured. He'd been there before. That firmed up the diagnosis.

"That's right," said Tari. "It'll make you more comfortable, because you know we've got to go on a little journey."

He seemed confused by that, but he squeezed her hand. He trusted her. She wasn't like the doctor or the supervisor, all brisk orders and no respect. She was considerate and polite, and her so-young skin felt good against his. For he was an untouchable now. He was very old and very disgusting, and good for nothing but this dark room hidden away from the world of youth and movement and thought and talk. When he had been well enough to sit on the veranda and watch the people rushing by, he had seen their faces close down in denial of the fate that one day would be theirs. He had seen their eyes twist away from his age-ravaged face and scrawny limbs, and he remembered when the girls had watched him and wanted him in the distant land when he'd been young.

"You're kind," he said.

"You're very brave," she said. It took courage to pass through the valley of the shadow. He was all alone, this wreck of a human being. The flickering memories locked inside would mock his helplessness. There was nothing left but the great mystery up ahead. Had he faith to help him in the last days? Had he the intellect to wonder why God had made this ordeal for him to endure?

Tari took the bottle when it arrived and held it out for him. He fumbled, trying to free himself, trying to find the opening. She helped him, totally unself-conscious, a servant to suffering.

He shook his head. He couldn't go.

"It's all right," she said. "We'll soon have you fixed up." She worked quickly, but cut no corners in the sterile procedure. The catheter pack came with a germ-free green surgical sheet, which she draped over the lower body of the patient. She slipped on the latex gloves and eased the anesthetic gel into his urethra. Next, she stripped the end of the plastic tubing from its cellophane wrapper. She waited a few seconds for the lignocaine to dull sensation. Then she threaded in the catheter. First she held his penis straight up, but she dipped it down to negotiate the kink as the urethra passed beneath the pubic bone and into the bladder. A bubble of bright yellow, concentrated urine poured into the end of the pack as confirmation that she had reached her target. Deftly, she nipped the tube and attached it to a receiving bag, which she lowered to the floor to allow gravity to exert suction. With an air-filled syringe, she blew up the bubble on the end of the catheter, which would hold the tube in place in the bladder.

"There," she said. "I bet that feels better."

His expression was her reward. Relief was all over his face.

He gripped her hand tightly.

"You're an angel," he said.

Tari stood up. "You're a very sweet man," she said.

Then she leaned over and kissed him, lightly, on the cheek. His eyes clouded with tears as he turned his head away from her.

She paused, but time was running out. There was so much to do.

The van held six, eight at the most. She selected the eight most immobile for those places. Next, she made a pile of their medicines, putting them in paper bags behind their individual chairs. She found a suitcase and filled it with things the old and the ill needed—Thorazine elixirs for agitation, catheter packs, disposable enemas, barrier creams for bedsores.

Now she had to organize the others. She shepherded the passive veranda group into the TV room, enlisting the help of the mobile, anxious contingent in this process.

They stood around in the gloom, twisting and turning in uncertainty. They muttered darkly among themselves. Their hands were in constant motion. Eyes darted this way and that.

"Hello, everyone," said Tari. They quieted at the tone of her voice. It was full of a vibrant reassurance. It was "up." It was totally confident.

"Listen, my name's Tarleton Jones, and I'm a medical student here at the State Medical College and I've come to help. Some of you know that there is a storm coming. Just to be on the safe side, we're going to move everyone to an inland shelter, away from the beach. As soon as the storm's over, we'll bring you back again. So it'll be a little bit of an adventure, and I'm going to stay with you through it all, until we're back safely."

"We're going to drown," wailed a small, tense lady.

"What about my photographs?" asked a tall, stooped man at the back.

"My son will be here to pick me up," said a sad lady in the front.

"There's only room for six in the van," said a shrewd, large woman.

"What I want you all to do," said Tari calmly, "is to trust me. I've got everything worked out. You're going to be one hundred percent fine. I guarantee it." She took a deep breath. God would make it all right. That she knew. The only question was how? "Now I want you to help each other pack just a few things that you need for the night, and any small, personal things that you feel you need. Your photographs, sir, and things like that."

She turned to the supervisor. "I need to make some phone calls," she said.

"You can use my office."

Tari worked quickly. There was apparently a shelter near the airport that had emergency medical facilities. That might be the answer. But it was still in the projected path of the storm, although it was fifteen miles from the beach. It might be better to travel north to the West Palm Beach auditorium. But how the hell would she get everyone moved sixty miles up a logjammed I-95? She looked at her watch. The evacuation was in full swing. The causeway would be rigid with traffic, and the road-work made travel a nightmare at the best of times. She called some taxi companies. The ones that answered all but laughed at her. Ferrying twenty golden oldies to West Palm in the middle of a category-four hurricane warning had to be a joke of sorts. The police couldn't help. The Red Cross wouldn't. It apparently contravened their famous small print.

She flicked on the TV on the desk.

"Andrew is an extremely dangerous storm, more powerful than Hugo, possibly the most powerful storm to make landfall in America . . . ever. We urge everyone to evacuate those areas in which a warning has been issued *immediately*. Do not delay. From Fort Lauderdale to southern Key Largo, all coastal areas should be evacuated. Winds of one hundred forty-five miles per hour have been recorded near the eye of the hurricane. It is imperative . . ."

Tari tried to stay calm. She should try the hospital. They, at least, would know who she was. There must be space on their buses.

She couldn't get through to the medical-school secretary. Eventually, she managed to contact the professor's secretary in the psychiatry department. She explained the problem quickly.

"The professor's right here," said the girl. "I'll ask her what you should do."

Tari waited. Good. At least Professor Hodges would have authority to make a decision. She breathed a sigh of relief.

"Are you a student on my psychiatry rotation?" Professor Hodges barked down the line.

"Yes, and I'm here in an old people's home on the beach, and we desperately need transport to get them out of here. I have immobile patients with heart failure and . . ."

"Why the hell aren't you here, helping move the psychiatric patients?" said Hodges.

"Well, I assumed everyone would be pretty well organized over there, and it's chaos here, and these people really need help, so . . ."

"What is your name?"

"Tarleton Jones."

"Listen to me, Ms. Jones. I suggest, if you want to stay out of big trouble, you get yourself here right now and help with our evacuation. Weren't you told you had to be at the hospital?"

"Yes, but . . ."

"I don't care who the hell you are trying to help. I want you at the South Beach where you belong. Do you understand?"

"No!" said Tari. "Do *you* understand? I have twenty people here, and they're abandoned. They haven't got the facilities of a hospital behind them. They're ill and they're frightened and they need my help and they need your help, too. And I'm asking for it."

There was a pregnant pause.

Veronica Hodges's voice was cold with fury when she spoke. "Do you want to be suspended from the medical school?" she threatened. Her voice trembled with rage.

"Why," said Tari, "don't you go take a flying fuck at yourself?"

She slammed down the phone.

That felt better. The professor had a reputation as a cantankerous, small-minded pedant, but Tari had never realized that a doctor could be so callous. It boggled her mind. Still, there wasn't time to think about Hodges now, or the damage that Tari had just done to her career. Shit! How the hell was she going to get these people to safety?

She ran out to the street. Chaos. Everywhere people were packing cars with pets, belongings, children. She debated trying to cadge a seat here, a seat there. No. These old people had to be kept together. She needed a bus, a truck, a Winnebago. She needed a miracle.

"Oh, God," said Tari out loud. "Help me to help these people."

12

UODIE SUMMERFIELD sat on the high bar and dangled her legs over it. Her microskirt hardly hid her underwear. Around the pool table, they couldn't take their eyes off her. Rickey Cage, however, chalking his cue, was planning the top left-hand pocket for the eight ball. He was thinking about nothing else.

"Rickey, why the fuck are we playing pool when there's a hurricane out there?" she whined, tossing the hair that sold the conditioner and netted her half a million a year.

"Top left," he said, not turning to look at her. He bent down to site the white on the black.

He didn't look like a movie star. His stubble was two days old, and his simple white V-neck T-shirt hung loose around stovepipe blue jeans. He smoked a cigarette, or rather allowed one to droop, Belmondo-style, from the corner of his mouth. A glass of neat vodka, no ice, no mixer, no shit, sat on the edge of the pool table. The harsh light from the table lamp emphasized his pallor. If he hadn't looked like an angel with a hangover, he could have passed for Count Dracula short of a blood hit.

The group around the table, his group, went quiet while he prepared the shot.

Bang! He shot the cue into the white and it ran like a rocket into the right rear end of the black. The angle was dead-on. The eight ball hit the net without grazing the edge of the pocket.

"Yesssss," he exclaimed, standing up straight and firing a victory fist into the air.

"Nice shot, Rickey," said someone. Several others murmured assent.

"Nice shot, Rickey," lisped Jodie, mimicking the compliment in a small-girl California accent. She was pissed. There wasn't a guy in America, apart from the one she wanted, who wouldn't have crawled five miles over broken glass to lick her feet. Yet here she was, passing up God knew what parts in Hollywood, to hang out in hurricane land with the antihero who hardly recognized her existence.

"What did you say, honey?" he said, turning to look at her as if surprised by her presence.

"I said, why the hell are we hanging around here waiting to get blown away?"

She looked at him defiantly as she spoke. Her dark brown eyes spoke about insecurity. She was on a fishing expedition that she knew was going to go wrong. The vulnerability in her expression emphasized her extraordinary beauty.

"Last I heard, it was a free country." Rickey smiled gently as he effectively told her to get lost.

She chewed on her lower lip as she took it. He didn't need her. He screwed her, but he didn't give a damn about her. That made him clever, because he alone had figured out the truth about her—that beneath her beauty she was a pretty inferior person. The others were taken in. They didn't know about the worm inside the glossy packaging. Rickey knew about it, yet he still did it to her, sometimes three times a night, so he must like her a little bit, mustn't he?

"You want me to split?" she said. The mist in her eyes was tears.

He shrugged with a bewildered laugh. "I just want you to do what you want to do, honey. I do what I want. You do what you want. It ain't difficult."

Nobody spoke as they listened to Jodie's public humiliation. How could anyone say things like this to a girl who looked like that? The question was on every mind, together with admiration for the stud who could pull it off.

Rickey walked over to the bar, scooping up the vodka on the way. He wasn't being aggressive. His body language said he liked her, fancied her, whatever. It was just that he didn't really care. One way or the other. She didn't touch him. She couldn't touch him.

Jodie clenched her fists. His disinterest only made her want him more. God, if only he cared. Then she'd show him the true meaning of pain.

He hitched himself up beside her on the bar and turned his baseball cap around the right way, as if paying lip service to the presence of a "lady."

"You know," he said. "There's time to finish the game and beat the Spaniards too. Sir Francis Drake, the armada," he added.

"Huh?" said Jodie.

"Yeah, well, anyway . . . I guess the game is over." He smiled suddenly, giving up the idea of making contact with her. What was the point? She was a gorgeous, extravagant, gift-wrapped parcel containing . . . precisely nothing. Beneath the fabulous exterior, she was nobody. He laughed out loud.

"Just stay beautiful, Jodie," he said. "It ain't such a bad thing to be."

He eased himself down and stood between her dangling legs, looking up to her face. It wasn't a put-down. Mother Teresa probably would have sacrificed a leper or two to look like Jodie. So what if she carried the fury of all L.A. women pickled in her heart? Her glossy exterior made up for it. Her medium was her message. She was form, not substance.

"You think I'm beautiful, Rickey? You really think so?"

She dripped insecurity on him, her voice husky with narcissistic desire. Which part did he like most? Her tits? She pushed them out at him. Her mouth? She licked the lips that pouted. Her crotch? It was his, at chest level, anytime he wanted it.

"Yeah," he smiled, smiling the careless, lopsided smile.

She leaned forward. She knew what to say now. She was Plato, Churchill, Oliver Wendell Holmes.

"You wanna do me in the john?" she whispered.

She had turned herself on. He could feel the heat beaming from her. She meant it. He allowed the steamy vision to play with his mind. He could see her long legs, wide open as she leaned back against the grubby wall. He could see her skirt, and those pure white bikini briefs, straddling her ankles. He could smell the musk, hear the gentle moans as the superstar model surrendered to his lust in the public/private place. For long seconds he paused, savoring the erotic dream. Then he stepped back from her.

"Nah," he said. "I guess it is time to hit the road."

There was a barely audible sigh of relief from the entourage. A couple of safe suites had been booked at the PGA resort in West Palm Beach, and outside a brace of limos stretched most of the block. Inside them would be booze, ice, TV, and air-conditioning that could freeze the balls off a brass monkey. Standing eye-to-eye with a hurricane seemed extravagant for a macho gesture in the circumstances.

Rickey looked at his watch. The cars were already loaded with luggage. On the street outside, the wind was up, the skies were darkening, and it had begun to rain. He looked around him, photographing the street for his memory. What would it look like when he returned? The beach at low tide? A pile of salty rubble? Exactly the same as this? There was no way of telling. Nature was calling the shots. His friends piled cheerfully into the cars, laughing and joking. Jodie held back, not certain which was the "best" seat, but knowing it would be the one next to Rickey. He, too, stayed on the sidewalk by the front limo. The driver hovered by his side, waiting for instructions, and the door-opening ceremony.

"Come on, Rickey," said Jodie.

But Rickey was thinking about something. Thinking about someone. Thinking about Tari. Where was she? Long gone by now, presumably. Her retreat from South Beach would have been well-planned and executed by now. She wouldn't hang around until the last minute to thumb her nose at a storm. He tried to push her out of his mind, but she wouldn't go. Damn! What was that building she'd said she lived in? That big one on Alton Road. He turned to the driver.

"Can you take Alton Road to the causeway?" he said.

13

THE WIND howled over South Beach, bending the palms flat. Rain splattered against Tari's windshield as she drove back toward the old people's home, and she leaned forward in her seat and peered out into the gloom. She was seriously worried now. She could cram maybe another four people into her car, but that still left ten or so behind, and all the luggage. She had left a note pinned to the deserted reception desk for Mary, giving her the Collins Avenue address and *ordering* her to get there as soon as possible with her car. But she knew it was in vain. Mary would have gone by now. One thing was for sure. Sunbathing weather was history.

She took the left on Collins and parked outside the home, behind the supervisor's van. Several frightened faces were flattened against the glass of the big picture window. She jumped out. The supervisor had been given a list of people and organizations to call while Tari was gone.

Now she ran out of the house. "It no good. Nobody can help. They say 'too busy.'" She looked frantic, but also relieved that this whole evacuation had somehow become the stranger's problem.

"Look, we've got my car now. And the van. Maybe we could do two trips."

Tari looked around. The weather was worsening by the minute. The sky had gone from gray to black, and the rain was more insistent. The wind was maybe twenty-five miles an hour, possibly more. The trip back might be difficult, and the police were probably no longer allowing traffic from the mainland to the beach. Tari tried to stay calm. Two trips wasn't an alternative. She should send the supervisor with the eight most seriously ill patients. Then she would stay and face Andrew with the rest. At sea level? Face a category-four hurricane with elderly people who couldn't even swim? It was out of the question. But what the hell was the answer? She could get twelve out if they all left now. But she couldn't leave the others behind. She hurried out to the rainswept streets. There had to be help somewhere. Once again, she prayed.

"Father, help me."

That was the moment she saw the limo. It sailed sedately out of the gloom like a great white cruise ship from a mist at sea. As soon as Tari saw it, she knew who was in it. It was a gut thing, a feeling of visceral certainty that came ready-made with relief. The car slowed as it approached, and now Tari could see that behind it was another limousine, as grand and as crass as the one in front. Both were bright alabaster, and bristling with radio antennas that looked as if they could speak easily to satellites in the sky. Thick smoked glass hid the occupants from view.

Tari leaped into the street and stood in the path of the lead limo like a student in Tiananmen Square before a tank. It was Rickey, but if it wasn't Rickey it would be someone else, some show-biz high roller with a liberal agenda and a conservative bank account.

The car stopped. The passenger door opened. Rickey's head popped out.

"Hi, Tari," he said. "I got your note."

"Rickey, oh, my God, Rickey. Thank God you're here. What note?"

She rushed up to him and made as if to kiss him. Then, at

the last moment, she held back. She was both ashamed of her joy at seeing him and guilty that a large part of it was because she wanted something from him.

"I went by your apartment building. I saw the note for Mary and thought I'd check if you were all right. It sounded sort of urgent." He swung his legs onto the sidewalk and smiled a lopsided smile at her, sizing her up, reminding himself of just how good she looked. She was wet now . . . not soaked, but damp enough for her hair to be a delicious mess, her shirt to cling to her chest, and her skin to be shiny with moisture.

"Oh, Rickey, a terrible thing has happened. I've found all these old people, and some of them are sick and they've got to be evacuated, and there isn't enough transportation, and they've just got to leave right now. It's getting dangerous." The wind sucked at her words, emphasizing their truth. A gust of rain ripped into them.

"Why have we stopped? Who the hell are you talking to?" asked a querulous voice from the bowels of the limo. Jodie Summerfield's head slid out into the horizontal rain. "I know you," she said accusingly. "You were the girl on the plane." From the tone of her voice, "serial murderess" would have been a less slanderous description.

"Do you remember Jodie?" said Rickey.

"Yes," said Tari. "Hi, Jodie."

"There isn't room for her," said Jodie nastily.

"Rickey, come and look at them, please. I just want you to come and look at them." She held out her hand to him. He took it, still smiling the funny smile. He allowed her to draw him out into the rain and then toward the broken-down building and away from Jodie's snarls of protest.

He wrinkled his nose against the smell as he walked through the front door, as his eyes adjusted to the gloom. He had never liked hospitals. This place wasn't much better. The old people flitted around him, muttering and complaining in a miasma of worry and angst. Accusing eyes followed him like dim searchlights in the semidarkness, passive and suspicious. They were the zombie "undead," walking the face of the uncertain earth. They were abandoned. They were lost. They were terminally unloved by a world they had all but left behind.

"Look at them," said Tari. "They need us." He looked at

her, hardly seeing them. There was fire in her eyes. He knew what she wanted. She wanted him to fill up his limos with these leaking hulks of former people, and take them all to safety. She was going to ask him for that any millisecond now, but what she *really* wanted was for him to offer to do it.

He thought of the limousines' cargo . . . Jodie Summerfield, smelling like the million dollars she earned each year; his business manager, quiet but all-seeing behind her horn-rimmed glasses; his valet; the couple of sparring partners; his personal trainer; the Harley friends; and the fan who'd been fun. There was room in there, but not *that much* room, especially when you factored in the Louis Vuitton, the booze, the boxing gloves, and the other paraphernalia of what had been shaping up as the ultimate lost weekend.

"Where are they going?"

"West Palm Beach auditorium?" said Tari hopefully.

"Maybe we can do a little better than that," said Rickey. "I presume that you go wherever they go?"

"Yes, I do."

"Then it looks like the PGA resort gets lucky," said Rickey with a laugh.

She jumped at him, arms around his neck, and he caught her in flight. She swung there for a moment, her head buried against his throat, her legs dangling half-on, half-off, the floor.

"Oh, *thank* you, Rickey," she mumbled against his skin. Then she climbed off him, almost embarrassed, her face flushed with excitement. She had saved her sick people. God had delivered to her the man who had promised they would be lovers. It was more than an answered prayer. It was a reward.

"But aren't those limos full? The front one looked kinda full."

"They are now," said Rickey with a smile. "Let's go empty them."

They walked out into the rain. Rickey tapped on the window of the front car and gave the glad tidings to the would-be fellow travelers. They didn't like it, but they lumped it. Easy come, easy go. Muttering darkly, they decanted themselves onto the wet, windswept sidewalk. The comfort and safety of the ritzy PGA resort was about to be exchanged for the uncertain charms of a tacky motel with a shingle roof somewhere away from the sea. And then there was the question of how to get there.

Jodie Summerfield was staying, but she still had no idea about exactly who her companions would be on the jam-packed I-95 to West Palm Beach.

The second limo was soon emptied, and there followed a nerve-racking hour as the elderly were arranged carefully amid the sumptuous pillows and pristine leather of the luxury cars. They had quieted when first they had seen their transportation. "My son sent the cars for us," one had insisted. "Reminds me of my wedding day," another had said. Rickey had stood back and watched Tari handle it, persuading, bullying where necessary, reassuring, joking, as she had made the old people at home. He had never seen anything quite like it, never known anyone quite like her. This was creative, competent caring on a giant scale, a tour de force of open-ended love. And it was contagious. These cars would never be the same again. The bill from the limo company would include reupholstering at the very least, but he couldn't care less. It was wonderful to be part of this kindness caravan. He laughed out loud as he watched the horror on the faces of the two drivers. His laugh deepened as he imagined the liquid shock that soon would be sloshing around the reception area of the posh West Palm Beach hotel.

She turned toward him, laughing too. It was an ill wind . . . From the jaws of disaster, hope could spring free. Was that God's point? Whatever. The limos were full of the people they had saved. And up ahead was an adventure she would share with the man she already three-quarters loved.

14

ARI WAS dressed. She'd thrown it all together in pretty much the order it had come out of her closet. The black miniskirt would show off her long brown legs on the bike, and the ankle-length pointed-toe boots were pure Rickey. She had a beaded belt that would do for Chanel, and a black T-shirt with a V-neck that plunged to her midriff and showed she wasn't wearing a bra. Crossed black handbags nestled at each hip, their plastic straps draped around her long neck like Zapata's bandoliers. The T-shirt was a dyed Jockey. The mini was a thrift castoff. The bags were Toys "Я" Us. The shoes cost nothing in a K mart sale. All in all, she cost about twenty bucks, but, as she twirled in front of the mirror, she saw no change from a million.

She turned to Mary.

"What do you think?"

"More dash than cash."

"Oh *thank* you, best friend."

"Just jealousy talking."

"Shit, will you just look at that sunset."

They wandered out to the veranda. The dramatic Miami downtown was more than usually beautiful. The sun was gone but it had left a burnished heaven as its memorial, a richer red and finer shade of scarlet than Tari had seen before. People imagined Miami to be about sea views, the beach, the horizon stretching away into the Caribbean. But to those who lived here, this was the view . . . the Miami light show, more beautiful than Manhattan, framed by bridges, the aquamarine water of the Intracoastal, and all tented over by a fiery sky.

They flopped down into chairs.

"I can't get over how lucky we were," said Mary.

"And how unlucky the others were," said Tari softly. Andrew's devastation had shocked the world. Homestead was a Hiroshima of destruction. Just four miles south of where they sat, the marine park on Key Biscayne was a matchstick box of toppled trees. Yet South Beach had been spared. Oh, there were trees down and water in some nightclubs. It had been irritating to do without power for a while, and the curfew had been an unnecessary drag. But compared to southern Miami and northern Key Largo, SoBe had been untouched by the storm. In the rush of leaving, Tari had left a plant on the balcony of her apartment. It sat there now, an Andrew survivor and a testament to the fickle ways of nature . . . and of God.

"It makes you feel sort of guilty that they caught it, and we didn't."

"Yeah," said Tari. "Everyone's feeling that. You want to help, but there's nothing to do unless you happen to be a roofer, a carpenter, or an insurance guy. It's the first time I've ever wished I had a bulldozer instead of a Toyota." She laughed, but she didn't feel good. It was six weeks after Andrew, but his legacy lingered. Whole worlds had blown away in his two-hundred-mile-an-hour winds. Houses had been flattened, jobs were gone, hope had disappeared. There were families that wouldn't survive the stress of this. Little children would watch in despair as the parents they adored were forced apart by the strain of financial disaster.

"I wish I'd come with you when you went down there with all that bottled water," said Mary.

"It was pretty futile. In a way it was for me more than them.

I mean, the road was stiff with ghoulish sightseers and the cops were turning people back. Okay, so they let me through and a few kids got a drink, but the army had it pretty well sewn up. When you need a brand-new life, a cup of water doesn't really hack it."

"Still," said Mary wistfully, "I can't help feeling yours was a better hurricane than mine."

"At least you didn't tell the professor of psychiatry to perform an anatomical impossibility."

"Shit, Tari, I still can't believe you actually said that."

"You know, the funny thing is that neither can Professor Hodges. She called me in and we had this sort of terrifying cold interview thing, but she couldn't bring herself to refer to it. She drilled on and on about failing in my responsibility to this and to that, and God knows what. She told me I was a little piece of dirt and morally bankrupt and hadn't the character to be a doctor, but she just didn't mention what I said to her. I wonder if she actually kinda blocked it out . . . you know, like patients do when you try and tell them that they haven't got long to go and ought to get things sorted out."

"Sometimes I think Professor Hodges has a pretty severe personality disorder. I mean, you really did something with those old people, and over at the South Beach there were about ten staff members to each patient and enough transportation to move an army. Of course, not in limousines. . . ."

"You should have seen the condition of those limos when we hit West Palm. You should have seen Jodie Summerfield! I honestly think that of all those old people, *she* was the one who most needed medical attention. She was hysterical, absolutely crazed. I gave her a dose of Amytal that would have sedated a horse, and she still ran for about an hour before passing out."

"Tari, it's illegal for you to dish out drugs like that."

"I acted in good faith," said Tari with a laugh.

"Tell that to the Summerfield attorney. Actually, I guess it was a pretty shrewd move to tranquilize the opposition."

"It wasn't exactly a party up there," said Tari sharply.

"I know. I'm sorry," said Mary quickly. She knew what had happened. So did Tari. The memory flooded back.

*   *   *

"Are you all right, Mr. Begelman?"

He sat stiffly on the edge of the bed. His breathing was labored. His lips, by the flickering light of the television, seemed blue. Tari leaned over him. He turned toward her.

"Difficult to get my breath," he said.

She picked up his hand. His pulse was thin and thready, with a poor volume. Its rhythm was irregularly irregular. He was in atrial fibrillation. Tari thought quickly. AF was common in old people, but from her earlier reading of the notes she seemed to remember that Mr. Begelman was not one of those being digitalized for it. It was possible that the lack of coordination in his atrial heartbeat was new. In conjunction with shortness of breath and mild cyanosis, that was sinister. The inefficiency of his heartbeat was apparently severe enough to reduce the capacity of his blood to pick up oxygen in his lungs.

She took hold of his head and turned it gently to the right. His jugular vein was distended with blood two inches higher than would be normal. That meant the heart was congested with blood. The failing pump was no longer able to circulate the fluid adequately. The resulting back pressure in the big vein was clearly visible. She bent down. His feet were swollen. She pressed the flesh with her thumb. It sank into the doughy skin. When she removed it, the flesh did not spring back. The white thumb-shaped indentation remained exactly as she'd left it. That was pitting edema. Fluid was not draining back to the heart from the feet, where it was pooling under the influence of gravity. Shit!

He coughed suddenly, a deep, gurgling cough. Tari pulled the stethoscope from her pocket. Her heart began to speed.

"I want to listen to your chest, Mr. Begelman."

He nodded. Was the blue coloration deepening on his lips?

She opened the buttons of his shirt and felt for the apex beat, the place where the tip of the heart tapped against the rib cage. It should be four fingers down from the left nipple. It wasn't. It was way, way lower, and out to the side. Okay, his heart was enlarged. The muscle had gotten bigger as it tried to compensate in increased power for the lack of pumping efficiency caused by the loss of rhythm. That meant the problem was not new. Whatever. Mr. Begelman was short of breath, and he was going blue.

She put the drum of the stethoscope over the apex beat. There was the hiss of a loud systolic murmur, which all but obliterated the sound of the two heartbeats. His aorta was all silted up. But the real problem was the rhythm. It was all over the place, like the beat of a bongo drummer who had lost the plot. He was on the edge of ventricular fibrillation, and in the absence of high-tech intervention, ventricular fib equaled death. Tari took a deep breath. Mr. Begelman needed lignocaine to calm his wriggling heart. Without it, the lack of rhythm could shift from the relatively unimportant top heart chambers to the vital bottom ones. Once two ventricles lost pumping power it would be all over, unless they could be shocked back into normal rhythm. But there was no way to administer DC cardioversion, no ventilators, no sodium bicarbonate. They had most things in the luxurious Jack Nicklaus suite at the PGA National Resort, but a crash gurney was not on the inventory.

"Rickey," she shouted.

He hurried in from the suite across the corridor. They had left the doors open in case of an emergency like this.

"Listen, Rickey, Mr. Begelman is not very well. Help me to move him to the bathroom, will you?" She spoke calmly, but her expression communicated her alarm.

"Is he going to be all right?" said Rickey.

"Of course he is," said Tari. "Aren't you, Mr. Begelman?"

He didn't answer, but his old eyes were frightened.

Together, they picked him up from the bed. All around the room the eyes of the elderly watched them. They were scattered all over the place, on beds, on the richly carpeted floors, in armchairs, on the sofas. The double-glazed windows were taped up against the storm and the drapes were drawn, but outside the howling wind screamed its fury, and inside the flickering TV told the little it knew of Andrew's devastation. The storm had gone south of Miami, the eye passing through Homestead, Florida City, and the Everglades. They were safe here, seventy miles to the north of the hurricane, but from the sound of the wind it seemed they had passed through the gates into hell.

In the brightness of the bathroom, Tari could see the situation was deteriorating fast. Mr. Begelman's face was darkening. The blue of his lips was deepening. He was fighting for breath now, his scrawny chest heaving with the effort of expanding his lungs. Tari kicked a bundle of towels onto the floor and they laid him down.

"Rickey, can you get some pillows from the beds?"

She tried to stay calm. The hand she held was clammy, sweaty and wet, as the peripheral circulation closed down in surgical shock. Mr.

Begelman's body was trying desperately to divert blood away from his extremities and toward the vital internal organs and his brain. If he went into ventricular fib he would be dead in minutes. And there was nothing on earth that Tari could do about it. Or was there? On the wall was the shaver socket. By the beds there were lamps and cords. Could she rig her own crude defibrillator and shock his heart back into sinus rhythm with 120 volts from the outlet? She didn't know. What she knew was that the alternative was to watch him die.

"I want . . . I want . . . my photographs," said Mr. Begelman.

He collapsed back in Tari's arms at the effort of speech. He knew. He could hear the horsemen.

His photographs? God, yes, of course! Mr. Begelman was the one who'd wanted to bring his photographs. And he had. There had been room in the cavernous limos for everything but the kitchen sink. Tari thought quickly. She shouldn't leave him. But, hell, why not? If he was going to die, why shouldn't he die with those he loved? She laid him down gently.

"I'm going to get your photographs," she said. "Don't you worry, it's going to be all right."

They were stacked against the wall to the right of the bed. Two large ones, and one small. Rickey was gathering pillows.

"Is he okay?" he said. He tried to sound calm, but Tari could see it was an effort. He wasn't used to being out of his depth, yet he had allowed it to happen for the good of strangers. Of all his attractive qualities, this was the most unexpected, and the best.

Tari shook her head in answer to his question, telling him to say nothing. The ancient necks craned and twisted in the semidarkness. Rain smashed against the plate-glass windows. ". . . landfall half an hour ago, the eye passing between Key Biscayne and the northern tip of Key Largo . . ." said the television.

She beckoned him to come close. "Listen, Rickey, he's got a heart arrhythmia. If we do nothing, he'll die. There's just a slim chance I can shock him back into normal rhythm."

"Oh, shit," said Rickey. This was way outside his domain. He was an actor, a boxer . . . he could be damn near anything . . . but he wasn't a doctor and he sure as hell wasn't a male nurse. But then he was with Tari. And being with her made everything different. It was like having a bright light in your life, in the darkness, in the night, whatever, whenever. He swallowed hard. "What do you mean, shock him?" he said.

*In the middle of the emergency, Tari couldn't help smiling at the look
of horror on Rickey's face.*

*"Not tell him ghost stories," she said. "Listen, pull that lamp out of
its socket and bring it into the bathroom. We can rip the wires out and
get some sort of crosscurrent across his chest."*

*Tari hurried back to the bathroom. Mr. Begelman was dark blue.
She knelt beside him.*

*"I've got your photographs," she said. "Here, I'm going to put them
on the edge of the bath where you can see them."*

He craned his neck toward them and smiled.

He tried to moisten his lips with his tongue.

"Thank you . . . thank . . ."

*Then he closed his eyes and breath rattled in the back of his throat.
Tari felt muscle tone disappear in the hand she held. His chest rose and
fell. He was still there, but only just. Now, he was unconscious.*

*She clamped the stethoscope to his heart. It was leaping like a bag of
worms. His ventricles were jumping and heaving in every direction. He
was as good as dead.*

"Quick, Rickey!"

He ripped the cord from the lamp. "What do I do?" he said.

*"We need four live ends, a couple of matchsticks to hold the wires in
the socket. Have you got a knife to strip the cord?"*

"There's a steak knife on the room-service cart."

"Great! Hurry!"

*Tari felt for the pulse. It was barely there. As long as his heart didn't
stop, there was a tiny chance she might de-fib it.*

*Rickey was back, tearing at the wire with the sharp knife. Matches
weren't a problem in a hotel room. He ripped the two wires apart at both
ends and plugged two into the socket with the matches. He handed the
other two live ends to Tari.*

*She didn't hesitate. She jammed them simultaneously, a foot apart,
across Mr. Begelman's left nipple.*

"Thy will be done," she said.

*He bucked with the shock, and the smell of burning flesh filled the
room. Tari held the wires aloft and felt for his pulse. No good. No
rhythm. She must try again. She leaned forward. As she did so, the
lights went out. The power cut was total. The bathroom was plunged
into darkness, and the TV clicked off, and a wail of alarm rose from
the suite. It lasted maybe twenty seconds, maybe less, but when the lights
came back on again, Mr. Begelman was dead.*

Tari was frozen in disbelief. She had felt him go in the darkness. He had drifted away from her, as she had held his hand in one hand and the powerless power cord in the other. It was a mind-bending trick of fate. "Thy will be done," she had prayed. Had God's will been done?

"Is he dead?" said Rickey, blinking in the light.

His chest was still. He was pulseless. She should check his pupils for reaction to light, but yes, he was dead.

Tears filled Tari's eyes. "I can't believe what just happened," she said. "I mean, why then?"

But she knew. There was a time, a time for every purpose under heaven. He lay there before her, and he was at peace. His soul was free, no longer old, no longer imprisoned in decaying flesh. Somewhere, out there, the young Mr. Begelman was flying on the wings of angels. What more had this earth to offer him? What sense had there been in her officious striving to keep him alive against the will of nature and the desire of God? There was a place for him now, beyond sorrow and pain. His valiant heart was still. He had gone to those that had loved him.

Through the mist of her tears, Tari saw Mr. Begelman's photographs for the first time. Where now was that thin boy with the dog, on the beach by the water's edge? Where the melancholy woman with the sad eyes staring out to the low horizon? What had become of the little girl, plain and pert in her party frock? Tari didn't know, but she knew one thing. Mr. Begelman was closer to them now than he had ever been.

She crossed herself and lowered her head.

"To die is to see the face of God," she said.

"What time is Rickey picking you up?"

Mary's question smashed into Tari's memory, fragmenting it.

"Oh, I don't know. I mean . . ." She looked at her watch. "Any minute now, I guess."

Mary stood up. "Well, it's time for me to hit the gym."

"You don't have to go, Mary. Don't you want to meet him?"

"Like when I'm more together."

Tari laughed. Mary wasn't together. She looked her usual chaotic mess. The illusion that one day she would improve on it was what kept her going.

"Do you think he'll have changed in six weeks?"

"In Hollywood? Nah," said Mary. "I mean, what better place than illusionville to keep you just like yourself?"

"Sarcasm is the lowest form of wit."

"Not when I'm telling jokes, it isn't."

"At least he didn't take Jodie with him," said Tari. "I keep seeing her Rollerblading on Ocean, looking like to die."

"Awesome thighs," said Mary with a leer.

"And the rest," said Tari ruefully.

"And talking of thighs and buttocks and tits and stomachs ... I'd better get downstairs and on the job. Have fun, sweetheart, and I want the *tiniest* details ... okay?"

She was gone. Tari sat still for a moment or two. So much was happening so fast. Rickey had gone to Hollywood the day after they had returned from West Palm Beach to talk about some movie. She had missed him, but she had been incredibly busy. She had started doing volunteer work for Positive Link, the AIDS charity, and in the evenings she would visit the old people's home that she and Rickey had evacuated during the storm. They were her friends now, the relationship sealed in the crucible of shared disaster. Now when she walked through the door, the whole place would erupt with good humor and animation. She had persuaded some of the students to help out with painting and renovation, and she had located the owners in Cincinnati and bullied them into spending some money on the place. She herself had put Mr. Begelman's photographs in a place of honor on the wall. When the supervisor had found one of Mr. Begelman himself, Tari had had it blown up. Now, the Begelmans stared down together, a family united at the last.

Tari sighed. Life was good, but it was frightening. Ever since the moment when the scissors had snaked into the eye of Dr. Seagram, her world had changed. Hardly an hour passed when she didn't try to make sense of what had happened. The memory had faded, but the fact remained. She had heard the voice of God in her ears, and she had seen his face in her soul. On one level, she felt big with knowledge and bowed down by responsibility. On another, she felt ridiculously normal. She could laugh and joke with Mary about boys and sex, and here she was watching the sunset and looking forward to a fun evening, far from God. Right now, she wasn't thinking about a lifetime's work in God's service. She was remembering Rickey's body plastered up against hers by the dog food in the Washington market. Could these things be reconciled? She had had a religious experience. God had seemed to talk to her. But many people had had an experience of being saved. Some even indulged in it on an ongoing basis, endlessly traipsing to the front of churches as slick evangelists made their pitches in atmospheres thick with music, incense, and group enthusiasm. Was that all it had been? What did it mean? Everything? Nothing? Something in between? She badly needed to talk to somebody, but to whom? Rickey wasn't for talking. He was for loving. Mary wasn't for talking. She was for laughing. Then who? The name that sprang into her mind surprised her. Marcus Douglas. Marcus Douglas, who doubled as priest and shrink. Douglas, who had been with her through all the tense excitement of the moment in the hospital. He had told her that he would be happy to talk to her anytime. And Dr. Seagram had told her that the psychiatrist had been asking questions about her. Yes, that was it. He would help get things straightened out in her mind. She had seen in his eyes the calm and tranquility that came from a lifetime of goodness. Then she remembered. His course of lectures at the medical school was starting tomorrow. There was all sorts of gossip about it. It was rumored that Professor Hodges had tried to cancel him, after her public humiliation on the "Donahue" show, but that the other members of her department had forced her to backtrack. That made it even better. Any man who had fallen out with Hodges was a guy Tari could trust. She would go see him after the lecture.

She felt better immediately, and as if to celebrate the return of certainty, the telephone rang.

Tari picked it up.

"Welcome back, Rickey."

He laughed. "How did you know it was me?"

"All my dates are called Rickey. *Casablanca* is my favorite movie."

"Well, I'm sure glad they've all been away."

"Are you in the building?"

"Yeah, sort of. I'm down here on my bike."

"You want to come up? The sunset's amazing."

"I'm there."

He was. He was leaning against the side of the door when she opened it.

"Neat outfit," he said. His voice was gentle, drowsy. It was as if he had just woken from a deep sleep and would fall in love with the first person he saw.

Tari couldn't hold back the blush. "Thanks."

He looked like the Wild One. His biker jacket said Harley-something that might have been Davidson if you had good eyesight. He didn't have a leather peaked cap, but his blue jeans had a chain belt. His boots looked as if they had walked deserts and climbed mountains. The message was that Rickey was no café biker. His look said he'd slept on his Harley for three straight years and not chickened out once in a motel room.

She stood back to let him in. He wandered straight to the view.

"Shit, this is beautiful," he said.

"You know, this is the first time we've been together in private," said Tari.

He turned back toward her, away from the skyscape.

"It's always felt like private," he said.

She half-laughed. It had. The world went away when they were together.

"I missed you. How was Hollywood?"

"Hollyweird, like forever. I missed you, too. I thought about you all the time."

"You did?"

"Yeah, and I missed our old people. How about *that*?"

"They're fine. I drop in most days. They ask about you. 'How's your *film* star?' "

"Jeez, what about that poor Mr. Begelman? You were so magnificent that night." His eyes went earnest. He took a step toward her. It was true. He had seen Tari Jones in action in her world. And he had never seen anything like it before.

"I think Mr. Begelman's the luckiest of them all," said Tari. She felt the mist build in her eyes. "What do you think of my apartment?" she said, moving to safer ground.

Rickey looked around him. People's apartments were essays

about them, like their clothes, like their body language, like their handwriting. It was people's words that usually gave out with the bum steer. Tari, through her apartment, stared back at him. It was a long, thin room, raised on a platform in the middle to take advantage of the view from the high window. A strip of lights ran along a central runway in the ceiling, and they were all turned one way toward a wall that was painted in high-gloss red. Black-and-white photographs dotted it like postage stamps. For a second, he stared closely at the pictures. The photos were of very nasty things juxtaposed with very nice things. A gurgling baby was next to a skeletal figure from Dachau, or some such hell. Beautiful, naked bodybuilding women were juxtaposed with old crones racked with disease. A plane dropped bombs inches from the spire of a quiet cathedral. He stood back for an overall view and it was then that Rickey noticed something else. The photographs in which the good and evil so nervously coexisted were not positioned at random. They were arranged in shapes, and the shapes were the shapes of crosses.

"You took these?" he said. There was no reason to know that, or no overt reason. Tari had not mentioned being a photographer. The photographs had no hint of amateur night out about them. They were very good, and at the same time intensely disturbing.

"Yes," she said. "I took most of them." Rickey had commented first on the view, next on her photographs. He knew how to pass personality tests.

"The question you ask is how can God allow evil if he is a good God," he said.

"Yes," she said simply.

"You live with that problem every day. On your walls. In your heart."

Again it was a statement, not a question.

Again she said, "Yes."

"And do you have an answer to the question in your photographs?"

"Nobody knows the answer to the problem of evil. Only God," said Tari.

"And he's not telling?"

"But if you think about it . . . really think about it . . . you can make some sense out of it." She flopped down onto a chair. So did he. He waited for her. He could wait. It was one of the many things she liked about him.

"All evil involves some kind of pain . . . physical pain, mental pain . . . and eventually death. But if there is a heaven and heaven is perfect peace, then death is the best thing that ever happens to us. To die is to be with God. Mr. Begelman is with him now. It is to *live* that is to be separated from him. When a baby dies it is no tragedy for the baby, it is only pain for the rest of us. For the baby it is death that is joy, and birth that is hell."

She paused. Why was that so difficult to believe? Because so few people embraced death. Because it was human nature to fight and kill to survive. Because fashion said that to want to die was failure. Because, in the world, there was so very little faith.

"And physical pain?" said Rickey gently, watching her so closely in the orange-blossom-tinged breeze.

"Pain protects us from injury. A child learns not to put its hand in the fire through pain. We're chopping wood and pain in the shoulder tells us to stop before we injure ourselves. It's very rare, but some kids are born with the genetic inability to experience pain. They're always damaging themselves. Pain is a protective mechanism. How would you know you had an ulcer if you didn't have pain? How would you know if you had a heart attack? You wouldn't know about the things that were going on in your body until it was too late for medical or surgical intervention."

"But pain hurts," said Rickey. "It's unpleasant. Why couldn't an all-powerful God simply have made us so that every time we are in danger of injuring ourselves a voice sounds in our heads, saying, watch out, you've got a problem in your back, with your heart, or something like that."

"Because we're free agents, and a whole lot of foolish people would simply ignore the voice when for sure they wouldn't ignore something as definite as pain. I think it's a pretty neat invention."

"And what about mental pain, all that anguish when a child dies, a lover leaves, when you don't get the part you wanted?" He smiled to keep it light.

"It's an opportunity to strengthen ourselves and increase self-respect by working through tragedy. How do you strengthen your arm unless you have a weight to lift? How do you sharpen your mind unless you have a problem to solve? Our gifts must be used. In use, we test them. Our prayer should not be for ease, but for the courage to face difficulty. In the absence of difficulty, sorrow, and sadness, we would have nothing to fight against. We'd just be great big vegetables in the cabbage patch of life. And remember, the time we spend here is a tiny blot on the face of infinity. Our sadness signifies nothing in the scale of cosmic time. Only our conceit blinds us to God's purpose."

He was looking at her strangely, his head to one side, quizzical, perplexed.

"Where did you learn to talk like that?" he said.

"I didn't learn."

Rickey was quiet. "It sort of makes me wonder if we're going to be spending a very worthy evening," he said at last.

She laughed. "Don't worry. I'm not on a pulpit all the time."

"Maybe you ought to be." He looked more serious than she had seen him look before.

She stood up, not wanting seriousness to undermine the fun.

"Come on, movie star, take me out."

He stood up, smiling at her, taking in the night sky, the pictures one more time, the door that would lead to her bedroom.

"You're on," he said.

15

"ARE YOU on?" he asked. She sat astride the back of his Harley, and rested her hands on his hips. It was surprisingly comfortable.

"You'd better wear this." He handed her a coal-scuttle helmet. She slipped it on, aware of her hair streaming down either side of it. He put on some dark glasses, turned the key, and revved the engine. Good vibrations shot between Tari's legs.

"Where are we going?" she asked, wanting to hear his voice.

"Let's just cruise for a while." He swung the bike away from the sidewalk in a sweeping motion, swooping, like a bird taking off from a high tree. The running board missed the tarmac by millimeters on the turn, but Tari felt as safe as if she were in an armchair in front of the fire. She leaned into the direction of the bike, mimicking his movements, and her body flattened against his back. She pulled in on his hips and felt the muscles harden beneath her hands as he tensed his gluteals. As part of the riding process? As a reaction to her closeness? He made a right on Alton Road and a left on A1A by the Miami Beach

Marina. Out to the right, brightly lit boats bobbed on the milky water of the bay. Tall schooners sported bearded hippies back from pot time warps in the islands; sleek drug boats with sexy radar arches shone with the psychedelic colors of special paint jobs that could hypnotize Lauderdale girls after the second shooter; megayachts with bathtubs and uniformed crews were piled high with rich toys for rich boys—Jet Skis, wave runners, twin boat bikes, and sailing skiffs for the long afternoons when the lunch had worn off.

She could feel the heat from the engine, and she could feel his heat too, radiating back at her. And then there was Miami's heat. The warm breeze of South Beach was in her nostrils, and, as she flew by, the hot colors of SoBe made neon patterns in her mind. They creamed past surf shops and bathing-suit boutiques, past the Harley-rental shop where café-bar cowboys could pose as policemen for the weekend on white cop bikes from the sixties. There were Rollerblade rentals, bike rentals, and little pink scooter rentals for guys who weren't Village People enough for a Harley.

Here and there were memorabilia of Andrew . . . a torn awning, an uprooted tree, a dented billboard. At Ocean Drive, Rickey hung a right, away from the action of the main drag and toward the relative dereliction of South Pointe, the Joe's Stone Crab area where shrewd Barry Diller was buying up the white stucco wrecks for God knew what purpose. It was old South Beach here, the Art Deco renovations half-hearted and spaced out. There were more old people and street drunks, blackened by the sun, teetering about begging for change and looking for a place to sleep beneath the underwatered palm trees. He slowed down to not much more than a walk, and the engine, like the end of a powerful cold, rumbled and croaked in sympathy as it tried to do low revolutions. Up above, a pink cake baked by an overambitious baker, was the towering apartment building that the unimaginative lived in. Out to the left was Penrod's, a beach-and-multibar complex that was saved from being mainline Fort Lauderdale by a funky weight place on the sand. He swung along the side of Penrod's, and parked the scarlet-and-chrome monster by the edge of the caramel sand.

"You wanna walk?" he said, killing the remains of the engine.

It was just a question. Clearly Rickey liked his control, but he wasn't chauvinistic. She could have said no and walking would have been history. But he made the walk sound like fun, and not just because the walking would be done next to him. Tari kicked off her boots and stuck them on the saddle of the Harley. He copied her. At the edge of the water, the ocean was quiet despite the breeze. It rippled near the sand, but the foam was half-hearted. The sea, bathwater flat, stretched out to the seven-mile horizon. A big cruise ship, lights blazing, headed north for a night in Palm Beach.

They looked back toward the now-distant bike, and away south to the pink-and-green neon ribbons of Ocean Drive.

"We're two refugees, aren't we?" said Tari. "You from L.A. Me from New York. Ain't that America." She broke into the phrase of the Mellencamp song.

"Yeah," he drawled. "Come to the pink houses." He knew the lyrics.

"There are two reasons for moving on," said Tari. "Dissatisfaction and hope. What was yours?"

He bent down and scooped up some sand, letting it run through his fingers. It was why he wanted to walk with her, to talk to her. Later, in the throbbing clubs, action would be heard much louder than words.

"Aren't you allowed both . . . dissatisfaction and hope that the dissatisfaction will disappear?"

"No," said Tari definitely. "This is a multiple-choice question, not an essay. 'All of the above' isn't an option." She laughed as she spoke. Black and white speeded "getting to know you." Death by a thousand qualifications slowed it to a snail's pace.

"You want to know why I moved here? Why I'm thinking of living here all the time?"

She nodded.

He paused as if deciding whether or not to let go of his secrets. He had been in Los Angeles for too long, and in Tinsel Town telling the time of day was considered a dangerous indiscretion. When you spoke, it was either platitudes or lies. The truth was for those who didn't want to be taken seriously.

He looked at her closely. She'd never been near a movie in development or production. Probably never been near a soul who'd been near one except him. She looked as safe as anyone he'd ever known, but then his aunt had sold a story about him to the *Globe*. Still, she seemed to want reality for some weird reason. Most people preferred illusion. He took a deep breath. God, her mouth was amazing.

"Well, let's start with dissatisfaction. In L.A. it would be pretty much inconceivable that you and I would be here on the beach. Over there, you are what you do. You are your bio, your *updated* bio, and believe me, bios get updated on a weekly basis. If my last movie is doing well, or is rumored to be going to do well, then I'm enormously lovable, likable, and my jokes are hilariously funny and when I puke in the pool I'm in the good old Errol Flynn hell-raiser tradition. However, next week, after the disappointing opening, I'm a boor who needs help with his drink problem and everyone prays like mad that the downturn picks up speed so that everyone can file by and spit on my grave. But somebody who isn't even famous, either successful-famous or unsuccessful-famous, someone who doesn't have a bio—like say a medical student—then they don't exist. They walk the earth in a state of suspended animation, vaguely seen, never heard. Attractive qualities of personality, intelligence, character, etc., are misleading irrelevancies. They are actually subversive, because they cloud judgment and result in people wasting valuable conversation time with people who could have no possible influence on their career."

Tari laughed delightedly at the acid analysis. She stuck both hands out by her side, and walked like a zombie, stiff and awkward.

"You can't hear me," she intoned in a Frankenstein voice.

He moved in front of her, stopping her with his body.

"But I can kiss you," he said.

She took a step back, and put a hand on his chest.

"I think I'd like to try some kissing in private for a change."

Her face was alight with a wonderful smile. Rejection didn't come any better than this. But his mouth itched for her. He held her hand against his chest so that she could feel his speeding heart.

They walked on in silence. Two girls approached, speed-walking toward them, arms flailing in exaggerated motion. They were talking to each other in German. Rickey checked out the long, sunburned legs, the bleached hair, the cold Nordic faces, and they returned the compliment. They exchanged "Hi" 's but there were no smiles. There was no hint of an L.A. come-on, the kind that would have turned into a "fuck-off" if you attempted to follow up and had no bio.

"I like beauty," said Rickey suddenly. "I love it. Physical beauty. Beautiful people. Men and women."

He paused. Men and women. The words hung in the hot evening air.

Tari said nothing, thought much. Was he trying to tell her something? Was she being invited to go for the tabloid headline? Or was that a trap for the silly literalist with the dirty mind?

"You sure are in the right place for that. Fifteen hundred models living in twenty blocks by six, not counting the mega ones that jet in. Not counting Jodie Summerfield."

That was a fishing trip. It substituted for a "men and women" one.

"Yes, Jodie is beautiful. Very beautiful. Maybe even incredibly beautiful, but she isn't as beautiful as you."

"Tell that to Weber and Meisel and Ritts."

"I'm telling it to you."

Again he stopped. He turned to her. Longing was on his face. She scooped the longing off hers. Later. Later. Please God, later, but there had to be more of this talk first.

"So, you were saying, you loved . . . beautiful people, men and women. Is that all South Beach is?"

"What I want is to have fun, be loose, not be serious. I want to just hang out, try to forget about the fucking future."

"But there's more, isn't there, Rickey? There's more going down in life than just the movable fiesta around the clubs with the beautiful people. There has to be more. What is it?"

"There's the art," he said in a low voice, as if someone might overhear on the vast beach.

"What art?"

"My art."

He looked down at his bare feet. The change in him was

devastating. He was like a little boy with a guilty secret. He had been forced to own up to something of which he was ashamed. Avoiding eye contact was the symbolic attempt to avoid the consequences of his admission.

"As in, art you did," said Tari.

"Yes, did. Not collected." He looked up now, and there was a sheepish smile on his face. He felt better now that it was out of the bag.

"You're an artist, too."

"I've done some paintings. I don't think that makes me an artist, or them art, for that matter."

"But you think they're good."

"Yes, I do."

"So *that's* what you're doing in South Beach."

"And the club, and everything, and walking on the beach with you."

But she had heard the clarion sound of truth. It was easy to joke about. Who didn't wonder sometimes if they could be an artist, a writer, a creator? How seldom the suspicion got tested, and when it did, how infrequently the results saw the light of day. Was the book in you the very best place for it to remain? Ditto the painting. And the photograph. She liked him more than she dared admit, but did that make it more likely that she would see the point of his "art"? Whatever, she *did* have to see it. It was clearly the most private part he had.

She turned around, walking backward as he walked on, facing him.

"Oh, Rickey, can I come with you and see it right now? This minute. Before we do anything else?"

"You interested in painting?" he said.

"Not particularly," she said. "But I'm incredibly interested in you."

"In the old days, 'You must come up and see my etchings' was something of a joke," he said.

"Well, be kind and don't tell that particular joke to Jodie Summerfield," said Tari with heartfelt sincerity.

16

T WAS a South Beach back street, a dirt-washed alley that had once been white. Rickey steered the Harley through the rubbish like a sapper through a minefield. There were broken bottles, discarded syringes, and a flat cat, squashed in the road, brown in the middle and marmalade at the edges. Flies were too lazy to circle, too well-fed to leave. They lay about on the ancient animals, and waited for the emptying stomachs that would allow takeoff. Two drunks sat in a doorway, hairier than Esau, a bottle of meth between them. They waved at Rickey, showing sparse teeth through extravagant smiles. They knew him not, but he was a human from planet Earth, and dollars might drop from him if they could dream up the password to the next drink.

"You live here?" Tari's question was rhetorical. Nobody could live here. It was condemned space, rat and roach land, a place of scurrying things beneath the sun and slithering creatures of the evening. No bicycle policemen, SoBe's user-friendly pop cops, would venture into this crack alley. It was a no-man's-land of nomads and outcasts, an outside pisshouse where the urine steamed the sidewalks for minutes and was gone; where excrement was baked solid before its smell could escape; where puke was paint that was gone in the rains.

He stopped the bike, jacked out the stand, and motioned for Tari to get off. The drunks laughed the too-loud cackling laugh that was no relation to humor. He cut the engine. Silence descended.

"Beverly Hills East," he smiled, grimly, she thought, when there was no reason for grimness.

Next to them was a hole in the wall. A grubby door looked solid behind a bundle of pointless sticks. A filthy mop leaned against the wall. A broken bottle was the bed for a used condom. A sign said something nonserious might happen to trespassers. Rickey reached into his jeans for a bunch of keys. He stepped carefully and opened the door. The door opened onto a six-foot-square space. It was clean, but empty. Another door, facing them, was the only feature of the vestibule. Rickey leaned back and let Tari past. Then he closed the outer door behind him and double-locked it. Darkness descended. At first it was total, and Tari caught her breath as she waited for him to turn on some light. But no light came. They were alone in the blackness. Still, not moving. She could see light beneath the door they had entered. And there was light beneath the door through which they would pass.

"Rickey?"

Silence. She could see the shape of him inches from her. She put out her hand and touched the leather of his jacket at the shoulder.

"Rickey!" Her voice was different now. Strain tugged at the edges of the word that was his name. Thoughts began to rush. A liquid tide of hormones began to move within.

"Yes, Tari." He knew her fear, the sudden excitement of the intense loneliness with a strong man in a small secret place. He knew she was weak and vulnerable, and his words told her that he knew.

"What are you doing?" she said.

He didn't answer her, allowing the mystery to grow in her mind. What was the game? Tari tried to control her breathing. She wanted to take a deep breath, but she knew it would come shuddering out in a moan of delicious anxiety. It was sex. It was unmistakable. She could smell it in the fetid air of the tomblike space. The man she desired was inches from her, wanting her. But there were manners, conventions, things that were done, and oh God, not done, and she shuddered in the darkness, afraid of what she wanted, and yet fearful that this frightening moment would pass.

Upstairs, in some loft, were his paintings. Perhaps! Down here, and now, was the weapon of his body, the muscles, the power of Rickey Cage, to whom a fight was a dessert, and a woman one too, sweet and light and frothy and fluffy, to be swallowed and digested and excreted and forgotten.

Her mind flashed into reverse. The tender kiss on the plane had been taken as she slept, or in the interface between sleep and wakefulness. It had been deliciously unexpected, and welcomed, but it had never been permitted by any language of body or tongue. She had never resisted it, never wanted to, and she had joined in it as a willing partner because it seemed so natural and felt so right. Then he had gone from her life, wafted away on a cloud of carelessness to the astral plane where superbeauties lived and movie stars cavorted. Then there had been the supermarket and their second kiss. It had started, she had thought, as a violent rape. She had fought him first, until she had known who he was, and now her body tingled with the memory of his and the things she had wanted to do to him and he to her, as they had stood knee-deep in the dog food and talked of lust. "We're going to be lovers," he'd promised. But they were not yet lovers, here in the darkness, so very close to each other.

Tari's thoughts picked their way across her mind, groping for direction in a darkness of the spirit that was at once frightening and stimulating. Games were beginning, but what games? Good games, bad games, games that hovered beyond good and evil where the rules of supermen applied? Was Rickey Cage ultimately beyond the law of lovers, past the pale, a creature so rarefied that a girl could suffocate on the air he breathed?

"Rickey!" She commanded him to speak to her, politely, but firmly, now in the blackness. The smell of urine wafted beneath the outer door. In the back alley, the laughter of the drunks was muted. They were alone.

Still, he didn't answer her. Another notch on the ratchet of anxiety. Another twist on the weird rheostat of desire. She could smell him, male sweat in the confined space, but she couldn't see him. He liked violent sex. Her intellect knew that. Memory said so, of tabloids, of her own experience. But her gut knew it too, and the blackness emphasized the knowledge. Her mouth was dry, but her heart was humming. She wanted to be bent against the dirty wall and flattened by his body. His stubble would rasp across her soft skin and his leg would grind against her crotch, and her wetness would come like the rains of spring to a parched valley. She tried to swallow, but her saliva had gone, gone somewhere else. She knew she was damp, and she wanted to feel her own dampness in the darkness, to make more of it, to stir the stew of sex that was already steaming in her body and her mind. She flattened her back against the wall, for safety and support, and she fell silent because the move was his, as it had always been. Everything was slow. There was no hurry, but fear scuttled about amid the physical sensations as she asked herself questions it was impossible to answer. How much did she want? When would be the moment to stop? Would she know it? Would he recognize it? Could communication fail in the interchange of bodies? Could anger and regret emerge from the tunnel of love and lust?

They had kissed before, but this would be more than a kiss. He might take her at any time, standing up in the filthy doorway off the deadbeat alley. He might just unzip his fly, now, and finger her panties aside and plunge into her. She would be pinned to the grubby wall by the force of him, her feet inches from the floor as he used her as a contraption for his pleasure. In a minute, it could be over. Then she would sink to the floor, full of his desire. It would drip from her, down her shuddering legs in the aftermath of the basest sex of all. She tried to recoil from the horror of that sex, unsafe sex, his sperm free inside her, with all its secrets and dangers and frantic irresponsibility. But she couldn't recoil from the fantasy. Instead, she was drawn to the flame of the vision with unreasoning force. In horror, she realized that it was what she wanted. She wanted to become a thing. She wanted the insecurity of tomorrow and the weeks to come. She wanted with a desperation that bordered on the insane the unsafest of unsafe sex with Rickey Cage, in the early evening, in the earliest hours of their very first date.

Once again she tried for sense. Once again it melted in the steam of desire. She was no longer damp, she was wet. She was liquid. Beneath her arms the sweat came, pungent with alarm and fear of him, fear of her own collusion in the mindless sensation. Her shirt slipped over the sweat slick on her stomach. Sweat rolled down the cleavage of her breasts and the divide of her butt. She tried not to show the fire inside lest it inflame some roaring conflagration in him. But her lips parted and a low sigh escaped, her breath shuddering through clenched teeth as she battled to stay sane in the mad moment of desire. In the eye of her mind she could see his black shape. She could see his bulging, pulsating jeans, vast with the glory of menace. His body would be coiled like a spring, ready to violate her, and she shook her head from side to side to banish the fantasy before it foundered on the rocks of reality. The voice in her mind was clear. *You want love,* it said. *You want tenderness from this man. You want the gentle touch of one who could learn to love you. Don't be rough with me, Rickey. Be soft. Don't use me, win me. Make this a memory for all time of our first time.* Ohhhhh! The flood tide of adrenaline burst within her as the bomb of ambivalence exploded over the dam that had held it back. No woman wanted rape, date rape, any rape. No woman wanted to be nothing but a receptacle for male lust in the dark and the dirt and the silence. It was a crime against nature, to be abused with no permission, to be entered and filled and discarded on the filthy floor like a tissue of nothingness, all messed up with the juice of a man's need. Clever words. Subtle thoughts. For the morning, the day after, for some other time than now. Now, there was the fire below, the aching, steaming fury of the cauldron between her legs. There was only one way to slake her crazed thirst for him. She didn't want to drink slowly and tenderly from the fountain. She wanted to be drowned in the waterfall, so that his delicious moisture could penetrate through the very pores of her skin. And she wanted it now, so immediately that the present would be forever frozen in a single frame of time. That would mean rough. Oh God, would it mean rough. He must tear the clothes from her so that the sound of them ripping could reassure her that release was near. Then she would open for him and pray only that he would come quickly, so that the first terrible conclusion could be reached, the first hurdle surmounted in the passion war they would fight through eternal time. Later, there could be her orgasms, much later tenderness, togetherness, and the sweet lapping sounds of lovers at the water's edge of intimacy. But now there must be only the animal power of his release in the soft prison of her inside. His mark must be in her, claiming her, naming her as his. There was nothing else. There was no kinder, more caring possibility. There was only the blind longing for his orgasm inside her.

She lowered her hand to her thigh, and her fingers slid on the juice of her lust. It ran in rivulets down the inside of her leg and she traced the stream to its source, without shame in the darkness. Her panties were wrecked. Their wetness already stained the front and the back of her skirt. But she didn't mind, because so soon the mess she had become would be the mess that he had made her. She slipped her hand inside. Her fingers slid in the slick hair, foraging for the lips of her privacy, dipping inside to handle the heat she had become. She arched her back and thrust herself out at her own hand, and she prayed for the moment when he would take over. In the back of her throat the noise was of an animal at bay, poised for an encounter more terrible and wonderful than any she had ever known.

The sound arrowed into her mind, parting the chaos of her thoughts. It was not the sound of tearing clothes, of an undone zipper, the roar of rampage. It was the sound of a key turning in a lock.

The street door behind them remained closed, but the door in front of them was opening. Rickey had opened it.

The light flowed in and lit Tari. Crumpled against the dirty wall, she was a wreck of a human being. Her knees were bent, her skirt hitched up, and a trail of wetness coursed down the exposed skin of her thigh. Her hand was still buried inside herself. The other clutched at a pulsing breast.

He turned to watch her in the light from the stairway. His

expression was awesome. It was focus, pure and single-minded, and it was aimed with laser accuracy at Tari's soul. In the silence and the darkness he had created the visual she had become. By lack of words and force of presence, by charisma, by aura, by magic language, he had generated this longing, this waterfall of lust. She was shocked by the light and by the knowledge of what it had revealed, but the sex didn't go away. That was the extraordinary part. She had dreamed up a fantasy so powerful that it had melted her. She had been turned by it into a lewd bundle of longing. She was crouched against the wall, weeping her desire down her bare skin, milking it from her core with guiltless fingers. It seeped onto the skirt she wore. Its musky scent filled the womb of thwarted pleasure. Still, Tari felt no shame. In the glare of reality the illusion persisted. He had not raped her. Perhaps he had never intended to, but whatever had happened was not over. Nothing so strongly experienced could be nothing. No dream so real, so intricate, with such devastating manifestations in reality, could have been uncaused. So there was no embarrassment in her wanton acts.

He put out his hand to her, and the faraway look in his hooded eyes merged with the trancelike one in hers. He drew her toward him, away from the wall, leaving the sweat imprint of her body on the dry whitewash. With her left hand she held him. Her right hand fell away to her side, her finger shining with lust. Her skirt fell down to cover the whiteness of her dampened panties.

His foot was on the bottom stair and Tari looked up past him to the bare pine stairway. There was a single rail. There were no pictures on the walls. At the top would be his room, his apartment, his studio, whatever. But Tari couldn't wait, for the steps, for politeness, for anything. He seemed to know that too. There was sweat on his upper lip, below the broken nose. Moisture glistened in the chest hairs at the neck of his open denim shirt. She tried to lick her lips. She tried to smile at him. But it was all too late. There were no manners left. There was only naked need. The hunger was frantic. Hers. His.

"Come here," he whispered. He moved her past him, and his hands were at her shoulders, pushing her down. She sat on the step that was the third from the bottom of the stairway. He stood above her. Her legs were together in a vain attempt at decency, but he moved them apart until they were splayed wide-open, the dark triangle of her love mound showing clear through her soaked panties.

"Oh, Rickey," she whispered, reaching out for him to draw him close to her. She could see the outline of him, huge as her dreams, crushed beneath the tight denim. It was in line with her face, with her mouth. She leaned in, pressing her cheek against the throbbing heat, rubbing her skin against the warmth, massaging it, nuzzling against the part of him that could not lie about what he wanted. But he was in control. He sank down to his knees, his eyes never leaving hers, until he was in position to give the ultimate pleasure. Now he moistened his mouth with his dry tongue, and she shuddered with the anticipation of the wonder to come. She knew to hitch herself up, and to push down her panties, exposing herself to him. She knew to draw up one leg, freeing it from the dripping material. She knew, too, to leave her panties, soaked and ruined, wrapped loosely around the thigh of her other leg. She looked down at herself, to see what he would see. Pink like the shell of a conch, her love lips nestled in the wetness. Full and swollen with pleasure, they were parted for him, releasing their captivating scent for him. All the time she waited in wonder for what he would do. For long seconds he gazed at her, in awe at her surrender. He knelt at the trembling heart of her, at the molten core of her being. This was her center now. The rest of her was the wrapping for this private, mystic place. Sinew, bone, muscle, nerve were incidental. She lived short, tantalizing inches from his face, from his mouth, from his tongue. He laid the back of his hands on the smooth skin of her inner thighs and he pushed gently as he leaned in to taste her. She threw back her head and moaned her acquiescence, and she tightened the muscles of her stomach to prepare for the delicious touch. His lips met hers, hot and dry against her warm wetness. They touched and left, touched, left again, pouting in the tenderest kisses against the symbol of her love. He breathed in, capturing the molecules of her sweetness deep in his lungs. He owned her intimacy now, and he lingered longingly at her entrance as he marveled at the power of this gift she was giving. He opened his mouth and his tongue moved where his lips had been, exploring with infinite tenderness the velvet surface of her. Drinking from her, he bathed the dryness of his mouth with the abundant wetness of her love lips. He moved to the top of her entrance with his tongue, meeting the pleasure source, licking it and dipping the tip of his tongue into the groove of her, pressing, drawing back, pressing once more.

Tari rocked her head from side to side as wave after wave of wonder crashed through her body. She thrust herself out at him, way beyond shame, trying to impale his tongue deep within her. She pushed out her arm and curled her hand around the back of his head, willing him to drown in her. With her left hand she steadied herself on the hard wood of the stair. She lifted up her butt, her muscles straining to make close closer, near nearest. His face was buried in the jungle of her need. It was slippery with lust, sliding magically over the cushioned surface of her love mound. He licked, sucked, probed at her with his tongue, and all the time the mountain of sensation grew, reaching for the peak that would have to come. She tried to slow his movement. Then, as her hand steadied his head, she sought only to speed it as the good became better, and the better best. She closed her eyes to focus down on the joy, and, nostrils flared, she breathed her own scent in a positive feedback of desire. The muscles of her stomach quivered with the effort of holding herself rigid at his face. She was shuddering with the strain, but her strength was limitless in the alien zone of ecstasy. He held his tongue still, and she alone moved against it. She took it inside her, rigid, tense, then expelled it as she shifted back from its reach, imprisoning it, once again an inch inside her so-soft prison. She was doing it to his tongue. She was the prime mover, he the constant. Locked between her legs, her strong thighs strained tight at his cheeks. She wrapped her legs around him tighter, locking her ankles together and forcing her thighs ever mo re powerfully around his head. She knew this would not last forever. Soon he would be the conductor, she the conducted. But now, in the eye of the storm of lust, she was riding him. His face was her saddle. The reins of her legs were around his head. She could feel him fight to breathe in the liquid pool of her longing. His hot breath sucked and exhaled in her fetid jungle, and she wanted to laugh and shout her joy at this power she had over the powerful. His tongue reached deeper inside her. She could feel its strong strokes exploring her. In, farther, up higher, then back to lap at her outside, to the source, to the bottom of her, to the thin, smooth strip of skin that separated entrance from entrance. The thrill of indecent excitement shot through Tari as she knew suddenly what he would do. His tongue was hovering at the edge of her forbidden place. Part of her held back, but the rest of her longed for the illicit act of love. She moaned her encouragement as her mouth formed a meaningless *no*. She thrust up higher, allowing him room to move. He twisted his head around, slipping it beneath her until his face pointed upward in the cleft of her buttock. Then his tongue slid into the alien darkness. She shook with the shock of the foreign sensation. His tongue was at the furrowed opening, bold at the edge of her privacy, and then, as she had dared to want, she was invaded. He pushed into the tight ring with his rigid tongue. He thrust through the outer defenses until he was firm in the so-tight channel, filling her up with warmth and wetness. She was joined to him in total intimacy. There could be no secrets now. The breach of her most private amulet of love was symbolic of a closeness they would share forever. It was a contract of body love, an act of homage that was spellbinding in its completeness. And it was joined to a fountain of longing that must end in orgasm.

Tari rocked against the tongue that pleased her. She reached down with her hand and parted herself, putting her fingers inside to stoke the coals of lust as his tongue roamed free in her secrecy. She bore down on him, thrusting him farther inside her. She tried to relax her muscles as she strained to allow him deeper access, to give herself more complete ownership of him. The feedback was faster now. Her fingers and his tongue made the pleasure and her brain sampled it and sent it back, amplified, as the bricks of joy built the glorious castle that would be made only to be destroyed. She didn't know when or if to warn him, but she knew that this orgasm must be hers alone. Later there would be a time for him, for them both, but this would be her personal peak of passion. She would drown him as she died, and in her rebirth he would surface from the deep, an accomplice and a witness to the shuddering intensity of her experience. He seemed to realize. His movements speeded. He was firmer inside her, more insistent, his whole mouth locked around her. His tongue, spearing her inside, fought to move in her muscular grip.

"Oh, Rickey," she moaned. "Oh please. Oh! Oh! Ohhhh!"

Her fingers drummed at her epicenter. The tight ball of ecstasy rushed from his tongue behind, through the glistening wall, to her fingers in front and back again. Up and down she thrust, and then from side to side in frantic rhythm, building to the moment. Her breath hissed through her teeth. Sweat hosed from her body onto her lover below. Her mind willed her on, frantic now on the edge of release. Her body too, past exhaustion, past failure, found the energy for the last dash to extinction. Higher she reached. Lower she pushed. She opened, and closed. She tightened and relaxed, breaking all records of extremes and excess with each shuddering, hovering motion. Then she was there. For a second there was the perfect peace of stillness before the storm. She stopped. Below, he waited. Then, she squeezed down on him, crushing the tongue that was within her, and she shouted out loud and long as she gave herself over to the orgasm. Like the earth in the strongest quake, she shook above him. Her legs danced in the air over him. They splayed wide open, and the dike that had but partially held the moisture within her gave way with her cry of joy.

"Oh, Rickey, I'm coming. Oooooooooh!"

The waterfall she had become crashed over him. The fingers of her hand were the sieve through which she flowed. On and on, more and more, she sprayed her longing. A fountain more full than she had ever known played, rushed, foamed from her depths. Her uncontrolled limbs thumped against the bare wood. Beneath her, he rode her like the bucking, rearing animal she was. Then, slowly, from the edges, reality crept into the chaos of bliss. It broke up the mosaic of brilliance, dismantling it piece by piece. Until she was still.

He moved from beneath her. Laying his soaked face against her bare and sweat-streaked stomach, he turned his head up to watch her at the end of ecstasy.

She reached down and stroked his glistening hair. Love and gratitude shone from her eyes.

"It's never been like that before," she said, her voice shaky.

"It will be better, I promise."

He smiled up at her, drawing patterns with his finger in the moisture on her thigh.

"We didn't make it to the top of the stairs," he laughed.

"There was a moment there when I thought we weren't going to make it to the bottom of the stairs."

"We nearly didn't."

He stood up, unfolding from her, leaning against the wall. He held out a hand to help her. Inside his jeans he was still diamond-hard. She pulled at his hand, as if to draw him down toward her. Unfinished business. A lifetime's worth. As well to get started. But he shook his head from side to side, smiling. It was his turn. She allowed him to draw her up, staggering slightly on India-rubber legs like a newborn colt in a field at dawn. He put his arms around her waist to steady her, and as he did so, the panties that had been stuck to her thigh by her own wetness fell to her ankle. She looked at him and smiled, her eyes thick with a film of lust. He bent down and she lifted up her leg on cue, letting him take the once-white panties from her foot. He put them to his mouth, sensing them, wiping them lovingly across his skin as he breathed in the musk of her. Together they walked up the stairs, hand in hand. With her other hand Tari held the rail for support. She felt so shaky, so deliciously weak, irresisting, irresistible. His shirt was soaked. She could see that. She tried to think of the minutes that would be the future. Was there a bed up there? Hell, was there a floor?

What there was was Rickey Cage's pictures. It was not his apartment. It was his studio. The room was dirty, like the alleyway outside, but this was wholesome dust. The sun came through a skylight. The four walls were obscured by the paintings. An old sink hung in the corner. Tari wiped the sweat from her eyes with the backs of her hands. It was a difficult moment to be an art critic. He stood back. He wanted to know.

She felt anxiety in the air, merging with sex in a cocktail she already wanted to taste. The paintings. Oh, yes, the paintings. She walked over to the one on the easel. She looked back at him. He smiled encouragingly. She looked down. It was still there. She chewed on her lip, and tried to clear her mind of the steamy mist. What did she see?

It was a photo collage. The photographs were of a woman's body parts. A shapely elbow, in fuzzy soft focus, or printed on superfast film, was twice the size it had been in real life. So was the vagina at which it pointed. Ditto the close-up of an armpit, complete with a sculpted latissimus dorsi muscle. That was a theme in the other photographs, too. Muscled women, very strong, showed lots of body parts but few facial ones. The faces that were on display belonged mostly to Jodie Summerfield. The blow-ups had been cut into severe geometrical shapes. These had been fitted together in a jigsaw that might have been assembled by the great-grandchildren of the original cubists. Acrylic, thickly applied, filled the gaps of the photo montage. The colors were largely Nazi. Scarlet, black, gold, and white. Together with the Aryan muscles, the effect was vaguely unsettling, and yet at the same time fiercely original. The paintings were also intensely sexual, autoerotic actually, as if the body in question derived its satisfaction from narcissistic and voyeuristic activities that rendered masturbation unnecessary although occasional. What did they mean? Paintings always meant something, whether the artist knew it, intended it, or not. Alternatively, paintings meant nothing, which was certainly something or other in terms of being difficult to achieve.

Tara's body was humming like a wire in a wind. She was still wet like a river, and her bottom tingled with the body memories. But the paintings, and Rickey's erection, and that dusty floor . . . She forced herself to think.

"I think they're wonderful, Rickey. They're Jodie, aren't they? All of them?"

"Yeah, nearly all."

"Even if I'd never met her, they'd make me know her. Sort of cold, distant, a bit self-obsessed. I don't mean to be rude. It's . . ."

He waved away rudeness, but not a feeling of surreality that was beginning to take hold. The tongue in her butt was about to curl itself around some words. Had his tongue been in Jodie's butt? Had they discussed art afterward? Was this something of a routine?

"On one level, bodies are just things, aren't they? However beautiful or ugly, they're just things. Bits and pieces that house people. Sometimes, often, like with Jodie's body, they get mistaken for the real thing inside. Only Jodie's house is kinda empty. Like it's not even haunted by the ghost of an actual person."

Tari had to laugh at the put-down of a rival. There was music, sweet music, and there was a beautiful rival being carved up verbally. She suppressed the frisson of guilt. He really *cared* about these pictures. But, really. It was a bit of a shock to realize that she wanted to be in one, or rather to *be* one. And it was unsettling to realize that her "bits and pieces" didn't match up to Jodie Summerfield's. But then again there was someone pretty interesting at home in her house.

"Are these tungsten lights?"

"Yeah."

"You taught yourself the photography?"

"It isn't so hard. Compared to getting the subject right. Compared to getting the subject *there*."

"I'm here. Could you get me right?"

"You might end up on a wall in public somewhere."

"Not so bad, if I can sit on your name."

"Like you sat on my face?"

"Mmmmmmmm."

She half-moaned her answer. The sex was all cranked up again. She'd started it. He'd finished it. Now they would get it on. Here. Soon. Before she got photographed. And afterward. Jeez, *during*? But Tari's heart was light as she realized she couldn't care less.

He stood there, and the sunlight caught him from above and from the side. It was Helmut Newton light, harsh and overhead, mad dogs midday, full of shadows and sunken eyes and tense flesh. He looked James Dean dangerous, a movie star pure and simple, and Tari couldn't remember seeing anything else as beautiful. She was hungry. She wanted food, and he was lunch. She walked toward him quickly, as if he were a cafeteria, not a fancy restaurant. He saw her coming. He knew what she wanted. He stood still, as she had first been still on the stair. She stood up against him and breathed warm breath in his face. With one hand she reached out for his butt. With the other she reached down for the other hard bit. She laid her hand on it in wonder. Her heart speeded up as the music began inside her. Their lips were millimeters from each other, but they didn't kiss. Kissing time was over. She watched his eyes as she found the tab of his zipper. She watched his eyes as she pulled at it. It caught once, twice, but she wiggled it about and it went all the way down with the noise that zippers should make. She reached inside like a looter in a store, hurriedly, grasping at the vast bulge so that it wouldn't escape her. She cupped it in her hand and felt its throbbing heat through the cotton. He blinked then, and exhaled, losing his famed cool in the sigh. Then she smiled right up into his eyes to show that she'd won that point, and there were others she'd win, too. *Watch out, male hero, macho man. You're going to howl at the moon and die the little death when I've finished with you. If I ever finish with you.*

She reached back between his legs, and then forward with her finger to find the little hole that Jockey shorts had. Forget it. There was no way. So she just yanked them down, impatient, and then he was in her hand. He was bigger by far than anyone had a right to be, and her eyes lost their certainty against his, and his gained their sureness against hers, and the glorious game went on. She pulled him free, still not looking down to see it, but wanting to, yet fearful. *Look,* said his smiling eyes, and she did. He reared against her hand, straightening, filling, pulsating, and she gripped him hard, her fingers surrounding him, but scarcely able to. With two hands she held him, at the proud tip, at the shaft, at the visibly expanding base. Her heart was pounding its confusion. This could not be done. But it had to be done. He grew as she waited and her eyes marveled at the vision, and her hands smoothed the shining surface of him. Down below, her helpless, hoping body tried to prepare for what had to be. Her eyes spoke her panic and her longing. Tari had tried for control. Now she had lost it completely.

"Help me, Rickey," she whispered against his mouth.

He took her hands away from him, and moved them up to his shoulders. His slow smile was the most reassuring thing she had seen in her life so far. Then, with his right hand, he reached around and held the cheek of her right buttock. With his left, he lifted the material that passed for her skirt. He rocked forward and pressed against her, and she felt the awesome thing hard and hot against her tummy. Then it was moving lower as he bent at the knee.

"It won't . . ." she murmured, her eyes wide.

In answer, he guided himself to her entrance, rubbing the head of him against the slick of her. She flowed out at him, thrust back, longing for the invasion she feared. He peered into her big round eyes, sensing the moment when her need would overcome all thought of pain. He waited patiently, but all the time he moved in the cascade of longing, testing, pressurizing, threatening the moment of union. She tried to relax, but she was standing up. Yet she wanted it like this, his pants still on, his hugeness poling out, disappearing beneath her skirt, totally ready to conquer her. She never knew the moment, but he knew. He knew precisely. He bucked down, and reared up, and one moment she was a void, achingly, agonizingly empty, and the next she was invaded, filled up with him. The force of his entry knocked the breath from her body. Her feet flew up from the floor and for one mind-bending second she hung there in space, a butterfly on a pin, unconnected to any world but this one bit of his body. She hung there. Her mind was dizzy with sensation. Deep in her guts, in her bowels, in her stomach, far removed from the inadequate space where it had a right to be, she felt the awesome presence of the foreigner.

"Oooooff!" was the noise she made, part physical, part mechanical, part mental. She was split wide open. She felt a wonderful, tearing completeness that she had never known. She had become him and he her. But there could be no movement. Entry itself was all there could ever be. Entry and exit, just once, never to be repeated. He would come out from her, and she would lie down on the floor and they would find some other way to make love. It was not sad. In its way it was beautiful. It was just a fact of life. But what did she know?

His hands were beneath her buttocks now, taking her

weight. His biceps strained, and his knees buckled, but he held her in front of him, lifting her up an inch or two higher, drawing himself that distance out from her. Then, he let her down again. She sank to the base of him, and the stars burst in her mind as once again his huge head rammed the anchors of her womb. The explosion of pleasure gripped her. She was being wrenched apart, but at last she was whole. And it could be done. This thing could move within her.

She looked down, her mouth parted in lust and wonder. They were both dressed. There was no sign of the magic place where their bare skin met. They could be dancing. Instead, they were making extraordinary love, and Tari had never felt more alive or more helpless, as she was penetrated more completely than she could believe was possible. Once again she sailed upward, slippery on the fulcrum of him. At the point of exit there was only the dread of emptiness. Then, once again, she was falling, deliciously descending, sliding down on the pole of longing. At the bottom was the zenith of sensation. At the top was the nadir of hope. In between was the mind-melting ride to a pleasure more complete than she had ever known. There were beads of sweat on his lip as he carried her, and she wrapped her legs tight around his hips, digging her ankles into the small of his lower back to steady herself in the dance of love.

And then she felt the beginning of her second storm. It flashed its soundless light in the distance, and she threw back her head to welcome it. She could see, at once, in his face that in her gesture of abandonment she had speeded the approach of his. His rhythm was measured now. Each powerful thrust, full of motive, strained for both his release and hers. He nodded once to tell her he knew and that it was all right. Now, in secret collusion, they worked together, magnifying pleasure in a widening loop of lust. She was looser around him, he bigger inside her, as she made the lubricant of love for the piston he had become. Tari focused down, loose with longing. She closed her eyes. Her ears were full of the sucking sounds of the flesh vacuum that was her body. Her nostrils flared to catch the animal scents of desire. And all the time the drama of absolute sensation engulfed her, until she was nothing but the feeling, a raw emotion suspended in space on the spear of her lover. She put her hands to his cheeks and leaned in close to his straining face, catching the frantic breath of him.

"I love you, Rickey. I love you," she murmured, her words punctuated by the shock of his relentless rhythm. He couldn't answer her, but his eyes flashed the recognition of her feeling and his reciprocation. Way past speech, he was living on borrowed strength for the end to come. Then she saw his eyes widen, and hers did too as the end of eternity approached. Their bodies slapped together, their skins lathered like the hair of horses. They were surreal with lust, cut off from existence, and yet in touch with life at last. No other time could mean so much. No pain could not be obliterated by this communion of the flesh. There was, for this brief time, an end to the loneliness of self, and in the oneness there was the pure and simple joy of the whole, of holiness. The rumble started at the back of his throat. It was a growling, low sound of a jungle animal, grand yet fearful, and it grew like the chorus of voices of a people oppressed. He opened his mouth to shout the warning, and she was shouting hers, as her body melted down, molecule by molecule, in the fission of passion. She was oil and water for him now, grease and sweat and the juice of love. She was squeezed down for him. Her bottled essence was the distillation of her being, waiting only for the perfect moment of release. She flew to the sky, ready to descend, but with his last strength he held her there, and, in the second before the last, there was total stillness.

His head, pulsing like a heart, was at her opening. It nestled there, hot and hungry, and Tari knew that this was the true moment. She tried to freeze it in memory. The imprint of this feeling must never be lost. It was like life itself, a microcosm of fear and joy. Before her stretched the possibility, the absolute probability of bliss. But between here and then, between the present's uncertainty and the future's promise, lay a thin fog of doubt. Could some perversity make him stop now? Could she be hovering in a no-man's-land of suspended longing, so near, yet so far from the explosion of happiness she needed so desperately? His stopping had been to pander to that fear, to wind it up, amplifying it, despite all reason and all prediction.

Still, he waited. She could feel him twitch against her love lips, feel him throb against her. He took a step forward, and then another, and, quite suddenly, there was hardness against her back. She reached behind her. Her fingers rested against the rough edge of a board. She was leaning against one of the paintings. Larger than life, it was against her back. She looked down to her side, her whole being on hold. Jodie Summerfield's hand was on her bare thigh, where it met the wrecked and rucked-up skirt. By her shoulder was the perfect Summerfield breast, the conelike nipple, wrapped in a sea of scarlet acrylic. Strung out on the edge of her orgasm, Tari was aware of the symbolism. She was pinioned to the painting. She was the butterfly against the page, a prisoner to lust. The features of her rival, naked and unashamed, were poking and plucking at her defenseless body. In the wilderness of sex, Tari loved it. In front was her lover, ready to fill and drown her with his most precious gift. Behind her was Jodie Summerfield, her beautiful mindless body, reduced to its parts, to its basics, bearing witness to this most private and fundamental act. And strangely, it was this that put Tari over the top. At the top of the cliff, poised for the jump to joy, perversely it was not the fingers of a man that pushed her . . . it was the feel of a woman.

She opened her mouth wide and she screamed out loud. "Ohhhhhhhhh, I'm going to come."

He thrust forward into her orgasm, banging her bottom against the cold plywood. He was falling apart, buckling, his legs shuddering, staggering. He leaned in against her, propping her up with the weight of his body against the painting. She was wedged there, held no more, and the vast piston inside her was now a pump. She felt the streaming ribbons of love loosed within her, felt them splash against the mouth of her womb, hosing the heart of her with essence of man. On and on it went. She could feel the molten warmth flowing inside her. And all around was the crash of her own moment, mighty and magnificent, and at one with his. She squirted back at him, meeting his liquid with her juice, drowning the drowner, in the glorious death of passion. He poured into her, and she around him, and together they flowed from her, down her thighs, around her bottom, dripping, rushing, cascading in the mix of

love. Together they soaked the dry paint, the smooth matte of
the photos, and her butt slid from side to slippery side of the
painting as her legs danced in the air at the execution of lust.
Her orgasm rolled around his. His climax surged over hers.
They were human no more. They were organisms alone,
locked in a timeless dance of nature, beyond control, beyond
meaning. Then, so slowly, it began to end.

Rickey Cage sank to his knees, still inside her, and Tari sank
with him. She put out her hands, sticky with sweat, to steady
her descent, and her soaked bottom slid down the painting.
She traced a pattern on its surface, a slippery silver slick of all
that they had become . . . over Jodie Summerfield's pert butt,
over her long legs, over the famous pouting lips. And then her
buttocks were on the floor, her thighs straddling Rickey's, and
her pubic hair, glistening with moisture, merged lasciviously
with his. They sat there for long seconds in the pool of their
mutual desire. He reached up and touched her cheek and she
nuzzled against his hand, still feeling the last spent twitching of
him inside her.

She smiled at him, the languid, earthy smile of a lover.

"We wrecked Jodie's painting," she whispered.

"Very soon we'll wreck the one I do of you," he whispered
back.

17

RICKEY NOSED the Harley into the curb, and kicked out the stand. On the terrace of The Marlin hotel, the diners watched. A rocker and a pretty girl were hardly noteworthy on Collins at dusk, but the paint job on the bike was motoring. Then Rickey plucked off his shades, and the cognoscenti got the whole picture, as they recognized the star. Interest perked up, but it was still SoBe interest. The sophisticated crowd vibed in on the fashion statement and the accessories more than the fame.

Rickey helped Tari off the bike. She put her arm around his neck as she swung her leg over the saddle. He was hers now. She was his. Their body language talked possession. Tari smiled. He was so courteous in his battered leathers, but she was aware that the other side of his chivalry was chauvinism. For now, that suited her just fine. Why shouldn't a male be all man? It made her feel warm and protected. The alien feeling was nice for novelty.

"Ready for goat stew and laid-back service? This may be the mainland, but The Marlin's an island trip."

"Ready for anything," said Tari. She was still tingling, high as a kite on body memories and lust for the future. She reached for his hand and drew him in close on the hot sidewalk, sighing her satisfaction.

The sidewalk was deserted, except for a lone man who walked toward them. He was big, and he got bigger as he approached. Tari immediately recognized the type. He wore filthy pants, and was stripped to the waist. Dirty, matted blond hair was scragged into a ponytail at the back. He wore no shoes or socks. It added up to a South Beach drunk. The remains of outsize muscles and an insolent swagger in his walk made him a threat. The diners on the outside terrace of The Marlin were separated from the street by a balustrade. No way would the wino cross that. He would go for the easy pickings. Tari and Rickey were going to get accosted. Rickey watched him come. He made no move toward the relative safety of the waitered terrace, although there would have been time to reach it. Tari looked at him. He stood tall. If there had been a neon sign over his head it would have read, "The guy who said 'Discretion is the better part of valor' was a weak-kneed sissy."

The street guy had arrived. He leered a glassy-eyed smile and swayed up to Rickey.

"Want to help a vet down on his luck?" he said.

Rickey didn't hesitate. "Yeah, sure," he said, reaching in his pocket. He pulled out a five and handed it to the guy.

Tari picked up on it. Yuppie man would have hightailed it to civilization to avoid the dilemma. Attorneys and dentists, etc., would have principles that forbade "encouraging" deadbeats to beg. They also would have had principles about not getting beaten up, spat upon, or verbally insulted, especially in front of an audience. Retreat would have avoided the conflict of interest. Rickey, however, could protect himself. At the same time he was sufficiently worldly-wise and caring to realize that some people were beyond helping themselves.

The man peered at the bucks, at the bike, at Rickey, at Tari. Then he got it wrong. What was left of his brain interpreted Rickey's gift as weakness. The hostility of the bully flared behind the unfocused eyes.

"That all you can afford for a guy who fought for his country?" he slurred.

Tari firmed up her grip on Rickey's arm and leaned away

from him toward the hotel terrace. The diners were interested now. Their collective neck craned toward the street. Dealing with panhandlers was such a nineties thing. Nobody had yet written the etiquette book on the subject. You had to make it up as you went along. How would the star do it? The drunk was vast and covered with tattoos. It was an appetizing moment.

Rickey didn't answer. He smiled a satisfied smile. Tari hadn't moved him. Now, he let go of her hand.

Tari wasn't used to being a spectator. By herself, or with a girlfriend, this would be a frightening experience. But she felt zero fear. Instead, she felt excitement, and an intense interest.

"Don't you fucking stand there and laugh at me," said the drunk. "You fucking scumbag piece of shit, you oughta have more respect for a guy who risked his fucking life for his country."

The guy leaned in over them. Spit spattered through broken teeth. The barrel chest flexed. The big, fleshy biceps switched to action mode. Then the guy reached behind him. From the back pocket of his trousers, he pulled a small and grubby knife.

Tari hardly saw the blurred movement. Her mind had to fill the gaps in the visuals. Rickey hardly drew back his fist. It pistoned forward and upward from his side and the sandwich of his knuckles was food for the still-open mouth of the mugger. There was a crunching noise that contained elements of both a slap and a thud. A fine spray of blood and saliva wafted into the air from the man's face, like scent from an atomizer in a well-lit room. He went backward. He didn't bend. Momentum from the blow straightened him. Falling reflexes were abolished by the onset of sudden and complete unconsciousness. His head hit the asphalt. His right leg twitched. Then he was still.

"Motherfucker," hissed Rickey.

Tari turned to him in shock as she tried to get a bead on what had happened. He was transformed. He was laid-back and cool no longer. His face was hungry, his mouth flattened back over his teeth in a snarl of cruelty. He was crouched down, energized, like a vampire after blood soup. In an instant, Tari saw a secret Rickey Cage. This was the Rickey that was in tune with his clothes, with his whole appearance, with the macho image that his behavior had always before belied. He was rigid with aggression. She could feel it pulsing from him, and she knew where it came from. His father had laughed while he'd beaten him, until one day his laughter had died. This was the child inside the man. This was the hatred below the surface for a world that had mistreated him. It was all anger and fury, and the terrible danger those emotions fathered. Rickey had been a boxer. What else had he been? A bouncer? A bodyguard? Muscle for men with grievances?

She looked at the broken drunk. She looked at the terraceful of onlookers. Not a butt lifted from a seat. Help was not on the menu. She ran forward to the prostrate loser. She picked up his hand and felt for the pulse. As she did so, she maneuvered him into the Trendelenburg position. There was no danger of any spinal injury. The trick was to get him into a position in which he couldn't inhale his own vomit. She turned around. Rickey was kneeling beside her. There was concern on his face. He was back. His demons had been boxed once more.

"His heart's pumping," said Tari. "But he has to go to the hospital. At best he'll have a concussion, at worst a brain bleed. Get someone to call an ambulance."

Rickey stood up. He called out to one of the waiters, "Hey, man, ring for an ambulance, will you?"

The emergency unfolded with typical American élan. The ambulance siren could be heard almost immediately, followed closely by the wailing electronics of several cop cars. In what seemed like seconds, traffic was diverted, lights flashed, and the wounded drunk was strapped immobile to a stretcher. The police were deferential, even complimentary, as they took statements. There was a terraceful of witnesses to the attempted mugging. The movie star had done the John Wayne thing. The wino was an irritant with a record. When the moment had been milked of the last drop of its drama, the road show disappeared, leaving Rickey and Tari alone on the pavement.

"You still feel like eating?" said Rickey.

"I'm used to blood," said Tari with a wry smile. "So, apparently, are you," she added.

"Sometimes I lose it," said Rickey. He didn't smile.

"You've got one hell of an uppercut," said Tari. Her

thoughts were spinning as she tried to tune into her bottom-line feeling. There was one sense in which he'd picked the fight. It could have been avoided if he'd retreated from the situation. But middle-class people knew how to walk away. It was part of being sensible, and being sensible was always the right thing to be. But on the corners of the dirty boulevard, walking had consequences. It meant you were a coward, and you would be tortured for that in a way far more horrible than the breaking of your bones. It was a question of image. In the land of the middle classes, what counted was success, education, position, and the possessions that kept the score. In the ghetto, what mattered were your balls. With them, you might one day escape. Without them, you were doomed. So Rickey had given his cojones an outing. What was that to her? What should he have done? Given the flyblown wino a lecture on the evils of drink and the virtues of abstinence? Should he have waxed lyrical about the merits of a college education, or extolled the advantages of the Betty Ford over the Minnesota method? She smiled at the ridiculousness of it all. What was the reality here? Her guy had protected her from a man with a knife on a street corner at dusk. How dare she be anything but grateful?

"Come on, street fighter, let's go eat. At least let's go drink. I think that's what I really need."

He smiled his relief. He was the sweet, old-world Rickey once more.

They threaded through the terrace, as two or three people clapped. Rickey ignored them. They pushed through the doors of The Marlin hotel. Inside, a strange world awaited. It was, thought Tari, a little bit like being under the sea, a Little Mermaid land of blues and aquamarines, of shell lamps and uplighters. The walls were done in the "distressed" look, a stippled effect saved from uniformity by patches of yellow and orange that mimicked rust, water seepage through wallpaper, and other signs of decay. To the right was the reception desk. To the left was a counter that sold everything from Rastafarian bracelets through reggae CDs to books about Jamaica and spices from the islands. The furniture was deco with a twist. Sofas and armchairs swirled around like waves. Down the steps was a bar area with a cluster of small tables, the chairs of which seemed to have no straight lines, heightening the impression of being submerged in some fairyland Atlantis.

Rickey headed to the bar. He drew out a stool for Tari. A couple of models sat nearby. The barman, lean, muscled, and great-looking, was there immediately.

"Good evening, Mr. Cage. What can I get for you both?"

They ordered rum punches under the influence of the cutting-edge reggae that wafted over the sound system.

"Christ Blackwell, the guy who owns this place, founded Island Records and discovered Bob Marley. English guy from some rich school."

"It's pretty original. I like it."

"Yeah, it just won some architecture award."

She watched her lover. He was the guy on the plane again, self-confident, charming, a man who knew things. But Tari knew now he was layers. Opening the gift that was him would be a never-ending process. Not all the surprises would be good ones. That didn't matter. In fact, it added to her interest, if that was possible. She sipped her drink.

"Were you a successful boxer?" she asked.

"Nah, not really. I won some, lost some. I could've scratched a living for a few years and scrambled my brains in the process."

"Acting's better." It wasn't a question, but, as she spoke, Tari wondered why she'd heard so little about his acting from him, and so much about it from others. He'd made five films so far. His reputation had grown with each, but *Double Dare* was his first hundred-million-dollar movie.

"Acting's the same," he said. "Scratching a living, scrambling my brains."

"You don't enjoy it?" Tari smiled her incredulity. The standard PR was, "I'm so lucky to be an actor. I get paid for doing what I love."

"I used to get off on it before I earned any money at it . . . before it became a job. But that's what it is now. I mean, you don't expect a construction worker to be like in love with his job. It's pressure. It's something you do all the time. And it's a little undignified, isn't it? Grown men pretending. Doing make-believe."

Tari added it up. Rickey was a tough ghetto kid in a

middle-class meritocratic world. He'd sold out for megabucks because it was the smart thing to do, but he was paying the price in terms of lowered self-respect. The kids on his block would be in jail now, on probation, or pushing up the daisies in the cemetery. The survivors would be plumbers, truck drivers, or sweeping the streets they'd once terrorized. If they could find anyone to listen, they'd boast about the days they'd beat up on the movie star, or gotten beat on by him, and how he couldn't get laid/was a faggot/and if only they'd really set their minds to it, they, too, could have gone to Hollywood. . . .

He drank hard on his drink as if swallowing memories. Tari's heart went faster. He was alien goods, a Martian to her. It was why he was so phenomenally attractive. There was a sense in which he had lived twice as long as she, despite the fact that they were more or less the same age. He had started living from the womb onward, maybe even *in* it. She had started as a teenager. She had had a "happy" childhood. He had survived his. It had been a war, and now he was a veteran who knew how to cheat and fight and how to hide hurt and to keep it all inside. While she had broken hearts at the prom, he had been busy breaking fingers in alleyways, and getting his nose fixed for cash in steamy gyms full of men who thought a woman was wrapping paper for their dicks. He made her feel frivolous and inconsequential, as if she had no right to worry or anxiety. And yet there was a sense in which he was damaged goods. It gave him the excitement of danger, but it also made him vulnerable. There would be things he would never get together because of his insecurities. His finger would always be snagging on the self-destruct button, just at the moment when his chutzpah had opened some door to glory. Was that what had happened to his career? Was his dislike of acting a rationalization of acting's dislike of him? On paper, he was box-office hot on the back of the megamovie. But how many feathers had he ruffled in the Hollywood corridors of power? Despite popular wisdom, businessmen *were* prepared to cut off their noses to spite their faces. She couldn't know, but the list of questions was growing. And that was how it should be at the beginning of love.

"Why do I get the feeling that your past has given you a problem with male authority figures?" said Tari.

He smiled, looked at her, then looked away.

"Part of this deal is that over dinner we get to do you."

"At the table!" Her eyes widened in mock surprise as she played the double meaning.

"Yeah," he said, letting his eyes slide over her. "Come on, let's go eat before anyone else interrupts us," he said, standing up.

Shabeen in Jamaican has two meanings—"cook shack" and "dirty dive"—and the Shabeen restaurant in The Marlin hotel had taken those two concepts as its theme without interpreting either literally. It was a low-ceilinged, long room, dark and yet full of bright colors. The walls were a collage of sticks, broken wood, and wrecked picture frames, some painted, others plain. Tables stretched down either side of the thin room, and each appeared to have been hand-painted by a precocious child, daubs of brightness merging with the haphazard artistry of a bunch of wildflowers. Great tubes of painted metal hung from the ceilings—the cook shack's air-conditioning—and along the walls bowls of paper sunflowers added to the feel of easy island living. Who needs cash and chic, said the room, when you've got the sun, the sand, and the sky. Each table came with a cluster of bottled sauces, but these were not Heinz, H.P., and French's. There was Pukka sauce, and Busha Browne's spicy tomato, and hot peppers in sherry, and each looked as if it could put a yuppie gastronome on an IV line for a week. The waiters, and an incredibly attractive waitress with brick red cropped hair and a body to die for, were black. So was the female maître d', who looked like a fashion cover of *Ebony,* and who ruled the lectern with a look that absolutely demanded slavish respect.

Rickey lingered at the restaurant's entrance in the laid-back way that Jamaicans liked, and soon they were seated and munching on the fried plantains that hit the table when they did.

"Do you wanna stay with the rum?" said Rickey.

It seemed the thing to do, with some St. Croix to even things out. Tari sat back and allowed herself to be wafted along on reggae dreams. The menu was fun. They ordered Jamaican patties as vehicles for the sauces; spicy jerk chicken wings and grilled pepper shrimp. Curried goat was said to taste a bit like lamb, and so they both wanted that with coconut rice, roasted sweet potatoes, and bammy, a.k.a. cassava cakes.

"Do you think that poor guy's all right?" said Tari suddenly.

"For sure. A tap on the chin, a bump on the head, and all under a general anesthetic. A night or two in a clean bed with good food and a chance to dry out is just what he needs."

"I guess you're right." Tari paused. "How does a guy get that far down?"

"By starting out on the bottom rung. He didn't have far to fall. There but for fortune. Shit, it isn't such a bad life. No responsibilities. No mortgage. No nagging wife. No kids to be ashamed of you."

"You don't sound too fired up on the joys of married life." Tari laughed. Somehow, it wasn't a belly laugh.

He was quiet for a second, thinking about it, not flip.

"I guess not," he said. "It's the compromise. To do marriage good, you have to fit in with others, wives, kids. You can't just do whatever. Can't just be yourself without hurting people. That kinda compromise doesn't fit with my honor. With my dignity. If I'm not honest to myself, I'm nothing. I'm just . . . like conversational Muzak, like some dummy goin' through the motions of living, but not really doing it. I'd just be actin' life with other people's lines, doin' scenes, and maybe even gettin' good reviews, but basically not me. That's marriage to me, unless you want to be some tyrant terrorizing your family, like my old man . . . and shit, that really is the end of the line. . . ."

"That's it, isn't it? You see bits of your father in you, and you're horrified by them, and yet you're drawn to those bits at the same time. As a kid you were fascinated by the power he had, and yet you loathed the way he used it. It's like you carry a loaded gun, and your nightmare is that one day you'll use it and blow everyone away."

"Sounds like Psychiatry 101. We are where we came from."

The rebuke was gentle, but the warning not to get too close was on the table. Bodies could get close. Minds were more dangerous to Rickey Cage.

"We don't have to be 'where we came from.' We can be 'where we're going to.' It's just that we carry the *baggage* of where we came from."

"And where are you going to, Tarleton Jones, with your invented name and Queens in your carryall?"

"Ah," said Tari with a smile. "Me."

"Yeah. Tari. Ms. Mysterious. Ms. Adopted. Ex-capitalist. M.D.-to-be. Future savior of kids or crazies."

"I thought I knew," said Tari.

He smiled an indulgent smile. *You see, it ain't that easy, mouthing about yourself,* said his expression. *Game plans change. Things happen. You will still be here tomorrow, but your dreams may not.*

"I thought I knew until a few weeks ago. Until this evening."

"What happened a few weeks ago?"

She looked down at her plate. She looked up at the ceiling. Goat stew in the cook shack. Shabba Ranks doing reggae. They didn't have the answers. She looked at Rickey, who was part of her problem and part of the solution. Then she looked inside.

She was a mess. It was impossible to know where to start in sorting out the chaos she had become. Yet she had to. She couldn't go on much longer like this. Two mighty things had happened to her. She had heard the voice of God, and she had fallen in love for the first time. The irresistible force of one had met the immovable mountain of the other, and she was frozen into an awed stillness by the magnitude of the meeting. Now she was lost. What did she want? Union with Rickey? Or union with God? It was as if she were being subjected to the ultimate temptation. Because she couldn't have both. Could she? Her life was at once in ruins, and yet poised at the beginning of an adventure that could shake history. Yet was this grandiose thinking? Could she be in the prodromal stages of a schizophrenic breakdown? Certainly, she experienced herself as being fragmented, her personality broken up into sections that seemed to be at war with each other. But on the other hand, it was a cohesive conflict. Love of God versus love of man. These were not the musings of a maniac. They were the internal arguments of a person chosen by God for a special purpose. Through history there had been such people. They might be numerically and statistically rare, but they existed. Somebody had to be a saint.

A broad smile opened up Tari's face as she thought that thought. It was tough work, but someone had to do it. Someone had to clean up the mess that was the planet. In the nineties a saint couldn't be too saintly. Bring love to the world.

Had the stairs of Rickey's loft been a beginning? Was it sacrilegious even to entertain the idea?

" 'A few weeks ago,' " said Tari, sitting up straight and taking the bull by the horns, "was when God told me I was his daughter and that I would bring love to the world. 'A few weeks ago' was when a murderous lunatic obeyed me, and I was instrumental in bringing about a medical miracle. 'This evening,' on the other hand, was when you fucked my brains out against your painting of Jodie Summerfield. I'm having a little trouble in reconciling those two particular scenarios," she said.

So, from the expression on his face, was Rickey.

When he spoke, he spoke slowly. "I've got a pretty good handle on 'this evening,' " he said. "But could you do 'a few weeks ago' again for me?"

So she did. She tried to explain it as carefully as she could, leaving out nothing, including the psychiatric speculations and attitude of Marcus Douglas.

Rickey tried to follow her, but as she spoke she could see she wasn't carrying him with her. People had their limits. She was beyond his. He was so many magic things, but he had never gotten around to getting metaphysical. Maybe that was why she liked him, a self-confessed action man who would rather do things than discuss them. Mean streets and the groves of academe were miles apart, and they both liked it that way. "Streets" reckoned too much thought was sissy. "Academe" believed too much muscle equaled a bonehead. Real men didn't read books. Bright guys didn't box. There were horses for courses, and when the going got tough, you needed the right mount. Tari petered out, dreading his response. The trailer for it was on his face, and it wasn't a movie Tari wanted to see.

"Uh. That all sounds just a little . . . weird, Tari."

"Weird?" said Tari.

The silence deepened. Rickey pushed a piece of meat across his plate. God hadn't happened in his life. God had been conspicuous by his absence in the nasty part of New York. He hadn't showed often in Hollywood, either. Okay, there were synagogues and priests and the Koran and the attitudes that went with them, but they were emotional mandarin to him. He had never met anyone who'd professed to having a religious experience until now, and what it sounded like to him was weird. At the same time he could see that he hadn't covered himself in glory in terms of his answer. "Weird" wasn't much help. He tried again.

"I mean . . . like maybe you should just forget it, and get on with your life."

"Forget that God talked to me."

"He didn't *talk* to you, Tari." There was exasperation in Rickey's voice. His eyes went up and he shook his head from side to side. "God doesn't talk to people. He just sits up there and lets all the shit go down."

"Oh, I see."

"Whaddya mean, you 'see'?"

"I see that you don't see."

"Meaning?"

"Meaning just what I say. That you haven't a clue what I'm talking about. Meaning I'm sorry I brought the subject up. Meaning I think that God is a little bit outside your experience."

Sparks were in the air.

"Isn't that what all the religious nuts say?"

Tari took a deep breath. She tried to keep herself rational. He was right. It *was* weird. Actually, *weird* was a very good word for it, shorn of pretension and psychobabble. And the "nut" crack wasn't so far off target. Hadn't she herself wondered about her sanity? Hadn't Marcus Douglas? Rickey might be a movie star, but before the fact of his fame there had been the fact of his obscurity. Not so long ago he had been John Doe with fast fists, a broken nose, and an attitude. It was naive of her to imagine that overnight he had acquired Solomon's wisdom. That was the mistake of the talk-show host, of the celebrity interviewer for the glossy magazine. The star-struck liked to cut out paper stars, and then expected them to shine in every direction. It made for major-league disappointment.

"I don't want to fight with you, Rickey," she said.

"You just want to fuck with me."

There was bitterness in his voice. Now he was angry. He was

angry because he really didn't do words. He was angry that she realized that, and interpreted it as a weakness. She thought he was thick. He felt the old fury build inside. He couldn't help it. It bubbled up from his basement, steaming and hissing and foul. Tari's patronization of him had opened the box, and the demons were free. Quite suddenly, she was his father and he was little Rickey Cage with nothing but his rage to protect him. She was trying to say he was thick, far thicker than she and all her medical people with their middle-class airs and fucking graces. Shit, the voice of God! Who did she think she was talking to? At least Jodie Summerfield knew the score. Jodie might be standing in the dirt, but she had both feet on the ground. Jodie dreamed of being a screen goddess, but she'd never claimed to hear the voice of God. This one was a loose cannon. She was unstable, despite the down-to-earth surface vibrations. But it was one thing to be a crazy. It was another to put him down. Girls didn't get to do that.

The waitress was hovering near the table—long black legs, a wide-open face, intelligent eyes sparkling.

"Can you get me a real big rum punch, honey?" he said, his voice like sugar. He wanted to tune out.

"I'm sorry, Rickey," said Tari, touching his knee.

"I'm never sorry," said Rickey. He'd reined in the anger. He smiled, gone away from her, gone to some distant place in his mind. He was nonchalant now. She had patronized him. She wouldn't get to do that twice.

Tari hunkered down for the silent treatment. She knew what she had unwittingly done, and she was sorry, but she couldn't say more. She looked around the room. It was full, and she had been too busy to notice it filling up. Who was that gaunt figure, hovering near the bar? She started. It was Marcus Douglas. And he was watching her.

Tari caught his eyes. She smiled her recognition, but he didn't smile. She tried to look away, but she couldn't. Then they were playing a game like chicken in a car. Who would blink? Who would look away first? When would embarrassment set in? At what point would decency be passed? Tari was suddenly confused, but there was no reason for confusion, and that made it more confusing.

By her side, Tari could feel Rickey fade.

Marcus Douglas had been watching them for several minutes. He dropped into the Shabeen from time to time because he found it relaxing after a hard day with the sick and the self-absorbed. Usually he had a drink at the bar, and then ate quickly at a table by himself. Tonight, however, it was full. He had nursed a beer, waiting for it to empty a bit, and then, at the back of the room near the juice bar with its neon sign, he had caught sight of Tari. And then of Rickey Cage. They had been leaning in close to each other, and he had concluded from their expressions and body language that they were either lovers or about to be lovers. Then, apparently, some sort of argument had occurred. Now bad vibrations were lingering.

At first he had decided to keep his distance. There was something about their intimacy, and something difficult to get hold of inside himself. He hadn't thought it through. He'd just decided that maybe a sandwich somewhere might be the best thing before returning to the article he had been writing. But now he had caught Tari's eye, and another decision had been made. Drawn by a force that seemed external to him, Marcus Douglas walked down the steps and into the restaurant. As he did so, his mind was on overtime. The medical student fascinated him. It was many things. Too many things. First, but not really first, were the amazing events in the ER at the South Beach. She had had some kind of religious experience—that was the priest's verdict—and it had been sufficiently powerful to communicate itself to a crazy man and avert a disaster. That was far from uncommon. The moment of conversion was one of awesome power to the believer. Those hearing the call at evangelical meetings achieved an infusion of serenity and certitude that others could all but feel. But it had been followed by a medical miracle, and the girl had seemed to predict it, or at least been in some way aware of it. That, to the priest in Douglas, opened up extraordinary possibilities. His church believed in miracles and their rarity. It investigated them in depth. On occasion, and in conjunction with other miracles and good works, the end result of that investigation was canonization. Could it be, just possibly, that within one hundred years or sooner, this girl would be a saint?

As he walked toward her, the psychiatrist laughed at the man of God. The girl was not a saint. She was sick. She had experienced an auditory hallucination. She had actually heard a voice she thought was God's. And it had apparently said she was his daughter and she would bring love to the world. The girl genuinely believed it. That was a delusion, defined as a false belief held with peculiar conviction in the face of all evidence to its contrary, a belief inappropriate to a person's cultural, intellectual, and social status. What's more, it was a grandiloquent delusion. Doctor Douglas said she needed chlorpromazine. Father Douglas said she needed investigation. But as he came closer to her, there was another part of Marcus Douglas to be counted. There was the man. The celibate man. The man whose lust for flesh had been bound forever in the promise of the priesthood. In chains it existed, but it lived on. So he approached her, as a priest to do homage to a girl who could be a saint; as a doctor to minister to a girl diseased; and as a man to long for a girl he could never have. The danger was everywhere. Danger for himself, for her, for all who could be touched by the discovery of whatever truth would be discovered. Maniac, saint, or mere woman? Which was Tarleton Jones? That was the mystery. Would he ever find out? Would she? Could there be two or more right answers?

He walked right up to their table.

"Hello, Tari," he said.

"Hello," she said. She put out her hand to him, and he shook it formally, but holding on long and joining his other hand to hers in a gesture of sincerity.

"I thought we would meet next in the lecture room. South Beach is full of surprises," said Marcus.

Rickey was stirring, like a lion from sleep. Someone was table-hopping. Someone he didn't *know*. A *man*! A good-looking one. His face took on a discouraging expression. The tension between him and Tari had not been resolved. It didn't need an audience. Or did it? Who was the intruder?

Douglas looked at Rickey, his expression neutral. Tari knew the time had come for introductions, and that they would not be successful. But she didn't mind. Douglas had come to the table. Rickey was busy doing a number. They would have to sort it out among themselves.

"Rickey, this is Dr. Douglas. He teaches at the medical school in the psychiatry department. He's also a priest and he writes best-sellers. Dr. Douglas, this is Rickey Cage."

"Don't I come with a bio, too?" said Rickey, pushing the sneer into his voice. He stuck out an unenthusiastic hand at the teacher. His butt didn't shift an inch from the seat.

Marcus smiled a mirthless smile. "I'm sure Tari realizes that everyone recognizes Rickey Cage," he said. It did for either a compliment or a put-down. You could take your choice.

"Dr. Douglas was in the emergency room when that 'weird' thing happened," said Tari.

For some reason she felt like living dangerously. Rickey was her lover. Douglas was somehow her champion. Where the hell did she get that feeling from?

"Ah," said Rickey. "A teacher-student relationship." He managed to get more into the words with a flick of his voice.

Douglas took his hand. The eyes of the two men clashed. They both knew what they were. The rest was bullshit. Already, in their guts, their hearts, and their souls, they knew. They were rivals. Tari watched them, aware of their rivalry.

"You're living here now?" said Marcus, letting go of Rickey's hand.

"I am," said Rickey. He was beginning to feel evil again. Tari had gotten to him, but you were only allowed to take just so much revenge on a woman. Men were different. The season on them was always open. And there were no bag limits. In a fight with this one, he held all the cards. First, he was the guy with possession. He could still smell Tari on his body. He was sitting at the table with her, Rickey Cage, the guy's guy and the woman's dream. He was rich and famous, and interesting as hell because of the dangerous "don't-give-a-shit" vibrations that made people worry from coast to coast. He had maybe fifteen years on the shrink-priest, even though the guy *was* good-looking in a Jesus-type way. And boy, did the male nun come with baggage? He wasn't allowed to jerk off, this one, without feeling guilty. He couldn't throw a punch, a party, or a tantrum without letters getting written to men in skirts who had his balls all tied up in conscience wire. He smiled at the thoughts. Shit, the loser couldn't even sit down. He was hovering there like some Hollywood agent trolling for business in Morton's and about to get the "walk-on" for his pains.

"I always thought actors had to be in Hollywood," said Marcus. What he meant was, "Hurry back there."

"I don't know about actors," drawled Rickey, leaning back on his chair. "*I* don't have to be anywhere."

He turned toward Tari to check how he was doing. She looked cross. Good. The bitch! This was fun. The braino had fallen at the first fucking fence. He would be a patsy. Probably wasn't used to being word-whipped. Nobody dared. Everyone too polite to zap the God botherer. Well, hang on, baby. It was time for blood.

"Are you eating here?" said Rickey. "Are you by yourself?"

Marcus was on to him. He was inside the mind of the movie star, reading his thoughts as they slipped like toys off the conveyor belt, stamped with little signs that said "Made in a Wounded Childhood."

"I was going to, but they don't have a table . . ."

He looked around at the crowded restaurant as if to prove his point.

"Why don't you join us?" said Rickey. "Tari and I were talking about that business at the hospital. You have to be the expert on that kind of thing. Come on, sit down."

Douglas looked at Tari. She looked at Rickey. Excitement and foreboding picked at opposite ends of her heart.

"Yes, please do," she said.

She stole a look at him as he sat down opposite her. He didn't look like a priest or a doctor. He didn't look like anyone, actually. He was an original, a hands-down winner on any panel game of "Guess the Occupation." He wore a pair of olive green slacks, comfortable but not baggy, held on his slender hips by what looked like a Brooks Brothers blue-and-white-striped belt. His faded blue denim shirt had been washed rotten, not acid-treated in some hot SoBe store. Feet were Gucci loafers that hadn't seen polish in a month or two. Compared to Rickey's Wild One, Marcus Douglas had come to the restaurant in comfortable style. The comparison was irresistible. Here were two extremes of male attraction. Rickey was excitement, unpredictability, danger, the cutting edge of sexual attraction for those days when you wanted to take life by the throat and shake it till it screamed. Douglas was security, the safety net that would pick you up when you fell, the oracle that would have the answer to any question you could ever ask. Rickey could love you and leave you, but you would remember the experience forever. Marcus would be a lifetime of commitment and gentle pleasure under the protection of the oak, and the sex would be slow and easy, comfortable as the velvet softness of his light blue shirt. Tari stopped, catching herself in midthought. Sex with Marcus Douglas? He was a priest. He wasn't allowed to. He was forbidden territory. Women were off-limits. *Celibacy!* And then, quite suddenly, the idea of sex with Marcus Douglas acquired a specialty all its own, and Tari felt her cheeks redden at the impropriety of her thoughts.

"So you're a shrink," said Rickey.

"I'm a psychiatrist."

"He's also a Roman Catholic priest," said Tari. Almost immediately, she regretted assuming the role of expert on Dr. Douglas.

"It must be hard to know which hat to wear," said Rickey. "Or to remember which one you're wearing."

He shifted position, sticking out a leg and folding his arms. The signals were aggressive.

"Do you confuse yourself with the characters you play?"

Marcus looked straight at him. The press often criticized Rickey for that. In the early films he had been touchingly vulnerable, funny sometimes, tough but mixed-up; James Dean kicking at a stone and wanting to be understood through the protective tough shit. Lately, he had become something of a caricature of a screen heavy. That had delivered the box office bacon in *Double Dare* and it had been easy to do. It had bolstered his always-precarious self-esteem, but at the same time Rickey realized that there was a sense in which it had been a cop-out. This pointy-headed guy wasn't supposed to know about the finer nuances of his career choices, and the press they'd got. He could hardly be a connoisseur of Cage interviews in the trendier rags, which were the only ones Rickey deigned to talk to these days.

"Method acting was last year," snapped Rickey. "That only happens to amateurs." He had fallen into the trap.

"Precisely my point," said Marcus Douglas.

Oh, shit, thought Tari. She knew they were fighting over her, and at the same time she knew it was incredibly bigheaded of her to think so. That didn't make it less true. The interesting thing was she was on both their sides.

"How do you know Tari?" Rickey said. His eyes twinkled with wicked mirth. Inside, the fires burned. There had always been guys like Douglas. They lived a Martian's life, always thinking, always worrying, forever twisting some knife in their immortal souls. They were awkward, and serious, and they held positions of authority, and there was one type of guy that they hated with a deadly hatred. Guys like Rickey Cage. Rickey was tough, macho, and male. He laughed and joked, and had a good time. He made money, whole piles of it, and he was famous and successful . . . and he got the girls. They loved him, the girls. They loved his ease and lack of complication and the way he gave them trouble, and they always did what he wanted. A girl knew where she was with a guy like Rickey . . . offstage, unless specifically invited for a turn in the spotlight. No decisions. No responsibility. No blame. Douglas's type resented that. They were awkward with women, always gabbing on to them, always yapping about this and that, confusing them, thinking too much. Whenever they got a chance, they stuck it to the Rickey Cages with the only weapons they had—words, IQs, and the power positions they had got from them. But there was a type of woman that went for bright guys. Women like Tari. She would go for Douglas's stuff. He taught her subject. And when she'd gone weird, she'd gone weird around Douglas. That figured.

"I don't really know Tari," said Marcus. It was true. He didn't. Didn't, but wanted to . . . as priest, as doctor, as man.

"I told you about Dr. Douglas," said Tari, suddenly uncomfortable. "You know, at the hospital. He was incredibly kind to me." She looked at Marcus. His eyes bored into her.

"Well, I guess I ought to thank you for looking after my little girl," said Rickey.

Tari turned and looked at him in horror. His "little girl"? Little? His? Where was Rickey Cage? Where was the cool, quiet guy on the airplane? Then she relented. Okay, Douglas had turned his motor. It was a male thing. There weren't too many people on this earth who could tweak Rickey's insecurity, but Douglas would be one of them. Her mind flickered back to the loft. She shuddered with the delicious memories. Suddenly, being his little girl didn't seem like too much to trade for genuine joy.

"I think Tari can look after herself. She looked after us all that evening. It may be . . ."—and Marcus paused to emphasize his words—"that looking after people is what she will do better than anyone." He felt the shiver inside as he spoke. He had surprised himself. The words had fallen out of him. Usually, he edited his speech in advance. Not this time.

His words arrowed into Tari. She looked stricken, confused.

"Are you in school tomorrow?" said Marcus suddenly. It sounded like a simple question. It wasn't. All the intensity in the world was in it.

"She hasn't decided yet," said Rickey. "It's a young night."

"Yes," said Tari.

"Can you meet with me after my lecture?"

"Sounds like a date," said Rickey, his lip curled around the sneer.

"Can you?" said Marcus, ignoring him.

"Yes," said Tari.

"In my office. Whenever."

"Yes," said Tari.

"Hey, what *is* this?" Rickey's voice crashed out so that people looked around. When they saw whose voice it was, they kept looking. "What the fuck is this?" He splayed out his hands in supplication to show that he didn't understand, or that he understood too well.

"It's med-school stuff," said Tari quickly. "He's a teacher, I'm a student. It's no big deal."

"Keep your fucking business off my time."

His eyes were narrow with jealousy and pride. He hadn't wanted to say it, but it had slipped out anyway.

"Your time?" said Marcus simply.

He stood up. He had had enough. He'd achieved something. He was going to see this girl tomorrow. She'd promised, and she would keep her word. Whatever was happening, she seemed to sense that she was in way over her head, and that he would be uniquely qualified to help her in whatever way was appropriate. He was worried by her and excited by her at the same time. But just who was it that he was so desperately attracted to? Was Tari a patient, a saint, or a troubled girl who was neither?

"I have to go," he said.

"Yeah," said Rickey.

Tari didn't stop him. She would see him tomorrow. In the meantime there was now, and, as Rickey had said, it was a young night.

"May I please have a large rum punch?" said Tari.

18

THEY STREAMED into The Whiskey, past the
sidewalk hopefuls. The bouncers stood back re-
spectfully, while the in-crowd on the terrace
eyeballed them. The muscled greeter washed his hands with
the very greatest respect. It was no longer just Rickey and Tari.
It was Rickey and Tari and "friends." Rickey's evil mood had
hung on in there at the Shabeen, but gradually it had lysed on
rum and merged into a devil-may-care insouciance. His old
nonchalance was back, but different, a little nerve-racking now,
and Tari, through the beginnings of her own rum buzz, was
wary. He had made a couple of calls from the restaurant, to
summon his court, and they had dribbled in over the next half
hour until the table for four was a table for eight and rising.

There was a huge man with a bandana who looked like
Willie Nelson on testosterone supplements. A pretty girl with
glasses brought her book. She was the business manager. Two
guys said they were stepbrothers, and were half-zoned on
arrival. There were a couple of partners in the Cage bar-to-be,
Dreemz, and a brace of guys from the Fifth Street Gym who

were what they looked like, sparring partners. Last, but not least, was an exercise trainer who'd been a model. She looked vaguely Polynesian and had an unbeatable body, with quads like a lifter. She revealed to Tari quite early on that she and Rickey worked out together. She would put on gloves and attempt to hit him for half an hour. Mostly, he tried not to be hit, but occasionally he let her through on purpose to keep it interesting. Well! Tari took it all in. This was an entourage . . . a star's court . . . and it had a distinctive group behavior that was quite different from the behavior of each individual that made it up.

Rickey led the way into the trendy bar. Tari looked around. She hadn't been to The Whiskey before. It was a Paris brothel on a short budget. Red velvet furniture was sparse on a plain stone floor. Over to the left were two pool tables, lit by lights advertising Budweiser beer. Waitresses bustled and hustled the cheerful crowd, haute slut in their denim cutoffs and dyed blonde hair. Everyone was having fun, sucking on Miller Lites and not bothering with glasses. The oldest guy in the room was on the sound system. Poor old Mick was singing out his middle-aged heart, unwithered by age, unstaled by custom. *Brown sugar, indeed,* thought Tari. More like Pepto-Bismol and carpet slippers, and check the insurance, dear, before the Alzheimer's of the fading years.

"Hello, girl," said Rickey. He put out an arm and brought her in close to him. He was booze-mellow, and Tari didn't mind. She was loosening up, too. She snuggled close in his strong grip, saying nothing. The hangers-on hung tight as if insulating the star's heat, basking in the stellar glow.

"You want some Mount Gay, Rick?" said the cowboy with the boots.

"Yeah, whatever," agreed Rickey. He rocked back on his feet and checked out the crowd. He felt good. The memories of the braino were fading. Here he was surfing his own turf. The gang around him proved it. They were his people. He paid them. He owned them. They owed him. Life was simple like that. You scattered bucks, and you bought lack of aggravation. Jokes always got laughter. Talk got respect. Deeds scored applause. He'd met a lot of famous people in his time, and they all went this way from the president and Eddie Murphy down. You moved on the grease of people who belonged to you. It was the smooth way to travel the rough road of life.

"You okay, Rickey?" she said.

"Believe it," he said.

Tari was wondering whether or not she should, when the voice cut into their crowd from the outside.

"Hi, people," said Jodie Summerfield.

She stood on the edge of the group, far taller than tall. She was nut brown from a beach shoot, and her aerobicized body was overkill. On her face was a diamond-hard smile. Her fingertips, apparently dipped in the blood of rivals, rested on high hips, and she curved and flowed like a roaring river from killer hair to feet you would die for. She leaned forward into her own hello, and the heads of the group snapped toward her like plants on fast film toward the sun. On South Beach, Jodie was still the number one girl, and in New York, Paris, Milan, and anywhere else you could think of. Her whole body said that, from the way she held it to the way it looked. She wasn't simply good-looking, she was Coca-Cola Classic, Elvis in a car with fins, Andy's soup can; an all-American icon of beauty that took away breath. Whatever was or was not going down in the Summerfield mind, Jodie's exterior rendered it deeply superfluous.

"Hi, babe," said Rickey.

He held out a hand, and she nuzzled against it, purring her pleasure at the unexpected welcome. She came out like a flower at him. Her lips relaxed over the dental dreams that were her teeth.

Tari's spirits sank. Life was timing, but this was ridiculous. For the very first time in her brief relationship with Rickey, storm clouds were everywhere, and now here came the rival, the "10." She wore a plastic-surgeon-approved catsuit, a black skintight thing that ended in shorts just shy of pubic hair. Above, the Lycra material cupped metallic toothpick tits that jutted straight ahead. Insects had fatter waists than Jodie Summerfield. Her body was so good it was a joke. The joke that was on you. There was only one hope. That she would talk. As if on cue, she did.

"Can someone order me some champagne?" said Jodie. "Dom Pérignon," she added, in case there should be any mistake about the sort of champagne she meant.

Jodie hitched herself up against the bar, next to Rickey. Tari was on his other side. The champagne, with a certain amount of ceremony, arrived.

"I'll have a Mount Gay and soda," said Rickey. "That stuff gives me gas."

Jodie said nothing, but her face registered the rebuke. Her eyes swiveled around and found Tari. Instinctively, she had located the enemy. Jodie had met her twice before. The first time, at the airport, Tari had made zero impression on her. The second time had been the nightmare hurricane weekend. For Jodie, the whole thing had passed in an Amytal haze, but she vaguely remembered the Florence Nightingale action in which Rickey had participated. And hadn't one of the disgusting old people croaked in the bathroom? Whatever. Jodie had split the minute the wind had died down and the drug had worn off enough for her to be able to walk. Rickey had stayed to help Tari ferry the living corpses back to Miami, but even at that point Jodie had not identified Tari as a rival. Now, however, the gossip on the beach was unequivocal. Tari and Rickey were an item.

Jodie peered at the competition, as if seeing Tari for the very first time. Whatever she was, she for sure wasn't a model. Compared to Jodie, she wasn't a tall girl, but something made her bigger than her height, and she was white, with soft, translucent skin. There were blue veins on her hands, and her brown hair, lustrous and cut in a pageboy bob, framed a face in which character shone bright. Jodie tried to analyze it, and she was no slouch at the job. She had got the drop on a hundred rivals at a thousand shoots, stealing their looks if their looks looked good, avoiding their mistakes, staying ahead of the competition. Most of the excitement was in the girl's eyes. They were large, round, Italianate, flashing and dancing like jewels in a crown. Her chin was big and definite, and her large mouth moved expressively over tidy teeth as she talked. Her voice was soft but animated, and when she spoke her long white hands conducted her message, emphasizing, downgrading, beating a rhythm that could clearly hypnotize. She was talking to one of the Cage stepbrothers, not an easy thing to do, and Jodie had never seen the boneheaded drunk look as interested. What the shit was it? Her body? It wasn't much better than better-than-average. It was the good body of the very young, pre-exercise, well-proportioned. Her breasts were firm, her legs long for her torso, her bottom high, her hips just a tad too wide. But it wasn't the parts, it was her whole that mattered. Mmmmm. Never an introvert, Jodie took a peep at her own feelings. She was a little drawn to the girl, and that was some sort of a first. Drawn to a girl? To a rival? She slammed the door shut on her finer feelings. Fuck them. They'd never paid the rent. She leaned toward Rickey on the bar.

"So, you shit," she said in a little-girl voice that could sandpaper boats. "Where have you been? I heard you were dating the dog with no name."

Rickey leaned back to watch the show. He hadn't totally forgiven Tari for the Douglas confrontation in the Shabeen. Now he would only step in to protect her if the psychic blood really started to flow. Jodie might be little more than a gift-wrapped Barbie doll, but she was still an L.A. woman. That meant she would know how to give good grief.

"You remember Tari Jones?" Rickey smiled as he reintroduced them.

"Would *anybody* remember Tari Jones?"

"Hi," said Tari, giving her one last chance.

"How are you enjoying the lifestyles of the rich and famous?" said Jodie.

"Lifestyles or knifestyles?" said Tari evenly.

"You can afford a scriptwriter?" countered Jodie, her lip curling like a whip.

"Some of us have been doing conversations without them for a while now," said Tari. "The tricky bit is learning how to think."

Jodie Summerfield took a deep breath. A stepbrother said "Whoa!" The speeded-up Willie Nelson figure chuckled. Jodie took a deep breath, which had the effect of thrusting out her superb chest, peacocklike, at the enemy. She needed to say something absolutely devastating, but thought had gone. It would be far easier and more satisfying to simply attack the nonentity. She could shred her with the red talons they'd coated in some space-age material at the salon. She looked at Rickey, her erstwhile screw. Shit, physical was a no-no. It would have to be the verbals. What would Mae West have said? What movies had she seen lately that had done clever put-downs? Jesus, it was a bummer when people weren't fazed by your fame.

"What did you say your name was?" she managed, playing for time. It wasn't a name anyone had heard of. It followed that repeating it out loud would cause some sort of embarrassment.

"Rickey said my name was Tari Jones. He was quite right."

"Well, Tari, I'd advise you to be careful what you say and how you say it to people like me."

Jodie tried to look incredibly famous as she spoke, to cover up the weakness of her repartee.

"I sure will," said Tari with an impish grin. "I'll speak real slow and use words of one syllable."

Rickey laughed out loud.

"You . . . bitch!" exploded Jodie.

"Whatever you say," said Tari, smiling broadly. "It's the one subject on which you have to be the expert."

Jodie had nothing left. She turned toward Rickey.

"Are you going to let her speak to me like that?" Ask a silly question.

Rickey splayed open his hands in a gesture of impotence.

"Yeah," he said. He, too, was smiling.

"Well, *fuck* you," said Jodie.

She was gone, striding through the crowd in her retreat from insult.

Rickey turned toward Tari. Respect was all over his face.

"You give good mouth," he said.

"So do you," said Tari, her eyes sparkling.

19

EYES CLOSED tight, her mind burning in a fiery furnace, Tari was awake. She lay there in the greasy dawn and the humid air came in off the balcony and licked her like a dog. She tried to open her mouth, but her lips were sealed by a superglue of grunge, so she gave that up and rolled over. Movement was a mistake. So was thought. But the kaleidoscope of memory was slipping into place.

Tari leaned in toward Rickey, shoulder-blocking a model with desperate eyes and a butt so small it could have taken money in a freak show at the county fair.
"I love you, big shot," she whispered.
"I love you back."
"You send my love back."
"No I don't. I'm keeping it. It's mine. You're mine."
She sat back and stretched her hands above her head, smiling her pleasure. She could actually feel her own eyes shining.
"Is this what it's like? Falling in love? I've never done it before."
"I'm not much of an expert myself," he said with a laugh.

Tari laughed, too. She felt wonderfully . . . weird, his word. It was like being hyperalive. Breathing wasn't done just for her anymore. Part of it was for him. She wanted to look great for him, be bright for him, to make him want her till the feelings hurt. It was an out-of-control emotion, like a roller coaster ride when your stomach got left behind. No wonder it was called "falling" in love. She tried to explain it, but it was crazy, and the madness was a potent part of the charm.

"Dance with me," she said.

"I don't do dancing."

"Then go stand on the dance floor, and let me rub up against you."

Tari was shocked by herself. Was it the rum talking? The words had shot out. But it was what she wanted to do, to rub up against him. She wanted the friction. If she couldn't have flesh, she wanted leather, and the smell of him, the feel, the touch.

He looked surprised, but a slow smile came up and his eyes flicked over to where they did the dancing he didn't "do." His smile deepened.

"Is that what you want?"

Tari nodded, and he took the nod for an answer. He stood up, his fingers still entwined in hers, and she stood with him.

The dance floor of the Van Dome was a multicolored rain of light. The strobes burst down, soaking the people with brightness, and the dancers surged like a sea, throwing up pockets of roughness, patches of calm.

"Here," she said. *A place had cleared for them. He stood there waiting for her to take the lead. Tari came in close, husky with sex. God, she was hot. She was on fire. Her fingers buried themselves in the tightening muscles of his butt. Her other hand was bent back on his stomach, massaging him. Her face was turned up toward him, her mouth half-open with a smile of lust.*

"You meant what you said," *he whispered.*

"I'm going to make you come," *she whispered back.*

Tari laughed up at him. Her hand crept lower. With her other hand she forced him in closer. He had only to collude with her. In one single gesture of acquiescence, he would be lost. She watched as he swallowed hard. His Adam's apple bobbed in his throat like a drowning man on a rough ocean. She was so near to her own way. Then he thrust back at her. It was the permission she needed.

Her hand was on him, separating him from her. She touched him through the denim. At the same time she touched herself. Together they slipped into the conspiracy. He ran his hands up the sides of her, feeling her heat. Up high, he went to bare skin, to her armpits, slick with sweat. He sank his fingers in the steamy damp, massaging her, almost lifting her, pulling her against him. It was as if he were positioning himself to enter her, but there could be no entry. He pistoned forward, and she shook with the force of his momentum. Yet she held her ground, jammed against him, smiling her lust and thrusting her leg and hip between his.

"You like it?" she murmured.

He groaned his assent and threw back his head. He was losing it. It was going to happen, just as she said it would. Tari swayed from side to side, back and forward, locked against him. The music conducted them. It washed over them, wiping them into one like surf over sand. Tari's skirt rode way up, exposing her panties as Rickey lunged against her. She fought to stay close, to mold with his body. She was hot and malleable like Plasticine, filling his curves and crawling into the cracks of him. There must be no space. There could be only two bodies creeping into each other's crevices, burning in the heat of the wonderful friction, cooled only by the bubbling juice of lust. There were the tracks of her wetness now on his cool blue velvet denim. There would be the weeping tears of his love on the inside. They must meet. They should run together in the final release, conquering clothes, and merging in symbolic union. She saw him wince with the pain of the love dance. In his faraway eyes she could see the goal.

"Yes," she whispered, and then much louder, "Yes."

Her assent was lost in the sound of music, but he could see her lips move as she gave the permission that was also a command. There was sweat on her breast. The strobe lights caught its brightness against her luminous skin. Her teeth were bared in a snarl of passion. Perspiration gleamed on her high forehead. There were beads of moisture below her nostrils. She wanted it this way. He would have ecstasy. She would have control. She watched him run toward the end, like a sprinter to the tape. He was so close. He dipped at the knee as she steadied herself to receive his final thrust. Then he arrowed upward, squeezing out, grinding forward against her body. His hands cupped her buttocks, and he pulled her to him with every ounce of his strength. Suddenly, his body was disintegrating. He was falling apart all over her, and she felt the pent-up lust stream from him. On it went, long and hard, the rain of passion. He moaned low. The sound gurgled in the back of his throat. His head was thrown back in abandonment. His eyes were closed to hold in the storm of feeling.

She held him through the throbbing, vibrating orgasm. She piled on the pressure, plastering her crotch against him both to experience and mother his climax. Wet against wet now, their clothes soaked by their mutual desire, they could feel each other at last. Their skins didn't touch, but their essence had merged. Here on the dance floor, among all the people, they were dancing for real the dance of love.

Tari nuzzled into him. Her mouth was warm against his ear, as he shuddered in the aftermath.

"You knew how to dance all the time," she whispered.

He leaned against her, exhausted. He buried his face in her neck, and when he spoke his voice was hoarse.

"I want you to be one of my paintings," he murmured.

Tari opened her eyes and stared at the ceiling. She ran the back of her hand over her clammy brow and tried to find the strength to get to the bathroom. There were things in there she needed . . . Tylenol, water, Pepto-Bismol for the nausea that sloshed around in her stomach. What the hell had happened last night? But she knew the answer. Basically, rum had happened. Everything else had flowed from that. Everything else? Yes, it had to be confronted.

She had been fine in the Shabeen, and cooking with gas in The Whiskey, especially after her victorious encounter with Jodie Summerfield. In the Van Dome she had been over the top, but still basically there. Then, it had all begun to unravel as the rum jag had acquired its own momentum. After the row with Rickey earlier in the evening, the making up had been spectacularly sweet. Lost in love, she had put her head on hold and let her heart lead. Somehow the urgent dance-floor sex had been a watershed. It had underlined what Rickey and she were. They were animals in the early stages of the most intense attraction. Later, their relationship could turn into mellow love, but now it was the hungriest lust. Each moment threatened the glorious outbreak of a fire that could only be extinguished by the waterfalls and storms of orgasm and climax. In the nightclub, Tari hadn't been able to wait for grown-up places like beds, or even floors. There had only been a need so naked it hadn't minded wearing clothes. On the dance floor, he had murmured about the painting he wanted to do of her; then, at the table, surrounded by his guardians, they had drunk most of a bottle of Mount Gay. She had watched him through the swirling mists and the vibrating sound waves of the trendy club, and she had loved him free of any inhibition. The drink had removed her censors and evaporated conscience and all that had been left was longing for the man both she and her body wanted. It had been a lot later when he had mentioned the painting again. Bits of the conversation came back to her.

"Only two things I care about . . . you and my art . . . so beautiful, your face and your spirit . . . I long to combine them, you and my art . . . only things that matter . . . so important . . . safe . . . love you always . . . live forever, my art, our love . . ."

He had wanted to take photographs of her for one of his collages and it had felt so deeply right, simply a consecration of the extraordinary passion they'd shared and would share. She had trusted him totally. To be in his art, to *be* his art, had seemed the logical way to lock up his heart. So she had agreed. At about that time the rum had really begun to bite, and her mind had begun to fragment. She could vaguely remember leaving the club, but not on the bike. Had they walked to his loft? Had she staggered there? Or had the quiet girl with the glasses and the book driven them? She had been there, the business manager, in the loft at the making of the photograph. Oh, yes, she had. Tari took a deep breath as she stuck the bits and pieces of memory together.

It was hot under the tungsten light. Tari lay back, bathing in brightness, as the motor drive whirred in the darkness beyond. She turned languidly, as if cooking herself on a slow fire, and the bits of her body came into hazy focus, part by part, for both the camera and her rum-soaked mind. She had never felt more beautiful, all alone, in floodlit splendor, on the grubby floor. Her body was at once familiar and strange. She was seeing it for the first time as an object, separate from her. It was a personal landscape of curves and corners. Shadows led unexpectedly to dappled fields of brilliance. There were cul-de-sacs and wide-open spaces. She could see the sheen of sweat on her skin.

Inside, too, she was warm with pleasure. She had laid herself out like artwork on a table. Her body had no meaning apart from its flesh and the shapes it was making. It was pure matter. It was totally physical. She no longer had a mind and a point of view. She was submerged in sensation. Heat, light, and the click of the camera's shutter were the edges of her world. Yet in that very detachment lived an incredible autoeroticism. So she lay back farther, and splayed her legs wide-open for the camera, her hands behind her for support. As she did so, she moaned her abandonment, shameless in her lonely ecstasy. All could give some for art. She could give all.

As she smiled her appreciation for the cleverness of her thought, it happened. The girl came from behind. One minute she had been alone in fantasy, stretched on the rack of sexual tension. The next she had been joined. Tari felt the girl first. Her long hair dripped down to brush Tari's shoulder. The shock of the touch merged instantly with an alien excitement. Tari had been sensitized. She had become an antigenic reaction waiting to happen. Now, the laser of unfocused desire within her was given, so suddenly, a target. The girl turned her face to the side of Tari's face. Then she put her tongue in Tari's ear.

It was wet and warm and soft as velvet. It probed inside her with a tenderness no man could imitate. Tari didn't resist. She lay there, still, her heart pounding, and the long chestnut hair of the stranger cascaded over her right breast. Breath was caught in the back of her throat. Her mouth was dry with desire. Her mind was a mess of confusion. The noise in her ear unhinged her. It was a moist, damp sound of liquid allure, and it was borne on hot, sweet breath that bathed her skin. She had no time to think of who, or why, or of the camera that captured the moment in the so-bright light. Because the tongue was gone now, and the girl's face, blurred and smiling, was an inch from her own. Now, it was a mouth that wanted her, and it was a mouth she wanted. And then she kissed her. Suddenly, Tari knew who it was. It was the quiet girl, who said so little and read so much. It was the business girl, the manager, who had smiled so politely and who was smiling with such unashamed desire now. It was a soft, gentle kiss, far more delicate and sensitive than Tari had known before. The girl's lips brushed across hers in a camel-hair caress. She put both her hands on either side of Tari's head, and for a second she cradled it with infinite tenderness. Then, firmly, she pushed open Tari's mouth with her tongue.

20

"**Y**OU KNOW they're going to lobotomize Sarah Perkins," said Mary.

"They're going to do *what?*" said Tari. She stopped in her tracks in the middle of the corridor. Mary stopped, too.

"Well, stereotactic modified prefrontal leucotomy, to be precise, but it's still hacking away at the brain to me."

"But Sarah's my patient. When was that decision taken? Why wasn't I told?"

"You're only a lowly medical student, Tari. The nurses knew yesterday. Hodges made the decision. Sarah's all shaved up and ready to go. Looks pretty weird with the Yul Brynner."

"That operation doesn't work!"

"Don't shout at me, Tari. I agree. So does Rivers, the psych resident. But Hodges is a fan. You know that boring paper she once wrote about it, and is so proud of. And the neurosurgeons are totally gung ho. Drill to skull in an hour. Do you want to come along? I've never seen one, and we'd only be missing Peterson on statistics, which is a must to avoid. Hey, are you all right? You look kinda pale."

"Yeah, hangover." Tari took a deep breath. All this morning she had been trying to come to terms with last night. Now, her own problems melted away in the face of Sarah Perkins's. The girl was an obsessive-compulsive, and the illness had wrecked her life. She was a hairdresser who had the compulsion to wash her scissors and her combs for hours on end. She realized that her compulsion was totally ridiculous and that her obsession with germs was irrational, even crazy. But it didn't make any difference. She would experience an almost unbearable tension, which could only be relieved by the washing ritual. It had started slowly, with an "obsessive" neatness that they joked about at the salon. Then it had begun to interfere with her work. She felt compelled to wash the scissors three times in disinfectant after each use. Then it had been three times three. And later on, three times three plus two. Pretty soon, her whole day had been taken up with washing, and there had been no time to cut hair. She had been fired, but at home the situation had gotten worse. She had begun to wash her hands and her hair constantly, and her fear of germs caused her to clean her apartment continually. Things had progressed to the stage where she was walking around with Kleenex boxes on her feet, and refusing to go out in case she came into contact with "dirt." She had become depressed, then suicidal, and eventually had been admitted to the hospital. The standard treatment, antidepressant medication and behavior therapy, had achieved little. Professor Hodges, whose patient she was, had given her a course of electroconvulsive therapy against the objections of everyone. Still, the compulsive behavior had persisted. A few psychiatrists in the biological wing of the profession, like Hodges, maintained that destroying brain cells in specific parts of the frontal lobes could alleviate the symptoms of the disease. Most mainstream psychiatrists disagreed. It was therefore something of a lottery as to whether or not you got surgery when all else had failed.

"Has she signed the consent?" said Tari.

"I imagine so. Nobody's going to drill holes in her nut unless she has."

"Well, she can unsign it," said Tari.

She hurried on.

"You're going to tell her to take back her consent? You can't do that. Hodges will kill you. Anyway, you can't worry a patient like that before an operation. Shit, Tari. She's depressed enough as it is."

"She'll be more fucking depressed if she has some butcher burning bits out of her brain to satisfy the dreadful desire of the unimaginative to 'do' something."

Tari was almost running now. Mary could hardly keep up.

"How was Rickey last night?"

"Fuck Rickey," said Tari, breaking into a run and leaving her friend behind.

She crashed into the ward. There was a curtain around Sarah Perkins's bed.

The anesthesiologist looked up as Tari drew back the curtain. So did the nurse. Sarah Perkins lay against the pillows. She was bald. Her head shone beneath the neon, shaved tight to the skin. A blue mark in grease pencil indicated the position where the electrode would be inserted through the skull.

"I'm Tarleton Jones," she said to the anesthesiologist's raised eyebrows. "Sarah is an assigned patient of mine. Hi, Sarah."

"Good. Are you going to be coming with us?" said the anesthesiologist. He meant to the operating room.

"Has she had her premed?" said Tari brusquely.

"I've just given it to her," said the doctor, not liking Tari's tone.

Shit! Tari thought quickly. The premed would have included a heavy-duty sedative. They would be going for deep anesthesia. In brain surgery, you didn't want your patients shifting about on the table. Sarah would already be under the influence of drugs. It simply wouldn't be feasible to get her to change her mind about consent now. Things had gone too far. The earlier consent would carry the weight. Any attempt by the patient to reverse it would be disregarded as a drug-induced decision, and not a rational one. There was only one person who could stop the show. Professor Hodges.

The professor would certainly be attending the operation. Leucotomies were rare, and she was the rare champion of them. She wouldn't miss the opportunity of playing high priestess at the ceremonial surgical exorcism of poor Sarah

Perkins's demons. But there was an hour till surgery. Tari could catch the professor in her office right now. She leaned forward and squeezed Sarah's hand.

"Don't worry about a thing, Sarah," she said. "I'm going to be with you all the way."

Sarah smiled wanly at her, and Tari was gone.

The secretary in the professor's office said, "Do you have an appointment? The professor . . ."

Tari walked past her and into the professor's office. She didn't knock.

Professor Hodges looked up, annoyed. On her desk was an open copy of *Gray's Anatomy*. Tari could make out an upside-down brain. The professor was reviewing. It was rare that shrinks got to see the inside of bodies. The professor would want to show off her anatomical knowledge to the surgeons.

"What is it? I didn't hear you knock."

"It's immoral," said Tari, "to perform a discredited and damaging operation on Sarah Perkins's brain."

"It's *what*?" The professor's "what" exploded like a whip-lash from her mouth. Her head snapped back in shock. She recognized Tari immediately. She was a troublemaker, an opinionated, outspoken renegade, and bright as a button academically . . . the very worst sort of student. Dr. Donovan had complained repeatedly about her. Doctors Boniface and Schwartz, in contrast, thought the sun shone from her back-side. Veronica Hodges, the only opinion that mattered, could still hardly bring herself to remember the extraordinary telephone conversation during the hurricane. Then, the girl had seemed to say something to her that couldn't possibly have been said. . . . The color came up on the professor's cheeks at the bizarre memory.

"Are you daring to question my judgment and the judgment of the department of neurosurgery . . . you, a mere . . . student? I'm not sure that I can believe what I'm hearing."

"Try," said Tari. "There is excellent evidence that even modified leucotomies do considerable harm to the patient, both psychological and physical. There is zero evidence that they do any good."

Professor Hodges couldn't resist the temptation. The right

thing to do was to chuck the little rabble-rouser out of her office, and then move heaven and earth to get her slung out of the medical school. But Tari had uttered the magical word "evidence." Veronica Hodges was being engaged in intellectual debate, albeit by an insignificant inferior. It was a challenge she couldn't bear to turn down, especially as the research to which she was about to refer was her own.

"Imagining that you are able to read, and that you have discovered where the library is, may I refer you to a paper of my own on the subject. *American Journal of Psychiatry.* June 1978. I think I demonstrated conclusively the statistically significant beneficial effects of this operation."

"You had a sample size of precisely five patients." Tari shot back her answer. "And they were suffering from chronic depression, not obsessive-compulsive neurosis. *And* you didn't investigate sequelae of the operation in your paper, merely its effect on mood, which, I seem to remember, was marginal at best. Lewin et al. at Columbia investigated the procedure, using a sample of one hundred ninety-four patients, and found no beneficial effect. Mathers at UCLA, in a prospective study, found no significant positive effect. Durlacher at Vanderbilt discovered significant postoperative psychological problems attendant on brain surgery for psychological symptoms. And then there are the one-percent risks of general anesthesia, not to mention the dangers of prolonged apnea as a result of electrical depression of the breathing center. Oh," said Tari, as an acid afterthought. "You'll find the breathing center down there, just north of the medulla oblongata, that little oblong bit in the center there." She leaned forward and stuck her forefinger in the middle of the brain section in the open *Gray's Anatomy* on the professor's desk.

Professor Hodges stood up. She was red with rage, and she had already begun to shake.

"How dare you even *attempt* to try to interfere with my treatment of my patient. You're a troublemaker, Ms. Jones. I've had to deal with students like you before. Don't think I won't be speaking to the dean about this. I see no future for you in medicine, let alone psychiatry. You have no judgment. You allow yourself to become emotionally involved with patients. In fact, I have serious doubts, serious professional doubts, about your personality. It seems to be disordered. Yes, disordered. Disordered!''

Her voice had acquired a strange shrillness. She was all but shouting. She could feel herself burning up with rage. Before her, the girl was calm as the sea in summer. Professor Hodges was not a very good psychiatrist, but she was good enough to know that it was she, and not the "disordered personality" who stood before her, that had lost it.

"Disordered," said Tari, "is a value judgment. In value judgments, the values and judgment of the judge are at least as significant as those of the judged. Yes, I do allow myself to become emotionally involved with my patients. I become specially involved when it comes down to protecting them from dangerous, harmful, and useless operations invented in the stone age of psychiatry. It may be that my personality is 'disordered.' Yours, however, is psycho-toxic, and that is never a good thing for a psychiatrist's personality to be."

"Get out! Get out!" screamed Veronica Hodges.

"Are you going to stop this operation?" said Tari, her voice cold as ice.

"Of course I'm not. Are you crazy? Get out of here!"

Veronica Hodges waved her hand in the air like an ineffective wand, as if hoping her gesture would make Tari disappear. Behind her, on the wall, were her diplomas. There were scores of them, memorializing each trivial step in the professor's painful journey to the great chair of psychiatry. But her power had gone. She felt it. The nonentity in front of her was far more than her match.

"Then I will see you in the operating room," said Tari.

"You will not. I forbid you to attend this operation."

"Sarah Perkins is my assigned patient. I have not only the right, but the obligation to be there. The dean is insistent on that. And it's not your operation. It's the neurosurgeon's."

"I'll talk to the dean. I'll . . ." stammered Veronica Hodges.

"You'll have to wait until he gets back from Jamaica," said Tari, and she turned around and walked out.

Sarah Perkins lay on the operating table, and she looked like something out of a horror movie. Her shaved head, glistening beneath the surgical lights, was encased in a monstrous helmet of metal scaffolding. It appeared to be some exotic instrument of medieval torture, a wicked mask worn by some tormented prisoner in a deep, dark dungeon. It had been screwed tightly to her skull, and at the places where it penetrated the skin, blood showed. The whole of her skull had been bathed in Savlon antiseptic, but the grease marks remained, little surgical doodles to remind the high priest of the procedure just exactly where metal should meet mind. The scaffolding around Sarah's head was both a measuring device and an anchor. In conjunction with the multiple brain X rays that would be pinned to light boxes on the wall, the surgeon would know, at least in theory, just how deep his probes were in the neuron mass, and at exactly what angle.

The chief neuro intern was setting up the geography. The surgeon himself, like minor royalty, had delayed his entry into the room until his minion had set the scene. The spectators— Tari, Mary, four surgical students, and Professor Hodges— stood distanced by several feet from the operating table.

"If he knows what he's doing, why the hell is he sweating?" whispered Mary.

Tari was thinking the same thing. The neuro intern didn't look happy. His cage, the instrument that would guide his probes to precisely the right part of the patient's brain, looked about as steady as a crane in a cyclone. The sweat stood out on his brow above the green surgical mask as he unscrewed one part of it and tightened another.

Tari felt the anger grow inside her. It was typical of this sort of surgery. None of them knew what the hell they were doing. They were going to insert an electrical needle into some part or other of Sarah's brain, and then they were going to burn holes in it in a vain attempt to destroy her crazy impulses. Theory said you defined a ridge one and one-quarter inches from the outer edge of the frontal lobe and placed six burns in a line abreast along it, like half a dozen soldiers on parade. But from the shaky hand of the neuro, and the slippery movements of the guide cage, any fool could see this was not pinpoint accuracy. It was a blunderbuss blast when it should have been a sniper's rifle. It was surgical smoke and mirrors, and these people ought to have known better.

The doors flew open. The surgeon had arrived. In contrast to the olive green operating gowns of everyone else, his was reddish-brown. It was an affectation for which he was well-known.

"We call him the Red Baron," whispered one of the surgical students to Tari.

"Good morning, everyone. Professor Hodges," he said, bowing slightly, like the minor star of a music-hall act.

He advanced on the table and peered at the positioning of the skull cage. "All right, Steven?" he said, his voice smooth as silk.

"I'm having a bit of a problem setting the angle," muttered the intern.

"Not to worry," said the Red Baron.

"Why not to worry?" said Tari out loud. Daggers flew from Professor Hodges's eyes.

Behind his brown mask, the Red Baron was smiling a patronizing smile.

"Because, young lady . . . because when we have the electrode in the vicinity of our target zone, we will pass a small current down it. If we are in the correct place, the patient will stop breathing. The current will suppress the breathing center and there will be a short period of apnea. Press the button, watch the chest. Ah, the wonders of science."

He chuckled. He was so very pleased with himself. He was playing God, and loving every minute of it. No wonder they called it an operating theater.

"Listen. Don't talk," hissed Professor Hodges at Tari.

"No, no, Professor. They have to learn. Have to learn. Ask away, people. Ask away."

"She starts to breathe again the moment you switch off the current, sir?" asked one of the surgical students.

"She does indeed," said the Red Baron, moving around the table like an Indian circling a wagon train. "Let's get on with it, Steven."

"I'm still not totally happy with the angle," said the intern.

"Nonsense."

"Okay, sir. Drill, please."

Tari froze inside.

"That's the way. X marks the spot," said the Red Baron in cheery tones.

Above her mask, Tari could see a grim smile on the face of the professor. What could have fathered it? Satisfaction that Tari was having to watch an operation that she felt was an abomination against nature? The pleasure of the sadist at the thought of those burning brain cells? The triumph of the biological scientist over those miserable optimists who dared to believe that minds were somehow bigger and grander than the matter that made them up?

It was a drill much like a Black and Decker, although it bore the proud name of International Surgical Instruments. It made the same noise as a Black and Decker as it ripped through Sarah Perkins's skin and skull. And it threw off the same colored shavings as a Black and Decker slipping through a third of an inch of red-painted plywood.

"Now we have a Burr hole. Next, we place the probe. I should say, for those that worry about such things, that our probe does minimal damage to the cells on the way in. It pushes them aside. Only when we give it heat does it cause the desired lesions."

The sweating intern slipped the probe into the hole he'd made. It ran on streetcar lines through the guide hole in the cage. At precisely one and a half inches he stopped.

"Let's have an X ray and see where we are," said the Red Baron.

Tari watched Sarah's chest wall. It rose and fell. The bag that contained the anesthetic gases and the oxygen contracted and expanded. She felt the panic inside her. It had been building slowly. Now, it had reached the boiling point. She had insisted on coming to the operation because somehow she had felt she might be able to stop it. But how the hell could she stop it? A hysterical outburst would solve nothing. The Red Baron ruled in this room. This was a totalitarian, chauvinistic autocracy. The probe was in Sarah's brain. The electrical box to which it was attached stood next to the operating table on its own cart. It consisted basically of some dials and a big switch. When the burning current flowed, Sarah Perkins's brain would never be the same again.

The portable X ray machine was wheeled over to the table. The radiologist took pictures from several angles.

"Won't be long," he said. He wasn't. He was back in minutes with the developed film. He flicked them onto the light boxes.

"There you are," said the Red Baron. "The probe is in the right place."

Tari closed her eyes.

Dear God, do something.

"Let's try a little apnea, shall we?" said the surgeon, as if he were deciding on an entrée in the staff dining room.

He flicked the switch. Tari opened her eyes. Sarah was still breathing.

"Ah," said the Red Baron, turning the switch back to the "off" position. "Shit," said the intern.

"Give it another two millimeters, Steven."

The intern eased the probe in deeper, reading off the depth on the gauge of the skull cage.

"Two millimeters."

Again, the surgeon flicked the switch. His hand darted into the air like a conductor bringing in the heavy brass. As if by magic, Sarah Perkins stopped breathing.

"There you are!" he said, his tone thick with self-congratulation. "Not as easy as it looks," he added, as if in some way switch manipulation had been the crux of the proceedings.

He turned to the student audience. "Now that we know we are in the right place, we can burn away," he said with relish. "We reduce the current and start the breathing, and then we can get cracking on the first lesion."

He twiddled a dial. "There! That's the end of the current. Behold, the breathing begins."

Tari stared hard at Sarah's chest. Nothing. It was still. She held her own breath in sympathy.

"Sometimes it takes a second or two . . ." said the Red Baron. His voice had lost its confident banter.

The silence in the room was total. Eyes bored into the patient. At the head of the table, the anesthesiologist looked nervous.

"She isn't breathing," said the intern.

"I can see that," snapped the Red Baron.

"I thought she was supposed . . ." tried the surgery student who had spoken earlier.

"Shut the hell up," said the surgeon, all vestiges of cool vanishing. "Why isn't she breathing?" He addressed his question to the anesthesiologist. He was in charge of breathing. The breathing buck would end with him.

Tari watched in horror. *Oh, God, please help.*

"I'll give it another minute and then go to positive pressure ventilation," said the anesthesiologist.

The seconds ticked by.

"This has never happened before," muttered the Red Baron, shifting his weight first onto one foot and then onto the other. "Take the damned probe out, Steven."

"She's cyanosed," said the anesthesiologist. "I'm going to intubate and go to PPV."

"That's it," said the Red Baron. "I'm not going to fool around with this one. I'm sorry, Professor Hodges, but I think we ought to get her off the table and up to intensive care right away."

"Breathe," said Tari in a loud voice.

The anesthesiologist was slipping the tube past Sarah's teeth when she took a mammoth breath, and then another, and then another.

"There she goes," said the Red Baron. "It was only a question of waiting." He paused. Discretion was the better part of valor. "But in view of her idiosyncratic reaction, I don't think it's wise to go ahead with the operation."

21

MARCUS DOUGLAS stood in silence at the lectern. He looked sternly around the crowded auditorium, noting the excellent turnout for his first lecture. When was the last time he'd stood in the pulpit and looked out at a full church? A long time ago. These medical students didn't want spiritual knowledge. They wanted the facts they could turn into M.D.s, into cash passports to the land of Lexus and Infiniti. The vast majority of the eager faces out there belonged to would-be millionaires and wannabe corporations whose medical practices would be nothing but the cash flow for real-estate deals and oil and gas plays. They'd heal a sick patient if they had to, but mostly they'd treat the elaborate tests they'd ordered to hedge against possible malpractice claims, as ingrowing toenails metamorphosed into major abdominal surgery and indigestion amplified itself into coronary bypass operations.

Not many of them would end up as psychiatrists. Only geriatrics was a less popular career choice for physicians in America. Out there were the knife men. Whip it in, whip it out and wipe it, and run like a rabbit all the way to the bank. And the gut guys, with their slimy tubes and smarmy chat. And the heart boys, pandering to the aged's desire to live forever, with their slick plumbing and winning electrical work, guaranteed to give you another few months of hell on earth in return for your savings. Still, they all had to know a schizophrenic from a psychopath. Otherwise they wouldn't pass the test. Good-bye, country club. Farewell, med school for junior and for Jock Stethoscope III. Au revoir, fawning respect, groveling gratitude, and the unconditional admiration of those who hadn't woken up to the fact that American medicine was turning into a giant cash-grabbing confidence trick.

"The most important thing to know about schizophrenia is that there is a lot of it around. There are about one hundred people in this auditorium. If each of us lives to be seventy-five, the statistical likelihood is that at least one of us will suffer a schizophrenic illness in our lifetime."

He paused. He looked around the room. The surreal impression was created that he was searching for the single schizophrenic. What he succeeded in finding was Tari.

She sat halfway up, in the middle, next to Mary, and her hangover was in remission. She leaned forward slightly in her seat as an eager student should, and her notebook was balanced on her knee. She wasn't writing, however. She was staring at Marcus Douglas, and now, quite suddenly, he was staring at her. They'd done this before. She half-smiled at him. He half-smiled back. Then he tore his eyes away from her.

"The other thing to remember is that it is a serious illness and one that is very poorly understood by the majority of the population. People know about heart attacks and diabetes and AIDS. Knowledge about schizophrenia is beset by myths. Myth number one is that the schizophrenic has a split personality. 'I'm a bit schizophrenic about that,' someone will say, meaning 'I'm in two minds about it.' It's simply not what schizophrenia is about. Split-personality disorder is a hysterical illness. And it's rare. The schizophrenic isn't in two minds about anything. He is suffering from a severe disturbance in his thought processes that affects his entire personality. He doesn't have two or more separate, different, yet coherent personalities. He has a totally fragmented and disorganized *single* personality. Dr. Jekyll was nice and organized. Mr. Hyde was nasty and evil.

Both made some sort of sense. The schizophrenic makes no sense. He talks and believes nonsense. It's an important distinction. If you get nothing else from this lecture, I want you to grasp hold of it. At the very least, it will stand you in good stead at the cocktail parties I suspect many of you are fated frequently to endure."

Tari smiled broadly. He was so dry, so pedantic, and so . . . angry, really. He spoke in a tight, clipped voice. Every word was carefully selected. There were no *ums* and *ahs,* no pauses, just accurate sentiments accurately expressed. But his grammar was aggressive. It was somehow scornful, as if daring the television-tuned minds of his audience to follow as he failed to split his infinitives, as he wrapped his tongue around Churchillian circumlocutions and conversational conceits. You, none of you, want to know about this, he was saying. Schizophrenics won't have the cash to pay your inflated bills, nor those of the insurance company. People like me will have to pick up the pieces of their broken personalities while you are worrying about stock-option hedging, CD changers for the Porsche, and whether or not you can get your leg across the pretty recep-tionist who pretends to be a nurse.

"He's rather attractive," whispered Mary by her side.

Tari nodded. He was. He seemed so deeply unapproachable, walled off in a private garden of forbidden fruit trees. And the intelligence was a turn-on. It was so fierce. So utterly unforgiv-ing. When a high IQ was combined with total moral conviction and the whole was packaged in a container as attractive as Marcus Douglas's body, sparks had to fly. Tari felt the thrill. This man liked her, and it was clear as a bell that he didn't like everybody.

"But I don't think he'd be a barrel of laughs." Mary's commentary sounded as if it had some way to go.

"He's sweet," lied Tari. It was a ridiculous word to use about Marcus Douglas.

"Bullshit," said Mary.

"The other great myth about schizophrenia is that it is an untreatable condition. That's nonsense. Certainly, the treat-ment of schizophrenia is largely the treatment of symptoms. Cure is beyond us. But then most of medicine is about symptomatic treatment. In the long run we all die. We can control diabetes, but we can't eradicate it. We can remove cancers, but we can't be sure they won't recur. We can't slow or stop the aging process, but we can help with the problems it causes. Schizophrenia responds to antipsychotic medication. Chlorpromazine usually makes the voices go away, or quiets them down. Its invention in the fifties emptied the long-stay hospitals of schizophrenics. So psychiatrists can help, and do help. Schizophrenia is an inherited disease, whose final common pathway is a biochemical abnormality in the brain. If you blockade the dopamine receptors in the limbic system with Thorazine, then your patient may no longer feel that he is controlled by radio waves from outer space, or that she has been sent to save the world . . ."

Tari sat up straight. Had that been done on purpose? Surely not.

"Whoops!" said Mary.

Tari swallowed. Sent to save the world. Was he talking about her? No. Schizophrenics often thought they were special people singled out for special purposes, like saving the world. It was an extraordinarily common schizophrenic delusion. It was absolutely to be expected that Douglas would use an example like that in a lecture on schizophrenia. But he had seen her in the audience. They had exchanged almost smiles. He couldn't be so insensitive as to make a reference like that. Could he? Why would he? To worry her? To raise the seed of doubt in her mind? To make quite certain that she sought him out for his advice? Yes. The reference had been made with her in mind. He had been talking to her, talking about her. He had been referring to her. Zap! The thought hit Tari hard. Was this an idea of reference? That was another common symptom of schizophrenia. The patient became deluded and began to believe that events had special reference to him, or to her, when there was no good reason for believing that. A patient might think that the song on the radio was being played *especially* for him, and that it referred to him and his life specifically. Douglas had produced an example of a common schizophrenic delusion and she had thought he was referring to her.

Panic shot through Tari. A primary delusion, plus a grandiloquent delusion, plus a voice, plus an idea of reference. Did *her*
limbic system dopamine receptors need Thorazine blockade?
Was this the thin edge of the wedge that would turn out to be
schizophrenia? Once again, she held out her hand to the life
raft. No. She had insight. Schizophrenics couldn't reason like
this about their illness. The disease consisted of a suspension
of reason. The reasoning process itself was damaged. Thinking
was all screwed up, and yet she was thinking clearly, rationally.
She was able to weigh things. On the one hand this . . . on the
other hand that. And there was an extent to which she did not
fully believe her "delusions." Or did she? Did they not exist
still? Were they alive and well, but simply camouflaged beneath
the hurricane of feelings that her crazy affair with Rickey had
unleashed?

The minutes flashed by as Tari sat in a daze of indecision and
anxiety. She lost track of what he was saying, turning inward to
her own thoughts. *You are my daughter. You will bring love to the
world.* It was so real. So unavoidable. It was so deeply . . . weird.

"One of the most difficult problems in psychiatry," said
Marcus Douglas, "is to differentiate between a genuine religious
experience and a psychotic episode." He paused and looked up
at the audience, catching Tari's eye. She sat transfixed, hardly
daring to wonder if he was talking to her or not.

"I, as a priest, believe deeply in God. Other psychiatrists are
agnostics or atheists, but we all believe that some people, on
rare occasions, have experiences that spring from belief in a
higher being. Whether or not the psychiatrist himself believes
in that higher being, we all recognize, as it were, a fellow
human's right to do so. There is no doubt in my mind that
some special people, saints if you like, are allowed to get more
than usually close to God. When that happens, the rules of
normal thought and behavior are often suspended. Strange
things can happen. Miracles can occur. The presence of the
Almighty can be felt here on earth, and to quote from the
Bible, like the shepherds on the hillside, 'we are sore afraid.'

"Humans are not very good at dealing with things that they
don't understand. We say somebody is mad if he says bizarre
things and behaves in an odd way. The Romans put Jesus to

death for claiming to be the Son of God. Today, some psychiatrists would maintain that he was suffering from schizophrenia. Did Joan of Arc need chlorpromazine for her 'voices'? Did Paul on the road to Tarsus suffer a rare visual hallucination when he 'saw' Jesus? Your answer depends to some extent on your faith or your lack of it. But we aspire to being men of science, doctors of medicine, and our definition of illness should not depend on something as unobjective as our own particular religious status.

"What we need is an objective measure of disease, a blood test, an X ray, something you can see. Alas, no such measure exists for the diagnosis of schizophrenia. We are left with our opinions, our experience, and sometimes, with our doubt. Nine times out of ten, perhaps ninety-nine times out of one hundred, our training will allow us to make the distinction between the deeply spiritual person and the deeply disturbed. But that one person, that one special person, may be touched by holiness. It is my fervent prayer that when I meet him . . . or her . . . I will not be found wanting. I pray to my maker that I will not be blind to the imprint of the finger of God . . ." There was a strange light in Marcus Douglas's eyes. His knuckles were white on the lectern. His voice had deepened. He was actually praying.

There was quiet in the room. There was stillness. His words echoed around the auditorium, shocking in their conviction. Marcus Douglas was ramrod-straight, his eyes ablaze with the intensity of his fervent prayer. It was no longer a lecture hall. It was a church. The students heard him at the fundamental level. They looked at one another. The rustle of their papers quieted. The scribbling of their notes ended. The impression was inescapable. The shrink was talking about someone he had met or would meet, someone who would be touched by the hand of the Almighty.

Tari began to shake. He was looking straight at her. They were following his gaze. One by one, and then in twos and threes, the students turned to look at her. The eyes of those behind bored into the back of her head.

"He's talking about you," said Mary.

"I know," said Tari.

22

"**Y**OU WERE talking about me," said Tari. Marcus Douglas pulled out of the lot and into the traffic. He looked straight ahead.

"I was talking about a problem I have. You were the cause of that problem."

Tari sat calm in the passenger seat. They had a lot of talking to do. Both knew that. It was a question of where to start.

"The problem is, you don't know if I'm crazy or a saint," said Tari.

Marcus didn't laugh at her outspokenness. He took a deep breath.

"Do *you* know what you are? Do you think you know?"

"Sometimes. Sometimes not. I'm confused."

Now he turned to her, taking his eyes off the traffic.

"I want to help you, Tari. I really do. Will you let me?"

"Why do you want to help me?"

He knew what she was asking.

"I'm a priest. I'm a psychiatrist. I was there at the hospital."

"And you're a man."

"Yes, I'm that, too."

He stared straight ahead, busy as he could be with the driving. She was onto every bit of him. In his tone, he'd admitted it.

"You like me," she said.

He didn't reply at first. She let the silence linger, punishing him for his lack of straightforwardness.

"Yes . . . it's true . . . I like you."

His words seemed to shudder out. He wasn't enjoying this. He was in his car, but there was a sense in which he was in the confessional.

"Like a man likes a woman." She wasn't going to let go.

"Yes . . . I'm attracted to you. Does it help to make me say it?"

There was exasperation in his voice now. Did he deserve this? Why was he admitting it? It wasn't so obvious, was it? He could have denied it. He could have ridiculed her for even suggesting that a priest and a teacher, a doctor, and a psychiatrist . . . His thoughts petered out. Lying had never been an option. She could see into his heart. She was special. She was far more than an equal.

"It helps to know you can be honest." She turned to him, smiling. She wasn't flirting. She was talking to him properly. She was communicating, cutting through to the deeper levels.

"It's not the point of all this," he said.

"I know it isn't." She looked down into her lap. "I mean, it shouldn't be, but it's part of my confusion. Men . . . Rickey . . . and God seeming to talk to me."

"You're in love with Rickey Cage?"

"I hardly know him. I'm obsessed by him. Sort of sexually obsessed. That means I can't be . . . special, doesn't it? That means I must be . . . whatever."

She couldn't bring herself to say it.

Marcus took a deep breath. She was sleeping with Cage. She was sleeping with the stupid, egotistical poseur of a movie star with neuroses so dull and obvious they'd put a fifth-rate psychiatrist to sleep in five minutes. Damn it to hell! Her "sexual obsession" didn't rule her out as a miracle worker. The mundanity and predictability of her choice just might. But, as he thought the silly thoughts, Marcus was aware of the jealous, green place they came from. He wanted to stop the car and take her in his arms and kiss the nonsense out of her. He wanted to be celibate no more and to hold this girl in his arms and teach her about God and love and sexual obsession firsthand, and forget the also-rans. He coughed, moving his hand to his mouth. Oh dear, oh dear, this was wonderfully terrible.

On either side, the seedy respectability of northern Miami Beach mocked his dilemma. The old hotels were full of the same old people. Life was on hold here, all around, and yet inside his car he was living as he'd never lived before.

"Tari, I don't know what's happening, but I've got to find out. We've got to find out. And I know how to. I've got to get information from you. A ton of it. I need a full psychiatric history. I have to know all about your past, your childhood, and your family. I have to do a formal mental status assessment. Without all that, I'm just plucking at the air. You know how we do it."

"To find out if I have a psychotic illness."

"To rule out the possibility of that."

"And to treat it if it exists."

"You don't talk like a crazy person."

"It could be an encapsulated delusional system."

"They exist. I wouldn't be telling the truth if I said it wasn't a possibility."

"It would be simpler if I were ill, wouldn't it?"

"I've never heard a schizophrenic say something like that."

"Because if I'm not ill, then I'm holy," said Tari.

Marcus felt the thrill within him. It was a burst of electricity through his body. His skin tingled. Something was happening at the nape of his neck.

"Yes," he said. "It might mean you were holy."

"But schizophrenia is common and holiness is rare. What are the odds against my being the daughter of God and destined to bring love to the world?"

"Long."

Oh, yes, long all right, long as infinity, long as the distance to heaven. But damn it, that wasn't what he felt, in his guts, in his heart and his soul. Those odds did not seem too long when

he was so close to her. They had not been long when he had
seen with his own eyes what she had done. And how long had
the odds been against Jesus? Not too long for those who
actually met him, from his disciples to Pilate, the hard-nosed
Roman governor and the very antithesis of gullible man. To
stand close to Jesus was to believe in him. To sit by Tari was to
do that, too. It wasn't blasphemy. The emotion sat in his chest
as real as righteousness. His car, his old Chevrolet, rust and
dust and three-quarters bust, contained something very like
the essence of the Holy Spirit. She moved him. In so very many
ways. But only the psychiatrist within him had a plan.

"We're here," he said. He turned right into the basement
garage of the Dr. Marcus Douglas Clinic.

"So we should go to your office and start sifting through my
family history?"

"Something like that."

"It won't be very easy. I don't know anything about my real
parents. I'm adopted," said Tari.

"Ah," said Marcus. "Adopted." The thought flashed before
his mind. Adopted children often fantasized about their
biological parents. Could this whole business have sprung from
some desperate need for a father in a manipulative, theatrical,
histrionic personality? Could Tari be exhibiting the scattered
symptoms of a pseudopsychosis of hysterical origins? But the
essence of hysterical illness, in which the patient dissociated
herself from reality, was the presence of some perceived gain
for the patient. Where would be the payoff for Tari? To gain
attention? To gain a father? To gain the interest of people like
Rickey Cage and Dr. Marcus Douglas, M.D.? No! The key to
hysteria was the character. Tari simply did not have a hysterical
personality. She was not shallow, manipulative, and prone to
exaggeration. She was not untruthful and unreliable, with a
propensity for role-playing. Instead, she was deep and serious,
a good, hard-working student with no need to stand out above
the crowd. She was not flamboyant, seductive, and flaky,
and . . . Marcus's thoughts slowed down.

How well did he really know this girl? Did he know her at all?
It was pathetically unprofessional of him to pretend that he
had anything but the most superficial bead on her personality.

He wanted so desperately to know more about her that his need had fathered the illusion of knowledge. It was not the sort of mistake he was used to making. As he pulled into his parking space, warning lights were flashing in his mind. *Be careful, Marcus. Take care. For the first time in your well-ordered life, you are out of your depth.*

She got out of the car as he did.

"You were wondering if I might have invented an over-the-top father," she said over the rusted top of the Chevy.

"Had that occurred to you, Tari?" Marcus batted her remark back in traditional psychiatrist fashion. Always answer a question with a question. But her remark hadn't been a question. It had been a statement of fact. She could read minds, the shrink's supposed trick. It made him uncomfortable. It made her even more interesting.

"No," she said. "I'm not an actress. I always got enough attention without trying for it."

"I believe you," he said, trying desperately to keep the compliment out of his tone, and not entirely succeeding.

They walked together toward the elevator. He stood back as she entered it, breathing in as he did so. Her scent was strong in his nostrils, a flowery, rich aroma of gardenias, orange blossoms, and night-flowering jasmine. He had noticed it in the car. Now he couldn't help commenting on it.

"That's beautiful perfume," he said.

"Thank you. It's called Miami."

"The one they call the scent of lovers?"

"You listen to commercials?"

"They're usually better than the programs."

She laughed and leaned against the wall of the elevator, at ease for the first time since she had climbed into his car.

The scent of lovers hung in the air.

"I don't imagine you watching TV," she said.

"I imagine you doing everything," he said. Immediately, he wished he had bitten off his tongue and swallowed it before making such an outrageously flirtatious remark.

"I mean, I have no preconceived ideas of you doing particular things and not others." He all but stammered the lie.

"Oh, *that's* what you meant," said Tari with a quizzical smile. *Ping!* The bell saved him. They were there.

She went out first. "Which way?" she said, splaying out both her hands. They were so delicate, white, her wrists thin. She was so young, yet so sure of herself. It came through her confusion and perplexity. She was worried, but she was deeply secure. Like a rock. On this foundation I will build my church. Marcus swallowed. He was in awe of her, or part of him was. But in awe of what . . . of her youth, her beauty, her closeness to God? She couldn't be ill. It was impossible. And yet the alternative was far more impossible. It was statistically unthinkable. All his life he had been ruled by reason, and reason was certain. But to be near her. To be with her. To walk beside her was to walk with possibilities so miraculous as to be mysterious. Was this the mystery of the divine? Was this the dearness, the nearness of God? Or was it the mere love of the poor priest for the young and the beautiful? Could it be just the lust of a bright mind unhinged by a fruitless desire for what he could never have? Marcus's hand shot out to point the way. He was too confused to speak, this doctor, this great man, to the medical student who wondered if she might be ill.

He felt stronger as they entered his office. This was his space. He was in control here. There was a couch against the wall, but he seldom used it. It would be deeply inappropriate now. He motioned toward a high leather armchair opposite his desk. Tari sat down. She placed both her arms on the armrests. Although she was lost in its bigness, her personality did not shrink.

"It's funny," he said. "In this room roles are usually so certain. I'm the doctor, the boss, and then there are the patients."

She laughed but said nothing, somehow emphasizing his unease.

Marcus sat down. In the normal way, each new patient would have a new file. The manila envelope would be on his desk, its contents carefully prepared by his secretarial staff and his nurse. It would contain a considerable amount of information. A referral letter from another doctor would lay out the bare bones of the case, the reason for referral, and a brief history of the present condition. There would be information about past medical history and the relevant points about the patient's work, her family and children, her marital status. His nurse would have measured weight, height, and blood pressure, and the details of those would be at the top of the form. The overall effect would be to reduce the patient to a manageable series of numbers and typed sentences. With Tari, however, it wasn't like that. She was far more than just a case. She was a fascinating enigma.

He pulled a piece of paper toward him, and took the top off his pen.

"I think we should start with your adoption, and what you know about its circumstances," he said.

Tari took a deep breath. She was nervous. At the same time, part of her was looking forward to this. She liked this man with his worried eyes and brilliant reputation. She felt safe with him. She knew that if anybody could understand her, he could. He would be able to sort out the chaos she had become because, in terms of his prejudices, he was at least balanced. "Priest" prejudices would cancel out "doctor" ones. Both would dilute "man" prejudices. Some sort of diagnostic truth would emerge from that system of checks and balances.

He seemed to pause at a thought.

"In all this, I'm afraid, I've rather bypassed the usual channels," he said. "I mean, I suppose technically I'm not your doctor. You haven't been referred. But then I'm having some difficulty in thinking of you as a patient. Do you have a family doctor down here . . . ?"

One who could make trouble, was what he meant. Some jealous territory-watcher who might think Douglas was trying to steal his patient. Then there was the question of the medical school, and the ethics of a teacher carrying on like this with a student. There was a medical school staffer who had overall responsibility for the health of the undergraduates. Should he be in the equation? But again, was this a health affair? Wasn't it more an investigation, an old-style inquisition? Wasn't he as much a devil's advocate as a scientist of the mind?

"I really want to talk to *you* about this. I do have a doctor in New York, but I haven't seen him in ages. If you don't mind . . . I mean, I think you are the best person . . ."

Tari knew what he was worrying about. Douglas would be well aware of medical ethics and every other sort of moral code. Guilt would be strong in him, and respect for rules. But sooner or later he would have to become her doctor. Any halfway decent psychiatrist could not ignore the possible differential diagnoses in the investigation of schizophrenia. Alcohol abuse and the misuse of both stimulant drugs and hallucinogens could cause psychosis. He should have her urine screened for those, and that would mean asking her to provide a sample. Then there were a whole series of organic diseases that could mimic schizophrenia, many of them central nervous system disorders. He should perform a complete physical exam on her, including a detailed neurological examination, and he should take some of her blood for testing. The tests should include a VDRL and a TPHA, the screening tests for syphilis. The third stage of that disease could be a spirochete infection of the brain, causing the psychosis known as general paresis of the insane.

Okay, all these were the longest of long shots, but good doctors were thorough. Tari knew that Marcus Douglas would be more than that. The bottom line was this. If this process was to start and finish, then at some stage she would be laying down on a bed and Dr. Douglas's hands would be on her naked flesh. She knew he was aware of that. So was she.

"I just think you should treat me like any other patient you were investigating for psychiatric illness," she said. "It'll be a good learning experience, apart from anything else."

"Okay," said Marcus. "Adoption."

"My father ... I mean, my adoptive father ... is in the immigration service at the Port of New York. My parents couldn't have children, so they got in touch with some lawyer to arrange a private adoption. One day the lawyer called and said he had a baby that was about to be delivered. The mother was already in the hospital, and was on the verge of giving birth. Apparently, she had made a spur-of-the-moment decision to have her baby adopted. Oh, and that was me."

"And the father?"

"There wasn't one. I mean, obviously there was one, but he wasn't in the equation. The attorney said the mother had had some one-night stand and gotten pregnant. So I guess I'm kind of a singles-bar baby. Out there somewhere is a good-time dad with a smooth line, and a daughter he knows nothing about."

"No father," wrote Marcus. It was the first thing he had ever written about Tari. "He never showed?" he said out loud.

"Never so much as a card." Tari's laugh was hollow.

"So the lawyer knows who your mother was?"

"Yes, he does. But he's not allowed to say. And my mother died. That was the whole point. She died having me. I killed her."

Marcus looked up. He heard the pain. Beneath Tari's matter-of-fact delivery, her soul was scarred. First, her mother had decided to give her away. Then Tari had killed her. Oh, and Dad hadn't hung around to see the show.

"Mother died in childbirth," wrote Marcus.

"So your mother signed the adoption papers first, and then died in childbirth."

"Yes. Apparently there were problems. She had a whole load of pregnancy problems . . . diabetes, hydramnios, hypertension. The lawyer said she had a premonition she wouldn't survive, and that's why she wanted her child adopted. She wanted to choose the parents and not have me looked after by some welfare agency. She was apparently pretty interested in what sort of people they were, good Catholics and stuff . . ."

Tari took a deep breath. She wasn't used to talking about this. It was taking its toll.

Marcus was listening. Tari felt angry that her mother had given her up for adoption. Most adopted children did. It was desertion number one. Being "not wanted" didn't get much bigger than that. Then her mother had died in childbirth, the mother toward whom Tari felt deep resentment. As a joke, she had used the phrase, "I killed her." But the truth was often revealed in jokes. There would be a part of Tari that felt guilty about her mother's death. There would be a small, irrational corner in her brain that did indeed believe Tari had murdered her . . . as punishment, perhaps, for abandoning her.

"What did she die of?"

"Uterine artery ruptured. Massive hemorrhage. She died of surgical shock."

"Do we know anything about her?"

"She was Italian. She'd recently emigrated to America. She

didn't speak any English. She had some money, about a hundred thousand dollars. She left that to me. It put me through college and med school."

"How recently had she emigrated?"

"The lawyer said just a few months."

"So the father was probably Italian."

"Probably."

There was silence. The voice that Tari had "heard" echoed in Marcus's mind. *You are my daughter.* Where was the earthly parent? He was a more shadowy figure than Joseph. He simply wasn't there. The mother was dead. The lawyer probably would have known nothing of her Italian past.

Yet another mystery was forming.

Then the thought occurred to Douglas.

"Most states have a system of adoptive parent and adopted child registers. Either birth mother or adopted child can place herself on the register. Then if, and only if, both want it, there can be a reconciliation. Your mother is dead, but maybe she placed her name on that register before she died. If so, you could get her name and trace it through immigration. It might be a way of finding out about your family in Italy."

"I checked that out. She wasn't on the New York State register in Albany," said Tari. "There was another thing that I found pretty strange. I went to see the attorney. I figured out that he might let me have all the information he had on her. After all, my mother was dead, and like it couldn't affect her. I'd expected some low-end attorney, but he was a million miles from that. He was a partner in this vast Wall Street law firm and he had an office out of some movie. You know, I'd pictured him as this seedy little guy, hustling a buck, only just on the right side of the law. Forget it . . . he was heavy-duty. Big-league. Smooth as silk. He told me it would be in breach of his confidence to a dead client to let me have any information at all about my mother. I argued with him and said that it couldn't be privileged information because it was like my *mother,* and I was her heir, and anyway, she was *dead.* He said I'd have to sue to get a sentence out of him about her, and that it would cost me every penny I hadn't got. And that was basically that. He told me to forget about it, and I was pissed off for a while, but I took his advice and got on with my life. That was it."

"How did your father, an immigration officer, and presumably not a millionaire, get mixed up with a hotshot lawyer like that, especially if the guy didn't make a business out of handling private adoptions?"

"I asked him once or twice. He told me some other immigration lawyer had introduced him to this guy. My dad—and my mom—were always sort of cagey about the whole adoption thing. I put it down to them being protective of me, a little jealous, and not wanting me to make some big deal about my 'real' parents. I respected that. I always felt it was kinda rude to go on about my biological parents in front of them when they'd raised me and changed my diapers, and stayed up nights I was sick and stuff like that."

"It's intriguing, isn't it?" said Marcus. Dead ends were. Especially Tarleton Jones's dead ends. The most important part of the psychiatric history in the investigation of schizophrenia was the family medical history. Schizophrenia was a genetic disease. If family members had suffered from it, then it was easier to make the diagnosis. But Tari's family had disappeared. How come? And $100,000 was a lot of money for a "poor Italian immigrant" to possess. Why the slick, expensive lawyer? Why his secrecy? And how had Tari's mother gotten a green card in the first place, when she spoke no English and had, presumably, no family in the U.S.? There were loose ends all over the place, and no way to tie them up. Immigration and hospital records couldn't be investigated without a name, and the powerful lawyer wasn't giving out names without mega lawsuits. He was the bridge to Tari's past, and the bridge was up. It looked as if Tari's curiosity might never be satisfied, and the family medical history would remain forever unknown. Would nobody ever know who was the father of the fatherless child? Once again the words echoed . . . *You are my daughter, and you will bring love to the world.*

Douglas felt the squirt of excitement within him. There were three lines of inquiry here, and, as the doors shut down on two of them, a third was wide open. He was getting to know Tari. He was moving closer to the girl, even if the "psychotic" and the "saint" remained shrouded in mists of mystery.

"Your own past medical history?"

"Appendectomy. Usual childhood illnesses. Nothing psycho-logical. Never been particularly depressed or anxious. Never been in the hospital, apart from the appendix."

Marcus wrote it down.

"Drugs, alcohol?"

"No hard drugs. The occasional joint. Maybe twenty over the last four or five years. I didn't inhale, of course." She laughed.

"Booze?"

"Ah," she said. "Usual medical-student intake. Sometimes heavy. Like last night."

"I remember those days," said Marcus. "And there are nights I can't remember. But no problem drinking?"

"No. It doesn't interfere with my work, my health, or my relationships. Those are the World Health Organization's di-agnostic criteria, aren't they?" Tari blushed. The photographs had been largely an alcohol production. Had they interfered with her work and her relationships? One day, would they?

"Alcoholics are best defined as those that drink more than their doctors," said Marcus. He smiled at his own joke. He didn't crack them often. Life was usually far too serious to joke about. But Tari was fun. She made the years melt away.

"Are sinners those that commit more sins than their priests?"

"Now *that* would be a way to abolish sin."

They laughed together. They were becoming friends. Or something.

"So, Tari, personal history. I don't think we're going to find much evidence of downward drift, or anything else, but we ought to do it."

"If this is the beginning of schizophrenia, I'd have a good prognosis, wouldn't I?"

"Let's see. Acute onset of illness, high intelligence, good social interactions, a clear-cut stressful event precipitating the onset of symptoms. Those are all good prognostic indications. I imagine you didn't show a schizoid personality prior to now. Yes, it would probably be 'good prognosis' schizophrenia. If there was no family history, it almost certainly would be, but we can't know about that. On the downside, you're single, and you're young. I hope you don't mind my being totally honest. I think we should tell each other everything, don't you? But anyway, I don't think this is schizophrenia, so it's putting the cart before the horse to start discussing outcome at this stage."

"I certainly wasn't a schizoid personality, the shy, introverted dreamer type."

"But you *were* religious?"

"Yes, but not hung up on metaphysics or obsessed by great mysteries and the meaning of life. I did CCD classes like a military campaign and I was in love with Jesus, and all that, but it was pretty natural religion. I wasn't a freak. I was just the little kid in the white dress, embarrassed by my tits, you know the kinda thing."

"Yes," said Marcus. He wrote hard to disguise his feelings. God, she was attractive. If she was ill, then he was an idiot, but they'd started this thing. They should finish it. They had to do birth history and birth weight, birth injury, and milestones. Had she walked and talked on time? Just how normal had she been in those early years? Then he would run through her first memories and schools, with all the dates and the exams passed. Had her childhood been happy, with friends, and love, and what about her relationship with Daddy, the first man in her life . . . and with Mommy, her first rival? And somewhere in there, after the date of her first menstrual period, would be her age at the time of her first sexual experience, and questions about sexual problems and sexual functioning, homosexual experiences, masturbation. . . . He swallowed. In this case, was that strictly necessary? Yes, it was on the list he kept in his mind. He was taking a history. He should do it the way he always did it. No stone should be left unturned.

Tari's periods had started when she was thirteen. She had lost her virginity to a stockbroker at seventeen. She didn't blush when she denied any sexual problems and admitted normal sexual functioning.

"Masturbation?"

"Occasional." He looked up. Now she was blushing. "Is that unusual at my age?"

"Not at all. People who deny masturbation are either lying or have extremely poor memories."

There was a laugh in that to ease the tension.

"Do you masturbate?" she said suddenly.

Marcus's head shot back. Nobody had ever asked him that. It wasn't allowed. It was breaking the rules. Alarm bells rang. It simply wasn't an appropriate question. Something was wrong after all. Tari wasn't as she seemed. The conversation so far had been sweet harmony. This was a note of discord.

"I'm not sure you're allowed to ask me that," he said.

He watched her closely. She seemed the same.

"You mean it's a doctor question, not a patient question," she said. "Or perhaps a man's question and not a woman's question."

"Ah," he said. He thought he heard her point, and was relieved that she had had one. Tari had taken an anarchistic/feminist objection to his masturbation question. He examined his conscience. *Be honest, Marcus Douglas. Cross your heart and hope to die and swear that your interest in this beautiful girl's masturbatory habits are one thousand percent professional and nothing else.* Where did it fit into an inquiry into the possibility of psychotic illness? Not anywhere. The justification for his question had been that it existed on a list in his mind. Perhaps that wasn't enough justification.

"In fact, occasionally, I do," he said quickly.

"I'm glad that you're neither a liar nor a forgetful person," said Tari. And she unleashed the full frontal force of her smile at him.

It conjured up one of his own.

"I think in the circumstances I'll put my usual inquiry into the nature of masturbatory fantasies on hold."

"Whatever you say, doctor," said Tari.

"Homosexual experiences," said Marcus. It lived after masturbatory fantasies under the heading of the sexual history. He took such a history maybe three times a day. It was second nature to him, but second nature wasn't always appropriate.

There was a long pause.

"As we're all being honest . . . yes . . . last night . . . not entirely voluntarily."

Marcus looked up. It was why the lists existed. If you didn't ask questions, you didn't get answers.

"I've never had ... a homosexual experience until last night. I got drunk. I did something stupid. And during it a girl made love to me."

She looked away from him, then down at the desk.

"What was the stupid thing?"

"I let Rickey Cage take some photographs of me. He's an artist. He does that. They were sort of intimate, well, nude really. I mean, I was naked, and pretty zoned, and this girl, I think she's his business manager or something, sort of crept up on me and we ... we ..."

"While he was taking photographs."

"Yes."

"And this was the first time?"

"Photographs or girl?"

"Both."

"Yes." Tari looked at him out of the side of her face. He was shocked all right, but he was also worried. "Do you think it's significant, I mean, in the context of everything else?" she added.

"I don't know. Why did you do it?"

"Because of Rickey. He wanted it so badly. And I was wasted, I mean, really gone, and you know how you get. His art is like really important to him. It's sort of ... his sensitive side. How the girl got into it, I just don't know."

"He set you up for it," said Marcus. "It was planned, especially if this girl worked for him." He was furious. Rickey Cage was bedbugs, but he hadn't reckoned him as low as this. The man in him felt fiercely protective, but the psychiatrist was anxious. Something told him that Tari was falling apart. A strange religious experience, a sudden and obsessional love, loosening of inhibitions, alcohol abuse, a bizarre and unusual sexual act. It was early days, but this would do for the initial stages of personality breakdown.

Was the attraction to Rickey the outer edge of a schizophrenic erotomania? With hindsight, would this period in Tari's life be the period when everything began to go wrong? So far her career appeared to have been an orderly procession of upward mobility. But this could be the beginning of the downward drift so characteristic of schizophrenic illness. Soon, she might give up medical school, take a job as a secretary, then a waitress, and then filter down to the ranks of the unemployed as the illness shattered her personality like a hammer on a plate of glass. His antennae had twitched violently when she had asked him if he masturbated. There had been an oddness about her question. He had rationalized it away into a fault of his own, but now, in the context of "last night," it was worrying once more. The priest, too, was disturbed. Religion had updated itself. The old school was in retreat. Trendy new thinking was everywhere. But whichever way you looked at it, photos of drunken lesbian sex were far from godliness. If this girl had really performed a miracle, if God had actually spoken to her . . . then his ways were more than usually difficult to understand.

Marcus tried to calm down and let his intellect take over.

"What do you feel about it all now?"

"Mainly confused. I mean, confused about how I allowed it to happen, even though I was drunk. Oh, and a little worried about what Rickey will do with the photographs."

"Not angry with him?" Was that hopefulness in his voice?

"I try not to blame others for when I screw up, but yes, I guess I'm a bit disappointed by him. Quite a bit disappointed."

It was true. Her relationship with Rickey had always been based on sex, but the sex had been based on respect. Last night, respect had seemingly been absent.

"But I suppose what I'm really worried about is that doing something like that is very unlike me. It's just not in character. Over these last few days, it's been . . . like I'm a new person, strange, unfamiliar . . . It's almost as if I'm not in control of me anymore, that I'm kind of a spectator to what I do and think."

"Do you have the feeling that there might be something wrong with your mind?"

"Not so much 'wrong' with it, but there is a sort of passivity. It's as if someone else is in the driver's seat . . . Rickey . . . God."

"You know about passivity feelings?"

"Yes, I know they're a symptom of schizophrenia. But I don't feel my thoughts and actions are *actually* controlled. I don't feel that they're someone else's thoughts and actions that are foisted on me against my will. My thoughts are mine, but they seem to be *influenced* by someone else. With Rickey, I wanted to do what he wanted, because I was so into him. And then I felt *owned* by God. Like not so much his servant as his slave. But it seems just crazy to be able to talk about sex and God in the same sentence. It's just so confusing."

"What time did you get to bed?"

"Late. Early."

"Hung over?"

"Yes. Very."

"Look, I think we ought to do this again tomorrow. Let's come back to it when you're fresh. Maybe early in the morning, before your day starts?"

"That sounds really good."

"I'd like to take some blood, listen to your chest, and get that side out of the way right now, if you don't mind."

"The physical?" said Tari.

"Yes, the physical," said Marcus.

23

"SHE'S NOT here," said Mary.
"Where is she?" said Rickey.
"I've no idea."

"Is she at the hospital?"

"If," said Mary, "I have no idea, how can I know whether or not she's at the hospital?"

"Well, fuck you," said Rickey and slammed the receiver down.

He got the hospital number from 411. The girl who picked up at the South Beach switchboard said, "Neat name. Any relation?" when he said he was Rickey Cage calling for a medical student called Tarleton Jones. When he owned up to being himself, she said she just loved *Double Dare*. Despite that, she wasn't up to finding Tari.

Damn! He needed to know if Tari had been spooked by the night before. He needed to know if she was okay, that *they* were okay. Shit, his head hurt. He was booze-bitten and bad-tempered, and now he had to do a thousand sit-ups to flatten his stomach. It was Felicity's fault. He hadn't asked his Sapphic business manager to make it with Tari, but when it had started it had been way too beautiful to stop. It had been so spontaneous, somehow so right, that he had just gone on taking photographs and let events follow their course. With an effort, he pushed Tari out of his mind.

"You gonna spar with me, honey, after I've fried my abs?"

For sure, she was. The girl pranced amid the machines of her workout boutique like a colt on cocaine.

"I'm gonna catch you good," she lisped in a Southern drawl, throwing a make-believe punch into the air. Her pectorals twitched beneath small, straight-up breasts.

"Dream on, babe," said Rickey. He pulled off his T-shirt. Sweat glistened in his chest hair. It was hot and sticky outside, and the air-conditioning hadn't reached him yet.

"How much weight do you want on your chest?"

"Fifteen."

He lay down on the incline bench and hooked his feet under the holders. The girl handed him the dumbbell.

"You want me to count?" she asked.

"Whatever."

He flicked himself up and down fast. He went for quantity, not quality, using his own momentum to ease the motion and letting gravity take him in the relaxation mode. She hung in close to his field of vision. Her upper-arm muscle definition was cool as hell. Her quads were a dream, where they disappeared into skintight exercise shorts laced at the front with a white silk ribbon.

The hundreds disappeared. The burn began.

"Get up the end there, honey, will ya, and give me a target."

She stood between his feet, pretty and turned-on. He tuned into her. Up to her face he went, up to her breasts, up to that mouth that smiled its welcome. . . .

"Where did you go last night after Van Dome?" she said.

"I'm . . . trying to work out, honey. . . ."

"Did you go home with that girl?"

"Nine hundred an' eighty-seven . . ."

"I'm gonna beat the shit out of you, Rickey."

He laughed. She laughed.

"One fucking thousand . . ."

He collapsed back and threw the weight out behind him. It clattered away amongst the machines. His stomach was twitching with the strain. He wiped sweat from his eyes and thought of Tari. He wanted to see her. Where was she? At home? Not taking his calls? Using the bitch roommate as a guard dog against him? He remembered last night. God, she had been so beautiful. She had been an amateur, full of love and sex and passion, and wanting so desperately to please him. It had gone way out of control when Felicity had started in, but he had the photographs he wanted. The moment he felt better he would turn them into a painting. Tari might be angry with him for the moment, but later, when she saw what he would make with her, she would forgive him and more. There was no question. It was going to be all right. He sat up. Half an hour of legs with this girl, and he'd be cooked.

"Okay, honey, get gloved and put 'em up. A hundred bucks says you can't draw blood."

"You're dead meat, Rickey."

They faced each other on the mat, and he smiled at her over his gloves. She rushed at him like a big sister, raining blows at his defense. He sidestepped her, forearms together, boxed away from her. No contact. No chance. She came at him again, whacking hard at him with a strong girl's fists. This time he opened himself wide, but swung his body back out of her reach. Her gloves windmilled in the air. She staggered, nearly losing her balance. He laughed as he saw the patch of moisture between her tits.

"Don't *run* from me," she half-hissed, half-laughed, and she came in again, unleashing a furious rain of blows. He picked them off one by one, catching her fists as she threw them. Then he hit a few back, timing his punch to meet the end of hers. A couple of times their gloves collided as he intended. He watched as she winced in pain.

"Ouch? Yeah?" he said. "Where's the dead meat, girl? Where's the hundred you were gonna score?"

She ducked down low, deliciously spunky, and she came in again. She thrust out her fists and followed them with her whole body like a battering ram.

"You trying to flatten my balls?" he grunted.

She led with a right. He let it whistle past his ear, and he snaked his left into the space she had opened. He rubbed her ear with the inside of his glove in a gesture of friendly patronization.

"Damn you!" She was sweating properly now, full of the fierce competition of a superb female athlete. She wanted to land one on this mother. She wanted to hit him even more than she wanted to fuck him. Oh, the joy of breaking his nose, cutting his lip, whacking out just one of those self-satisfied teeth. It was the age-old sexual struggle. The men always had their strength. They might not be able to get it up, but they could always knock you down. They might be verbal cannon fodder, emotional milksops, childish games that could be played with the ease of an automatic piano, but in the end, they could beat the shit out of you, and they knew it. Worse, they knew you knew it.

"Hit me, honey," begged Rickey, dancing like Ali, arms down by his side. "I'm nothing but a great big target, little girl. Zap me if you can. You wanna see the color of my money or the color of my blood. What's all those muscles for if you can't land one on a hungover bum like me?"

The taunts got to her. She redoubled her efforts. Her superb legs worked the floor, pushing in close to him. Sweat glistened on her upper arms. There was a growing patch on her shorts, between her legs. Wet hair straggled across her forehead.

Then Rickey slipped. His foot caught in a corner of the mat as he danced back out of reach. He stumbled. It was all the time the girl needed. His right arm went out behind to guard against falling. His left reached up in the air for balance. Her big red glove came in like a missile and landed on the end of his broken nose. Bang! The blood erupted in an aerosol spray. A gob of it floated across his cheek like a dab of paint. There was a crunching noise. Rickey dropped to one knee. His right glove was on the floor. He smeared his left over the damaged area. He pulled it back and looked at the blood in astonishment. His mind was fuzzy. Oh, boy! She'd hit him. Really. His nose was stinging like shit. Jesus, the bitch had hit him. Really hit him.

She stood over him like they did on TV, bouncing backward and forward on those long brown legs, waiting for some imaginary count. Her face was a triumphant mask. Her mouth was parted in a smile of joy. "I got you, you bastard. I got you," she yelled. "Gimme my hundred bucks, or get up and let me whack you some more."

He got up slowly, shakily. Up from the count. His head was clearing, but he wasn't totally together. He was upright, but his legs felt like rubber and his nose hurt like hell.

"Okay, okay!" she yelled, high as a kite on adrenaline. She headed in to finish the job. Her right floated toward him. He swatted it aside with his left. Her face swam into focus. She was laughing. Her lips were wide-open. She was just one helluva great, fantastic-looking, healthy hunk of worked-out chick. He hit her hard with his right, in the mouth, below the nose, and his glove wiped the smile from her face like a wet cloth mopping a dry blackboard. Her lip split, up from the top, and now it was the girl's turn to bleed. She went down hard, onto her butt, and the blood ran up her face into her right eye as she went down.

"Ooooooof!" was the noise she made as she thumped into the mat.

She sat there, stock-still, in disbelief and before the beginning of pain. Rickey stood over her, between her legs. She looked up at him in surprise. She tried to clear her head as she wondered how she'd got there.

Rickey undid his gloves. The fight was over. The session wasn't. He slipped out of his shorts. She looked at him, in double vision and astonishment. What!?

"I'm bleeding," she said.

"So the fuck am I," said Rickey.

He knelt down between her legs, and he reached forward and wiped at the blood on her face. He brought his hand back to his nose and smeared her blood into his.

"Blood brothers," he whispered.

"Blood sisters." She tried to laugh.

"Whatever," murmured Rickey.

Their blood was on his glove. He made a mark on her T-shirt between her breasts, where her chest rose and fell.

His voice was soft. "That's my mark," he said. "It's my brand. You belong to me."

She wasn't sure. But she was almost sure. He shouldn't have

hit her. That was wrong, but she wanted him. She always had. She wanted to have him, and now he wanted to be had. So what, he had shitty timing.

"You shouldn't have zapped me, Rickey."

"I wanted to," he said.

"Okay, so what else do you want to do?"

"I want to do this."

He reached forward to the string that did up her pants. He undid it.

"You just take, don't you. You just do what you fucking well like." The ambivalence was thick in her words. She hated him. She loved him. She wanted to knock his head off, and she'd damn near succeeded. Now she wanted to be screwed to the floor, and she'd damn near succeeded in that, too. Oh, and she wanted to murder him, and marry him, and show him off to her friends, and steal his money, and have his babies, and ruin his life, and swim forever in the surf of his fame. It wasn't so very much for a virgin to ask.

She braced herself against the floor with her hands and licked at her lips. Her mouth was full of the salty taste of her blood. Her head still sang with the force of his blow. Her love lips were parted for the next assault. She watched him in fascination as lust merged with pain, and he moved in toward her like a snake to music.

"Did I break your nose?" she asked hopefully.

He didn't answer. He lowered himself down on her and his wounded face was close to hers. His eyes were wide with lust. He could see the separation in her deltoid muscles, the definition of biceps and triceps as she raised herself up from the floor. Her skin glowed with a sheen of health and sweat, and her teeth were white against her sun-bronzed face and swollen lips. Her shirt was wet from exertion. It was stained with drops of her bright blood. He could smell her heat as he smiled down at her.

"Pull down your pants," he said.

"You fucking pull them down."

He laughed out loud at her rebellion. But he allowed her the victory.

She eased her butt up to help him, her superb body pulling

off the feat like a floor exercise in class. Her tummy was flat as the sea in summer, muscle ripples flickering across its surface. He pulled down her pants to the neat mound of pubic hair. She had shaved it to a pointed triangle for the high-cut leotards that turned on the aerobics crowd. It was trim and neat like the girl herself, squeaky-clean and oiled with body juice. Pink lips pouted out at him, unbruised lips, fresh and ready, in contrast to the wounded ones above. He drew her pants down farther, below her muscled butt, down the long four-headed quads, past her knees to the rounded gastrocnemius muscles of her calves.

She still wore her vagina-pink candy-striped sneakers. Color-coordinated for nakedness, she was every bit the fashionable semi-undressed aerobics instructress.

"Rickey," she said, her expression a mask of conflict.

In answer, he thrust forward into her, collapsing his body down on her.

The air rushed from her lungs, through her hurt mouth, bathing his face with her heat. She gripped him tight. She had the equipment. Her gluteals were rock-hard from lunges and squats. Her abdominals were sheet metal, her abductors were steel struts. The walls of her vaginal musculature clamped around him, and for once in his life he was the captive and not the marauding invader. She ground back at him, her mound locked to his pubic bones. Almost before he could find his rhythm, she was milking him of the moment that should be his alone to command. She was a vacuum around him, sucking, drawing at him, gripping him in a power vise of wet heat. Silk and steel, she surrounded him, strangling him in the noose of lips. Rickey was sucked into her warm whirlpool, and already the feeling was there. But it couldn't be. Not yet. It was too soon. Ridiculously so. But it was too late. He'd lost control.

His eyes flitted up to the ceiling. His movements lost their coordination. Below, on her face, was a look of triumph. Rickey let go. His thoughts had lift-off. He sailed on stormy seas to the waterfall at the end of the world. One minute he was there. The next he was in space, soaring on clouds of spray into the river valley below. Up ahead were the calm, still waters and meadows where he could lie down to rest. But now there was the glorious flight to peace, and the strong wind beneath his wings. Down below, there would be Tari . . . forgiving, forgetting, loving him, like a woman should . . .

The girl's face swam in and out of focus beneath him. She was smiling, and she was saying something.

"So soon, Rickey?"

But he was saying something, too. He was shouting, screaming the word he wanted to scream and shout.

"Tari, Tari!" yelled Rickey Cage as he collapsed into orgasm.

He did not see the door open behind him. He did not know there was a witness to his moment of truth.

But there was.

Jodie Summerfield was ten minutes late for her training session. But she was not late enough.

She stood there as Rickey came on cue. She stood there in shock and horror and surprise as he howled the name of the girl he loved into the bloodstained face of the girl below.

24

ARCUS WAS acutely aware that it was time for the physical. Analysts and talk therapists, the fringe members of the psychiatric profession, avoided these like the plague. For a medically qualified psychiatrist to fail to examine his patient, however, would constitute malpractice. Physical disease from anemia through thyroid disease to cancer often presented with psychological symptoms. No mainstream psychiatrist would dream of omitting a full physical exam and the pathological investigations, blood tests, and X rays that went with it. Marcus might be a priest, but right now he was wearing his medical hat.

He washed his hands and dried them carefully. Then he drew back the curtain and stepped into his examination room.

Tari was lying on the table, covered by a sheet. Her clothes, neatly folded, were on the chair next to it. Her head poked out. She looked mildly apprehensive.

"Psychologists dispense with this," he said in what already sounded suspiciously like an excuse. "You get to miss a lot of brain tumors that way." He paused. "Not that there's much chance of those."

"You know what they say about the rectal exam," said Tari. "If you don't put your finger in it, you end up putting your foot in it."

He laughed, thankful for the easing of a tension that simply shouldn't be there.

He picked up her hand and felt for the pulse. Fifteen seconds times four gave the rough pulse rate. Thirty times two was more accurate. Sixty seconds was the most accurate of all, but hardly decent in the circumstances. He took the middle way.

Her hand was warm and white, soft and smooth. But her pulse was running ninety. Why? Him? For God's sake, Marcus, get on with it. He laid her hand down on the examination table. Heart rate was regular, good volume, and of normal character. So what, she was ten beats faster than he might expect? Hyperthyroidism? Forget it. Blood pressure was the classic 120 over 80. He put his hand on her brow, not bothering with the thermometer. She wasn't running a fever. The fast pulse was nerves. He wondered what his was. Raised, he suspected.

They both knew what was next. Heart and lungs.

"Can you sit up for me, Tari?"

She did so, dropping the sheet to her waist. She took a deep breath and looked straight ahead. Her breasts hung there, stiff with youth. Her prepregnancy nipples were rosebud pink cones, turning up so slightly at the ends. They moved as she breathed . . . faster, as he watched. It wasn't the first time he had been sexually attracted to a patient. At one stage or another, every doctor was. It was the volume of the feeling . . . the violent strength of it, the quality, the breadth. He stood there, transfixed by her beauty and awash with a tenderness that was as inappropriate as it was dangerous. His feelings were as natural as birds in a clear blue sky. But in this context, in the context of him and who he was, of what he represented, they were as indecent as exposure.

He buried himself in action. He leaned forward and pulled down her lower eyelid with his thumb. Pink. Not anemic. He turned her head to one side. The jugular venous pressure wasn't raised. He stuck his fingers into the hollows behind her clavicle. No big lymph nodes. Then he reached below her left breast to feel for her apex heartbeat. Her heart banged back at his fingers in precisely the right place. His own heart throbbed in excited sympathy, mercifully unheard. He clamped the stethoscope to her ventricles, listening with the drum. *Lub-dub. Lub-dub.* Two sounds. One and two. No extra beats. No murmurs. He moved the stethoscope over the atria. As expected, everything was apple-pie normal.

"I can never hear diastolic murmurs," said Tari.

"Neither can I," said Marcus. "In the exams, I always used to ask the patients if they had one. They always knew exactly what they had."

He paused. He had an ethical dilemma. Before moving on to lungs, he usually checked a woman's breasts for lumps. Breast cancer was the number one woman-killer. It was nothing to do with psychiatry, but he was a physician. He'd found an adenocarcinoma about five years back. Apart from a few thwarted suicides, that was a life he'd definitely saved.

"I'll just check your breasts for lumps," said Marcus.

The decision made itself, as most decisions did.

"Sit up straight, both hands above your head."

He looked carefully. There were no skin indentations, and no tethering, the characteristic wrinkling of the skin that might point to a tumor just beneath the surface. He took in the extraordinary beauty of her body. Her pectorals were a milky white ski slope to her breasts. Her stomach was flat beneath them, her tummy button a neat slash across smooth skin. Her arms reached for the ceiling. A film of sweat glistened in the center of each armpit. That was where he was heading. His mouth was dry. Insects fluttered in his stomach. He reached for her right armpit with his right hand, feeling for swollen nodes, checking the five separate groups in turn. Her sweat was on his hand as he withdrew. He was anointed with it. It was like a blessing. With his left hand, he felt the other armpit.

"Lie down flat, please."

It sounded businesslike. At the same time, to him, in his private chaos, it sounded like an invitation to make love.

Her chest rose and fell. He laid the flat of his hand against her right breast, and he pressed down. He joined his left hand to his right, both sets of fingers probing the upper outer quadrant where most tumors lived. Then he was back again, covering the other three quadrants, and her nipple, and the perfect pink of her areolae.

Tari stopped breathing. He was leaning over her. His face was inches from hers. She could see the little patch of hair below his nose that he had missed shaving. She could see the tiny streaks of gray at his temples. She could even smell him, the honest smell of a man, the hint of some no-nonsense cologne. Her right breast was molded to the shape of his cupped hands. And, oh, Lord, he was attractive, and dear God, she shouldn't think so at a time like this, in this place. The thought did it. With horror and fascination, Tari felt her nipple harden beneath the fingers of the doctor who was a priest. He sensed it instantly. She watched him stiffen. His hand withdrew a millimeter, as if she had burned him with her skin. But his hand didn't leave her breast. It couldn't. He was not free to move it. Blood rushed into the closed space of her nipple. In an instant it was erect and it pricked like a hot needle at the hand that held it.

Marcus felt the rush of her arousal. It was unmistakable. Threat and excitement collided. It was impossible. It was magical. Her feelings fed into his. His response was instant. He felt it happen. He was on the move. But it couldn't happen. Nothing he had ever done in his life would be as bad or as mad as this. He actually prayed for strength as he longed for her. And then his hand was free. But there, on the other side, was the other breast. How could he not examine it? How could he?

"No lumps?" she said.

She was helping him. Or was she helping herself? She was trying to bring this fire under control.

"No lumps," he said.

It hadn't helped. He could actually see the other nipple hardening. It was expanding visibly at the very anticipation of touch. He had to examine it. To avoid it would be to admit what they could both pretend to ignore. He tried to analyze his predicament, and to focus in on himself—Marcus, the man, cut off for too long from the joy of this; Marcus, the male, living in the wasteland of mind minus feeling. Sex was a distraction from the love of God. Without it, there was so much extra energy to channel into his service. There was so much love, or at least good work, to share and to give. But the tigers of lust came at night, growling in the darkness, and frightening him with their animal strength. For how long could it be healthy to starve the flesh? What pent-up river of foaming desire lay behind the dike of denial? Was this the end result of celibacy, the making of secret love to an innocent girl, a patient, who was all but young enough to be his daughter? Self-disgust tore at Marcus Douglas, but there were other more powerful forces at play. He knew that because his hands were moving toward Tari's left breast.

She shuddered as he touched her, but her eyes, wide-open, faced the ceiling, not him. He moved fast, forcing himself to do so. There was only one lump there, and it was a glorious, rock-hard parcel of throbbing blood as far from disease as the Devil was from grace. Marcus fled from it even as he wanted it. He touched, and remembered, and marveled at the supreme strength of sexual desire . . . and then it was over.

She sat up. Behind her now, in safety, he listened to her chest. He heard the delicious air, ebbing and flowing into perfect lungs. He was aware, too, of the speed of her breathing. Her respiration rate was on overdrive—twenty-two to the minute, maybe more. She said "Ninety-nine" as he held the flat of his hand against her back, and he tried to think of equality of lung expansion, to listen for crepitations and rales, and to wonder whether or not this area or that was resonant or dull to percussion . . . but it was all irrelevant. He was touching her. His hands were on her body. A song was in his heart. Never again would he do this. When they lowered him into his cold grave, this would be the nearest he got to the joy of sexual encounter. As he thought that thought, a voice inside Marcus Douglas howled in sorrow at the pity of his predicament. Here, beneath his hands, was the miraculous girl of his dreams. Her body was responding to him. He sensed that. She was attracted to him, despite herself, and the situation. She didn't want to show desire. She couldn't want to, but she had. A crazy part of him wanted to acknowledge this, to get it out in the open where it could either grow or be destroyed by reason and common sense. Another part of him wanted to bury it where it was. It should be forgotten or ignored. It was a lapse of manners, taste, and self-control that was as unforgivable as it was understandable, but should never be repeated.

He tried to recapture the tattered remnants of his scientific detachment.

"Let me look into your eyes," he said. "It's CNS time. You know the drill. Pick a corner on the ceiling and focus on it."

His face was close against hers as he hid behind the ophthalmoscope and peered into the back of her eyes. Soon he would feel her warm, sweet breath on his cheeks. She held it in as long as possible, but he was long in looking, and her oxygen was gone. It shuddered out against his skin, against his lips, and he breathed in guiltily, taking the molecules of her breath into his own lungs. He had part of her inside him now, and her sweat was on his hands, and the excitement of her was in his soul.

He roamed over her retina, over the tiny veins and arteries, over the blind spot of the macula where the optic nerve was the gateway to her brain. He was near her center. Her feelings lived here, just inches from the part of her he could see. Was he in there? Was he an idea in her mind? Was he part of the complex neuron web, of the singing telegram of brain bio-chemistry that had made her nipples harden at his touch? He forced himself to remember why he was here, in the depths of her eye. There was no swelling of the optic disk. He drew back and shone the light into first one eye and then the other. Each pupil contracted down, reacting to light. They were equal in size. It was all but certain that Tari had no space-occupying lesion in her brain.

"All clear?" she said.

"Crystal clear."

He slipped his hand into hers.

"Squeeze as hard as you can," he said.

She squeezed. It was a test of her motor power. It was a test. She crunched at his hand, aware of him as never before. Her body had not slowed down. It had speeded up. First her breasts, now the beginnings of the rest of her. The more she tried to calm herself, the less successful she was. It was involuntary. Her body had a life of its own. In vain, she tried to bathe the physical in thought. Was she attracted to this man? No. Not really. Not like Rickey, who flicked her switch as if she were a light. But yes, in a way. He was so stark. He was an ascetic roped off behind walls of brilliance in a prison of his own making. He was like an H-bomb. In his life there would be but one explosion. Rickey, in contrast, was a cannon. He was going off from dawn to dusk. This one would need a detonator, but when he blew, the sky would not be high enough to contain him.

He was holding her other hand. She squeezed again, but more gently, savoring the contact like a movie hand-holding ceremony. His eyes caught hers, hunted, haunting.

"Push out. Pull in. Can you feel that? Does it feel the same on both sides?"

He ran a finger up both arms, testing for sensation.

"Yes. Yes," said Tari. *Yes, yes, doctor. Yes, yes, priest.*

Her nipples taunted him, and, quite suddenly, Tari felt wicked. Wicked and turned-on. What was wrong with tempting? It was just raising the tempo. It was only upping the ante. She put both hands behind her on the table and she sat up straighter, pushing out her chest a little, thrusting it up higher. She knew what was next. Feet were. The legs, and if he was thorough, the thighs.

Her toes turned down beautifully in the correct Babinski response as he ran the end of his pen along her instep. He did the power in her feet, and the sensation. Then he was moving upward, until his hand rested on her right quadriceps.

"Lift up for me," he said.

She thrust up hard, lifting her leg and part of her pelvis from the examining table, and she watched him carefully as she did so. His eyes were level with her breasts, and leaning forward to put downward pressure on her leg, he was close to them. His eyes were directly above her bikini briefs, and in the middle of them, slap-bang in the center of them, was a patch of dampness the size of a quarter. Tari couldn't help it. And now she didn't want to help it. Her biology had taken over. He was a doctor. He ought to understand that.

Marcus hung there, suspended on the knife edge of ambivalence. He had never felt like this before. He was rigid with desire, and there wasn't very much else left in his being. It had been a slow build, and at every point there had been no return to a lesser state of arousal. Now he was at the peak. She was excited. He could see it. But how strong were her censors? What did she want, this woman, this girl? Did she know? Oh, God, dear God, help me!

Marcus stood up straight. His voice hardly belonged to him. "Tari!" he said.

25

THERE WAS an atmosphere of muted panic. Shindler, the professor of medicine, liked to keep it that way. His ward rounds were the weekly event, and for two or three hours every seven days he got to be a cross between an irritable John Wayne, an irritable Albert Schweitzer, and an irritable Adolf Hitler. Behind him trailed his victims—about forty students, his medical team, a handful of postgraduate students, and three or four visiting foreign physicians. These last were the most nervous of all. In the bloodthirsty questions-and-answers game that would follow, they had the most to lose and the farthest to fall.

Tari and Mary were tucked in the middle of the group. Neither had been hitting the books as hard as usual for the last few days. There had been distractions.

The professor's eyes roamed the ward like searchlights looking for escapees. The patients who had been "worked up" for the grand round had red ribbons tied to the feet of their beds. *For danger?* thought Tari. On the bedside table of each examinee were voluminous piles of notes, X rays and lab-test results. On the faces of the victims were wary smiles. Most had been through this before, and they knew they were not the targets of the professor's practiced ire. The unfortunate students were.

"Ah," said the professor, zeroing in on a middle-aged lady with glasses who sat up straight in bed, neat and nervous. "Good morning to you, madam."

The professor had once worked in England at St. Bart's. He had been enormously impressed by the old Etonian doctors and their exaggerated, but patronizing, courtliness. It seemed a wonderful way to retain both your distance and superiority, and yet to avoid criticism for those vices. Now it was an integral part of his medical act. It had earned him the nickname Smarmy.

"Dr. Sugarman, could you please outline for us the bare bones of Mrs. . . ."—he peered at the bedside chart—"of Mrs. McArthur's condition? That is, ma'am, if you are kind enough to have no objections."

Mrs. McArthur had about as many objections as she would to the Almighty's questions on Judgment Day.

Dr. Sugarman stepped forward, cocky and confident. He was the professor's protégé because he was shit-hot at his job. That was good for both the professor's golf game and peace of mind. Sugarman's roachlike charm was beside the point.

"Mrs. McArthur is a forty-five-year-old lady with two young children, who presented a week ago with severe shortness of breath after running for a bus. Recently she has run an occasional fever, especially at night. Nothing of note in her past medical history, except for rheumatic fever as a child . . ."

"I think that will do for a start, Doctor. Don't let's make it too easy. Severely SOB on exercise, febrile, rheumatic fever as a child. Immediately, you are all thinking . . ."

He gloated around the terrified faces. The lucky ones were thinking. The nervous ones were praying. The rest were calculating the odds of getting singled out by the professor's spotlight.

"You," said the professor. "You, what are you thinking?"

His finger was in the face of a boy in the back. He'd skipped around the well-read front-runners to the juicy victims in the rear.

"Heart," said the hapless student. "Or lungs," he added, covering his bets.

"Hah!" The professor's exclamation was full to the brim with scorn. "Heart or lungs? What about broken legs or skin problems? Or a psychiatric condition, perhaps. Maybe something gynecological. What on earth do you mean, 'heart or lungs'? Ask her some questions, for God's sake." He turned to the patient. "Please try to humor this poor student, Mrs. McArthur. He is going to try and dream up some questions for you."

"Did you have any pain?" asked the stuttering student.

"Good," barked the professor.

"No," said Mrs. McArthur.

"Have you had a cough recently?"

"Good, go on. Go on."

"No," said Mrs. McArthur.

"Give him some hints, Sugarman. What did we find on admission?"

"She was mildly febrile. Temperature ninety-nine. Respiration rate twenty. BP one forty over ninety. Pulse regular at ninety. On examination, she was not cyanosed. The chief finding on listening to the heart was a diastolic murmur of inconstant character."

"That's enough. Don't give it to him on a plate. Make him work for it. Okay, what investigations would you have ordered up, 'Doctor'?" He loved calling the students that.

"Chest X ray . . . and culture of sputum . . ."

"Wasn't any sputum. Chest X ray was normal. What else? What else?"

"Full blood count, and differential, oh, and an EKG and . . . and . . ."

"Differential showed a raised white-cell count. EKG was normal. Come on, man, what's the one we're waiting for? What's going to clinch this diagnosis? Quick. Quick. Staring you in the face."

It was no good. The curtain had descended on rational thought. But something had to be said. Something almost certainly silly.

"A CAT scan?" he tried.

There was scattered laughter.

The professor drew himself up to his full five feet four. "Of which particular body part would you like a scan, 'Doctor'? Her big toe, perhaps?''

There was more muted laughter.

"Frankly, sir, for all the use it would be, you might just as well do a CAT scan of the good Mrs. McArthur's cat." He opened it up.

"Anybody?"

"Blood cultures," said Tari.

"*Thank* you," said the professor. "Because you think this patient might have . . . ?"

"SBE."

"Precisely. Subacute bacterial endocarditis resulting from . . . ?"

"Rheumatoid arthritis as a child."

"Of course. And so you will start empirical treatment with . . . ?"

"Two to five megaunits of intravenous benzylpenicillin q.d.s. until I get the results of the cultures and echocardiogram, which I expect to show heart-valve infection."

"Ah," said the professor. "I see we have here an embryonic doctor who won't single-handedly destroy the underwriting profits of our beleaguered American insurance industry. What is your name, ma'am?"

"Tarleton Jones."

The professor looked at Tari. She looked bright. In fact, she looked terrific. This could be his next year's house physician. He would test her some more. Something a little more exotic. He thought for a second. Yes, that would do nicely.

"Perhaps you'd all be kind enough to follow me." As an afterthought, he turned to Mrs. McArthur. "Many thanks for your help, Mrs. McArthur. I am pleased to report that our excellent penicillin has cleared Mrs. McArthur's mitral valve of all unwanted flora and fauna. In future, she will be able to pursue buses with her muscles full of oxygenated blood."

He smiled grandly as he set off across the ward to a cubicle separated from the other beds by a glass partition.

"Okay, Ms. Jones, you are on a winning streak. With no help from the oracle in the shape of Dr. Sugarman, perhaps you would lead us into this next patient, who is, I'm afraid, not very well. This young gentleman is twenty-one. He, too, presented with severe shortness of breath, coughing up clear sputum, mildly disoriented. On admission he was febrile, with a tachycardia of one hundred, and a BP of one twenty over eighty. Please do us the favor of examining Mr. Peters, and telling us your findings, Ms. Jones.''

Tari stood at the end of the bed. The young man was pale. His face was covered with a thin film of sweat. An IV line dripped into an arm vein. His hands were above the bed covers. They plucked at the blankets as if they were too heavy on his skin. On the back of one hand was a purple lesion the size of a tomato. Tari went cold. She felt the clammy touch of horror on her back. She felt her stomach turn in terror. She knew this boy. A few weeks ago she had held him in her arms and he had cried because he couldn't tell his mother about the antibodies inside him. Then, he had been HIV-positive. Now, he was far more than that. The lesion on his hand was Kaposi's sarcoma. The shortness of his breath was caused by PCP pneumonia. He was dying of AIDS.

"Please examine the patient," said the professor.

Tari felt the change within her. She looked around, at Mary, at the professor, at the students. They were the same, but they were different. They were different because *she* was changing. She seemed free of her body, moving up and out of it, around it, flitting back to visit, and then away again. She felt weightless, enormously light, and yet stronger and more powerful than she had ever felt. The familiar roles of so-called reality were fading. She was no longer a student, a friend, a young girl, a lover. She soared above all that simplicity into a great white space of light and love where disease did not exist and there was no more pain. Doctors and death were illusions in the space she knew now. It was the far, far better place they would all go to. It was the paradise of which all mankind dreamed.

"God loves you," said Tari.

"What?" said the professor. There was silence. Mary looked at Tari in astonishment. The students exchanged glances. Dr. Sugarman looked bemused.

Tari stood by the boy's bed. Now, she walked to its head. She picked up the hand that bore the lesion.

He turned to face her. He recognized her. He tried to smile. A big tear formed in his eye.

"Hi," he said.

"Your mother understood," said Tari.

"Yes, I told her. How did you know?"

"What on earth is going on?" said the professor. "Do you know this patient?"

"God told me," said Tari.

"What is all this nonsense?" spluttered the professor, but his was not the voice that Tari heard.

The voice in her head was loud and clear. It spoke with warmth and love and pride. It was infinite, this voice, resounding with a conviction and resonance that made belief superfluous and denial impossible.

"You are my daughter," said the voice of God, "and you will bring love to the world."

Tari felt her body begin to vibrate. She shivered with the force of the feeling, and then, as it grew stronger, she began to shudder and shake with the intensity of the emotion that coursed through her. She could see the shock in the eyes around her. They didn't understand. They couldn't understand what was happening. They had no idea who she was. In her power, she pitied them. In her glory, she cared for them. They were her children, lost in a world of make-believe, at sea amid the trivia of their pursuits. They were far from God and from salvation. They cried out for leadership, and they knew not their genuine desire. In the jungle of mammon, the path to perfect peace was hidden in the tangled undergrowth of unneeded want. But she could show them. It was her duty. Her father had told her who she was, and what she would do. She would bring these people love, and she would bring it now.

She turned around.

"Hold the hand of the person next to you," she said.

Nobody spoke. There were smiles on the faces of some of the students, indecision was in the expressions of others. About half a dozen immediately obeyed her. None of the doctors did. The professor's face was going red. His mouth opened, but no words came out.

"Take the hand of the person on either side of you," said Tari, her voice full of power. "We are going to pray."

Maybe a quarter of the students now obeyed her.

"I will not have my . . ." said the professor, but he stopped in midsentence as Tari's eyes burned into him.

"Dear Father, help us to know the beauty of death, and the relief it gives from farness from you. In the passage from body to soul, in the journey from illusion to the reality of holiness, we will find ourselves at last in the glory of your grace. Touch us with the power of your love so that we, too, can love as you do. Let us shine the burning light of that love at the dark corners of disease and wickedness. Let us behold the darkness brighten and the shapes of the night melt away in the new dawn of your morning. Give us the faith to believe in the nothingness of Evil and the infinity of Good, and fill us with the courage to rise above the narrow reason and faulted knowledge of our limited existence." Tari listened to her own words in wonder. They had come from her mouth, but they had never been in her mind.

Six or seven of the students, and a professor of hematology from Sri Lanka, said, "Amen."

The professor found not faith, but his voice.

"Who on earth do you think you are, disturbing my . . ."

Tari's voice cut him off.

"I'm the daughter of God," she said.

26

MARCUS DOUGLAS lay back on the sofa. The four other men leaned forward in their seats. It was clear from the body language that they were the ones doing the wanting. Douglas had what they wanted.

"What we want from you, Marcus . . . is commitment. The deal is immaterial. We will pay what anybody else will pay plus twenty percent. You get total carte blanche to do what you like. A children's book. A cookbook. Ha! Ha!"

They all laughed at that—the publisher, the head of distribution and marketing, the head of publicity, the reprint guy. A Douglas cookbook. Jeez, what a joke. The laughter petered out like a barbecue low on butane. Douglas was only smiling. Smiling was suddenly the game's name.

The chief executive of World Publishers looked at his high-gloss nails. He was searching for the words that would seal the author to World with Krazy Glue.

"I like to think we have had a good relationship . . . a family relationship, because that's what we try to be at World—one

big, happy family. I know you have been pleased with the way
we have handled your book. Hell, we've all been thrilled with
the way things have gone. Not to say delirious.''

The smiles dared to be chuckles, wanting to try laughter
again. Marcus Douglas's smile, enigmatic, held them in check.

''We've had a good run,'' he said, holding the past imperfect
tense over their heads like a sledgehammer. ''I don't think any
of us dared to believe that God would be so good to us.''

God, yes. Oh, yes, God. Not the sweat of the sales force, the
fortune spent on TV advertising, the print media campaign,
the special deals with the bookstores. Not the clever cover, the
World PR clout, the cunning manipulation of the talk-show
circuit. God's goods. That was what the book had been. And if
that was the way Douglas saw it, then by God, nobody was about
to disagree.

''Yes, God has been kind,'' said the publisher through
tensed teeth. He wondered whether or not he could get away
with it. He couldn't resist trying. ''And God has benefited. I
gather all your royalties go to the Catholic church.''

Douglas picked up on the dig. God as the guy who looks
after number one, was the idea in the air.

He priced the jibe at around $250,000. That's what it would
cost World extra in the deal. Expensive for a sly remark.

''When you say 'commitment,' Mark, what exactly did you
have in mind?''

''Something that would tie us together through several
books. That's all. We want to know that you are with us. We
want to build on the megasuccess we've had with you. We want
to build together.''

''But you want to know what I want to do.''

''Of course we want to know that, Marcus, but I'm saying it's
deeper than that. It's a more fundamental relationship than
just subject matter. I'm saying that we want a commitment, and
you get total freedom. Isn't that a writer's dream? Go with your
heart. Go with your gut. Experiment. Go out on a limb if you
like. We'll travel with you wherever you choose to go, and we'll
sell you like we did last time. And we'll all be happy. With
God's help, of course.'' The publisher jammed in the afterthought in the nick of time.

Marcus knew what he meant. The success of his book was such that he was now a name-brand author. In fact, he was *the* nonfiction name brand. His next book would go to number one if it contained nothing but blank pages. He could screw up for book after book, and it would still take years for the success juggernaut to stop. He had built-in buyability, and World knew it, and he knew it, and, out there, other publishers knew it, too. Only Scott Peck came close. Douglas was the one they had to have, and that meant unthinkably large bucks.

"How many books?"

"Three, more. The sky's the limit."

"And the time frame? I have my medicine. There's the church."

"We can work with you on all that. It's detail." The publisher waved away the small print. He was getting close. He could feel it in his guts, where he felt such things. Douglas's medicine! His church! Shit, the church should be so lucky he should type till he dropped. As for the patients, he would personally provide each of them with ten replacement psychiatrists if he could have the time they wasted in typescript. The older he got, the less he understood people and their pathetic priorities. Here was the man with the golden fingertips, and he actually preferred to do something other than write. It was ludicrous. It was bizarre. Douglas was probably worth seven million bucks a book. It worked out at seventy dollars a word. It was more than $15,000 a typed page. That bought a lot of candles, and a whole load of incense. It was bells, smells, and popery for serious amounts of people. Couldn't Douglas see that?

The telephone rang. He picked it up. "Listen, Liz, I said on no account was I to be disturbed. . . . What? Who? . . . Oh, I see . . . yeah, right. . . . Hang on . . ."

He held the telephone in the air.

"There's someone called Mary Allard trying to get hold of you urgently from Florida. Says it's something about . . . Tarleton Jones."

Marcus stood up. He walked quickly to the publisher's desk.

"This is Marcus Douglas," he said.

"Oh, Dr. Douglas, thank God I got through to you. Your

office wouldn't give me your telephone number, and I..."

"What's happened to Tari?"

"Well, that's it. I'm a friend of hers at the med school, and she told me she was seeing you, and I know all about the night when the doctor got the scissors in his eye..."

"Is she all right?" barked Douglas.

"Sort of yes and no. She went really weird on a ward round. She's been admitted to Robert E. Lee Memorial, to the psychiatric wing. They say she's having a schizophrenic break-down, and they've got her pumped full of Thorazine."

"Damn it to *hell!*" shouted Douglas. "Who organized her admission? Who made the diagnosis?"

"The professor of medicine. It was his ward round, and she started praying and saying she was the daughter of God. They've brought in Professor Hodges and she agrees Tari's psychotic."

"She would," snapped Douglas.

"Tari didn't want to be admitted, but they organized it anyway, and she didn't want Thorazine, but they put her on a treatment order. They're trying to get hold of her parents, but they're away on vacation in a Winnebago somewhere. Tari said you were her doctor, but they said no, you weren't, because it wasn't cleared through the medical-student office, and I think that both Hodges and the professor were worried about you being a priest, and Tari's ... Tari's delusions are kind of religious..."

Douglas looked at his watch. There was usually a lunchtime plane. He could be there by midafternoon.

"Tell Tari I'll be there before five. Okay? I'm leaving now... oh, and Mary, thank you. You're a good friend. I'm incredibly grateful."

He put down the telephone. Tari on Thorazine. Tari in the clutches of the mind mechanics. They couldn't know what he knew. They could never suspect what he suspected. On paper they were right. But paper knew nothing. He had to get there. He had to save her from the narrow stupidity of the scientists. But even as he thought that, he wondered if, after all, they might be right and he might be wrong. She had chosen the professor of medicine's ward round to tell everyone she was the daughter of God. It sounded about as crazy as anything could.

"Listen," he said. "I have to leave immediately. One of my patients is in trouble in Florida. I'm sorry, but we'll just have to do this some other time."

They looked at him in horror. This was their lives, their jobs, their company, their balls. They had been gearing themselves up to drop millions of dollars on the supershrink, and they were minutes away from the actual figures. None of them had slept last night. Now coitus was being threatened by dramatic interruptus. Surely he wouldn't pull out on them so close to the moment of truth.

"You have to go this minute?" said the publisher, disbelief at war with disappointment on his face.

"I'm gone," said Douglas, and in the time he took to get to the door, he was.

Douglas erupted from the elevator on the fifth floor of Robert E. Lee Memorial. The receptionist looked up.

"I'm Dr. Marcus Douglas. I've come to see a patient called Tarleton Jones. I gather she's on Siddons ward."

"Just a minute, please."

The receptionist ruffled through some papers on her desk.

"I'm in a hurry."

"Everyone is," said the receptionist. She found a piece of paper. "Yes, Tarleton Jones. She's under Professor Hodges and the professor of medicine, Professor Shindler."

"Why the hell is she under the professor of medicine when it's a psychiatric ward?"

"I'm just reading what it says here, and anyway Professor Hodges is the professor of psychiatry. Oh, and it says 'no visitors.' " The receptionist brightened. She was about to be the bearer of bad news. She was going to get to use her favorite word . . . "no."

"I'm a visiting lecturer at the medical school."

"I'm afraid 'no visitors' means just that, with no exceptions."

"The hell it does. Ms. Jones is my patient."

"No. It says here she's Professor Hodges's patient. And the professor of medicine is on her card. So she's his patient, too. She's not yours. Not while she's here."

Marcus was always nearly angry, seldom the genuine article. He was now. He leaned over the desk like the Tower of Pisa. A burning-oil equivalent flowed from his eyes.

"I don't care what it says on your silly little list," he said. "I'm going in to see Tari. I'll take full responsibility. My name is Douglas. I'll spell it for you . . ."

"Can I help at all?" said the voice at his shoulder.

Marcus turned around. An intern stood there.

"Ah, yes. Maybe. Who do you work with?"

"I'm Dr. Sugarman. I'm the senior intern on the professorial medical unit."

The enemy, or, at least the enemy's standard-bearer.

"I'm Marcus Douglas. I'm . . ."

"Yes, I recognize you from TV," said Sugarman rudely.

"You've got my patient in there. Why wasn't I consulted?"

"We're talking about Tarleton Jones?"

"You bet we are."

"I think there has been some mistake," said Dr. Sugarman. "This patient has suffered an acute schizophrenic breakdown. We gather you weren't treating her for anything. Had you diagnosed schizophrenia?"

"I'm not sure she has schizophrenia."

"Precisely. You didn't think she was ill, and you weren't treating her. That hardly makes her your patient."

"I was investigating her," snapped Douglas.

"Well, since you 'investigated' her last, she has become acutely ill. Her parents couldn't be contacted, and the physician responsible for the health of medical students referred her to Professor Hodges and Professor Shindler."

"You've got no right to treat her without her permission or to hospitalize her without her consent. She's not a danger to herself or others, and she's not a minor."

"She believes," said Dr. Sugarman, "that she is the daughter of God. In the history, she gave a classic description of a primary delusion, of a grandiose auditory hallucination, and other softer symptoms of schizophrenia. She's a textbook paranoid schizophrenic. I'm surprised you didn't think so."

"Are you a psychiatrist?" hissed Douglas. As an intern on the medical unit, Dr. Sugarman had been trained in psychiatry, but was not a board-certified specialist in the field like Douglas.

"Are *you?*" dared Dr. Sugarman.

"I hope," said Marcus, "that you are a very rich man, an extremely well-insured man, or that your father is an excellent attorney. If you are none of the above, you are, believe me, in deep trouble."

Dr. Sugarman was none of the above. Supremely at home in matters medical, he was all at sea in things financial, and far, far away on problems legal.

Pale already, he now blanched.

"I'm sorry for that last remark," he stuttered.

"You will all—all of you—discover the true meaning of sorrow," said Marcus as he turned and headed for the elevator.

27

TARI WOKE up. Her eyes were still closed, and she didn't know where she was. She opened them. Neon brightness poured in. She was in a cubicle. She was in bed. She realized immediately where she was. They had locked her up on the psycho ward. She tried to sit up, but her muscles wouldn't work. She was made of rubber. Tari flopped back on the pillows, hardly able to control her neck as she hit them. Her head lolled to one side, burying her nose in the foam. For one ridiculous second she thought she might suffocate, lying in bed, drowning in pillows because she was too weak to move.

Her mouth was dry. Her mind was cotton candy, great billowing clouds of nothingness. Her head was a pink ball of fuzz, held up by a neck stick that had ceased to work. She tried to focus, but everything was blurred. Through the surreal experience, a word kept repeating itself over and over. *Thorazine. Thorazine. They've filled you full of Thorazine. You're in the chemical straitjacket, Tari. You're in the asylum. They've tattooed the diagnosis to you. You're mad.*

"No!" she said through sticky lips. The sound of her own voice, faint as it was, encouraged her. "No!" she said, more loudly.

She lay still, exhausted by the effort of thinking and speaking. *I think, therefore I am,* she thought. *I know they think I'm mad. Therefore, I'm not mad. Hang on, Tari, hang on tight to Descartes and the ropes of reason.*

She closed her eyes. It was easier to think without the fuzzy visuals. They'd got her on a ton of phenothiazines. That she knew. She was heavily sedated. She was damn near comatose. But Thorazine hardly had any sedating effect on true psychotics. She clung onto the thought. It was an argument for sanity. But there was nobody to listen to it. She was all alone. They'd locked her up and thrown away the key, and they would never, ever let her out. The squirt of panic wafted through the chemical calm. She had to get out, but she couldn't stand up. She had to get help, but from whom? She tried to remember. What had happened? How the hell had she gotten here?

It came back in bits and pieces through the drug haze . . . the ward round, the voice of God, the prayer and its extraordinary aftermath. They had taken her away to a room, and the questions had started, and she'd told them everything because everything had become so beautifully simple. The time for doubt was over. The stupid thoughts of possible mental illness had melted away in the blinding light of God's presence, and she had been able to explain her experiences perfectly clearly. She had been touched by God. He had a purpose for her. She was his daughter and she would bring love to the world. She had told them this, her face alive with relief and joy. She had talked of God's message, of his voice, and she had laughed when she had described Dr. Douglas's doubts, but his deeper faith in her, and she had thrilled with exultation as she had thought of her future, and her duty. Even now, she could see their faces surrounding her. Professor Shindler's head had been cocked to one side, quizzical. Dr. Sugarman had smiled constantly, his expression full of the fascination of the expert for a peculiarly interesting specimen. They had brought in Professor Hodges and she had asked all sorts of questions and Tari had told the truth, because at last she knew for certain what the truth was.

Professor Shindler had huddled with Hodges and the others, and then he had been quite definite.

"Tari, I am afraid you are not at all well. I don't expect you to believe that, but I want you to try to trust us. You know who we are. We are doctors, experts, trained in psychiatry. And Professor Hodges, as you well know, is the professor of psychiatry. We want to admit you to the hospital. And we want to give you some medication."

"But I'm not ill. Don't you see? That was what I was trying to explain. I used to wonder if I might be ill. But *that* was the crazy part. I was wrong. Now I know what's real. I've been sent by God. I have a mission. I have insight. Surely you can believe that."

Silence. They didn't believe. They thought she was mad. And they were the doctors, the men and women with the keys, the straitjackets, the syringes, the tranquilizers, and all the sanctions of society on their side.

She had gotten cunning then, but it had been way too late.

"If you don't mind, I'd rather not admit myself to the hospital," she had said. "Perhaps I could come in as an outpatient and talk some more about all this. We can discuss the possible medication then."

She had stood up, a watery smile on her face.

"Sit down, Tari," Professor Hodges had said, her lips tight, her eyes gimlet-small.

She had disobeyed her and taken a step to the door.

"I think I'll call Dr. Douglas. He's a psychiatrist, you know . . ."

She could remember Dr. Sugarman's arm on hers, and Professor Hodges calling sharply for a nurse. She remembered the male nurses, several of them, firm and clean-smelling in their white jackets, and quite definite that she would be all right and just to leave things to them, and "You take her leg, Paul, and I'll get her arm" and "Watch out! Oh shit!" as she'd started to fight and landed with a kick. On the floor she'd struggled and screamed. They had lifted up her skirt, ripped down her pantyhose, and jammed the needle in extra-hard as punishment for the pain and irritation she had caused. Pinned to the floor, she had known just exactly how "okay" she was. To rub it in, the professor of medicine had said, "That's the

most florid case of paranoid schizophrenia I've seen in ten
years. What on earth can that idiot Douglas have been doing
letting her wander around? Stick her on a section. You sign it,
Veronica. I'll countersign. And a treatment order, too, and I
wouldn't hold back on the phenothiazines."

Tari tried to take a deep breath as the horror slipped
through the chemical cordon of the major tranquilizer. But
even breathing was difficult. She tried to plan. She had to get
out of the hospital. She had to get to Marcus. Or she had to call
him. He wouldn't know where she was. Or would he? Mary had
been at the ward round. Wouldn't she have told him by now?
But, if so, where was he? Why hadn't he come to see her? Was
he in on the plot? The plot against her. The plot to manufacture her "madness" and to foil her mission. The wicked
scheme to keep the world loveless and far from God. No! What
on earth was she thinking? It wasn't a plot. Paranoid schizophrenics dealt in plots and plotters. It wasn't a conspiracy. It
was a misunderstanding. They were simply those dangerous
kinds of people who didn't recognize the folly of their wisdom.
They hadn't eyes to see or ears to hear. They were so pleased
with their brain-power, they had forgotten how to look with
their hearts. Father, forgive them, for they know not what they
do. They needed the love she would bring. They were part of
her mission. They were the problem to which she was the
solution . . . but she was in bed, too weak to move, and she was
their prisoner. She had to escape.

She went feetfirst, letting her heavy legs drop to the slippery
floor. Her whole body followed them, slithering from the bed
and sliding into a crumpled heap on the linoleum. She folded
her feet under her, and grabbed onto the bedclothes. They
came off the bed and landed on top of her like a tent
collapsing in the night.

"Fuck!" she said.

She crawled out and propped herself up against a wall. She
was wearing a hospital nightgown. Nothing else. She peered
around the room. Everything was out of focus, but there were
no clothes. She made it to the door. It wasn't locked. She
opened it and peeked outside. The nurses' station was over to
the right. It was empty. A television was carrying the local news,
its sound turned down low. The effort and the motion had

cleared her head a bit. She was beginning to think. The nurses' station was deserted. A window of opportunity had opened. Shit! Clothes. She had to get some clothes. She'd never get through the crowded hospital in a patient's nightgown. She wedged herself in the doorway and gathered her thoughts. The cleaners had a room on each floor for their mops and buckets and their . . . uniforms. Yes, that was it. She should be able to find a green smock and some loose slippers of some kind. If she could just stay standing and not stagger or fall. She crept along the hallway, moving backward, keeping her eyes on the nurses' station.

She had to get out of there to the protection of someone who would help her. If not Douglas, then . . . Rickey? He might not understand, but he was enough of a rebel to disapprove of people being put in hospitals against their will, crazy or not. And they would listen to him. In America nobody messed with a star. But that was down the line. How the hell could she get out? The main doors to the ward would be locked for sure. The nurses' station wouldn't be empty forever. She had no chance.

Tari crept along the wall, still desperately weak, but stronger with resolve with each step. She found the door marked "Staff Only." She eased it open. A buzz of conversation came from inside. Shit, it was an interview room. She closed the door, praying the doctor would be too deep in the magnificence of his insights to investigate the intruder. He was. She moved farther down the corridor. A clatter of feet at the other end signaled the return of the male nurse. If he looked, he would see her in the corridor. A door said "Utility Room." She opened it and hurried inside. Empty or not, she had to take the chance. The smell of disinfectant was more welcome than the perfume of sweet roses to Tari. This was what she was looking for. Mops, buckets, uniforms, plastic bags stared at her from their serried ranks. She grabbed a green smock and slipped it on. Then she picked up a bucket and filled it with sponges, Pine-Sol, Clorox, and ammonia. She took a mop and stuck it under her arm. Then she peeked out into the corridor. The male nurse was doing paperwork at the station. All was quiet. It was five-fifteen. The cleaners were usually long gone by now. Would the nurse notice?

She couldn't afford to wait for him to leave his station again.

It might not be till midnight, if then. She set off down the corridor. The nurse looked up as she got closer, then looked back down at his desk. She didn't recognize him. He wasn't one of the ones who'd been called in to jump on her after the ward round. She could feel her heart beating. She hadn't much of a plan. She would just ask to be let out.

He looked up again. His expression was irritable. He had to waste valuable time letting out a cleaner. Tari put her head down low and tried to pick up her feet. Actually, the cleaners mostly walked as though they were on Thorazine. It was the doctors who charged around as if they were on speed.

"You wanna go out?" said the nurse.

Tari nodded. Oh yes, she did. Would he ever know how much?

He picked up a bunch of keys from the desk.

"You on overtime or something?" he said as he came out of the station. He walked toward the heavy twin glass swing doors that were the exit to the locked ward.

"It's my first day," said Tari. "I had trouble getting things done."

He looked at her closely. Tari had never been more acutely aware of the fact that she did not look like a cleaner. Still, the drugs had taken the edge off her. She was pale, wore no makeup, and her face was devoid of its usual vivacity.

"What do you think of the crazies?" said the nurse, at the outer edges of a come-on.

"They look pretty much the same as you and me," said Tari.

He had the key in the lock. He was turning it. She was almost there.

She looked through the glass doors. In the distance some white coats were approaching. The doctors were talking animatedly among themselves. And in the middle, surrounded by interns, was Professor Hodges. Tari looked around in desperation. Retreat was impossible. The doors were opening. It was now or never.

"Funny you should say that," said the nurse. "They admitted a medical student this morning. Apparently looked totally normal. Thought she was the daughter of God."

Tari slipped through the door.

"I thought it was an only-child situation," she said. Hodges was coming up fast. There was a corridor off to the right. A door said "Fire Escape." She pushed through it and in seconds, she was on the stairs, hurrying downward. She was free.

28

"OH, GOD, I'm tired."

Tari slipped into wakefulness. She felt like lead. Every part of her was heavy, and her mouth was so dry talking was an effort.

"Just rest. It'll wear off in a few hours, and you'll be back to normal."

Marcus sat at the end of the bed. He squeezed her foot through the blankets.

"Am I really safe?" said Tari.

"You bet you are," said Marcus grimly.

"But I was on a commitment order, and I escaped. Isn't that a problem?"

"Not really. As long as you stay with me at the clinic, nobody can get too upset. You're in 'care.' I'm a board-certified psychiatrist. You want me as your doctor and you're not underage. Hodges and Shindler can moan to the ethical committee all they like, but it won't make any difference. It's a question of habeas corpus. I have the body. And possession is nine-tenths of the law!"

"But I would be free to leave," said Tari.

"It just wouldn't be wise."

"I'm not ill. I know that now."

"I'm not saying you are. But it would be crazy for you not to stay here until things quiet down. I can protect you here. You're safe."

Tari lay back on the pillows and closed her eyes. The horror of the hospital was still so real. She had found a phone and collect-called Marcus. Then she had waited in terror behind a plant in the lobby until he had arrived to pick her up. Seeing him had been the definition of the feeling of safety, but now she was not so sure. He possessed her body. He had just said so. And he was a psychiatrist, who had at least some doubts about her sanity.

Then she remembered the other day. The day he had examined her. They had started so professionally ... the doctor and his patient, going through the motions, doing all the right things. It had hardly ended that way. Something had happened that was beyond the control of either of them, and only the exercise of Marcus's iron will had prevented disaster. He had said her name once, his voice strangled by desperation and desire, and then he had walked out of the room. After she had got dressed, he had been distant and coldly polite and he had told her that he would have to go to New York the following day and that he would be unable to see her. She had known exactly what he was doing and how he was feeling, and she had gone along with it. She hadn't seen him from that moment until he had picked her up at the hospital.

"Can I get some coffee? I want to get out of this feeling."

"Sure. Caffeine'll help." He got up. "Be right back."

"Oooooh," Tari moaned her frustration and her irritation. She had to get going. There was so much to do. The little energy she had she'd used up in the escape. Getting out of the locked ward had been her only priority, but now that she was safe, there were others. Somewhere inside her was the mission. She had heard the call, and found the faith. Now she had to find the way, or carve the path. She closed her eyes. The prayer welled up inside her.

"Oh, God, Father in heaven, help me to know what to do."

She lay still, calmed by the closeness to him. Peace crept into her mind. She was not alone. From now on she would never be forsaken, because doubt had died.

Once again her flesh was tingling. Her awareness was heightened, as it had been twice before. She sat up in bed. Her eyes were closed as she waited for what she knew would be the answer to her prayer.

His voice would come. She could feel it. The room was full of his presence. It was warm and cold, and bright as the sun behind her eyes. She held her breath.

"Write down what I say, Tari, and bring love to the world," said the voice.

She opened her eyes wide. The empty room stared back at her. But God was there. He was with her, all around her, in her heart, her mind, and her soul. There was a pencil on the bedside table. And a copy of *Time* magazine. She picked them up and she waited.

"Love is the blood of the soul of man. It is the essence of his existence. It is his reason and his explanation. Only through love can man come to know who he is. Through love alone, can he learn to live."

Tari scribbled the words, as if taking dictation. She scrawled them in a big round hand over an article on the budget deficit. The voice spoke slowly, pausing for her to catch up. Then it stopped. There was silence. Tari was on fire with excitement. She read through what she had written. It made sense, but it was not her sense. It was the sense of God.

The door swung open. Marcus stood in the doorway, holding a mug of coffee. Immediately, he sensed some change in her. She was wide-awake, sitting up in bed, reading *Time* magazine and apparently taking notes. Where had the Thorazine zombie gone? Changes weren't that dramatic, *shouldn't* be that dramatic. Alarm bells rang.

"*Time* magazine?" he said.

She put it down in her lap. She looked at him. Her whole face was ablaze with excitement.

"You've heard another voice," he said.

"God has spoken to me."

He walked toward her. He put the coffee on the table.

"What did he say?" On purpose he didn't ask, "What did the voice say?"

She thrust the magazine at him. "He said, 'Write down what I say, Tari, and bring love to the world.' Then he dictated this."

Marcus took the magazine from her. He read the scrawled words.

He felt the strange buzz of spirituality he had felt half a dozen times before . . . at Lourdes once; at a Marian "sighting" in Tuscany; at St. Peter's, a few minutes after the election of the pope. But at the same time there was confusion. The doubt of the scientist was still locked in combat with the spirit of the priest.

"God told you to write down these words."

"Yes," said Tari. "God said those words in my head."

"He didn't put them in your head."

"He spoke them. I heard them. Like I hear you. But he has a nicer voice than yours." She laughed her confidence at him, and her humor was a shock. She could joke about God. She believed that strongly. She showed no self-doubt now, no "insight." She was talking about the voice of the Almighty as she might the voice of a friend, a neighbor, of a father. She hadn't stopped to wonder how weird this was, despite the fact that she was hot from the hospital and full of antipsychotic medication. Tari, of all people, ought to realize the significance of that, but it made no difference to her. She no longer wondered whether the "experts" might be right, and that she might be ill with schizophrenia. Now she knew she was sane. She knew who she was. She was God's daughter, and she would bring the world love. It was a watershed. There could be no return from this. She was either mad . . . or she was holy.

Marcus Douglas shuddered at the enormity of the crossroads that he had reached. Should he be reaching for the Thorazine? Or should he be falling to his knees? There was precious little in between. He felt the rack begin to tighten in his mind. Above was the pull from one direction. Below was the tug from the other. And this had hardly started. Before long, his body and his soul would be screaming with the pain of indecision. He knew that. And he knew, too, how beautiful she was in either her holiness or her psychosis. His heart ached for her, as his mind wondered just exactly what, in heaven or on earth, Tarleton Jones was.

He read through the words again. They were not crazy words. There was a thread to them. They cohered internally. They followed a sequence. There was no tangential discursion from the central theme. In contrast, the writing of the psychotic was all over the place, jumping from idea to idea and often traveling in crazy directions over the page itself.

"Don't!" she said. "Don't try and explain it. Feel it. Open the door to the Spirit. You're a priest. Don't shut God out."

He sat down on the bed and ran a worried hand through his hair.

She touched his arm. She was telling him that she understood his dilemma. It was a gesture of comfort.

In all his psychiatric experience, Marcus could never remember a schizophrenic doing something like that. There was a barrier that existed between the psychotic and the sane. He didn't have that feeling with Tari. He felt close to her, and he wanted to feel even closer. He wanted, really, to take her in his arms and to hold her because he . . . because he . . . because he . . . oh, God . . . because he loved her. Marcus sat up straight with the shock of the revelation. Who was mad now? Who needed the doctor? He was locked in a diagnostic puzzle, but it was the physician who needed help. It was the priest who needed forgiveness.

"You're falling in love with me, aren't you?" said Tari.

"Yes," he said. "I think so." He couldn't add lies to the list of his sins.

"I'm sorry," she said. "That's difficult, isn't it?"

"That's very difficult," he agreed. He swallowed hard in his confusion.

But as Marcus, the man, took the mighty step into the quicksand of confusion that was love, Douglas, the psychiatrist, was confused no longer. Tarleton Jones was not mad. He knew that now. You couldn't love a psychotic. They were walled off from the world by their weirdness. And psychotics didn't read minds, didn't empathize, didn't sympathize. Deep within him, Marcus Douglas heard the rumblings of upheaval. Because the chain of cause and effect, of logical entailment, was alive and well in his emotionally clouded mind. If he was not in love with a psychotic, who then was he in love with? With a saint? With the only daughter of God?

He went cold as the enormity of the thought sank in.

"Do you think this is the beginning?" he said. "That there will be more?"

"Yes, there will be more. It will be a book like the Bible."

"And you will write it down?"

"And you will help me."

"I will help you?"

"Yes."

"I don't quite know . . . what's happening . . . exactly what I should do."

She could all but touch the chaos in his mind, and she was full of love for this man who wanted so very badly to be good.

"I know what you should do," said Tari. "You should kiss me."

29

"IS IT like automatic writing?" said Marcus. He perched on the edge of the table.

Tari looked up at him. She sat back in the chair. "I don't know. I mean, I can stop when I'm interrupted, like now. Then I can go right back to it. Just like this." She began to write again. "I'm not hearing a voice like I did the first time. It's coming from me, but it's not coming from my mind. When I read what I've written, it's as if it's been written by someone else."

"Can I see?"

Marcus looked over her shoulder. He read out loud.

"Love is a feeling, but it is also a pathway. Learn to lose yourself in love until it takes over your mind. Then the way forward will become clear. You must practice this loss of self in love. Each day, love more. Each day the self will recede, and the soul will emerge more fully. When the universe is full of souls and empty of selves, then all will live together with me in paradise."

They looked at each other.

"What is it?" said Marcus. "Is it sort of spiritual self-help?"

"It's like a manual for living, I guess. You can come at it from all sorts of levels. I suppose the know-it-all intellectuals would say that it's psychobabble with spiritual topspin. They'd ask questions like, 'What exactly is meant by love?' But I know what it means, don't you?"

Marcus wasn't quite sure. "Maybe I do, if I let myself."

"That's it, isn't it? You have to let go. You have to make the faith leap. Stop thinking with your head and start thinking with your heart. God only wants us to open the door an inch to him and he'll be in and he'll never leave. But everyone bolts the door and puts the bar across, and hides the key, and God won't cross that barrier. Letting yourself love is opening the door. Loving nature, loving animals, loving truth and kindness and gentleness, and yes, people, too. Love is letting go. It's letting go of selfishness, of me and mine, and then flowing out into the oneness."

"What about love as possession and jealousy and all the crimes committed in the name of love and passion? Freud said love was neurosis. How does that square with love as the path to God?"

"It's just a word. It means what your heart wants it to mean. It means what your heart *knows* it means. If you want to be clever and intelligent, you can pick holes in this. But then you wouldn't be practicing 'love,' would you, and the path forward will be dark and your big old self will get bigger and grander and more self-satisfied and sit on your soul till it can hardly breathe. And you'll be far from God, out in the cold with only your brainpower to keep you warm. Does that sound like a good deal, Dr. Marcus Douglas, M.D., scholar, scientist, and semantic genius?"

She laughed up at him, far from fanaticism and full of the life that love made.

He smiled back.

"You know, something like this has happened before," he said.

"It has?"

"Do you know about *A Course in Miracles*?"

"No. Well, vaguely. Isn't it what Marianne Williamson talks about?"

"Yes, that's right. There was a woman called Helen Shucman,

who was a professor of medical psychology at Columbia University's College of Physicians and Surgeons. She was an atheist, and a rather ambitious academic at what, I guess, is perhaps the most prestigious medical institution in the country . . . I mean, no flakes, the real McCoy. She had an explosive relationship with the head of her department, a guy called Bill Thetford. Some people say she was in love with him, but that he was gay . . . whatever, it was sparks flying all the way . . ."

"Sounds exactly like us," said Tari with a smile.

"One day, Thetford sat this Helen Shucman down, and said they had to find some better way of handling their relationship, because it was too much hassle fighting all the time. She said she agreed, and more or less immediately she started having strange experiences and odd dreams full of symbols and things. She heard a voice saying, 'This is a Course in Miracles' and she felt compelled to take it down in shorthand. Thetford helped her, and seven years later *A Course in Miracles* was completed. So far, it's sold about a million copies."

"What's the book about?"

"Some people think it's New Age gobbledygook. Others think it's the most important book since the Bible. It's very dense in parts, metaphysical, hard to follow, but it's enlightening. It's religious, but it's wide-open to all religions, a bit like a twelve-stepper's 'higher being' . . . you know, room for God and Buddha and Mohammed all around the same table."

"The difference is that this is God's book," said Tari.

He didn't reply. There were too many questions and too many answers. The problem was matching them up. Had Helen Shucman been touched by holiness? Or had an unstable woman found a cunning way to spend time with a man she loved? Had she achieved some hysterical dissociation in which there was a sense that even she did not really "know" she was manipulating the situation to her advantage? Could an atheist write such a book, rich in religious and spiritual insights? Would two professors at such a prestigious academic institution collude to manufacture a fake, or was it true that God did, after all, work in mysterious ways his wonders to perform? Could an intended fake mutate into the genuine voice of truth and enlightenment? And, if it helped people and filled their lives with sense and comfort, was not that the only true and important reality?

"What will we do with it?" said Marcus.

"We'll finish it," said Tari.

"But what will we do with it then?" He asked the question because he was fascinated by the way he had already answered it in his mind.

"I don't know," she said. "God will tell me."

"We'll publish it," said Marcus. "Under our joint names. We'll call it *All for Love*. I promise you, the whole world will read it."

Marcus Douglas sat at his desk and stared out to the sea. It was hardly light, but there were joggers on the beach, and a yoga model already twisted into limb knots. The ocean was flat in the gray, greasy dawn, and the glow on the horizon heralded the fierce heat to come. He looked down at his desk. The pages of handwriting were in a neat pile. Already, it looked like a book, way past the stage of notes, or an essay, of an in-depth article.

Marcus put his head in his hands. Here were his two worlds. Out there was the reality of the beach. This was Miami, the lush, throbbing, tropical city that was his home. He lived here, his feet firm on the sizzling sidewalks, his mind at home in the steamy caldron that doubled as a melting pot. Here was where he thought good thoughts, and prayed and loved God. Here he went to church, and wrote for Catholic magazines, and attended seminars thick with words and intellectual bonhomie. In Miami he was at home in the world of food, feeling, and fantasy. But now he was confronted by another world, the world of the spirit. It stared up at him from the pages, shimmering in mysticism, wondrous, yet terrifying in its ghostly presence. It had been three weeks now, and Tari's *All for Love* was growing.

Every day he sat down to read the pages. Every day his excitement and his fear grew. He was thrilled by the beauty of the words. He was mesmerized by the strange truths they told. He knew their importance. His silly mind told him that, but it was his heart that really understood. Yet, at the same time, a part of him recoiled from the vastness of what was happening. He was not equipped to understand it. And yet, if not he, then who? He was a priest, technically God's man on earth. And he wasn't just any old priest. He was a learned academic and a scientist, too. He was consulted constantly by the hierarchy in Rome. He was a man who moved easily in and around the inner sanctum. He had the ear of the cardinals, of the monsignor politicians in the Vatican. The pope himself valued his judgment, and had sought it indirectly on several occasions, and twice face-to-face. If anybody was qualified to unravel this mystery, he was. But still the feeling of impotence cloaked him. He was certain that Tari was not mad. He had explored every inch of that avenue and found no evidence of mental illness. Did that mean she was holy? Were there other possibilities? Could she be hysterical? Was this some bizarre personality disorder? Could it be that she was playacting, merely pretending to be hearing voices? If so, then the book in front of him was not God's book. It was Tarleton Jones's book, nothing more, nothing less. But Tari was in her early twenties. She was a medical student with no training in literature or writing. She had worked on Wall Street, of all places, before going to med school. Whatever she knew about love, it couldn't conceivably be enough to write a book like this about it.

He picked up a page and read through it.

Have you tasted, smelled, and heard the union of the love with God? No, you say, and you are right. And you are right, too, when you say that no possible or hypothetical experience related to the five senses could ever prove to your satisfaction that love and God are one and the same. However much science advances, whatever measuring devices are invented, there will never be a way to determine the truth or falsehood of what I say to you. But you are wrong if you conclude that it is meaningless to say that God is love. And you are wrong again to maintain that it is false to say it. The error you make is to put your faith in narrow science. The mistake you commit is to trust only your senses. You are lost in awe at the power of your intellects. You have set yourselves up as gods on earth, when all you are is my creation. I say to you now there is a religious way of knowing. I tell you now that the mightiest sense of all is faith. Faith will show you a truth more bright and more full of wonder than any poor truth you have learned in a consideration of earthly things through the meager senses of your bodies. Through faith, you will come to know that I am love. There is no other way. It is your choice. You can live the cosmic minute of your lives in the dark insignificance of the little truths. Or you can brighten the fleeting moment of earthly existence with the shining light of the great and ultimate truth that you will come to know through love.

A religious way of knowing. That was it. It arrowed through to Marcus's heart, making sense of the confusion there. There was a religious way of knowing, and it was the only way to the important truth. All the arguments and discussions of the existence of God had bypassed this central point. The argument from Design; Anselm's ontological argument; the first cause argument; and all the others depended exclusively on the laws of logic, the laws of science, and on a consideration of the "real" world as experienced through the five senses of man. It was why the arguments always foundered. It was why the agnostics always won them. The essence of God was that he remained unexperienced directly. All the so-called direct experiences of God could be explained away by other phenomena—by lunacy, charlatanism, lies, misconceptions. Nobody could know if the experiences were genuinely God-related because nobody knew beyond doubt the essence of God, what he looked like, felt like, sounded like. But what if there was to be a religious way of knowing? What if faith was a branch of knowledge superior and more reliable than sight and touch? What would it take to make it such? Itself. Nothing more, nor less. Faith would be its own validator. The old saying "Seeing is believing, but touching is the truth" could be revised. Faith would be the one sure path to the truth. The rest would be mere illusion.

Had Tari invented this concept? He, the Bible scholar, the philosopher, the priest, had never heard of it. He could hardly contain his excitement. There was no way she could have dreamed this up. It was Wittgensteinian in its philosophical elegance. At a stroke, it rendered argument irrelevant in discussions about the existence of God. There was simply a religious way of knowing. Some people possessed the sense. Others didn't. Some people were blind. Others weren't. And intelligence and intellectual pride were the "blinding agents" that clouded the faculty of faith. The simple, the humble, the children, could "see." The sophisticated, the worldly "wise," the materialistic, were blind to real knowledge. The sense it made was perfect. It was so clear. It made the complex simple and the difficult easy. There was a religious way of knowing.

Marcus stood up. This was not the first revelation. His mind was spinning with them. On every page of *All for Love* there were others. Tari could not have written this by herself. However completely she might have dissociated herself from her previous personality, she would still be bound by the confines of her education, her memory, her IQ, and her past experience. It seemed impossible to deny the agency of a higher being in the writing. If so, her personality was not disordered. She was not hysterical. She was in communication with God. She knew his mind as a daughter could, as the Son of man once had.

Marcus knew what he had to do. He was shivering with excitement. He had to find out everything about Tari. He had to discover where she came from. He had to solve the mystery of the Italian woman who had spoken no English, yet emigrated to the United States with $100,000 and died bearing the child she had already decided to give into adoption. He had to talk to Tari's parents, and meet the lawyer with the secrets. He had to find the earthly family of the girl who claimed the heavenly Father.

30

ICKEY CAGE stormed into the reception area of the Douglas Clinic like a category-5 hurricane from the sea. He knew that bullshit was waiting. He also knew he wasn't taking any. The girl at the reception desk recognized the movie star at once. She knew already what he wanted. The telephone calls had paved his way. He had been trying to get to see Tarleton Jones for three weeks, and he wasn't allowed to.

"Listen," he said. "Are you the girl I've been talking to on the telephone?"

"If you're Rickey Cage, then yes, I am."

She was quite brave about it, because her instructions were explicit. Nobody was allowed upstairs to see Tari . . . especially Rickey Cage.

He saw from her body language that she wasn't going to be a pushover. He saw from somewhere deep in her eyes that she hadn't met many movie stars.

He softened himself down.

"I guess I should apologize." It came with the little-boy smile.

"That's all right," said the girl.

"I'm an impatient kind of guy, I guess." Again, he smiled. The receptionist looked like she was drawn to impatient guys. In the Intracoastal bars she frequented, all named after Irishmen or days of the week, the macho males would be terminally impatient.

"I am afraid the answer is still no. Ms. Jones is having no visitors. Dr. Douglas was quite definite about it. Look, he even wrote it down." She held up a piece of paper to prove it. *Don't shoot the messenger, she could be a fan,* was the subterranean message.

"You remind me of someone," he said suddenly.

"I do?"

"Yeah, I'm sure I've seen you before. You go down to my club, Dreemz?"

"No, but I heard it's great."

"You should get down there."

"Isn't it members-only?"

"Girls who look like you are always members. What's your name? I'll leave it with the door guy, so's you can always get in."

The receptionist was pleased by that, but she was not so stupid that she didn't know something was wanted in return.

"Thanks," she said, waiting for the rest of it.

"Actually, I came down here wanting to see Dr. Douglas, not Tari."

"Oh, I see." That was different. No written instructions there. She had leeway. Dreemz would be a fun place to take Chip. Very fun.

"Well, you haven't got an appointment," she said, "and he's pretty busy . . ." She scanned the Douglas appointment book. "But he does have half an hour free in about five minutes. I'll call up and see if he can see you." Then she had second thoughts. "Except right now he's with a patient and he doesn't like to be disturbed."

Indecision was all over her face. Chip would really like Dreemz. And Rickey Cage was real cute.

"Don't bother him. It's cool. I'll just go sit outside his office. I only want a couple of minutes of his time. Promise. He said to just drop by anytime."

"He did?"

It seemed just about as likely that Marcus Douglas had recited the lyrics of a Sister Souljah rap song.

"Yeah, he's a pal of mine."

Rickey couldn't quite keep the grimness from his voice.

"Well . . . okay . . . you go to the second floor, and there's a sofa there. You just wait, and Dr. Douglas should be out pretty soon."

"Thanks, babe, you're a doll."

"You won't forget about Dreemz? My name's Karan Michaels . . . Karan with an *a.*"

"It's etched forever on my memory," said Rickey, banishing it instantly from his mind.

He sauntered toward the elevator and pressed the floor marked three. It was the top one. Chances were the "patients" would be there. If not, he would work his way down from the top.

The third door he tried, he found her. She was sitting at a desk, writing something. She didn't hear him come in.

He walked over to her, wanting to do the hands-over-the-eyes bit. Then he remembered how much he hated it being done to him.

"Tari," he said.

She swiveled around. Her face said "surprise." One half of her expression said "pleasant," the other half didn't.

"Rickey!" She paused. "You're not supposed to be here."

"I'm never where I'm supposed to be, remember?"

He stood back waiting for the rest of it, hoping for the rest of it.

She said nothing.

"What's going down?" he had to say. "I'm out of the loop." He splayed his hands apart to show he was. "That Mary chick said there was a problem at the hospital. You weren't well or something, and now you've been here forever, and I'm not allowed to see you or talk to you."

Tari watched him. At the same time she looked inside. What did she feel? Oh, dear, he looked so *good*! He'd just washed his hair. His shirt was so white. His butt in the blue jeans was so very neat. He stood there, confused and confusing, trying to figure out the scene, and yet there was no way on earth he would ever begin to understand what had happened, what was happening. He came from another planet. He was the world of yesterday. He was part of the old Tari. Yet, at the same time, he could not be ignored. The power was in him. The Devil's power. The power of temptation. She remembered his body, his flesh, the noises he'd made. She remembered the love with which he'd filled her body.

"Are you ill, Tari . . . or what? You don't look ill."

"No, I'm not ill, Rickey. I'm incredibly well." She smiled, and some of the affection came out. Enough for him to build on.

"I've missed you, girl."

He took a step toward her, putting out his hand for touch.

Reluctantly, she held out hers. He reached for the bridge to her, hoping he would be allowed to cross.

Tari felt the old excitement. He'd missed her. Had she missed him? If so, should she say so? His fingers fired up hers, twining into them, squeezing them in a grip that was so soon a caress. Boom! She felt her heart start to move. It was that quick. That automatic.

"Listen, Tari. You never let me say sorry."

"It wasn't your fault, Rickey. It was mine. I drank too much. I just lost it."

"No, it was my fault. You were just so beautiful. I wanted you so much. I want you . . ."

"No!" The word shot out, surprising her with its force.

His eyes registered the vehemence of her denial.

"Tari, what are you doing here? If you're not ill, why are you here with Douglas, and not taking my calls?"

"Rickey, we've tried talking about it before. It doesn't work."

"Shit, Tari, I love you."

"I love you, too, Rickey." And she did. She loved him. She simply loved.

"You do?"

He smiled in triumph, not knowing what she had meant. He walked toward her. He drew her up to him, into his arms.

Tari let him. There were so many ways to love. There were so many ways to care. There could never be enough of it. It was not diluted by being spread wide. It was strengthened. The goal was not to love one person completely. It was to love everyone with the same intensity that one could love one person. In the reciprocity of that love, possession and jealousy would melt away. Her book said so. God's book said it. In paradise, there would be only clouds and cushions of unconditional love. Nobody would be excluded. Everyone would bask in its warmth. It would never end, because love was eternal. Life and love might seem to die in the land of illusion, but in the reality of heaven, they were infinite.

"Can I kiss you?" he said, suddenly afraid at the edge of intimacy. In his arms she had changed. She did not feel like the old Tari. She felt new. She was charged with a power that he couldn't understand, and it made him uneasy. He loved her, but he was no longer sure exactly who it was he loved. She had left him behind. She had moved on. He felt like a child, cunning and tricky at the edges of the adult world, but also acutely aware that he lacked the answers. Her face was turned up to him. Warmth shone from her eyes. But inches from her lips, he drew back. She was too good for his crude embrace. Once before he had shamed her. He had taken advantage of her as men like him did. Later he had worried, not so much for her, but for him, worried that she would respect him no longer. Now, he knew just how sorry he was, because it seemed that a barrier had grown between them. He could feel it. Once again he moved his head toward her, and his lips to hers. Once again, he stopped at the brink.

"It's all right," she said.

She could feel his uncertainty. It was so out of character, but nice, too.

His lips brushed against hers, and she kissed him tenderly. She was full of affection, but lust was muted. It was there, but no longer in the foreground. The sexual harmonies played softly in the wings, but in her heart Tari was singing another song.

He drew back. "You've changed, Tari. Something has happened to you. I can feel it."

"Yes," she said simply. "I have work to do."

"Work? Med-school stuff?"

"No, God's work. Important work."

"God's work?" His voice was thick with lack of understanding.

"I have to tell the world about love."

She saw the pain and the hurt race across his face as she spoke. She knew what was coming.

"This is Douglas's thing, isn't it?" Anger bubbled in his words. "He's the one who's filling your head with all this crap. He's fucking brainwashed you, Tari. He's turned you into some cult groupie weirdo. He's playing with your mind, do you realize that, 'cause all he can think of is playing with your body. I ought to knock his fucking, hypocritical egghead off. I should have done it that night."

"Please go, Rickey."

He put up his hands. "Okay, okay, I'll go, Tari, but this isn't it. I may be just a know-nothing actor, but I'm not going to hang around and let some souped-up Svengali screw around with your mind. You understand what I'm saying? You tell Douglas that when he messes with you he's messing with me, okay? Okay?"

He backed toward the door.

"I love you, Rickey," said Tari.

31

"I CALLED this meeting," said the dean, "because I think we should be quite clear about what we want to do, and how we want to do it. Dr. Douglas is a person of considerable reputation, however ill-deserved that may now appear to be. He is rich and well-connected, and he is famous. I have the reputation of the school to consider. I will have to weigh that against any responsibility I might have toward Tarleton Jones."

"Here is the bottom line," said the professor of medicine. "My patient and Professor Hodges's patient was diagnosed as having an acute psychosis. That diagnosis will hold up. She was committed to Robert E. Lee. The commitment was legal, and in the best interests of both the patient and the community. She escaped. On being discovered, she should have been returned immediately to our care. It is as simple as that."

"It would not be stretching it too far to say that Douglas has kidnapped her," said Veronica Hodges.

"But he is a trained psychiatrist and he says she isn't ill," said the dean.

"That's for a properly constituted review board to decide when asked formally to investigate the commitment order. Douglas can't preempt the correct procedure in this situation. He is way out of line." Professor Shindler had once wondered about a career in law.

"How can anybody say she is not ill? She thinks she's the daughter of God, for God's sake. Does Douglas actually believe that? If so, he's crazy too. We should get some phenothiazines into him."

Veronica Hodges was equal parts fury and excitement. It was a wonderful and rare moment in life when moral duty and revenge coincided. There were few enough people on this earth that she liked, but there was only one person that she loathed. That person was Marcus Douglas. He had humiliated her in the most public forum in the land. Her intellectual poverty had been revealed to millions, and he had been to blame. Scarcely a minute passed when she didn't relive the horror that had been her "Donahue" Waterloo. It had been the ultimate nightmare. The cloak of her achievements had been rudely ripped away, and beneath there had been nothing but her naked mediocrity.

But now fate had dealt her at least a full house, if not a straight flush. The chance had arisen to destroy the man she hated. If she played her cards carefully, Douglas's professional reputation could be ruined. Malpractice, breach of ethical codes, stealing patients, lack of the most basic diagnostic skills, all could be proven against him. And what was so magnificent was that right was on her side, and more important, a potent ally in the form of the formidable professor of medicine. If the dean would join them, the trinity would be irresistible. Together they could ensure that Douglas as a serious psychiatrist would be history.

"Then there are the . . . the photographs," said the dean. He fingered the brown folder on his desk as if it were contaminated.

"Just how did you get hold of them?" said Veronica Hodges.

The dean winced. He had taken an instant dislike to the famous model when she had presented herself in his office, but he had not been able to ignore the story she told. She had

had a key to the studio of the movie star Rickey Cage, with whom, apparently, the Jones girl was "involved." Jodie Summerfield had been "shocked to her core" to discover the pornographic photographs of Tari making love to another girl. She had known that the dean was responsible for Tari as a medical student and she had felt it was her duty to take Polaroids and to show them to him so that he could act in the best interests of the State Medical College and to safeguard the moral character of one of his students. The dean hadn't bought any of it. Summerfield had stunk of the green fumes of jealousy. She had reeked of revenge. But the Polaroids told the truth, and it was a truth that dovetailed neatly into the course of action that the dean and his colleagues were now planning.

He brushed away Hodges's question. "The bottom line is that they exist," he said.

"Well, they're just another nail in the diagnostic coffin," said Hodges, unfazed by the dean's failure to answer her question. "The girl is falling apart. She lets herself be photographed in homosexual poses. She hears 'God's voice' telling her that she's his daughter. With the benefit of hindsight, there have been other pointers. Dr. Donovan complained that she was inappropriate in a lecture. I myself have had problems with her. She was disobedient and offensive during the hurricane. She behaved in an odd way with regard to a prefrontal leucotomy. I thought she was merely a difficult student. Now, I see clearly what was happening. If I were writing a textbook, I couldn't have dreamed up a more classic case of progressive schizophrenic destruction of the personality," said Hodges.

"Okay, okay, I agree with you both, but just exactly what can we do?" said the dean.

"We can apply to the Florida State Medical Board to have Dr. Douglas's medical license revoked," said Veronica Hodges. Her mouth was a surgical scar across her face.

"That'll take forever . . . longer," said Professor Shindler. "I think the thing to do is to go to the police with the commitment order. It's still in effect. Legally, only Veronica and I can revoke it. I say wait until Douglas's out, or away, and then go in there with a warrant and take her back. Once she's been on medication for a week or two, she'll probably begin to gain

some insight and see that she was ill, and that it's Douglas
who's nuts. Then, in the fullness of time, we can nail him."

"Snatch a patient from another doctor's clinic, against her
will?" said the dean, shaking his head.

"*We* wouldn't be doing it. The police would be doing it
under the still-extant commitment order. Think of the patient.
She's one of our students. She's getting no treatment. Douglas
is apparently colluding with her delusions. She needs Thorazine. She needs our help," said Shindler, as Veronica Hodges
nodded vigorous agreement.

"Do you really think the police could be persuaded to take
a patient away from her doctor?" said the dean.

"Hell, he's *not* her doctor. He doesn't think she's ill. He's
never treated her. She's never been referred to him by a
primary-care physician. Technically, her doctor here in Miami
is the medical-school doctor who examined her prior to her
starting her studies. That physician referred her to Veronica
and myself, after the ward round. I make a point of doing
things by the book. Douglas hasn't a leg to stand on if he
pretends to be her doctor."

"Oh, there is one other thing," said the dean, wondering if
this was the best time to drop his thunderbolt. "I just had a call
from my editor in New York, the guy who does my textbooks.
The trade division of World Publishers has just commissioned
a new book, and they've sent around an internal memo about
it. My editor thought I'd be interested because of Douglas's
connection with the medical school. Douglas's producing
a book called *All for Love*... and he's coauthoring it with
Tarleton Jones. My guy, who knows about these things, says it'll
do a million five in hardback. If you get her back, Tarleton
Jones is going to be the richest and most famous psychotic you
ever had."

32

ARCUS DOUGLAS sat back against the cushions of the stretch limo. He was lost in the pages.

Life can be a prison. A person is locked in his body, looking inward, unable to escape except into the frightening unknown of death. Through love you can begin to belong to the universe I have made, and to understand the joy of my peace. You are afraid of love, because you fear that love will put you in the power of others. You look out for yourselves because you do not trust others to do so. You decorate the palace of self and you fortify the castle of ego against intruders, but you fail to install the drawbridge of love. As a result none can enter, nor can you leave. You see love as the greatest risk. You fear it will weaken you, and put you at the mercy of others. But I say to you, the risk is to live a loveless life. In doing so you will be consumed by the flames of meaninglessness in the empty halls of self, and the cries of your helplessness will echo in the void of your existence. You have the choice. It is yours to make. On every day, during every minute, salvation from self is a commitment away. Start with love. Start with one simple act of love. Then, as darkness melts into dawn, another act of love will follow and, as the river runs from the hills, the reservoir of your love will rise. You will flow out into the space of forever, and togetherness will be your prize, and meaning will be your reward. Through love you will come to know me. Through love, I will live in you.

Marcus put down the pages. Here was an ultimate truth. The human predicament was loneliness, and the fundamental cause of that loneliness was the human being's imprisonment within his body. The mind could not escape from the confinement of the flesh. But here, in this book, was love as the antidote to self. Here was death as the ultimate freedom. Here was only hope and joy and an escape from the prison of the physical into the love-filled world of the soul. In the world this book described, Marcus could see humans flowing out to each other, connecting, becoming one with nature and with God. You were not asked to believe in God as a first step. You were asked instead to believe in an emotion with which everyone had a nodding acquaintance. You were simply asked to give love a chance to work miracles. God would follow . . . because God *was* love, the blood of our souls, the reason and the explanation for our existence.

He picked up the telephone. His whole mind was filled with the importance of this. It was so clear. It was the clarity of holiness. The sense it made was not only perfect, it was the sense of perfect peace.

"Amoy? Marcus Douglas. Is he in?"

"He's in ten meetings and a sales conference in Buffalo, but, yes, of course, he's always 'in' to you." It was a joke, but one of those jokes that dressed up embarrassing truths to make them more palatable.

In seconds, the mighty publisher of World was on the line.

"Marcus, Marcus, how are you? How can I help you?"

"I just wanted to talk a bit about *All for Love.*"

"Ah, yes. *All for Love.*" The trumpet had an uncertain note.

Would the sales force, the PR people, and all the others be preparing themselves for the battle? It was the reason Marcus was calling.

"Listen, I know you're lukewarm on this project. Tari is an unknown, and you think she'll dilute the brand name, and you're worried about the whole idea because you think it's wacky. . . ."

"No. No, Marcus, not wacky. Not at all. I've read the early pages. I think they're very inspirational. We all do here at World. Of course, it's a departure . . . some might say a big departure from the last book. But listen, if we knew what the public wanted we'd be gods, not publishers . . ."

He petered out, suddenly aware that in this context his remark had been a little inappropriate.

Marcus didn't seem to notice. "You remember you said I could do anything I wanted, total freedom, a children's book even . . ."

"A children's book. Ha! Ha!" said the publisher. It was the laugh you managed when a supremely important person had made a joke in astoundingly poor taste.

"Well, here's what I propose to do. When I met up with you a few weeks ago you were talking about my commitment to you for a multibook deal. You said, I think, that you would pay more than anyone else in terms of a guarantee against royalties . . . twenty percent, if I remember correctly."

"That was the substance of the conversation, I think," said the publisher. Did shrinks record conversations? Did priests?

"Well, I want a media blitz on *All for Love,* the likes of which has never been seen before in publishing. I want subscription deals with the bookshops, return postage paid, all and every incentive your marketing people can dream up. Then I want wall-to-wall TV advertising, radio saturation, print and magazine overkill . . . you name it, and the rest. Get your special promotions people to hand out goodies that make the bookshop people drool. Do you understand me? I'm talking a major, megamajor campaign. There mustn't be a person in the country who doesn't know about this book."

"Now, hang on, Marcus. I don't think we should get carried away here. You can take a horse to the water, but you can't make it . . . you know how it is. If they don't want the book, they won't buy it and then all the promo money is blown away. I think you just have to trust us to . . ."

"I'll sign for a three-book deal, on the royalty basis of the last book, and I won't take a penny up front."

"Oh." There was silence on the line. The limo purred out over the bridge.

"Listen, Marcus, bad line. Could you be very kind and say that last bit again? I'm not sure I heard it correctly."

Marcus repeated it word for word, smiling grimly as he did so. Here was a man with a price.

"That would be extremely acceptable," said the small voice at the end of the telephone.

"I'll drop by tomorrow and we can write something down," said Marcus.

The conversation was over. The publisher was still murmuring about the excellence of the idea of writing things down when Marcus cut him off.

"You know where we're going?" he said to the driver.

"Yes, no problem. I have an uncle who lives a few blocks away."

"Good," said Marcus. He was excited. He was on the trail. Where would it lead? Would Tari's parents point the way?

The house was all-American, a little yard in front, and presumably a little garden at the back. A Buick, neither old nor new, sat in front of the closed garage that would contain the number one car. The borders were well-tended. The paint on the windows and front door was faded, but not chipped. Not much exciting had gone on in this house. And the excitement had almost certainly not been missed. The Douglas limo pulled up outside. Marcus peered up to the top floor of the small house. Tari was the only child. Would she have had the top left-hand bedroom? Was that where she grew up, woke up in the morning on Christmas Day with the sensible-sized stocking on her mantelshelf; rode out the rigors of the chicken pox, the heart-wrenching woes of first love, survived the humiliations and hopes of high-school happy days?

"Just wait, okay? I don't know how long this will take."

The driver said, "Sure, Dr. Douglas."

He got out. The front gate had a latch. The doorbell made a tune somewhere inside the house.

The man who answered it was short and neat with a bureaucrat's mustache and a distantly polite manner.

"Dr. Douglas. You found us all right."

"Yes."

"Come in. Frances? Dr. Douglas."

He stood back to let Marcus pass as he called to his wife. She hurried out, very pleased to meet him. She had read his book, and she had never met a famous author before, and it was an honor . . . and . . .

Marcus answered her platitudes with a few of his own. Already he was sizing them up as a psychiatrist learned how. It was all in the actions. Forget the words. The man had opened the door. His manner said he wore the pants. She was the mousy wife, talking nonsense to hide her nervousness.

"How's Sarah?" said the husband.

"Ah, yes, Sarah. I know her as Tari, of course."

"Yes, she changed that," said the father. It was clear from his tone that it was not something that had pleased him.

"Used to be Sarah Bennett. Now she's Tarleton Jones. Funny what matters to people, isn't it?" said Frances. "We always think of her as Sarah, though."

"I'm sure you do," said Marcus.

"How is she?" The father repeated his question.

"We're so grateful to you for . . ." tried his wife.

Her husband's look cut her off. They had arrived in a dark, severe sitting room. There was no television. The chairs were uncomfortable, but expensively upholstered. A photograph of Tari was above the mantelshelf. She looked happy, young, and innocent. And beautiful, even then, at maybe fourteen. Marcus walked over, drawn to it.

"She's fine. She sends her love, but she says she talks to you most days."

"Yes, she does," said the surrogate mother called Frances. "She's a good girl. Always has been."

"We've been very worried," said the father. "Two doctors have called, and the head man at the medical school. Two professors, one medical, one a psychiatrist. They said Sarah wasn't at all well, and they said you shouldn't be looking after her."

He was an immigration officer. Directness might not be merely a duty for him. It might also be a pleasure. Marcus couldn't resist the feeling that "Daddy's hands" had not always been gentle. To Frances? To Tari?

"But Sarah sounds just fine," said the mother.

"Yes, she does," agreed the father, somewhat grudgingly.

"So we just didn't interfere," said Frances. "Especially as I'd read your book. Father Hartnett at the church speaks very highly of you, and he says the monsignor does too, and even the bishop . . ." She tailed off, clearly in awe of such important figures in the Catholic hierarchy.

"Please sit down, Doctor," said her husband.

"Or should we call you Father?" said his wife.

"Tari calls me Marcus. That would make me feel most comfortable."

"When in Rome," said the father and laughed quickly. He stopped. His wife looked at him reproachfully. Marcus smiled. Tari would have gotten the Catholicism from the wife.

"Can I get you a cup of coffee?" said Frances.

"Thank you." She scurried away, relieved to escape the heavy-duty conversation.

"What exactly has been going on?" said the father. "Oh, I'm Tom, by the way. Tom Bennett. I should have said."

"Tom," said Marcus, as if making an effort to learn the name by heart. What was going on? It was a good question, and one that Marcus had not fully answered. It was why he was here. To find out. Still, something had to be said.

"I don't quite know how to explain this, but . . . are you a Catholic?"

"Yes. But my wife is the real one, if you know what I mean." Tom laughed, nervously this time.

"Well, I think that what has basically happened is that Tari has had some rather significant religious experience."

"Oh."

"And unfortunately some of the doctors down there in Miami have misinterpreted it as some sort of a nervous breakdown."

"They were saying it was you that had misinterpreted it." Tom was blunt. The implication was that he didn't necessarily share his wife's faith in Douglas. As far as he was concerned, the jury was out, although Sarah's "normalness" on the telephone was a factor that couldn't be ignored.

His wife was back with the coffee. Conversation went on hold while she poured.

"Of course, I was always against her going to Miami," she said. The relevance of her remark wasn't clear to anyone.

"It is not *that* unusual, in our church," said Marcus, relieved that the true believer had returned, "for miracles to occur. From time to time people have visions of God or of the blessed Virgin. In fact, Marian sightings are getting quite common, and of course, the stigmata are far from unknown . . ."

"Has our Sarah experienced something like that?" said Tom. He sounded deeply skeptical.

"Something like that. Yes, I think she has."

"Something like what?" said Frances, revealing a tougher side to her personality. "She never mentioned anything funny on the telephone."

Marcus fought against the surreality of the situation. Tari had never mentioned being the daughter of God on the telephone. It wouldn't be the sort of information you'd send by fax, either, or by postcard, hardly even in a letter.

He took a deep breath.

"I think, for instance, that she has performed something that might well turn out to have been a miracle."

They exchanged glances, saying nothing. All this was way outside their experience. It was hardly in the mainstream of Marcus's, either.

There was more. "And I personally believe that she has a very special relationship with the Holy Spirit."

"You mean . . . like a . . . like a saint?"

"I think that is what I do mean."

"She wasn't a saint when she was a child," said Tom. He was quite sure about that.

"No, I don't suppose she was," said Marcus.

"But she was a lovely child," said her mother. "She was kind and gentle and warm, and everyone loved her. And the boys loved her. My word, they did."

Her father's mouth had set in a straight line.

"I'd rather hoped you could let me know a bit about her childhood. More about her character: warm, you say, and kind . . . Was she very religious? I mean, was it a big thing with her?"

Tom answered. He appeared bemused. It was not every day that one's daughter was described as a saint and a miracle worker.

"She wasn't a fanatic. She was a normal girl. Frances brought her up in the faith and she went to church and believed in God, and said her prayers. But nothing odd or out of the ordinary, if that's what you mean."

"And she wasn't shy, introverted, a dreamer, withdrawn? No friends?"

"Good gracious, no. None of those things," said Frances, laughing at the thought. "But she was headstrong. Always a leader. The other children would do anything for her. And she was fair, but a bit impatient. And very bright. If she hadn't gone into medicine, she'd have made a fortune in business. Everyone always said she'd be a success of some sort. Worked hard and played hard, that was our Sarah."

"What was this 'miracle'?" said the father.

"It hasn't been formally investigated by the church, and so we can't technically use the word miracle, but she seemed to save the sight, if not the life, of a young intern who was attacked by a psychotic in the hospital where Tari was working."

"Good gracious," said Frances. It was another thing Sarah hadn't mentioned on the telephone.

"And the special relationship with the Holy Spirit?" said Tom, the immigration officer who was clearly used to interrogating people.

"She's heard voices. And she is writing a book. Much of what she is writing appears to be communicated to her by . . . by . . . well, for want of a better word, by God," said Marcus, wondering why he wanted a better word than God.

"A book?"

"Yes, actually a very important, very brilliant book. And I think a very holy book."

"Sarah's writing a book?" said the father.

"It's going to be published. Under her name. And under mine."

"Sarah's writing a book with you?" said Frances.

She could see the point of that even if the point of everything else was beginning to elude her.

"Yes, she is. It's going to be a very famous book."

Again they looked at each other. Their eyes were saying something. Marcus wanted to know what it was.

"Actually, I wanted to talk to you both about Tari's adoption."

They both stiffened. The immigration officer sat bolt upright in his chair. His expression was guarded. Frances was looking at him. This would be his conversation.

"What did you want to know?"

"I've talked to Tari about it, and so I know as much as she knows, which is basically what she's heard from you. What I think we both find a little mysterious is the attorney, Bertram Applegate, through whom the adoption was arranged. I gather he's a corporate lawyer on Wall Street, who doesn't specialize in private adoptions at all."

"He was recommended to me. He found us Sarah. I never thought any more about him." The father's jaw was set.

"Well, anyway . . . he was extremely unhelpful—actually downright confrontational—with Tari. He refused to reveal the name of Tari's dead mother. I can't think why he would take that attitude, can you?" Marcus watched them closely as he spoke.

"I don't know the legal business. He must have had his reasons. I can't see why it was important for Tari to know about all that. We are the only family she's ever had," said Tom.

There was a silence. Frances looked down in her lap.

Marcus pressed on. "It seems so odd that the mother would have a hundred thousand dollars, and yet speak no English, and be emigrating here when she was pregnant with no family to go to . . . and that she would get a green card so easily, and then hire this rich man's lawyer, Applegate, to get her daughter adopted . . ."

Tom shrugged.

"Not as odd as miracles, and books, and professors ringing me up to say my daughter's crazy and that she shouldn't be anywhere near you."

The hostility was out in the open now.

"Why do you want to find Sarah's family?" said Frances. "Are you in love with her?"

Marcus hadn't expected that one. He could see where Tari got her directness, and even her insight. The flush exploded on his cheeks.

"No, of course I'm not," he lied.

"She wants to find her family," he added. "It's quite an understandable desire in an adopted person."

"Are you her doctor, or her priest, or what?" said Tom.

"I'm her friend," said Marcus.

"You, and the movie star she's always talking about," said Tari's adoptive father.

Marcus's flush was deepening. He would learn nothing more from these people. They had closed down on him. Why? He had to find out. He had to know just who Tarleton Jones was.

The building didn't scrape the sky, it impaled it. It was a vast granite phallus, hot from a Freudian dream, and it sank into the pale blue of the heavens in coital triumph. The lobby was marble. Busts of Roman figures were scattered about to provide suitably Augustan grandeur. A reception desk was manned by many men in gray. Above and behind them, in gold lettering on a mahogany background, were the names of the nabobs who "worked" here and the companies they owned. Many of them seemed to be variations on the theme of the mighty Wall Street legal firm of Applegate, Myers, and Runne.

Marcus approached the desk. As he did so, he looked up at the names of the other companies. He didn't recognize any of them, but most appeared to be Italian, and, from the similarity of the names, the companies were apparently related.

"I'm Dr. Marcus Douglas. I have an appointment with Mr. Bertram Applegate," he said.

The receptionist consulted the leather-bound oracle that was the appointments book.

"At noon," he said. The word "high" seemed like an omission.

"You take that elevator to the fourth floor, and the receptionist will direct you further," he said.

When he got there, he had a few minutes to wait. He sat down in the intimidating comfort of the reception area. Everyone would get to cool his heels here as the financial importance of Applegate and his partners sank into the psyches of those waiting. Marcus was supremely unimpressed. As a priest and a psychiatrist, he had learned that appearances were designed only to deceive. Patients and penitents spent most of their time lying. So, he imagined, did Wall Street lawyers . . . in spades. He flicked open his briefcase, ignoring the trendy eighties art. He pulled out the manila folder. Once again he was deep in *All for Love.*

In learning to love, you will not try to feel. The battle to feel love when love is absent will not be won. Here is the struggle that so many lose. Hate and indifference, boredom and pride, leave no room for love in so many of the minds of man. But even when the mind is full of negative emotion of this kind, there is a way to love. It is through action. If you cannot think a loving thought, then perform a loving act. It will break the chain of antipathy. It will be the water that allows the flower of gratitude to grow in others. You will see the rewards of love before you know the feel of it, and a speck of light will emerge in your darkness. That tiny point of light will grow until your whole mind is full of the brightness of love. And then you will be near to me. The first action may be small, a minute reaching out through the barrier of alienation. But it will be a seed planted that will one day make the desert bloom. A kind word when a cruel one was intended, a genuine compliment to an enemy, an act of charity to the stranger in a street. These are the foundations of love in the loveless. They must be built like a building, brick by brick. They must be written like the pages of a book, word by word. Do not recoil from the impossibility of building an entire building. Do not draw back in impotence at the prospect of writing a complete book. Take one single step, then another, and another still. As time passes, you will build my temple. In the fullness of time you will write your own book of love.

"Dr. Douglas." The girl was leaning over him.

Marcus started. He had the impression she'd said his name several times. He had been lost in the manuscript. Its emphasis was extraordinary. It was almost behaviorist in its philosophy. The mind was discussed as if it was inferior to, even dependent on, the body. The old idea of the mind as the vital prime mover, and the body as its servant, was absent from these pages. "Act first, thought will follow," was the message. "Learn to love not by mental gymnastics, but by doing things." "By your deeds shall you be known" had acquired new significance. Deeds were not merely a window into your thinking. They were the *cause* of your thinking. And it was true. How many times had he ignored his patients' stories, and learned about them from their actions? It was as simple as the wheel, but it was directly contrary to popular "wisdom." "Think right, then you will act right," was the accepted truth. First, change your thoughts, get them straight, get them "shrunk." Only then, sound in mind, could you proceed to sound actions. But to straighten your mind was a crossword puzzle of awesome intensity. It was like building a castle from the dry, shifting sands of the beach. The moment the orderly edifice was constructed, it was washed away by the churning surf of life and experience. To act, however, was relatively straightforward. How hard could it be to force yourself to say something kind, to make a gift of your time, to praise, to encourage, to take the first faltering step on the road to love?

"Dr. Douglas!"

"Oh, yes. I'm sorry. I was far away."

"Mr. Applegate can see you now."

The Applegate office was designed to intimidate. The industrial-strength art alone would have bought all the attorneys in a medium-sized town in Wisconsin. The partner's desk was a helicopter landing pad covered with faded red leather. And then there was Applegate himself, WASP suave, with his Brylcreemed graying hair and his Brooks Brothers look, sliding across the carpet like an oil slick on a calm day in the gulf.

"Dr. Marcus Douglas. This is an honor. Your book . . . your book, what shall I say . . . it changed my life!"

Applegate had come out of his mother's womb like this. The only things that had ever changed about him had been his diapers and his mistresses. Marcus had never been surer of anything.

"How kind of you to say so," he said.

"Do please sit down. Yes, sit, please do . . ."

The lawyer made small upper-class gestures with his hands as he muttered the meaningless, half-finished, upper-class sentences.

"Might I ask the nature of your next literary project?" said Applegate.

"It's a book not unlike the Bible," said Marcus. He didn't laugh. The silence expanded. Applegate sensed a joke, but there was no overt evidence of it. Maybe Douglas's sense of humor was as dry as the claret Applegate enjoyed.

"Aim high," he said with a little laugh.

The silence deepened.

"So, Doctor, how can I help you?" Time was lots and lots of money.

"I have a . . . friend in Miami called Tarleton Jones. She came to see you once about her mother. She was an adopted child and you acted for her mother, who died soon after giving birth to Tari. Apparently, you did not feel able to help Tari in discovering her mother's name and circumstances. Do you remember the case?"

"Ah," said Applegate. He drew his fingers together and smiled an uneasy smile. "Yes," he said. "I do remember the girl. Your . . . friend, you say."

"Yes," said Marcus, failing to amplify on the word "friend."

"As I remember, it was a straightforward question of client-attorney privacy. I was instructed by my client, Tari's mother, not to reveal her identity. I saw it as my duty . . . I still see it as my duty . . . to respect her wish."

Applegate's lips were pursed. What was left of a smile still lingered.

"There were several questions that Tari wanted answered," said Marcus. "We found it difficult to understand how a woman who spoke no English was able to emigrate to America, having no family here, and presumably no job. And there is the question of how she came by you as an attorney. It is clear from ... from many things"—and Marcus waved his hands around the office—"that you do not specialize in the arrangement of private adoptions."

"With respect," said Applegate, the warmth of his voice notching down a few degrees, "this is my private business. As a psychiatrist and a priest, Dr. Douglas ... Father Douglas ... you are surely aware of the importance of professional privacy."

Marcus could see the end of the cul-de-sac. It could only get worse from here on in. He was going to get the same cold shoulder that Tari got.

It was then that he decided to try the shot in the dark.

He watched Applegate like a hawk as he spoke.

"I couldn't help noting the large number of Italian companies that are fellow tenants of your building," he said. "From the similarities in many of their names, one could imagine that perhaps they are owned by a single entity."

Applegate's cheeks revealed twin pinpoints of red. His eyes darted away from Douglas's and then hurried back in case their absence had been noted.

"I hardly see what that has got to do with ..."

"Only that Tari's mother was an Italian from Italy ... with one hundred thousand dollars," said Douglas quickly. He felt his pulse quicken. He was onto something. Suave Applegate now looked like shifty Watergate.

"I can assure you that is coincidental," said Applegate.

The lie was in neon. If Applegate had nothing to hide, he would have ended the interview by now with another short speech on attorney-client privilege before showing Marcus the door. But Douglas was still there. That meant Applegate wanted more time to assess Marcus's objectives, to discover just how far Marcus was prepared to go in reaching them.

"I'm sure it is," said Douglas. "And I mustn't waste any more of your valuable ... of your very expensive time. But to save me the trouble of satisfying my curiosity about all these Italian companies, could you let me know the identity of the controlling interests?"

Applegate paused. He was weighing something in his mind. If Douglas wanted the information, it would be available in public records. If Applegate withheld it, then Douglas's suspicions would be increased.

"I believe they represent the American interests of the count of Lonza."

"The Italian industrialist?"

"Yes, I suppose you could call him that."

"And your firm represents him?"

Again, it would be a matter of public record somewhere.

"Some of my partners do," said Applegate. His voice was now colder than the snows of winter.

Douglas stood up. "Thank you very much," he said, "for your help. It has been a pleasure meeting you, and I am so glad that my humble book was some sort of an influence for good in your life."

Applegate could hardly bring himself to utter the word "good-bye."

In the elevator on the way down, Marcus's spirits were going up. He was sure that he had a lead. What he knew about the count of Lonza wouldn't make up a small story in *USA Today*. But he had friends in Rome who would know everything there was to know about the plutocratic aristocrat since the time he had been nothing more than a gleam in his parents' eyes.

33

TARI WAS tired, but she worked on. Her back was stiff. Her butt was numb. Her hand was cramped, yet still she wrote.

"Love will be clearer, not at the beginning, but at the end. In the early days, love can blind with its brightness. It can be kidnapped by alien emotions, by obsession, by possession, by jealousy. But in the evening of life when faculties fail, then the clarity of love will point the way to me."

Tari stopped. A chill had fallen on the room. A draft of cold had caught her heart. In the evening of life, the love would come. She buried her head in her hands and sighed. The desk was piled high with pages. Now, suddenly, she sensed the end. For two months, nearly three, she had sat here, writing down the words of the inner voice that was both hers and his. It had been a time of incredible excitement and intense loneliness, even though Marcus had been there at every step of the way with encouragement and support, and with the sad warmth of the love he hardly dared admit to her. She had slept and eaten and exercised in the gym, but mostly she had written and read.

Dawn had become midday, noon had turned to dusk, and now she knew the *All for Love* was nearly finished. And she knew something else, the thing that had chilled her heart. Her mission to bring love to the world would end with this book. It was her task . . . her one task . . . and it was all but over. Tears welled up in her eyes, suddenly, like a storm at sea.

The knock on the door was Marcus's.

"Come in," she said.

He walked toward her.

She turned toward him.

He saw her tears. "What's the matter, Tari?" His voice was full of concern for her.

"It's nearly finished," she said simply.

He looked at the pile of pages.

"The book?"

"Everything," she said.

He caught her strange premonition of death in midair with the fine net of his feelings. He was attuned to her now, in love, in awe, in reverence.

"Tell me what you mean, Tari."

"When I finish, it will be over," she said.

He waited.

"When the *All for Love* is written, the mission will be complete. I know that. You will sell the book. The world will read it, first because of you, and then later, because of the words of God."

"But you won't die," he said. "That's ridiculous. I understand where you have the idea from, but . . ."

"You're right. There was no prophecy. I haven't been told. But I know, and you mustn't mourn for me. How can you be sad for someone who will leave to live in perfect love?"

"How can you know these things?" said Marcus.

"How did I write this book?" she answered. She laid her hand on the pages. Down below, two typists were at work on the transcription. It was big now, the *All for Love*, perhaps three hundred thousand words, maybe more, written with no revisions and unedited by human hand.

Marcus's stricken face stared at her. He didn't have to ask her how she knew such things, and he felt the fear. He looked wildly around the room. From where could the threat come? How could she be harmed? How could death reach her? Through disease? Through violence? Through what earthly agency could the will of God be carried out? Even as he thought the thoughts, he rebelled against them. Surely here at last was a genuine delusion in the girl he had come to believe in. No good God could kill her. No good Lord would harm her.

"How?" he said.

"I don't know. When the time comes, I will know it."

She smiled and wiped away her tears. The premonition was in place. Later, through dark nights of the soul, she could confront her demons as Jesus had. But there was still work to be done. The games of ambivalence, doubt, and fear could be played later . . . as they had been played so very long ago.

"Can we eat?" she said. "I'm so hungry."

"Oh, Tari," he said. There were tears in the eyes of the doctor, and of the priest, and of the man.

34

THEY FILED into the room like conspirators, two men and one woman, with good in their mouths and evil in their souls. They were the hypocrites, scribes, and pharisees of their secular religion, and, as they sat down in the armchairs of the gloomy office, they were already polishing the words that would make acceptable the anger in their hearts.

Professor Hodges spoke first.

"It is intolerable. This situation simply cannot be allowed to continue," she said, her voice low with loathing. "The press is full of this Tarleton Jones/Douglas book. I can't open a paper without reading about it. My staff knows the girl was on a commitment order. They know I diagnosed her as a paranoid schizophrenic, and now all they read about is how she's been paid vast sums by a thoroughly reputable publisher to write a book about her delusions. I'm the laughingstock of the hospital. Me, laughed at. I'm not used to it."

She fumed in her angst, smoking in it like a trout in a box. Her most precious sin was her intellectual pretension. She had grown it through the years like a prize tomato. Red and robust, plump and livid, it sat inside her, threatening to explode. The last time they had met, her hopes had been high that the situation could be turned to her advantage. There was an outside possibility that Douglas's reputation and career could be ruined. Instead, the unbelievable had happened. "Her" psychotic was about to become a megarich celebrity. The fact that a renowned publishing house was prepared to publish Tari's "delusions" gave them respectability. It was a powerful indicator that the outside world believed Douglas, and not Veronica Hodges. It followed that her diagnosis was a joke, along with her commitment order and her professional "expertise." There was only one way to set the record straight, and the law was on her side. She must get Tari back into the hospital under her and Professor Shindler's "care." Then everyone would have to accept that Tari was crazy. At a stroke, Tari's book would be exposed as either the cruel hoax of an unscrupulous psychiatrist or the metaphysical claptrap of a priest blinded by his religion to the harsh reality of madness.

The dean's fingers were together as if in prayer. All things to him were the art of the possible. He was the trimmer, the Vicar of Bray, all the chameleons through all the years who had tried to be everything to everyone, and ended up as nothing at all.

"I have talked several times to the police department about this," he said carefully. "They are quite adamant. They are not prepared to apply for a warrant to get the girl out of the clinic. They point out that Douglas is not only a board-certified psychiatrist, he is also a famous and well-connected one. They simply won't do it. The chief was quite candid. He lives with his butt on the line. In the police department, there are no tenured professorial chairs."

"He's not doing his job," snarled Hodges.

"It won't be the first or the last time someone hasn't done that," said the dean with a tight smile. "In fact he was refreshingly honest about it. He said it's his policy never to irritate anyone who has instant access to 'Oprah' and 'Donahue.' Rather perspicacious in our present age, don't you think?" said the dean.

"It isn't your reputation that's on the line," said Veronica Hodges, her face filling with thunder.

"Something simply has to be done," agreed Professor Shindler.

Unlike Hodges, Shindler was clever. A brilliant diagnostician, an original thinker, and possessed of a brittle charisma, he nonetheless suffered from a deadly insufficiency. He was neither a kind nor a caring doctor, and he was acutely aware of it. He instilled no confidence in his patients, despite his skill. They simply didn't like him. Shindler was bright enough to realize this, and he knew deep down that his deficiency meant he would never be a good physician. His lack of empathy made it vital that he maintain his intellectual stature, which was the basis of his self-respect. Now, in this whole Douglas business, it had been seriously diminished. He simply had to get it back.

"It may be," he continued, "that the poor girl will step outside the Douglas clinic one day. Presumably the police would have no objection to acting upon the commitment order in that situation."

"Ah," said Professor Hodges.

"And who do you propose funds the twenty-four-hour-a-day surveillance of the Douglas Clinic that would be required to discover her exit? Certainly not the police department, I can tell you that. And certainly not the medical school," said the dean.

There was a silence as everyone contemplated the spending of money . . . and discarded the idea.

"Might she not be 'encouraged' to come out?" said Shindler. "I mean, she must have friends who are worried about her. There must be fellow students who could be persuaded of the truth . . . that she is being taken advantage of by this dangerous and unscrupulous man."

"There was one girl," said Hodges. "I remember her quite well from the time of Tari's original commitment. She seemed to be the best friend. In fact, I think she said she shared an apartment with Tari. She was extremely worried. Yes, she was. And she seemed a sensible girl, both feet on the ground."

Shindler leaned forward.

"If this girl could be talked to, and made to see how it would be in the very best interests of Tari to be handed over to us, then perhaps she could . . . succeed in getting Tari to come out of the clinic and then this girl might alert us. . . ."

"I could certainly speak to this girl," said the dean. "Do we know her name?"

It was one of the many marginally useful skills of Veronica Hodges always to remember names.

"She was called Mary Allard," she said.

"You're asking me to betray Tari," said Mary.

The dean laughed indulgently.

"No, no, my dear. You've got it all upside down. I'm asking you to help your friend. She's ill. She needs your help. Surely you must see that."

"But getting her to come out with me, and then tipping you off so that you can put her in the hospital, would be what a traitor would do. It would be telling lies."

The dean took a deep breath. Moral convictions in the young were so tiresome. Thank God, they grew out of them.

"Mary, let me just ask you this. Do you believe that your friend Tari is the daughter of God, the sister of Jesus, the only begotten daughter of our Lord? Just answer me that, will you?"

There was a pause.

"No," said Mary.

"Exactly," said the dean. "But you must remember that Tari *does* believe that. Deeply. Truly. With every ounce of her strength. Now, that's madness. That's psychosis. If you don't believe she is the daughter of God . . . and you've just admitted that you don't . . . then you have to believe she's psychotic. I mean, you've nearly finished the psychiatry rotation. If you haven't learned that yet, you're not going to make much of a doctor."

"But it's one thing saying she needs help, and another lying to her," said Mary stubbornly.

"It's a means-to-an-end dilemma," said the dean definitely. "Frankly, if she's psychotic, and she is, she needs treatment. The last thing she needs is someone like Douglas feeding into her psychotic delusions. It's the worst thing for her. It might make all the difference to her prognosis. If we let this schizophrenic process take hold, it could destroy Tari forever. I can't let that happen. Can you? Would you want that on your conscience, when there's something you can do about it?"

Mary twisted around in her seat.

"Why can't *you* do something about it? Or the police, someone?"

"Because, my dear, we live in an imperfect political world. Douglas is a powerful man. A lot of people in this town don't want to upset apple carts. I've been as good as told by the police that if they can act quietly, secretly, out of the spotlight, then they will help. But they are not going to stir things up by being confrontational. As long as Tari stays where she is, we can't help her. She's in the clutches of a man who is using her for his own purposes. As we all know, he's got plans to write this book with her . . . full of nonsense, I imagine . . . and I've been told by psychiatrists who know about these things that nothing could be worse for Tari. It would literally be disastrous for her mental health to have her delusions pandered to and strengthened in this way. We've got to shift them with medicine. Then she'll see the light. Then she'll realize that we've been acting in her best interests all along. Believe me, she'll thank you. You'll be acting as a true friend."

"I don't know . . . I mean . . ."

"Are you in contact with her?" said the dean, watching Mary weaken.

"I haven't seen her for two and a half months, but we talk on the telephone about once a week."

"How does she sound?" asked the dean.

It was a question Mary had asked herself endlessly.

"Not crazy," she said. "But not quite normal, either, I guess."

"She's deluded?"

"Yes, she is. But she talks about it in such a natural way."

"What's she doing?"

"Writing, writing all day. She says that a voice speaks to her or dictates to her. Or there's a voice in her head, or something . . . I don't know. I've given up trying to get to the bottom of it. We mostly talk just junk about things at school, and friends, and TV and stuff."

"Will she leave the clinic?"

"She says that Douglas doesn't want her to."

"And you think she won't disobey him?"

Mary thought hard. What should she do? What the hell was the right thing to do? Here she was in the office of the dean of the medical school. He had already explained at great length the views of the professor of medicine and Professor Hodges, the senior psychiatrist in the Florida State Medical College. They were Mary's teachers. She was their student. If they didn't know what they were talking about, then what the hell was Mary doing in their medical school? She was going to be a doctor, a scientist. She'd read the textbooks. What were the odds on Tari being sane when she believed that she was God's daughter? Next to nil. Did Mary really want to be the one that condemned Tari to a life of madness? If there was anything she could do, surely she should do it, up to and including treachery, lies, and betrayal. She was being asked to smuggle Tari out into the night and deliver her to the doctors. She would not be handing her over to enemies. She would be putting her in the hands of healers who only wanted to make her well, who only had Tari's best interests at heart, as Mary did.

"I don't know that I would be able to persuade her to leave the clinic," she said.

"You can't dream up something that she'd really like to do? No birthdays, or parties, or anything like that?" prompted the dean.

Mary thought for a moment. No, none of those.

But there might be a way. There was somebody Tari had talked about a lot, especially recently. There *was* somebody Tari wanted to see.

The name roaming around in Mary's mind like a wolf in the night was Rickey Cage's.

35

THE TELEPHONE blasted in Marcus's ear, yanking him from the deepest sleep. He grabbed at it, to stop it ringing as much as to answer it.

"Marcus, Marcus, my friend."

"Paulo? Paulo!"

"Greetings from Rome, dear friend. I hope I haven't woken you."

Marcus tried to clear the cobwebs from his mind. He flicked on the light and looked at his watch. It was five A.M. His brain was starting to work. This was the call he had been waiting for all these weeks. His heart began to speed.

"No, Paulo, not really. Just dozing."

"I have news for you. Fascinating news."

His friend was excited. He could hear it in between the words. Paulo, the smoothest, suavest monsignor in Rome, and by far the best-informed, was not given to hyperbole. "Fascinating" would be just that.

"What have you got, Paulo?"

"An amazing story . . . and, in the context of your story,

doubly amazing, perhaps miraculous ... perhaps even more than that ..."

"No!"

"Yes. I have had my people on this ever since you contacted me. They were concentrating on the count of Lonza's businesses and his political situations, his big-city activities. Nothing much of interest there. Nothing I didn't know or suspect. But then they started to dig in the personal area. A couple of my Jesuits are just back from Santo Pietro in Northern Italy. It's a tiny village up there, but the count keeps a country place outside the town. It's one of his favorite houses. My people have an extraordinary tale to tell."

"Can you talk about it now?"

"I can give you the bare bones, but I honestly think you should fly out and meet me at the Vatican. On the evidence so far, we have prima facie grounds for a major investigation. I've asked for an audience with the Holy Father. I'm seeing him at noon."

"Serious enough for the pope?"

"Yes. I'd like to be able to tell him that you will be coming to Rome. He will want to hear your end of things, and any hard evidence you have of the miracle. And if you could bring copies of the writing so far ..."

"Paulo, talk to me. Tell me what you've found." Marcus couldn't contain his impatience. Yes, he would fly to Rome. But first he needed to know everything.

"It all started about twenty-three years ago," said Paulo. . . .

The voice was quiet. The writing had ceased to flow. Tari's conscious mind was creeping back. She was wondering what came next. Nothing did. It was the end. She felt it strongly. She sat still in the chair and took a deep breath. Then she read the last sentence.

"In reading this book, you will come to know me. It is your passport to paradise. I love you."

It was over, but Tari did not write "The End." That had not been dictated. *All for Love* was not so much a book as a map for a journey. It did not have a beginning or an end. Instead, it was a circle. The last page led back to the first page. In the traveling and the loving, you reached the destination. A weight was lifted from Tari's shoulders. The vital part of her mission was successfully completed. But there was more, and she shivered in the cool morning as she thought of what must come.

She stood up and walked over to the window. The dawn breeze came in from the east, off the sea. She wanted so badly to get out of the chair. She wanted to walk on that beach. She wanted to run down the street and watch the people, to drink fresh orange juice in the market on Washington, and most of all, she wanted to laugh and be light, and to giggle with Mary . . . and to see Rickey again. That she wanted most of all.

But she remembered Marcus's words.

"Promise me you won't leave the clinic while I'm gone, Tari. Promise me." The look in his eyes had been scary in its intensity as he'd made her promise. "You're only safe while you're in here. Do you understand that?"

"I'm safe everywhere," Tari had answered. "If you believe in me, you know that."

"You were meant to choose to stay here . . . to finish the book."

Marcus had been cunning in his answer. God's purpose was fixed. What would be, would be. And men's and women's "wills" were part of that grand design. But however much decision might be illusion and thought predetermined by a greater power, in the real world one had to go through the motions of "deciding" what to do.

"Yes," said Tari. "I will stay. It's best to have no distractions. But must *you* go? Is it *that* important?"

"Yes, it is. Trust me. We will find out about your mother. Isn't that what you've always wanted?"

It had been what the old Tari had wanted, but there was a sense in which it was merely history now. Soon, she would meet her mother. Soon, she would be one with the past, hers, everyone's, and their futures, too. But Marcus had to go. There was doubt in him. He wanted proof of what she knew, of who she was. It was so hard for him to believe. He and his friend Paulo would perform their ritualistic dance around the facts, laying them out and exposing them in the way that clever people must. They would ask brilliant questions and leave no stone unturned until all the "truths" were in, and still they would wonder and vacillate, because neither had reached perfect faith through perfect love. But it was meant to be. After her, there would be them. They would be the standard-bearers of the love she had brought to the world. They would distribute the book, and in their canonical courts they would sift the evidence of her divinity and their conclusions would make it easier for others to make the leap of blind faith. She would miss him, and his sad eyes, his good heart, his impatience, and the gentle way he loved her.

"I don't want to leave you, Tari. You know that, don't you?"

"I know that. Hurry back."

The loneliness had closed in when he had gone, and she had listened and written with renewed vigor. Now she had finished, while he was still away.

The telephone rang. Great. It would be Marcus or Mary. She wanted to talk to someone.

She picked it up.

"Tari, hello, honey. How are you? How's it going?"

"Mary, great. I'm so glad you called. I was just thinking about you. I'm so relieved. I've finished the book."

"You have? That's wonderful! When do I get to read it? All the newspapers and magazines are full of it. It's going to be a huge success."

"It will bring love to the world."

"Yeah, Tari, and big bucks to you and Douglas."

"It's God's work, Mary."

"You still believe that, I mean, really believe it, Tari?"

"You sound like a doctor, Mary."

Suddenly Tari could sense her friend's anxiety. She could feel the tension on the line. Something was happening. What?

Mary took a deep breath. It seemed to Tari she was making some sort of decision.

"Is Marcus still away?" she asked.

"Yes. Why?"

"Oh, I just thought that maybe if the book was finished we could all go out, go dancing, have a blast. You need one."

"I sort of do. I was thinking about it, too, when you called.

It would be so great to hang out and do the clubs . . . just once more. But I really can't. I promised Marcus. There are reasons why I can't. It would be difficult to explain them to you."

"Oh, come on, Tari. Does God have a rule against fun?"

Tari thought for a second. It so often seemed he did. Maybe that was because "fun" was so seldom what it pretended to be.

"It *would* be fun to go dancing. And have dinner. Is Cassis still hot?"

"Boiling, and Les Bains is finally opening tomorrow night. *Big* party. Should be killer."

"Tomorrow night?" Tari could feel herself weakening. So could Mary. She decided it was time for the trump.

"I saw Rickey last night at his club."

"You *did?* How was he? Is he back with Jodie?" Tari's voice was full of excitement and so suddenly was her body. She had thought about him so often. He had never really gone away. Rickey had bridged the gap between the new Tari and the old. The intensity of the passion they had shared had seared him onto her soul. She was branded by his body. Whether allowed to or not, she would take those memories with her to paradise.

"He was by himself, in the middle of his usual crowd of hangers-on."

"Did you speak to him?"

"Yes." Mary waited, baiting the hook.

"And? Mary!"

"Hey, Tari. What is this? Still interested . . . ?"

"Just tell me what he said, Mary."

"He said he really wanted to see you again, but that you weren't allowed out of your fucking clinic. His word, not mine."

"He did?"

"That's what he said. And then he said some things about Marcus Douglas you probably don't want to hear. Then he said that he'd given up calling you because you never take his calls."

"And what did you say?"

"I said he should give it one more try, because I knew that deep down you were really into him."

"Mary, you didn't. You shouldn't say things like that."

"True, isn't it?"

"It may be a little bit true." Tari laughed. It felt good to laugh.

"Anyway, he said he was going to call you. He's really neat, Tari. Why don't you go out with him one more time, now that the book is finished and Douglas and the thought police are away? We could all go out somewhere . . . you know . . . a real South Beach evening. Remember those?"

Tari remembered them. Bits of them, anyway. It was perfect timing. It jelled completely with her mood. Rickey, again. The touch, the smell, the feel of him. Out there was the world she had retreated from. Out there was music, laughter, sex, and good times.

Tari felt the thrill of excitement . . . and then the feel of something else, too. She would go out with them, for the innocent night on the town. But at the end of it, when dark met dawn and the music began to die, when the party broke up and high spirits collapsed into the jingle-jangle morning . . . Tari knew that Mary was going to betray her.

36

THEY SWUNG over from Collins to Washington, and Tari clung on tight, burying her head in Rickey's back and nuzzling there in the soft leather. He squeezed his shoulder blades together, gripping her face with them in a gesture of affection. Tari was out of the clinic, back in the high life again, and she smiled against the leather as she remembered. This was life with Rickey—bikes and brawls, high times and low times, blacks and whites on the cutting edge of whatever. As if to emphasize it, the bike slowed at the junction of Washington and Espanola and slipped into the street where Dreemz was. They were waiting for him. Maybe ten Harleys were in line abreast, already loaded up with the entourage. They screamed their welcome, and Rickey waved back as he slowed the bike to walking speed and growled past them. Then he U-turned in the narrow roadway, scraping the foot platform against the hot tarmac, sending off a shower of sparks.

"See y'all at Cassis," he hollered, and he roared off down Espanola in the direction he had come.

They peeled off behind him, one by one, an honor guard of bikers for the king and his new queen, and soon the narrow street throbbed with the roar of engines. The passersby stopped to watch the display . . . bright colors in the early evening, flashing chrome, the bare brown legs of the biker girls, the streaming ponytails of the riders. Tari looked back at the procession of Harleys, and excitement exploded inside her. Oh, this was wild! She wanted Washington to last forever, but Cassis, the trendiest restaurant on South Beach, was already coming up. There was a cluster of waiters and valet parkers on the sidewalk. One by one, Rickey in the lead, in what seemed like carefully choreographed synchronization, the bikes were backed into their parking slots.

It was nearly dark, and the sky over Miami was ablaze with the bloodred of the sunset. Inside, the restaurant twinkled in candlelight, as the other diners peered out of the long windows to watch the show. Two waitresses hurried out of the main doors of the restaurant. In their arms they carried a dozen flaming torches. Each waiter took one, and proceeded to form a gauntlet that stretched from the front door of Cassis to the place where Rickey and Tari were dismounting from the bike.

Tari looked at Rickey. "Oh, Rickey," she said.

"Welcome back to my life," he replied, and he swept her up in his arms in front of everyone . . . and he kissed her.

The cheering and the clapping of the crowd, burning torches in the twilight, and the warm envelope of steam heat were the accompaniment to the kiss.

Tari let herself go. It didn't matter that this was public. Nothing mattered, except her suddenly melting body . . . and his. There was desperation in their lips. Their mouths knew this was not for long, and they grabbed hungrily at the moment, greedy for touch and sensation. His body was painted against hers, as rock-solid as the time was fleeting. His arms were tight bands around her, molding her to him. His tongue invaded her with its angry lust. She kissed him back, cruelly. Her mouth was alive with panic because she knew there was an end waiting. Make it last. Thrust it into memory where it could live again. Remember the taste, the wet softness, the feel of this, until bodies were no more and only spirits stalked the ghostly mountains of eternity. She twined her fingers into his hair, and forced his face against hers. He bent her over with his body power, thrusting her backward as he feasted from her mouth.

The audience was silent now, in awe at the passion so violently released. The torches still flickered as they watched. The expressions on the faces of the small crowd were strangely unself-conscious. There was no embarrassment at the public display of affection, because it was so much more than that. It was primeval in its intensity. The longing of a man for a woman, of flesh for flesh, was distilled into its essence before their eyes. It lived there as they loved, magnificent, frightening, burning into the minds of those who watched like the flames of the torches they bore.

She pulled away from him at last and looked up into his face, wet with her wetness, moist with her moisture.

"I love you, Rickey," she said.

"I love you too, girl."

And then they were back. The sensual spell was broken, the wound of longing was partially healed. Once again there was clapping around them, and boisterous shouts. Hand in hand, they ran the gauntlet of flickering flame, and they erupted into the restaurant.

Inside, Cassis was a cavern of magic. The whole room was lit only by candles. Light danced from the ceilings, and flashed in dark corners, while the regulars of SoBe, and the tourists that knew, clapped and cheered as the lovers made their entrance. The rest of the party thronged the long bar, waiting for the host. Rickey and Tari, entourage in tow, headed toward their welcome.

They clustered around, and Rickey introduced Tari to the guests. She was overwhelmed by the throng of party people. She had been alone so long. For an age, she had been shut off from this world of jokes and repartee. Now, she hardly knew how to handle it. She was lost in a maze of clever banter and knowing smiles as she allowed Rickey to lead her through the bronzed bodies and the extra-strength beauty. All the time, she thought of the kiss and what it had meant, and how very much

she had to lose. She squeezed Rickey's hand tight, drawing him
back until she was close to him. She felt good there in the lee
of his island, a ship in safe anchorage in a storm at night. He
turned toward her, sensing her sudden vulnerability.

"Let's go eat," he said. "We're sitting together at dinner.

"Food," he shouted. On cue, everyone converged on the
center table that threaded down the restaurant like a back-
bone.

He drew out her chair for her.

"Hello, honey," said Mary from across the table. She was
already seated.

"Hi, Mary," said Tari.

"We have to thank Mary for this," said Rickey. "She gave me
the courage to try just one more time."

"Mary wants only the best for me," said Tari. She looked
straight into the eyes of her friend.

Mary's blush was instant. It rushed to her cheeks like a stain
of blood.

"Sometimes I think that all my friends want only the worst
for me," said Rickey.

"You should change them," said Mary, glad of the new
subject.

"Nah," said Rickey. "The only thing I care about in a friend
is the length of time I've known them. Only thing you can't
replace. Loyalty is an unexpected bonus."

"Yes," said Tari, "but friends do betray."

"What on earth do you mean?" said Rickey. "Bad-mouth
you? Don't worry about it. Happens all the time."

Mary looked at the tablecloth. For the thousandth time, she
reviewed her conscience. Was this really for the best? Was Tari
really crazy? Did she really need Thorazine and a commitment
order? Yes. Yes. Yes. There was no other possibility. The
professor of medicine, the dean, and Professor Hodges were a
trio Mary simply couldn't ignore. They were dispassionate
scientists who had no motive to do Tari any ill. It was Douglas
who was the evil influence, manipulating Tari's psychosis for
his own ends. Yes, she must go ahead with her plan for the
good of her friend. Tari must be rescued from herself. But,
despite her certainty, Mary couldn't help feeling like a female
Judas. Somewhere out there, in the steamy night, she would be

doing the job of a traitor. And now she sensed that Tari knew.

"It has to happen," said Tari, as if in answer to Mary's thoughts.

"Are you okay?" said Rickey. He leaned toward her. Beneath the table, his foot found hers. Suddenly, she looked pale.

Tari smiled back at him, brightening. "Yes, I'm fine. Just a gloomy moment. All gone now," she said with a laugh.

The place next to Tari was still empty.

"Who's sitting here?" she said, picking up the nameplate.

"Chris Blackwell," said Rickey. "Guy who owns the Marlin. Real neat guy."

"Never been accused of being that before," said the upper-class English voice at his shoulder.

"Hi, Chris," said Rickey, smiling. "Sorry about giving you the bad press. Do you know Tari?"

"Only by reputation. I hear you're about to be a famous authoress."

He shook Tari's hand and sat down. He didn't look or sound like the founder of a major record company. But then old Harrovians specialized in not looking the part.

"You've been reading the papers?" said Tari.

"Well, occasionally, but actually I heard about you from the girl who handles my company's publicity, Susan Magrino. She used to work for a big publisher in New York. She says *All for Love* is going to be the publishing event of next year. Advance orders in excess of a million, a reprint sale to Ballantine for a nonfiction record . . . sounds pretty serious stuff to me."

"It will change the world," said Tari simply.

Across the table, Tari saw Mary's eyes narrow. Next to her, Rickey was suddenly uncomfortable in his seat.

"I felt like that about signing Bob Marley," said Blackwell pleasantly. "Unfortunately, the world was more resistant to being changed than I'd imagined."

"Everyone's ready for love," said Tari. She turned toward Blackwell as she spoke. Her intensity focused in on him.

"Can't argue with that," he said. Now he, too, was uncomfortable. Englishmen were nervous in any discussion about love. And they mistrusted both hyperbole and fanaticism. The fire in Tari's eyes was burning just a little too brightly.

"But hasn't love been around for a while?" said Richard

Pollman. Bronzed and good-looking, the model-agency guru and South Beach night impresario had a sharp mind and tongue.

He leaned back to allow the waiter to serve the vichyssoise.

"Electricity has been around for a while," said Tari. "It's a question of knowing how to use it."

"And your book tells us?" said Richard.

"God tells us, through my book," said Tari.

"You mean your book is the word of God?" said Blackwell, a faint smile playing around his lips.

"Yes," said Tari.

"You're saying," said Richard, who was also a journalist who liked to have his facts straight, "that God told you what to write."

"Yes," said Tari. "The words in my book are the words of God."

"Can I quote you on that?" said Richard.

"Tari doesn't mean it literally," said Mary. "She means that she lives for God, that everything she does is for him, and that he has created all things . . . you know how it is when someone takes religion seriously."

"Sort of like God is responsible for everything," said Rickey.

Together, they were the "protect-Tari-from-ridicule" damage-control team.

"That's not what I mean," said Tari. The table had gone mysteriously quiet. The bush telegraph was signaling a possible drama at the top end of the table. On South Beach, nobody wanted to miss those.

"What I mean," said Tari, "is that God dictated the book to me, and I wrote down his words. I was merely a stenographer. I had no part at all in creating the ideas in the book. It is God's work."

The words dripped like acid into the silence.

"What about Douglas?" said Rickey.

Tari turned to him. "He knows the truth. He lent his name to the book so that people will buy it and read it. He had nothing to do with it. God wrote it."

She sat up straight in her chair. She was apart from them, from their trendiness, their fashion, their beauty, and their success.

The table could feel her separateness. Christy Turlington, the waiflike ice beauty, felt it. Naomi Campbell, exotic and erotic, was in tune with it. Gianni Versace, South Beach's hero, was aware of it. Mickey Rourke, in his surfer shorts, pink baseball cap, and Hawaiian shirt, said a soft "Wow."

"Doesn't that make you rather special?" said Chris Blackwell gently. "I mean, having your own personal hot line to God?"

Somebody down the table couldn't suppress a giggle.

"When we pray, we talk to God," said Tari. "Is it so very odd that he should answer back?"

"There's answering back," said Blackwell, not unkindly, "and there's dictating books. Okay, you heard a voice, but how do you know that it was God's voice? It could have been a creation of your own mind. If I hear a strange voice on the telephone, then all I know for certain is that a voice is speaking to me. I don't know whose voice it is. Even if the stranger tells me his name, I have no way of checking it. He could be an imposter."

"That's because you think all knowledge comes from the senses. Seeing is believing. Touching is your truth. You only believe a voice belongs to someone when you hear it coming out of his mouth, and when you see his lips move. But I'm telling you there is a more fundamental form of knowledge. There is a religious way of knowing. It's called faith. With faith, you can know and be blind. With faith, you can touch yet have no hands. With faith, you need no ears to hear. I have faith in God, my Father, and I know what you do not know. One day you will see by the light of his love. One fine day, through love, you will hear his message. In the pages of my book you will learn the feel of your Lord. Then the ignorance of your 'wisdom' will be washed away like castles in the sand."

The silence was contagious now. It spread down the table of open mouths and stillness. It flowed over the edges of the group to the lesser tables. Farther away, the diners sensed the diminution of sound, and they lowered their own voices as they looked around for its cause.

Richard Pollman dared break it.

"But Tari, if there is a religious way of knowing, how can you test it? If I see a person and I want to test the validity of my eyesight, I can go touch him, and smell him, and listen to him speak. If you know God only through faith, by what process do you test your knowledge? The God I know may not be the God you know. What you experience as God may really be an experience of something entirely different. It may be created in your brain, as Chris says, or by drugs, or fever, or by illness, even . . ."

He dared to touch on what everyone was thinking. Tari was out of the loop. She was either on something, or she was dangerously unbalanced. God was okay up to a point, but there was a line. Tari sounded as though she had stepped over it.

"Oh, the mighty faith you put in your poor senses," said Tari, with a laugh. "Yet look what LSD does to them. Don't you believe your dreams are real when you're asleep? Yet they are full of fake sense experiences. Any philosophy student will tell you that knowledge derived from the senses is deeply suspect. At the end of all knowledge is mystery . . . infinite smallness in subatomic particles, infinite largeness in the vastness of a universe without end. We can't experience the essence of matter with our miserable senses."

She looked down the table to see where her words had gone. They stared back at her, not convinced. This was not normal. That they knew. Something odd was happening. It was a question of the quality of oddness and of the direction from which it was coming. There were Tari's words. And there was Tari . . . message and messenger. The one was indivisible from the other. She was a young girl, a medical student, and she was the lover of Rickey, the movie star. She wasn't famous as they were, but, because of the buzz on her book, she stood at the edges of fame. That was her reputation and her bio, but Tari was more than that. She was her beauty, pure and simple, and her body language, sincere and certain. She was the power in her voice, and her unblinking eyes. She was her charisma, the force field of strange charm that clung to her in a shimmering aura.

Rickey watched her. The script stank. The performance was magnificent. He was proud and ashamed of her at the same time. But through the ambivalence, he wanted her. That only got stronger. The kiss on the sidewalk had fired up the memories, and the sight of her so close had fanned the flames of his desire to a white heat. He couldn't wait to touch her. He couldn't wait for this dinner to be over, and these people to be gone. It had been a crazy idea to even dream of sharing her. She was a girl for heroes, not for the universal soldiers of these meaningless trend wars. But if she'd just shut up for a minute about God. Here he was, beside her, loving her. What the fuck was this other shit going down? He reached for her hand over the top of the table. What he wanted was a private walk on the beach. Now. Ten minutes ago. Really.

It was the moment Jodie chose for her entrance. She had somehow managed a minicommotion at the door of the restaurant. Now, she burst through it. She stood there, looking around for the respect that only her fame and her beauty could provide. Her eyes swiveled around the room to locate the pockets of interest and to amplify them with haughty looks and ice-cold smiles. But her eyes never got much farther than the center table, where the action was. She took it in fast. Rickey was at the top. Tari was by his side. The movers and shakers of SoHo south were scattered about as courtiers to the lovers. Across the crowded room, Rickey could actually see the sudden pain in Jodie's eyes . . . and the shock. Her attenuated band of hangers-on, a couple of male models and a black booker from one of the smaller agencies, clustered at her back. His heart sank. Overhead was the fan. Now the shit had arrived. And it was going to fly.

Jodie's world had stopped. This had been intended as another quiet evening in lotusland, surrounded by losers who would at least pick up on the L.A. names she was knee-deep in. The brace of male models, gym rats with biceps for brains, wanted to be in both music *and* the movies . . . uh . . . uh . . . like . . . you know . . . wouldn't that be cool, man? So, to upgrade their "careers," they fucked the supermodel who had fucked producers in Hollywood they'd actually heard of. Although any form of concrete thought was a problem, now at least they could enjoy celluloid and vinyl dreams. The beefy losers would have done for a normal dinner, but this would not be one of those. Oh, no. Jodie felt the bile rising. Here she was with the B-minus team. There, at the center table, was the A crowd. At the head of it was the guy who'd been hers, the

movie star, the erstwhile open sesame to Jodie's movie future.
Next to him was the jumped-up nobody who'd actually written
some *book* that apparently everyone was going to *buy*. It was
impossibly impossible. A book? With words all strung together
to make sense? Goddamn it, a best-seller and Rickey, too? And
Jodie left behind with the steroid closet queens and their
pinkie dicks, miniminds, and pumped-up ambitions.

She took a step forward into the restaurant. It was time for
psychic blood. Oh, yes, it was. Because she still had some
Polaroids. She had the ones she hadn't given to the dean of the
medical school. She still had the pix of the hot writer in the hot
action. And there, hidden down the table, was the partner in
the body crimes. There was Felicity Business Manager, with her
horn-rimmed spectacles, and doubtless her book beneath the
table. Yes, it was time for all that to come out now. Inquiring
minds had a right to know, in democratic America, just exactly
what their celebrities had been up to. She would be performing
a service in the sacred public interest. The mighty media gods
must be appeased. The truth would set Jodie free.

She marched up to the table. A couple of top tablers waved
"Hi" at her. She stood between and behind Rickey and Tari.

"Hi, Jodie," said Rickey.

"Hi, Rickey," said Jodie.

Tari turned around.

The table fell silent once more. Practice was making perfect.

"Oh, lord!" said Richard Pollman.

"Hello, Tari," said Jodie.

"Hi, Jodie," said Tari.

Jodie primed herself like a pump. Her magnificent fake
breasts ballooned out like the chest of a cock robin on a cold
morning. The only question was where to start.

"Been on any porno shoots recently?" said Jodie in a voice
that echoed around Cassis.

Porno shoots! *Porno* shoots? Nobody had misheard.

"Fuck off, Jodie," said Rickey, standing up. His face darkened with instant rage.

"But Tari the Good hasn't answered my question," said
Jodie. "I know she likes to make it with chicks while you take
the pictures. I've seen the results. Not bad for an amateur. I

must show you the Polaroids I took, Tari. If publishing doesn't pay off big, you could always try skin flicks. I showed them to the dean of your medical school. I think he thought you were sick. No way, I said. Just a good, strong sexual appetite and a penchant for exhibitionism."

Jodie turned down the table.

"And look, there's Felicity, your film fun lover. What's she doing tucked away down there? Yesterday's news, is she, Tari? Oh, the fickleness of lesbian love. One minute a hot, tasty morsel, the next a cold, greasy leftover on the side of the plate. Isn't life hard, folks, on the Rickey Cage mystery tour to a broken heart?"

Rickey took a step toward her. His face was black with fury. But Tari put up a hand, holding him back.

She looked straight at Jodie.

"I love you," she said.

"What?" said Jodie. Her face was a mask of surprise.

"I love you. God loves you. I love you."

Tari looked up at Jodie. Her expression said she meant it.

"What the fuck do you mean, you love me?"

Jodie was deeply suspicious. She suspected a flanking movement. It was a ploy. The cunning bitch had some plan. It wouldn't be allowed to succeed.

Tari said nothing. Her words hung in the air. They were over, but they hadn't gone away.

Tari was calm. In the middle of the incredible and unexpected verbal assault, she was at peace. On paper, she was in trouble. Somehow Jodie had got into Rickey's studio and photographed the painting. She had shown the pictures to the dean. Now she had told South Beach about Tari's lapse from grace, and tomorrow New York would know. The publishers would know. The world would know. But Tari didn't care, because God was in control, and there was nothing left in her mind but love. Love could make wrong right and the bad good. It could cancel evil and dissolve wickedness, and the more inappropriate its presence, the greater was its power. The world paid lip service to the truth of this . . . it was the other cheek of the Bible, God's famous love for the sinner, it was the beauty of forgiveness.

Right now, she loved Jodie Summerfield. It was as genuine and as complete a love as she had ever known. She looked at the wounded model, her values upside down in the muck of her Hollywood longings, and she saw only the beauty of her immortal soul. God loved this L.A. woman. He had made her in his image, and she had chosen to reject him as he had made her free to do so. Yet there was no millisecond of her tragic life when Jodie could not choose to wipe her slate clean of horror. A simple prayer, a single act of faith, and she would be full of the good God she had so mistakenly shut out. At this moment there was no decent desire in Jodie. Today, tomorrow, and forever, there could be nothing else. It was as easy as opening a door. It was as difficult and as straightforward as finding the humility to return to love.

"Is it so hard to understand that God's creatures and creations can learn to love one another as he loves us?"

Tari spoke the words into a silence so complete that you could all but hear it. Even the waiters seemed frozen in midtask. The telephone didn't ring. The muted music seemed to have lost its sound. People didn't just not speak. They didn't move, either. Their expressions were fixed in fascination on their faces. Mouths lolled open. Food hovered on forks before faces that simply weren't ready to accept it.

And then there was the most extraordinary sound. It was the sound of sobbing. Jodie Summerfield, way too tough for tears, was weeping. One by one, in shock, the diners turned to look at her.

Jodie, too, had amazed herself. Teflon was bubble gum compared to the stuff her heart was made of. The nearest she came to a fine feeling was her "Have a nice day," which, for sincerity, matched a computerized voice recording. Jodie Summerfield rasped through her days on a cloud of external-ized loathing and internalized self-hatred, and she survived her nights on Halcion and disposable lovers. Now, for the very first time, somebody had told her that she loved her in a way that left no doubt at all that she meant it. Of course, her father had said he'd loved her when he'd screwed her as a child. And her mother had said it, when she'd telephoned after a silence of twenty years to ask for a handout on the day that Jodie landed her first big shoot for *Vogue*. Then there had been directors in Hollywood who'd said it during the preclimactic part of the head she'd been giving them, but it hadn't sounded for real. Nor had it been the genuine article when the toy boys had got lucky with her American Express Platinum Card, nor when the obsessed photographer's assistant from Omaha had discovered her unlisted telephone number. But now, it had happened. She had hit out at the nobody who had latched onto Rickey, and the girl had turned around and told her that she loved her. It wasn't just her words. It was the context, the way in which they were spoken. There was no motive for Tari whoever-she-was to love Jodie Summerfield. In fact, there was the best reason in the world for her to loathe her . . . rivalry. It made it all the more poignant.

At this expression of love, Jodie's loveless life flashed before her eyes as it was supposed to when you were drowning. She saw everything crystal clear . . . the hatred, the cruelty of her upbringing, the warped values, the brittle, useless "strength" that had flowed from the trial by emotional fire. She had migrated first to Hollywood, the only place on earth where emotional deprivation could be turned into the "success" of fame and fortune, and now, here on South Beach, she was confronted by an amazing revelation. She, Jodie Summerfield, proud possessor of the body that an angel would weep for, was in fact nothing more than a twisted cripple. Her sobs deepened. Her breasts heaved with grief. She bowed her head as the diners looked on in horror, and the tears poured down her haughty cheeks. Nobody comforted her. Nobody knew about the dreadful pain inside the high-gloss exterior.

But Tari knew. She stood up and took the sobbing supermodel in her arms and she cradled her head against her shoulder. She wiped the tears from her cheeks with her fingers.

"Are you all right, Jodie?" Tari whispered.

"Yes, I'm all right," Jodie mumbled through the sobs. "How silly. How silly."

"You're not silly, Jodie. You're magnificent. You're strong and you're wonderful, and you will live to see the face of God."

Tari felt the tingling power as she spoke. This girl in her

arms would be converted. She knew it as she had known that
the doctor would see. She would be converted to love, to being
and becoming, and she would never again be lonely and lost in
the middle of plenty's land.

Jodie looked up at her. "You mean it, don't you? You really
mean it."

"Yes, I mean it," said Tari quietly.

"But it's more than that, isn't it?" said Jodie, the tears still
rolling down her cheeks. "I mean, you can make it happen."

"*You* can make it happen, Jodie. You just have to ask God.
You just have to let him in."

"No," said Jodie. "It's you. *You* can make it happen."

Rickey's hand was on Tari's arm. "It's enough," he said.
"That's enough. Come on, we're outta here."

He disentangled Tari from Jodie's embrace, and he led her
away from the table and out of the restaurant.

37

MARY FOLLOWED them. The hot night air filled her face as she stood on the sidewalk. They were heading for Ocean Drive. After that, she was pretty sure they would go to the beach. But she couldn't be certain, and certain was what she needed to be. Damn! She hadn't counted on Rickey walking out of his own party and taking Tari with him. She looked down the side street. The van was parked maybe a hundred yards away, discreet and quiet in a dark corner. Inside, they would be waiting, the white-coated snatch squad who would take Tari away from the world and make her different.

Mary took a deep breath. The dinner party hadn't solved her dilemma. Tari had produced more than enough evidence of psychosis, but then she had seemed totally sane, too. If you slipped on the tinted spectacles of religion, you saw a saint. With the horn-rimmed magnifying glasses of science, here was a psychotic. It simply depended on your point of view. Her breath shuddered out through clenched teeth. It was academic now. The die was cast. There could be no turning back from this. The wheels had been set in motion. As Tari herself had said, what must be must be.

Mary made the decision. She turned left down the side street and headed toward the van. When she reached it, she knocked on the back door.

"Who is it?" asked the muffled voice from inside.

"It's Mary."

The door opened. Dr. Sugarman's head poked out.

"What's happening?" he said. "Dinner can't be over yet."

"They've left the restaurant. They're headed for Ocean Drive. I think they're going to the beach."

"Shit!" said Sugarman.

The door opened wide. Mary could see inside the van. Dr. Sugarman was flanked by two large male nurses, both black and muscular. A police sergeant in full uniform made up the foursome.

"As long as she's on public property, I have no problem," said the cop. "If they go into some private club, we're in trouble."

"If we lose them, we're in trouble," rasped Sugarman. "Listen, Mary, you go try and find them, okay? Don't let them see you. We'll bring the van to one of the side streets off Ocean Drive. Keep an eye out for us, and one eye on them, okay? God, if she gets back to the clinic, this whole thing will be a disaster."

"She won't go back yet," said Mary. "They've got a few things to discuss."

Mary turned away and hurried back in the direction from which she had come. Behind her, the van crept away from the curb. She felt like a conspirator. She should have a black cloak and a dagger in her belt, some stiletto that she could plunge into the back of her best friend. But the doubt was in the background now. Events were moving too fast. There was the feel of destiny in the air. *Que sera, sera.*

She walked fast past the meandering people. On Ocean Drive, she crossed the road and peered into the flickering shadows of Lummus Park, searching for Rickey and Tari. Part of her wanted to find them. Part of her didn't. If she lost them now, she would have tried and failed. Her conscience would be clear ... or would it? Tari needed treatment. She was the friend in need who needed the caring friend. It was the ultimate test of friendship to risk a friend's wrath in order to do her good. Bullshit! Tari was close to God, some latter-day saint, perhaps. Mary, in contrast, was the blind hypocrite. She had sided with the forces of mediocrity and reaction to silence a voice that embarrassed the status quo and dared to be different. She was condemning Tari to the chemical crucifix, because she, Mary, was too small to see greatness ... or too mean of spirit not to be jealous of it.

Mary's heart hammered in her chest as she confronted her demons. Still, her eyes searched the shadows of the park.

There! There they were. Rickey and Tari were sitting on a bench at the edge of the sand, deep in conversation.

Mary turned around. The ambulance crept along the boulevard.

It was decision time.

"I'm sorry," said Tari. "I spoiled your party. I couldn't help it. But I'm sorry anyway."

"Screw the party. Who cares about parties anymore? I'm just worried about you."

"Don't," said Tari.

She put her hand on his, touching him tenderly. She smiled into his eyes.

"I mean, all that business ..."

Tari put her finger to his lips, as if to close them, quieting him.

"Rickey," she said, "strange things are going to happen, things that you won't understand, perhaps for a very long time. But one day you will understand them. I love you, Rickey. Don't ever forget that."

"Tari, do you know how odd you sound? It's like you're talking about endings, when it's just the beginning for us. I blew it for a while, but we're back. It's gonna be different. What's all this 'strange things' shit?" He held her hand as he spoke, genuinely bemused, genuinely worried and yet pleased to have her alone, pleased once again to own her.

Tari looked over her shoulder to the neon brilliance of

Ocean Drive. Sometime soon, they would come for her. She
felt the fear.

She turned back to Rickey.

"It will be hard for you to find the faith," she said. "But you
will. I promise. Perhaps even with Jodie, after I am gone."

Rickey threw back his head in exasperation.

"There you go again, Tari. What the hell do you mean? . . .
'after I'm gone.' Where are you going? Are you telling me
there's nothing between us anymore? Is that it?"

"No, that's very far from it. I love you, Rickey."

"Then fucking marry me," he said. His voice broke as he
spoke. The words burst from him. His hand tightened around
hers. He stared into her eyes. There were tears in his.

Her eyes widened.

"Marry you?" she said.

"Yes, marry me," he said.

She hadn't been ready for that. The words exploded like a
bomb in her soul. Never for one moment had she dreamed of
it. Her surprise was total, and it had scrambled her mind.

"I . . . I . . . oh, Rickey, marry you!"

He leaned toward her, following his words, backing them up
with the burning intensity of his gaze. Now he knew what he
wanted. He wanted marriage, children, commitment, all the
things he'd hated and despised for as long as he could
remember. He was Rickey Cage, free as the road was long, his
hair streaming in the wild wind, rich and famous and with the
world at his feet. But now he wanted to be chained to this
perfect girl forever. He wanted to wake with her in the
mornings, and sleep with her through the long nights. He
wanted to watch the wonder of life bursting from her body and
to see their children grow and their household prosper until
the morning was noon and the noon evening, and it was time
at last to part in death. He wanted to fight her battles and win
her respect and admiration. He wanted to love her and shield
her from the hardships of life. He wanted to fill her table, and
calm her heart until there was no more pain, nor doubt, only
security, and happiness, and the bliss of togetherness.

And a part of her wanted it. Her body longed for him. She
wanted desperately to grow his child inside her. She wanted it,

like the woman she was . . . marriage to a hero, a wild, strong man she could tame in love, a father to her son, a husband, a champion to protect her. Tears filled her eyes.

"Oh, Rickey, I can't marry you. But what a wonderful thing to ask of me."

He looked stricken by her refusal, and she wanted to try to explain the inexplicable. Then, at that moment, she felt the chill. Dread touched her shoulder. It was near. It was now.

Tari stiffened. "Rickey, kiss me. Hold me," she said.

He took her in his arms and held her tight as if he would never let go. His cheek was on hers, rough and unshaven, and he turned up his face, burying it in her hair. She knew he was crying.

"Oh, Rickey," she whispered, and her own tears came, flowing free, here at the end of freedom. She wrapped her arms tight around his strong shoulders and she prayed with all her heart for the strength she would need.

The voice came creeping out from the shadows.

"Tari?"

It was Mary, and she wasn't alone.

They stood around her in the gloom, the big men in their white coats and the policeman and the doctor.

"Yes, Mary," said Tari. "You've brought them for me?"

Rickey unraveled from her arms.

"What is this . . . ?" he said, peering out through the film of tears in his eyes.

"Are you Tarleton Jones?" said the policeman, stepping forward. "I have here a commitment order, signed by two authorized physicians, to deliver you to the Robert E. Lee Memorial Hospital for admission and treatment," he said.

"I'm sorry," said Mary, her voice breaking with the strain.

"She's not going anywhere . . ." said Rickey, jumping up.

The policeman drew his gun.

"Don't do a thing," he said.

"I'll go with you," said Tari. "Rickey," she said, "it has to be like this. Please trust me. Let them do what they have to do. Don't fight them."

He stood there at gunpoint, his fists clenching and un-clenching by his sides. His face was a mask of incomprehension and impotency. There were the tracks of tears on his cheeks. He looked at Tari, at the policeman, at the doctor, at the nurses, as if they had turned his whole world upside down.

"What's *happening*?" he shouted, his voice cracking with frustration.

"Ms. Jones is not well. She has paranoid schizophrenia and two authorized physicians have certified that she is—" said Dr. Sugarman.

"Be quiet," said Tari. There was absolute authority in her voice. The doctor stopped in midsentence.

"I want to say good-bye," said Tari.

She went to him. Nobody lifted a finger to stop her. She stood against him, her breasts on his chest, and she put her arms around his waist and she looked up into his eyes.

"Be strong, Rickey," she said. "This will pass. Do nothing until I am gone. Trust me, and always love me. You will, won't you?"

He reached up to touch her cheek. "Oh, Tari, Tari, I don't understand any of this . . . I love you. I've never loved anyone before. Don't leave me."

"I'll never leave you," she said. "I'll always be with you. At every moment. In the quiet, in the storm, I'll be close to you. When you sleep, when you wake, and when you love, I'll live in your heart. When you hear the wind in the trees and see the sunlight on the water, please believe it will be me."

She stood up on tiptoe and she kissed him, and then she turned around to face those she would allow to torture her.

38

SHE LOOKED back at him, her face screwed up with a childlike fear. Rickey stood there. The memory of her lips was on his. A sudden breeze picked up from the sea. It rustled the palm fronds above his head, and the echo of her words lingered . . . "please believe it will be me."

On automatic pilot, he began to walk, not toward Tari, but away to the left, on a divergent path from hers. His pace quickened with his pulse. His legs speeded with his heart. It was coming together. In the aftershock of Tari's abduction, he was beginning to think. He broke into a jog as the fury built. Then he was running, fast, now faster, as the plan formed and the rage grew. They were taking Tari away from him, the girl he loved, the only one he had ever loved. They. Them. All the men, through all the years. The men—the rivals with their guns, their lip, and their attitude; with their badges, their uniforms, and their authority—were daring to take away the girl he had asked to marry him. He sprang like a panther through the strollers of Lummus Park. He burst onto the neon strip of Ocean Drive and his eyes were wide with the adrenaline rush. He could feel the power in his muscles. There was a delicious tightness, the tension before the fight. He sucked the warm, wet air into his lungs and he let it out in a growl of fearsome purpose. They would have a car, or an ambulance, to take her to the hospital. It would be parked in one of the side streets off Ocean Drive . . . the one toward which they were heading now. They would need time to load Tari aboard. There would be no rush. They would be thinking that the hard part was over.

His bike ruled the curbside. Neon caught its chrome. Light strobed from the sixteen coats of its gleaming paint. It was surrounded by a small group of envious admirers. Rickey pushed through them. He swung his leg over the saddle. He was hardly aware of the murmurs of recognition, the couple of compliments, but he heard the howl as the twelve hundred horses of the Harley brayed their response. He thrust back the throttle. As the sound of the exhaust cracked out its threat, he kicked down on the gear. The bike sailed into the road, big, shining, and snarling its menace.

He cruised to the top of the street, not hurrying. He leaned into the right-hand turn, doubling back toward the parallel street where they would be. At the end of it, he stopped. He took the middle of the road. It was his. He owned it. He stood there holding the bridge. They would have to pass him, but they would never pass while he lived on this earth. The street was empty, but it was not long. At the other end he could see the unmarked van that now held Tari. He twisted the throttle, gunning the engine, and the throaty roar was the threat they should fear. Like a horse, anxious for the race, he allowed the mighty bike to inch forward in the road. Then he stopped again, and the finger of the headlight probed the point where they would come to him. He heard the van's engine start. He saw the blurred face of its driver. Its lights flicked on. Its indicator blinked. Then, it slipped away from the curb and crept down the road toward him.

Tari wept gently. In the back of the van, sandwiched between two male nurses, her dreadful ordeal was just beginning. Any minute now, someone would break open the vial of Thorazine.

Then her mind would be captured and she would no longer be able to trust her thoughts and plan her deeds. The bending and twisting of a body in physical torture was nothing compared to what she would have to endure now. With drugs they would rape her essence. They would take away "her" in a murderous assault on her soul that only God in heaven could forgive. So she sat very still and tried to sob silently so that she could be Tari just a little while longer.

What did she feel, here, so near the ending she had chosen? Frightened? Yes. And sure that she had done the thing she must do . . . ? No. No! She didn't feel sure. What was it all about? What was this craziness? Reality had been the touch of Rickey's lips on hers. Realness was his proposal of marriage. Truth was the hardness of his body, and the passion he could create in her. Lust and the love of a man were the things she felt sure about in the first long minutes of her captivity. And the extraordinary thing was that they dwarfed her love of God, and of martyrdom, and of saintliness, and they rendered irrelevant the love she had sworn to bring to the world.

Tari took a deep breath. No! She was being tempted. The Devil was at work, as he would be. There was a precedent for this. Part of her triumph would be the renunciation of the flesh with all its hollow pleasures and cunning joy. But her intellect did not comfort her. Her feelings were what mattered. She wanted to live. She didn't want to be sacrificed. She wanted to be human, not divine. She wanted to swap the eternal bliss of paradise for Rickey and marriage, and babies and the future here on earth. That was what she wanted. Shit, she wanted to be *free*.

She looked at them. They watched her. The first sign of resistance, the first move of a muscle to escape them, and they would be all over her. There was a straitjacket in the van. She could see it hanging on a hook at the back. Dr. Sugarman's bag would be full to the brim with quieters, and his itchy little fingers would be longing to use them. Despair filled her mind. This was her doing. She had known what would happen, and she had permitted it. She was acting the part of the scripted play of divine passion, and now in the final act she wanted the plot changed. But where were the new lines? What could possibly stop what she had started? Not her. Not God. Then who?

Helplessness closed in on her. Doubt welled up in her heart. Could these people around her be right after all? Had her divine imaginings been nothing more than the product of biochemical imbalances in her brain? Now, as she felt certainty fade in the hour of trial, she began at last to wonder about the possibility of that. She bowed her head into her hands, as if by doing so, she could make her thoughts more secret.

"Are you all right, Tari?" asked Dr. Sugarman briskly.

"Yes," she murmured, not looking up. But she was not all right. She was very far from all right, and was racking her brains to think of a way to get the hell out of there. Thoughts heaved in her head. They rolled this way and that, but through the chaos a blinding light was beginning to shine. It was a turning point. Now, at last, she knew what she wanted, at the very moment it was too late. Suddenly, her frustration exploded. She threw back her head, and she opened her mouth, and she screamed at the top of her voice . . .

"Rickey, help me . . . !"

Rickey laughed in the neon glow. Nothing mattered now. His slippery flesh might ooze through the twisted metal. His spirit might fly from a blood-soaked sidewalk. But the possibility of death, destruction, and disfigurement was merely a comic sideshow to the purpose that throbbed within him. He racked open the throttle and the bike surged forward. Like an arrow from a bow, the Harley flew toward the hood of the van, a blur of crimson chaos and crystal chrome. The driver of the van could not go forward, could not go back, and stopping would not save him. In the milliseconds left, he tried to compute the alternatives. There was no room to the right, none to the left, and in the middle was a superbike flying toward his heart.

Rickey saw the eyes of the driver widen in terror. He steeled himself for the shock. He opened his mouth wide and he screamed at the top of his voice . . . "Tariiiiiii. . . ."

The driver's face, feet from Rickey's, was whiter than the white coat he wore, and his mouth was open in a soundless shriek of fear. His right hand darted downward, and the van's headlights veered to the right as Rickey wrenched at the handlebars and stamped on the brakes. The crash of metal and breaking glass melded with the smell of burning rubber as the Harley's tires churned the asphalt. The right exhaust pipe gripped the rough road, sending a shower of sparks into the night. He careened past the van as it piled into a parked car, and his shoulder slid along its panels as Rickey and death all but touched. Then he was behind it, crossways to the road, and the protesting engine of the Harley stalled as the stillness descended. Briefly, before the yells of the passersby could take up the story, there was silence.

Everything, everyone had stopped except Rickey. He was action man in a paralyzed world. He switched on the stalled Harley, kicked out its stand, and in an instant he was off it, and at the back of the van. He gripped the handle of the door, praying that it wasn't locked. He pulled it open. A pile of bodies writhed on the floor. Dr. Sugarman, his glasses broken, was trying to sit up. Tari, dazed, lay on the floor, her back against the side wall of the van.

"Tari!" said Rickey. His voice was sharp as a pick as he fought to get through to her. She hadn't wanted to be rescued, and there was no time for a debate. He had to make her obey him through the sheer force of his will. He jumped into the van. One of the male nurses, the biggest one, was uncoiling himself from the floor. "Quick, Tari! Get onto the bike. For God's sake, *do* it." Rickey shouted his command. He reached down to help her, and she came up with his hand, a disorganized smile across her face.

"Rickey," she said, in shock, "there's been . . . an accident."

He scooped her up, half-carrying her, and he lowered her down onto the road.

"Are you all right?" There was no blood. She could stand. But she was out of it. So, thank God, were the opposition. But they were coming back together. There was zero time. The cop wasn't there. That was something. No guns. Obviously, the guy had felt his job was over with Tari's apprehension.

"Yes, I think . . . so . . . ." said Tari. She staggered against him. He sat her on the bike and jumped on himself. "Hold on tight, Tari. Don't let go."

"Where are we going, Rickey?" She was bemused. It was all happening too fast for her. And for him.

The male nurse was standing in the back of the van six feet from the bike. "Stop them!" yelled the shaky voice of Dr. Sugarman. The huge white-coated man hurled himself into space, landing on his knees next to the back wheel of the bike. He recovered quickly and reached out. One of his hands hooked into the spokes of the Harley's back wheel. The other curled around Tari's ankle. Rickey turned around to the danger. He threw all his weight to the left and heaved the handlebars to the right as he let out the clutch. The bike shook as the power was unleashed and the rear wheel slid in a slalom skid toward the white-coated man who gripped it. His fingers disappeared in the spokes of the spinning wheel like soft frankfurters into a blender. At the same time, the burning chrome exhaust that could cook eggs slammed against his face, searing a brand mark that would last a lifetime. Letting go of Tari's leg was the very least he could do in the circumstances.

"He's hurt," yelled Tari as they roared down the street.

"The fuck he is," yelled Rickey.

He stopped at the intersection with Ocean Drive and looked back. The other nurse was peeling his colleague off the sidewalk. The little doctor was running around barking orders. But, in the flurry of activity, only one thing mattered. The van was backing up, untwining itself from the car it had hit. It was still a runner. Shit! It wasn't over. In seconds, they would be coming after him.

Rickey thought fast. Losing a van on a bike was no big deal. But they might manage to stay close enough to see where he was going ... and he was going to the boat. It took long minutes to get that untied, fired up, and away from the dock. That would be the window of danger. Every second of headway would count between now and then.

He screeched into the jammed traffic of Ocean Drive. The high-priced cars fled from him, a pathway opening like the Red Sea for his exodus. He didn't just use the road. Round the valet-parker stations of the restaurants where the cars were thickest, he took to the sidewalks. Rollerblading models dipped delicately into doorways to avoid him. The odd skateboard time-warper cruised out of reach. And everywhere the Euros, the seen-it-all regulars of South Beach, and the tourists jeered, cheered, or tried to take photographs as the crimson dream machine roared on.

"Where are we going?" yelled Tari.

"Far away," yelled Rickey.

The wall of traffic ahead looked impenetrable. The sidewalk, solid with pretty party people, was as bad. Rickey heaved the bars to the left, and took the concrete walkway through Lummus Park. It was as if a real-life locomotive had decided to try the toy railway. He weaved along its convoluted course as little old ladies cursed and nocturnal strollers took evasive action. Then he was at Fifth, the road that led to the marina. He looked back. He could see the van stuck in traffic. That meant they could see him. Shit! He opened up the Harley as he made the turn on Fifth. Tari's arms were tight around his waist, her head buried in the small of his back. Getting to the dock before the van would be no problem. The difficult part would be to put to sea before the white coats swarmed all over his express cruiser. If he could achieve that, all their problems would be over. Out there was the Caribbean. He had a full tank of gas on the boat and a pocketful of credit cards. In a couple of hours he could be in the Bahamas, lost in the islands of the Gulf Stream in a sea full of fish on a boat with the girl he loved. Nobody would find them out there. Nobody would even bother to try. Committal documents didn't cut it for extradition warrants. The open ocean was where the real safety lay . . . *after* the moment of greatest danger.

He went flat out on Fifth. The road was sucked under the wheels. The hot breeze howled in their faces, threatening to pluck them from their seats. He hardly slowed for the turn into the marina parking lot. The tires screamed on the road as the bike half-skidded, half-slid into the turn. He straightened it out and aimed the Harley at the entrance to D dock. They had lift-off as the bike hit a parking block, but it crashed down again and screeched to a stop at the dock's entrance. The bad news was that the van had seen them take the marina turn. A white arm waved excitedly from the passenger window. It would be close. Perhaps too close.

Rickey eased the bike onto the pier and roared toward his boat. Five black ropes attached it to the dock and the wooden pilings. The engines had to be started. Damn it, there just wasn't going to be enough time. He jumped off the bike, pulling Tari with him. They half-fell into the boat. The van was pulling into the parking lot, its horn blaring. Rickey pulled open the radio compartment where he kept the engine keys, and the key to the main cabin.

He opened the door to the cabin and thrust Tari inside. "Lock it from the inside," he shouted. "Don't open it to anyone but me."

He jammed one key into the port engine, and another into the starboard. He thrust forward on the throttle levers, priming the engine with gas. Please God, let it start! Usually, he would have run the blower for five minutes to get rid of engine fumes below decks. If you didn't do that, gas boats could explode. His didn't. The port Mercruiser coughed into life. The starboard followed it, and the twin three-fifties roared together in the quiet of the marina. The ropes still had to be cast off. They were the only barrier remaining between the boat and the open sea.

The van had stopped at the water's edge. White-coated men were flowing out of it. Already one of them was running onto the pier. Rickey lifted up the driver's seat. From the storage space beneath, he pulled a knife that would have drawn a gasp of admiration from Crocodile Dundee. Rickey kept it sharp enough to shave with. He ran along the companionway to the forward ropes. With a single swipe of the razor blade, they were free. He caught the spring line on the way back. That left the two crossed lines at the stern. The huge man was nearly there. Rickey slashed at the remaining ropes. The boat was free now, but it was swimming in a mess of severed lines. Any one of them could foul the propellers when he thrust the engine into gear. This wouldn't be over until way after they dredged up the fat lady to sing. The man was there now, big and brutal in his white coat. He was gauging the distance of the jump that would put him aboard. Rickey looked to the left. The others were nearly there. What should he do? Throttle up and get the hell out of there? Or fight off the boarders from the stern? If he did the first, then he might get away from the dock, but with a crew of enemy in the back of his boat. If the latter, he might be overwhelmed and everything would end there and then.

He ran to the wheel, jammed the boat into gear, and hit the throttle. The boat surged forward in the slip. At the same time, the white-coated man jumped. He landed on the transom swim platform, steadied himself, and began to climb on board. At the wheel, Rickey tightened his grip on the knife. The boat was away from the pier now, but there was a boarder to repel. Rickey's knuckles whitened around the knife that was so sharp it could separate a tongue from its spit. He would slit him from the nape of his neck to his nuts. But there wasn't the luxury of time. The boat was out of control in the narrow marina. Sailboats and speedboats were everywhere. He pulled down on the wheel with his left hand and threw the port engine into reverse, grinding gears as the engine screamed in protest. The man on the stern all but lost his balance as the boat changed course. Rickey seized the moment. He scooped up the boat hook, took two steps back from the wheel, and swung it in a lazy arc, shoulder height, at the uninvited guest. The end of the hook caught the man a glancing blow on the shoulder. It was more than enough to destroy what was left of his balance. He went sideways into the aquamarine water, and Rickey didn't wait to see him surface. He spun the wheel, avoiding several collisions, and thrust toward the harbor entrance. Now he made the left turn into Government Cut, past the dredging boat and an outbound tanker. He turned up the revolutions to max and the boat shuddered as it powered toward forty knots. He hit the buttons on the Loran. The course to Bimini was in storage memory. At present speed, and from this location, the display said they would be in the Bahamas in less than two hours. They had escaped.

39

RICKEY DIDN'T relax. He wanted three miles between him and America. He wanted out of territorial waters. In the time available it would have taken a miracle to alert a Coast Guard chopper, and longer to get a patrol boat to intercept them. Anyway, it was hardly a Coast Guard problem. But still, he wanted to be international. The Gulf Stream wide would be safety.

He flicked on the all-weather radio operating out of Coral Gables. Thank God! Seas were forecast at two to three feet, with the winds out of the southeast. There was zero tropical storm activity from Jupiter to the Tortugas and out to the Bahama Bank. His boat could handle three times that and still come up smiling. And now Rickey smiled. His smile widened, opening up the cracks and crevices of his handsome but battered face. Yeah! He'd done it. He'd rescued her ... on a crimson Harley rather than a white charger, and now he was bearing her away to an island paradise on a sleek white boat rather than a bejeweled carriage. He laughed into the salt-sprayed wind. No fairy tale yet had dared to give the prince's coach the seven hundred horses that he had running beneath the deck!

The knocking on the cabin door cut into his thoughts.

"It's cool, Tari," he yelled. "You can come on out."

The door slid back and Tari was framed in the entrance, hanging on to keep her balance on the heaving boat. She looked around at the open sea and the skyscrapers of Miami over the stern.

"We're outta there," yelled Rickey into the headwind.

She could hardly hear him, but his smile did the talking.

She stepped up onto the deck and edged in close to him at the wheel.

"I wanted you to rescue me," she said. "I called out to you, and you were there for me." He pulled her up onto the seat beside him, and put his arm around her, squeezing tight.

"I'm going to look after you from now on, Tari. Do you hear me? I look after you. Okay?"

She nodded and leaned her head against his shoulder. She wanted that. So much had happened, and she could understand so little of it. She was overwhelmed by events, and feelings, and strange imaginings. But she did know she was starting to love this man, and now he had rescued her. It felt so good to let go. It was wonderful to have Rickey in control.

"What happened?" she said.

"It's over," he said dismissively. "They wanted the wrong thing. I wanted the right thing. And they got fucked."

"But how did the van crash? How come you were right behind it?"

"How come I'm in love with you?" he said. He shut her mouth with his, covering it like a silk sheet. His warm breath fanned her upturned face as he leaned into the kiss. Tari felt the delicious letting go. She melted from her outside in, until the core of her was touched with a physical feeling she hardly dared to remember. This was body business, far from intellect and all the fuzzy business of faith, instinct, and convoluted thought. Her man was in her arms. She was alone with him at the edge of a great adventure on a wide, blue sea. He had rescued her from a terrible ordeal by drugs at the hands of a secular inquisition that could never understand her. Now he was kissing her . . . this man who an hour before had asked her to marry him. Was there anything else that could matter? Now, or ever? Her tongue, as it crept into his mouth, didn't think so.

She climbed up his body and kicked her leg over his as she clung to him in the kiss. Then she was straddling him, her skirt rucking up to midthigh, her body braced against the wheel of the boat. Her knees were level with his shoulders. Her arms were tight around his neck. The vibrations of the boat's engines, still at maximum thrust, throbbed against her back. Tari's mouth was wet with lust . . . slippery and greedy for much more than this mere bliss.

She backed away from him, her eyes hooded with desire.

"Can you see to steer?" she whispered.

"I can't think to steer," he said, laughing.

"We should get there . . ." The "first" hung seductively in the air. "But where are we going?" Tari was suddenly aware of the speed of events. How could things move this fast? Minutes ago she had been heading for the psycho ward, now she was halfway to nowhere.

"We make it up as we go along. The Bahamas, basically, or we could head west to the Dry Tortugas. We'll have to stop for fuel on Bimini, then we could hit Eleuthera, then way out to the Abacos, and the Exumas."

"Don't we need passports? I forgot to bring mine." Tari laughed at the ridiculousness of the idea.

"I keep mine on the boat. Anyway, these are the islands. They'd sell three hundred gallons of fuel to Hannibal Lecter with no questions asked. We'll anchor off deserted islands. Cook the fish we catch. We've got a generator, so we have our own power, and the deep freeze is loaded. I keep the boat organized so that I can just get up and go. It's my freedom train."

"But what about Hodges and the others at home? I mean, have we committed a crime? Are we fugitives? I don't feel like a fugitive."

Tari didn't look like a fugitive. She looked deeply adorable.

Rickey tried to concentrate on what she said, not how she looked.

"I don't think so. Once we're back in America, the whole

thing just starts up again. But outside the U.S.A., we're fine. One country's idea of who should be in a hospital isn't another's. Look at the Soviet Union before it fell apart, and all those 'schizophrenic' political prisoners. The nearest thing to a crime was my driving. I'd need a super lawyer to get me off a dangerous-driving charge, but that's peanuts. And I didn't hurt anybody except the guy who tried to hijack my bike and the bozo who tried to pirate my boat. I mean, that would all be self-defense."

"But it does mean that until everything is sorted out, we can't go back," said Tari, heading toward the bottom line.

"Let me promise you something, Tari," said Rickey. His voice was husky. "In a couple of days you're not going to want to go back."

And he leaned forward, and he kissed her, and she believed him.

40

MARCUS DOUGLAS threaded his way through the packed tables of the American Bar. Wherever the English recession was biting, it appeared to have no teeth here in London's Savoy Hotel. The pinstriped brigade were tucking in. There was champagne in buckets beaded with moisture, Havana cigars going up in smoke, delicate smoked salmon sandwiches going down. Marcus headed to the back of the room where the small bar was. He sat down on one of the stools and angled himself so that he could see anyone approach.

"Can I get something for you, sir?"

"A tomato juice, please."

Marcus felt his anxiety build. He looked at his watch, then at the crowd. He wondered if this had been a clever place to meet. There were other bars at the Savoy, but this was the most famous. There shouldn't be any confusion. He took a deep breath and exhaled. He felt like a detective, hot on the trail. He was so close to the answer . . . perhaps minutes away from the truth and its incredible implications.

He sipped at the drink. He had arrived from Rome late last night, a few hours after Paulo had set up this lunchtime meeting. Now it was just a question of waiting, of asking the right questions, of squeezing the right answers from the only man on earth who knew.

For the hundredth time, Marcus went over the details of the extraordinary story that Paulo and his investigators had discovered. Twenty-five years ago, a beautiful and deeply religious woman, Maria Mirabella, had been a maid in the country house of the fabulously rich Lonza family. She was a strange and charismatic person, and there were even rumors that she had performed miracles. Antonio Lonza, the spoiled son of the billionaire, had fallen in love with her, but Maria, devout, ascetic, and obsessed by God, had not returned his affection.

One day, walking by the river with Maria, Antonio had kissed her against her will. One of the villagers had seen it happen. A few weeks later the bombshell had dropped. Maria was pregnant. The villagers, who loathed Maria for her extreme piety and closeness to God, had jumped to the inescapable conclusion. Everyone believed she was carrying Lonza's child. In the uproar that had followed, Maria had added insult to injury. She had claimed that God, not Lonza, was the father of her unborn child. It had been an immaculate conception. Her baby was divine.

Old Lonza had moved fast to defuse the crisis. He had persuaded Maria that she and her precious baby were at risk from the fury of the villagers. In no time at all he had arranged for Maria to emigrate to America through his friend and lawyer Bertram Applegate. But Maria had had a premonition that she would die in childbirth and, in the event of her death, she had arranged through Applegate for her baby to be adopted by a good Catholic family. Maria's prediction of her own death had come true. About how many other things would she be proved right? Paulo's final words echoed in Marcus's memory—"If God is not the father of Tarleton Jones, then Lonza is."

Marcus recognized him instantly. He was better looking than his photographs, tall and straight, yet rangy and athletic. He walked with a loping gait, a bit like a bullfighter, weaving through the tables as if playing them with some invisible cape.

He wore a sleek, khaki-colored lightweight suit of Italian cut. His black hair was swept back from a sunburned face in a shiny sheet of what looked like patent leather. He locked eyes onto Marcus immediately. As he approached, he didn't let go of his gaze.

Marcus stood up. The man was there, reaching out his hand. Marcus took it.

"Antonio Lonza," said the man.

"Marcus Douglas. How very good of you to see me," said Marcus.

"When Paulo Percevaldi and Cardinal Vincento ask, one doesn't refuse," said the count of Lonza. His smile wiped the sting from the remark. Its effect, however, lingered. Marcus Douglas's request alone would have been insufficient to secure the meeting.

"You're in England for the polo?" said Marcus politely. This was the old world. Business would have to wait. Bottom lines meant lines beneath bottoms over here.

"Yup," said the count. "Actually, I come over here quite a bit in what passes for their summers." He laughed, enormously sure of himself. His British accent made Robert Morley sound like the middle-class actor he was. He had even picked up the English trick of talking about the weather to strangers.

"Can I get you something to drink?"

"Are we going to hang about here, or should we sit at a table?" said Lonza. It was clear from the emphasis that the count was no barfly.

"Let's get a table," said Marcus. He tried to fit Lonza's face to Tari's. Both were intensely good-looking, dark, Italianate, but there was no obvious facial similarity.

"Can you arrange a table for us?" said Lonza to the barman. It was said with aristocratic firmness. It was not the barman's job to organize tables. The barman knew that. So did Lonza. And both knew that the other knew it. On the other hand, each knew the other, and each other's position in the delicate hierarchy of the European class system. Lonza was a wop to the working-class Englishman, but he was a nob wop. The barman was a peasant to the Italian aristocrat, but an English peasant. The courtly "arrange a table" was a concession to that. At some level deep in the genes, the deal was done. The barman left his position to speak to the man who seated the tables in the American Bar. Minutes later, Lonza and Marcus were sitting at a deuce in the corner that combined privacy with a panoramic view of the room.

"Paulo tells me you are an old friend of his," said Lonza.

"Yes. We go back twenty-five years."

"Good, good," said Lonza. Anything old was good. "And you live in America? In Miami, Paulo said."

"Can I get you anything, sir?"

The waiter deposited the remains of his tomato juice in front of Marcus.

"Oh, I don't know . . . I'll have a glass of champagne," said the count.

"Yes, I have a clinic in Miami. I'm a psychiatrist there."

"And a priest. An interesting combination. What brings you to London?"

"You do."

"Ah, the 'something important' that Paulo spoke of. But of what possible interest could a . . . a . . . frivolous person like myself be to a serious man like you?"

There was a hint of mockery. It was the amateur's view of the professional, here, in Europe, where professionals didn't rate at all.

Marcus wondered how best to put it. This man would have firm views on just about everything. He would shut up like a clam if he was rubbed up the wrong way. Approached correctly, however, he would talk all night. Upper-class Europeans were incredibly indiscreet. But Marcus was an American. Over the years, subtle diplomacy as a skill had slipped away from him.

"I need very badly to talk to you about someone you knew many years ago. Do you remember a girl called Maria Mirabella?"

Marcus said the name as the count of Lonza's champagne was arriving. The waiter was leaning over to place it in front of him. The effect was startling. The aristocrat's hand shot up to his face, caught in the waiter's arm, and sent the flute of wine sailing across the table. It broke on an ashtray. Champagne flew in a fine spray through the air. The conversation at the surrounding tables faltered. But it was on Antonio Lonza's face where the real accident was happening. It went white and rigid. His mouth twisted to one side. His eyes widened in shock.

"Maria Mirabella," he said in a choked voice.

The waiter cleared the mess. Marcus helped, trying not to stare at the disaster area that was the Lonza expression. His heart was racing. He was near. And what was the truth that could have such an effect on a man like Lonza? His previous demeanor had insinuated he would find a firing squad nothing but a minor irritation.

Marcus waited. The table was mopped clean. The shards of glass were removed. Lonza's face was returning to some semblance of normality. His composure was partially regained.

He took a deep breath. "Maria Mirabella was a maid in my father's house near Santo Pietro," he said. His face began to turn red. Once again he was starting to lose it. His voice was stretched out as if it were on some rack. It positively quivered with an alien anxiety. In all his professional life, Marcus could not remember a personality change of such extraordinary proportions in such a short space of time . . . and all at the mention of a single name. The adrenaline was zipping through his own body. What had happened all those years ago that could produce an effect like this twenty-five years later? Some vivid traumatic experience, no less. It was almost enough, single-handedly, to restore one's faith in Freud.

"You may know," said Marcus, turning up the heat, "that Maria emigrated to America and died in childbirth. She had a little girl, who was adopted."

Marcus leaned in over the table. In front of him, Lonza's face continued to change color. The redness deepened, but patches of white were beginning to emerge in scattered locations. His suntan was now simply irrelevant.

"I know," he whispered.

Marcus took a very deep breath. It was now or never. He had to take the risk.

"Look, I have no right to ask these questions and please believe me, as a friend of Paulo's and of the cardinal's, that I have no ulterior motive here. I am not trying to place you in a position that will compromise or embarrass you. I'm after the truth for my own information, for my own peace of mind."

The count of Lonza nodded. It seemed speech of any kind

had become a problem for him. There was a bead of sweat on his forehead, another on his lip. A damp patch had appeared on his immaculate cream silk shirt.

"I know that some sort of relationship existed between you and Maria." Marcus plowed on. "What I need to know is whether or not you are the father of her child."

"Yes," said the count.

Marcus's heart stopped.

"Yes, you are the father?"

"No. Yes, I understand what you're asking me."

Marcus's heart started again.

"And?" he said, unable to contain himself.

"I loved her," said the count in a small voice. "I was in love with her. She was the most wonderful person I have ever met in my life."

His eyes dropped to the table. His shoulders sagged. Suddenly, he seemed weighed down by an almost unbearable sorrow. Marcus wanted to put out his arm and touch him, so vivid was the pained language of his body.

"I need to know," said Marcus, gently but firmly, "if you are the father of the child."

"Why?" said Lonza. He looked up. His eyes were full of tears. "Why do you need to know?"

"It's nothing to do with anything legal . . . with paternity . . . with anything like that. You have my word as a priest. But I must know if you had . . . sexual relations with Maria Mirabella. . . ."

"Father," said Lonza in a halting voice. "What I have to tell you . . . I want it to be God's secret."

"You mean you want me to hear your confession?"

"Yes."

Marcus was in a turmoil. He looked around the crowded bar. He looked back at Lonza and at the silent tears streaming down his cheeks. He felt the chill on his back, the explosion of curiosity in his soul. He would get the answer now, but he would never be able to repeat it to a living soul. He wouldn't be able to tell even Tari.

Marcus leaned forward. He nodded his head.

"Forgive me, Father, for I have sinned," said Antonio, count of Lonza.

41

"THIS BOAT'S like a home," said Tari. She paused. "How come you never showed it to me before?"

"It's like my secret place. Where I get away to be me." Rickey smiled a childlike smile, aware that grown-ups weren't really allowed secret places.

"So I need to learn about a whole new you," said Tari, laughing. "I was getting rather fond of the old version."

He put out his hand to her as she sat, swinging her legs over the edge of the big bed. She took it and held it playfully as if it were a toy. She turned it around in her hands, and then, very slowly, she put it to her lips.

"Thank you for saving me from myself," she said. Her voice was suddenly low and intense. The conversation darkened. The whir of the air conditioner was loud in the silence. There would be time to talk demons . . . and gods . . . but it wasn't now. They had been free and alone together for such a short time. Both knew they should indulge that freedom to the full.

"It isn't every day a damsel in distress gets rescued by a

knight in a secret white home," said Rickey, breaking the potential seriousness of the moment.

"So what do we do now?" she said. "I mean, how long can we stay out here?"

"Until you get tired of paradise . . . or me. Or both. I come here all the time. By myself. I like to do the islands by myself. No timetable. No hassle. I catch my food. Cook it. Listen to music moored out on the bank with no land in sight. I've got everything on this boat. I guarantee you won't think of a thing that isn't on board."

"Tampax," said Tari cunningly.

"Actually, I do have that. Unopened." The question of whether or not Jodie had been to the islands on one of Rickey's lonely trips had been asked and answered, in a way.

"Okay," said Tari. "Let's think. Grenadine," she said suddenly.

"And fresh limes," he said on cue.

"Mount Gay?"

"And Myers, and Angostura and powdered nutmeg and an ice-maker. Fresh O.J. and pineapple juice."

Tari clapped her hands together. "Okay, Captain Cook, let's *do* it."

He took control. The Key limes were in a Ziploc bag in the refrigerator. The Barbados rum went at the bottom of each glass with five cubes of ice. Fresh O.J. came from a sealed container. The pineapple juice was canned. He added a dash of Angostura, maybe four drops, and a splash of grenadine, just enough to give the drink a tinge of pink, not sufficient to make it sickly sweet. He squeezed a lime into each glass and stirred briskly with a vast knife. Right at the end, he layered one and a half fingers of brown Jamaican rum over the top of the drink and sprinkled some powdered nutmeg on top of that.

"Let's drink them on deck and watch the stars. They taste better that way."

They did. The boat was anchored in a U-shaped Robinson Crusoe bay on South Bimini in five feet of the most beautiful water in the world. Above them, stars lit a cloudless sky. Water lapped against the boat's hull, and a soft breeze came unexpectedly, like the warm breath of a lover. The moon was full, and palm trees from the beach dipped into the edges of it, their fronds barely moving in the quiet night. A flight of pelicans flew low in military formation across the water. To the right, a ballyhoo skidded across the bay leaving silver ripples on the moonlit sea.

They sat in the stern on the white leather banquette as the boat tested gently the fore and aft lines of the Bahamian-style anchorage that Rickey had set up.

Tari sipped deep on her drink. "I've never been anywhere as beautiful as this," she said.

"Not many people know about it. You can only get here by boat. There's no road to the beach. Most people like to be in a marina at night. Sometimes, a couple of boats are here. We got lucky."

"So we sleep out here?"

"I was thinking we should sleep on the beach. Make a campfire. Grill some fish. There's a tent and sleeping bags. Everything, remember?"

"Rickey, how do you know all this stuff? I mean, you're a movie star. You play pool, and hit people, and make people like me fall in love with you . . ."

"Do you love me?" he said. He turned to her, deadly serious.

Tari stopped. Did she love him? What she felt about Rickey was never still. It changed. There had been moments when her lust for him had filled her mind and body. There had been others when her soul's longing had elbowed him out of the way. He was an imperfect man. He was damaged, and therefore dangerous. His childhood had wounded him so deeply, his character would always bear the scars. But shouldn't love be blind? Should real love not notice these things? Shit, shouldn't her mind shut the hell up?

"I think I do," she said.

Rickey nodded gently, digesting some secret truth, some private perception. His smile was wry, but his expression said he was not discouraged. There was a time for him, and it was now. He would take the tide at the ebb and it would lead to the fortune of goodness and beauty that would be Tari. She, like him, came with history. She was adopted. She was not like other women. Things happened around her that walked with miracles. Things happened inside her head that some thought crazed, and others thought holy. It wasn't a question of opposites, it was a question of them coming from different planets. For Rickey and Tari to come together in marriage would be the greatest miracle of all. Yet, as he sipped on the rum punch beneath the twinkling stars, Rickey felt for the first time in his life like a miracle worker. If faith could move mountains, then desire alone could make Tari his wife.

"Hungry?" he said.

"A little."

He was gone for hardly any time at all. Now there was a tray of canapés—Beluga caviar on Carr's water biscuits, with a sliver of lime; smoked salmon from Scotland on thin slices of brown bread; a bowl of nuts—cashews, macadamias, and pistachios.

"Rickey, how did you get this . . . ?"

"It's easy. The caviar is from a jar. The salmon is vacuum-wrapped. And the fresh stuff is all around us, always." He waved a hand at the phosphorus sea, sparkling in the moonlight. To emphasize his point, a fish jumped in the shallows near the beach. The *plop* it made on reentry touched the silence. Tari could see the rings of water spreading out to infinity from the place it had disappeared.

The smoked salmon, the caviar, and the punch were making her feel really good. She felt the bubble of happiness build inside her. At a stroke, she had been cut off from her past and stranded from her future. There was only here, only now, in a place of incredible loveliness with a man she adored. She looked at him in the moonlight—so strong and brave, and yet vulnerable, too, beneath the tough-guy exterior. Each minute he showed some unexpected new angle to his personality. On the boat he was in another element. He knew navigation and the mysteries of the Loran. He had showed her the harbor entrance on the radar when they were way out of sight of land. He had known how to anchor, how to take advantage of the shore's shelter in terms of the wind's direction. And now he was orchestrating the next adventure . . . dinner, and a night on the sand beneath the stars on a deserted island so very far from the ordeal she had just escaped.

"So we catch fish?" she said.

"There are lots and lots of things we do," he said.

He threw open the storage hatches and began to unload supplies. He blew up a rubber dinghy and loaded it with a tent and a vast cooler full of soft drinks, champagne, and white wine. There were sleeping bags and ground sheets, battery-operated storm lanterns for keeping away the mosquitoes, fishing tackle, knives, and a large net surrounded at the edges by lead weights.

"What's that for?" said Tari, watching him in fascination.

"It's for netting pinfish in the shallows. We'll use them as bait to catch a pompano or two for dinner. The only thing you need to be a good fisherman in the Bahamas is live bait. Okay, are you ready?"

"For what?"

"To swim ashore," said Rickey with a laugh.

"We don't get to go in the dinghy?"

"No, that's for ferrying supplies."

"Oh," Tari laughed nervously. "I am afraid I didn't have time to do much packing. No swimsuit." She splayed open her hands in a disarming gesture.

"So luck hasn't deserted us on our desert island," said Rickey.

"Rickey!"

Tari could feel the sexual tension building all around her. It was everywhere. It was in the smooth, slippery texture of the caviar and the salmon. It burned with the rum in her belly. It shone from the stars in the sky, and it was lighting a slow fire around her heart. Soon, once again, they would be lovers. The only question was when. Both knew it. She could see it in his sultry eyes. He could read it on her flushed cheeks. Her bathing suit, any clothes that covered her, would merely be wrapping on the gift she had become. It would exist only to conceal the present. Its purpose would be its removal. It could be ripped from her, or removed gently . . . the moment would dictate which . . . but it would change nothing. She was his and he would be hers on this magic evening, far from the chaos and confusion of the outside world. They were spinning alone on their own personal star. They were merely waiting for the moment to become perfect, and they were waiting for nothing else.

Tari found a big T-shirt in the cabin and she slipped it on. That, and the plain cotton panties she wore already, would do for the island night. Tari felt her heart bang in her chest as she returned to the deck. His eyes washed over her white simplicity, and she felt rather than heard the moan of longing within him.

"Any sharks?" she said, trying to push back the lust that bubbled within her.

"A few." He laughed. "That means you have to hang on to me, real tight, for protection."

Together, they slipped into the warm water, and Tari did stay close although she was not thinking about sharks. Rickey swam strongly, dragging the laden dinghy behind them, and she swam beside him, her heart full of adventure. The shelf of soft, clean sand rose up to the beach, and they emerged dripping from the water. Tari's nakedness was only emphasized by the soaked T-shirt that modesty had seemed to require. Her breasts, hardened by the water, now hardened further as they were exposed to Rickey's gaze. She stood there, uncertain what to do. It was so close. Was it now? He, too, seemed to sense the nearness of the moment.

He took a deep breath. "First, we secure our camp. Build the fire. Put up the tent. Catch the bait fish. Then . . ."

His "then" melted into the ether of mutual longing.

The fire was fun. Driftwood was everywhere. Tari collected it, while Rickey dug a pit in the sand. The wood had been bleached by the sun, and some bits were twisted into weird sculptures that seemed almost too fine to burn. There were big planks that had to be dragged to the fire, and Rickey showed her how to place them across the pit so that the fire would saw them into manageable pieces for later in the night when the temperature dropped. Dried seaweed was the kindling. Charcoal fuel from the boat and a long barbecue lighter were the cheats from civilization. In no time at all, the fire was blazing. They huddled around it, their minds lost in the flickering flames. The smell of warm salt air melded with the scent of the different woods. The sound of crackling dry timbers merged with the swish of the swell against the pure white sand. Rickey stood up and placed two storm lanterns seventy feet away to each side of the fire to draw mosquitoes away from them. Together, they hung the ground sheet across two huge uprooted trees, hurricane victims of Andrew, forming a roof that the clear sky said would not be needed. There seemed no excuse for a tent, and so they laid it down as a ground sheet and placed the twin sleeping bags side by side on top of it.

"I wish we had one bag," said Tari suddenly.

"It'll be too hot to get into them anyway," said Rickey, laughing.

Both knew what they were doing. They were letting the hunger build before the feast of bodies. They were tantalizing each other and themselves, as the desperation of their need grew.

"I'll show you how to catch the bait fish."

Tari followed him into the shallows. He arranged the weighted net carefully, like a gladiator in the Roman arena. Then he drew back his arm and swung it out in a smooth motion from the shoulder. The net fanned in the air, made a big circle, and flopped down on the flat sea, sinking immediately to the bottom. He waited for a few seconds, and then drew it in slowly. Three cylindrical pinfish struggled in the mesh. He disentangled them and dropped them into the bucket at his feet. One more throw. Two more fish. That should be enough.

"It looks so simple," said Tari.

"When I started this, each time I threw the net it took me half an hour to untangle it."

"Life's so uncertain, isn't it? I mean, the chances of us arriving here, now, and catching those poor little fishes and feeding them to some bigger fish, and then eating that."

"And those medical sharks in Miami wanting to pickle you in medicines when you can feel things like that about little fishes."

Tari wanted to say something about the mystery of God's purpose. But then she just didn't want to say it. Here, in this paradise on earth with the man she loved, it seemed so superfluous. Yes, one day she'd have to go back and start again, and sell *All for Love,* but this was this. This was now. This was meaning, as meaningful and as wonderful as any of the metaphysical longings that had preoccupied her for so long. Here in this most beautiful of God's little acres, strangely God was absent. She felt the love flow out of her, directed at last toward a single person, no longer to the bleeding crowd. No more did she want to be God's daughter. Or his bride. She wanted merely to be one of his created beings, loving, lusting, wanting, and longing like all the others. Above all, she wanted to take this man, this strong man who had rescued her from others but chiefly from herself, and she wanted to make love to him in the moonlight, in the shallows of this deserted bay.

So she took hold of the extra-large T-shirt that clung to her throbbing body, and she drew it up over her head. She stood there in her panties, beneath the full moon, and it lit her from behind and from one side, and the moonbeams danced from her nakedness in celebration of her naturalness. She stood there, legs apart, and there were drops of saltwater on her rock-hard breasts, and her hair was tousled and tangled. She threw back her head in defiance of her need, and she dared him to ignore it. To emphasize her point, she kicked out at the bucket of pinfish, upturning it and watching the silver streaks dance away to freedom.

"There," she said. "I free you, little fish. And I spare you, big pompano, because I haven't got time to catch you or to eat you."

Rickey took a step toward her.

"What about me?" he said.

"That's different," she said. Her voice caught as she spoke, and she tumbled into his arms.

He took her fast, standing up in the water. He pulled down his trunks, hard already, and she pulled down her panties and she was already soaked for him. He bent down quickly, pushed up, and slid into her. Joined, they swayed there, their arms tied in a knot their hearts had tied long before. They hardly moved as they savored the communion of their bodies and the merging of their minds. Her wet breasts thrust at his chest and he buried his head down low on her neck, whispering her name.

"Tari, Tari, I love you. I love you so much."

She moved around him then, inching up on her toes. Then she lowered herself again, the better to feel the hugeness within her. His back was so strong beneath her fingers, and she pulled him in closer, thrusting down to push him deeper into her body. Her mouth was by his ear, and she put out her tongue and licked it so that he could hear the sound of her lust.

"Don't wait. Don't stop," she whispered.

He moaned his acquiescence. He bent her over backward, until she lost balance in his arms. Then he lowered her gently into the inches of water at their feet. He knelt down with her, still deep inside her, and her legs splayed out around him to hold him there where he had to be. Their faces moved apart and they could see each other's longing now, lust mirrored in faraway eyes, twin expressions with but one purpose under heaven. The sea that received them was silver with moonlight, the sand soft beneath Tari's back, the sky above very bright with stars. Palm trees waved above the face of her lover in the so-slight breeze, and still he filled her with his love. She clamped around it, softly sucking at it with her body. Together, they twisted and turned in the watery clay of shifting sand. The sea had created a bed for them, softer and more subtle than any man-made place for love, and she heard him groan at the gate of ecstasy as her own feeling grew. He moved now inside her, and she poured out around him, the juice of her love melding with the salty waves of the sea where life had begun. They slid together down the slopes of passion and climbed the cliff again in the remorseless motion of humanity's creation. She sat up in the shallows and held his shoulders, grinding herself around him, hungry for friction in the smooth ride of love. He thrust himself at her, hard and strong, and the muscles of his buttocks shook her core with the shock of his most wanted invasion.

"Oooooooh!" She moaned loud in the moonlight to the careless sky. All around, the beauty of nature framed the bliss of their moment. Soon this would end, but only for some new beginning . . . by the crackling fire, and later on the bow of the boat, rocking gently while infinity watched. And Tari marveled that she had never been so far from anywhere, yet so close to anyone. Her body wanted to say that, and it could, it would, soon.

He had slowed his movement inside her, as if frightened of

the little death to come. And she was floating on the glory of sensation, strangely light in the warm buoyancy of the water. They danced together, some delicate waltz from long ago, entranced by magic music they composed themselves. Tari felt so beautiful. Naked beneath the sea, she was clothed in a phosphorous fabric of the moon's making. She shone with the brilliance of her moment, and she threw back her head to let her hair dangle in the water at her back, while God's moon painted a necklace of light at her moment of ecstasy.

The slow, easy feeling gathered within her, and within him. This was far from the frantic longing of before. This was the making of love. Lust and passion were the wind and the wings, but not the essence of the unity they now shared. She arched her back. Her eyes widened. Her hands slipped lower on his back to his buttocks, the better to feel him when he showered her with his soul. She tried to stay still, impaled on the point of him, so that she should fall by an act of his. Her whole body was suspended in that perfect paralysis that would one day be nothingness, but was now everything. She couldn't move, yet there was not a sinew of her body, a muscle, a nerve, that wasn't singing to her mind in perfect joy. Here was the secret harmony that some never heard. Here was eternity captured in a moment. If life needed a meaning, this was it. It was worth living and dying for, and it was no accident that it was also the moment of creation.

He stopped, as he had to, because now motion was spent. All conscious action was superfluous in the face of this mutual moment of fate.

"Yes," she said.

"Oh, Tari," he whispered.

He felt the long ribbons of love tear away from him, like the moonbeams that danced over their bodies. She felt them, too, alive inside her, full of the future. Her legs quivered as she received him, and he shook and shuddered as he gave himself to her.

She was a vacuum for him, a glorious receptacle to the distillate of the man she loved. She wrapped herself around him tight, not wishing to lose any part of the wonder that was him. She dug her fingers into his back and her legs hugged him where her arms could not. And all the time she, too, melted into the maelstrom of her climax. Out of her body's weakness at this moment broke the full force of the strength of love. On the sands of this island in the Bahamas, in the warm sea that had given birth to mankind, Tari was reborn. It was an epiphany. She had learned at last that love could be for lovers, too.

42

MARCUS HADN'T slept. He had spent the previous night praying, and the flight from Heathrow to Kennedy thinking. He hadn't had much comfort from the prayer, and far less from the thought. Which was basically how life was. Comfort was action. Now he walked fast because there were many things to do, and so many more emotions to discharge . . . fury, vengeance, jealousy, and love, of course. He had managed to do without love for the better part of a life, and now it had caught up with him when he was least able to handle it.

He hurried through the crowded airport, stopping only to buy the tabloids that told him in garish detail most of the things he didn't want to know. The headlines were vintage garbage:

"Movie Star Abducts Mental Patient. Miami Shrinks Go Crazy"

"Rickey Cage and Schizophrenic on Boat in Caribbean. Florida Cops of Two Minds About Pressing Charges"

"Sick, Holy, or Just Star-Struck; Shrinks Fight Over Med Student's Diagnosis"

Marcus stood there, rage rising, as he speed-read the facts. Unforgivably, he had been out of the loop. Usually, he kept in the closest contact with his clinic, but the chance to meet the elusive Lonza in London had come up at the last moment. He had dropped everything and flown to London immediately, and in the aftermath of his extraordinary conversation with the count of Lonza, he had been too preoccupied to call home until late into the night. When he had eventually gotten around to it, his hysterical secretary and house doctor had told him the news. Tari had left the clinic to go to a party with Rickey Cage. Somehow, Professor Hodges had found out about it, and had taken steps to enforce the still-operative commitment order against her. There had been some sort of confrontation, during which a male nurse had been injured, and then Rickey and Tari had disappeared. Nobody knew for certain where. The papers, whose newsprint was already coming off in his hands, suggested it might be anywhere from Key West to Mexico or the Bahamas. Doubtless, the supermarket tabloids would already be researching wider possibilities, up to and including heaven and outer space.

Douglas looked at his watch. It was three o'clock. There was still time to get things done, if not to work out what they should be. One thing was certain. The news that was flowing like sewage was not being managed by the good guys. The quotes were from Professor Hodges; Shindler, the professor of medicine; and the Miami City Police Department, trying desperately to stay out of what looked like an incredibly unpromising situation for them. He hadn't time to go through the serious papers. But he had to make some calls. The first was to his heart, which was making no sense because it was heavily engaged. Lonza's bombshell, handed over in the sacred secrecy of confession, had shattered his world. It made all sorts of impossible things possible, and it had totally destroyed the moral compass that he had used so far to guide his life.

The second call was to Mark McKinley, the chairman, CEO, and publisher of World Publishers, Inc. This whole thing had to have a major impact on *All for Love,* now well down the publishing pipeline, and already hailed as a blockbuster of monumental proportions. Tari's name was on the book. She was its principal author. Now the reading public was learning that serious psychiatrists had serious doubts about her sanity; that she had ducked a commitment order in a situation involving violence; and that she had disappeared into the Caribbean or some such place with none other than the latter-day James Dean, for those old enough to know who he was. It stretched to the very limit the notion that all PR was good PR.

He found a quarter. The chairman of World Publishers seemed to have been hanging around for his call.

"Where the *hell* are you, Marcus? What on earth is happening? I'm fielding the entire media here, and I've got no facts. Nothing I can even *pretend* is a fact."

"Where are they?" said Marcus. He didn't mean the media.

"I don't know where they are. I was hoping you did. The movie guy's boat's gone. That's all anyone knows. Where does Cage come into it? Is he the Jones lover? I thought she was all locked up in your clinic."

"Shut up," said Marcus. "Shut the hell up."

There was silence on the line. McKinley knew instinctively the words that had caused the loss of the Douglas temper. "Is he the Jones lover?" It was true. And Douglas didn't like it. Why? Because *he* wanted to be the Jones lover. The priest. The psychiatrist. The lion's share of World's profits . . . now, and for years to come.

"I'm sorry, Marcus. Forgive me. I'm upset. We're all upset. I didn't mean to speak out of turn."

"Listen, this can be turned around, Mark. If we all keep our heads. Tari's not crazy. Believe me. Those idiots in Miami are going to pay with their bank accounts, with their licenses, with their departments, with their immortal souls for what they've done. Trust me. I swear it before God in heaven."

McKinley took a very deep breath. This was heavy-duty talk from a priest. It was industrial-strength talk coming from Marcus Douglas. McKinley started to feel better. Someone else seemed to be in control.

"What do I do?"

"You call a meeting for four o'clock. All your lawyers. All your PR people. Bring in some legal heavyweights—Arthur Liman, Alan Dershowitz—if you can get them. If not, set up a

conference call, and also with a hot criminal guy like F. Lee
Bailey—he's dynamite. Oh, and get the top guys in from the
ACLU. This is their field. Pledge them a hundred thousand
dollars from me today, okay? This is your authority to do that.
Get the PR people onto the *Times* and say there's a major story
brewing . . . assaults on personal freedoms; professional jealousies in the psychiatric profession; psychiatry being used as an
instrument of repression; belief systems being suppressed for
lack of conformity to conventional norms . . . you know, we're
taking over where the Soviet Union left off . . . get all that
started, and I'll see you at four."

"Shall I send a car for you? Where are you, anyway?"

"I'm at Kennedy. I'm just in from London. No, I don't need
a car. Oh, and there is one other thing you should know.
Tarleton Jones is . . . Tarleton Jones is . . ." He tried to say the
thing that would make the difference, but his whole past life
screamed for his silence. He couldn't break the silence of the
confessional. What he had learned from Lonza might change
everything, but it was a card he couldn't play. Or could he? For
Tari? Hell and damnation, for himself? One last time, he tried.

"Mark, Tarleton Jones is . . ."

"Is what, Marcus?"

His hand put down the *receiver*. He didn't. And he stood
staring at the kiosk in the crowded airport, and the man
behind him was coughing politely to show that he wanted to
make a call.

In a daze, Marcus wandered away from the phone. The night
of prayer and the day of thought had come to this . . . paralysis
of the will. His vows held him prisoner. He was a priest. He was
a servant of God. He had never been anything more nor less
than that, but now he wanted to be much, much more . . . and
much, much less. Out there, somewhere, was Tari with a man
she would be learning to love. Here, forever alone in the desert
of his spirit, was Marcus Douglas. He wanted her. He knew that
now. He wanted Tari. He wanted her for him, and he was
beginning to come to grips with just what that meant. Celibacy,
the church, God, his priesthood, everything he was and had
become was at risk in this madness. And for what? Would he
sacrifice everything for a child who had never pretended to

love him? He was old. He had never until this moment known just how old. Any respect she may once have had for him had been based on all the things he had been. It had been based on none of the things he now dared to dream of becoming. To love her, to stand a chance of being loved by her, he would have to become a mere mortal. All of the mystique of his unavailability would blow away into the sad reality of a man whose life had become a broken promise. If he could not look at the face in the mirror, who else could bring themselves to gaze at it? Not his readers, not his friends of a lifetime, not Tarleton Jones.

He began to walk, and the old solutions presented themselves to him. Pray. Confess. Call on the army of the church, the good friends who would know the right words. He should talk to Paulo in Rome. But those were not the solutions for now. On an island, this moment, the girl he loved was being loved. She was being loved by an icon of the age in which she lived. Marcus had seen the damage in the eyes of the wounded boy whose fame was no protection from the terror of his childhood. But Tari would not see that part of Rickey. She would not know of his danger because she would be too beguiled by the energy and enthusiasm that were both youth's blessing and its curse. She would see his hard young body, and dream his dreams. And it would be the wise men like Marcus who ended as the fools because they had committed the sin of growing old.

He sat down on a bench and buried his head in his hands, and he felt the tears come because all he could see ahead was hopelessness. Above him and around him, the world went on. It hurried to catch planes and make money, and to run away and to run back. It wanted, and it made silly sense of itself, as the disembodied voice told about departure gates, and flights canceled, and places that sounded depressing, and some exotic, and others grand. He heard it all, and he heard it not, because his heart was breaking and because he held a secret that he could not let out.

There was one quarter remaining in his pocket, and he felt for it. There was another call he could make, but it would change nothing. How could the godly ever be free? Was freedom only for sinners? Was freedom their reward? Their punishment?

He stood up, swaying slightly. He should have eaten something on the plane.

The phone booth was empty again. The phone book gave him the number.

"This is Applegate, Myers, and Runne," said a computerized female voice.

"May I speak to Mr. Bertram Applegate? This is Dr. Marcus Douglas calling on a matter of supreme importance."

He didn't expect to get close. A "meeting" would all but certainly be in progress, if not a "business trip" of uncertain duration. He well remembered his last visit to the pompous patrician Wall Street attorney. They had not parted friends.

"This is Walter Hiscocks, Mr. Applegate's assistant," said a polite voice, after what seemed like no more than thirty seconds.

"I'm calling from a phone booth," said Marcus quickly, "and I haven't another quarter."

"Please give me the number. Mr. Applegate will call back directly. He is anxious to speak to you."

Marcus felt the dart of excitement pierce him. He gave the number quickly and hung up.

He guarded the telephone against a couple of would-be callers. It rang almost immediately.

"This is Bertram Applegate. Dr. Douglas?"

"Yes. Hello."

"Where are you, Dr. Douglas?"

"I'm at Kennedy Airport."

"You've just flown in from London where you saw my client, Antonio Lonza."

Again the excitement sparked.

"Yes, I have. How did you know?"

"He has been calling me constantly since your meeting with him last night at the Savoy Hotel."

Silence. Applegate was being positively free with his information. The patrician beating about the bush was nowhere in evidence. Marcus knew to hang on and say nothing.

"He was much impressed by your meeting. Greatly affected

by it. I hardly think I am understating things when I say that."

Again Marcus waited, his heart on hold.

"He told you some things, some very personal things, that during our former meeting I was not at liberty to disclose to you."

"Yes," agreed Marcus. His voice was faint.

"He told me that he disclosed to you information ... information that was given to you on the basis of it being a confession ... I mean a confession in the true sense of the meaning in the Roman Catholic church, with all the implications of privacy and secrecy that I don't have to explain to you, Dr. Douglas, in your role as a Catholic priest ..." Now Applegate paused, aware at least that he had been the provider of information and as yet had received not a morsel in return.

"What you say is correct," said Marcus.

Applegate cleared his throat in a way that called for the sharpening of ears.

"He has done much thinking in the night, and he has made this decision. He communicated it to me by telephone this morning, and he has confirmed it by facsimile. I have a copy of his fax message on my desk right here."

"What does it say?" said Marcus. The feeling of unreality was intense.

"It says that he releases you from your vows vis-à-vis his confession. The count of Lonza has asked that you treat the information he gave you as unrestricted information. You may use it as you like, and in the best interests of all concerned."

Marcus felt the weight lift from his soul. Was this a gift from God? Was this the mercy of the Almighty for someone on the verge of deserting him?

"I am free from the constraints of the count's confession," said Marcus.

"You are, indeed, but may I say that that is far from all. Very far from all. As you may know, all sorts of problems have arisen in Miami in your absence. The papers are full of them. Are you aware of the situation with regard to Tarleton Jones, the girl about whom you spoke to the count and to me on that earlier occasion?"

"Yes, I am."

"Well, you should know this. I informed the count of Lonza of the situation. This was a few hours ago. I have just received a very important document from London and another from Rome. You are to be told their contents."

"I'm listening," said Marcus, wondering if you could listen in a dream.

Applegate was genuinely excited now. Here was the voice of a man who was finally talking about something he both loved and understood, something that far surpassed in interest the trivial dramas of conscience, confessions, and secrecy. He rolled his tongue around the facts as if they were the choicest morsels at Lutece, and when he had finally finished, Marcus was left with the distinct impression that, Chinese-style, Applegate was about to burp.

"So there it all is," he said at last, seemingly reluctant that there it all was. "Rather dramatic, I think, don't you?"

Marcus spoke quickly.

"Mr. Applegate, I know how valuable your time is, but could you cancel whatever meetings you have this afternoon and meet me, with the documents about which we have just spoken, in the head office of World Publishers at 560 Fifth Avenue within the hour . . . in the office of Mark McKinley, the chairman?"

Whatever else Bertram Applegate could or couldn't appreciate, he was an aficionado of drama.

"In the circumstances, I should be pleased to," he said.

43

THE BUZZ of conversation quieted as Marcus was ushered into the boardroom at World Publishers. Mark McKinley, immaculately pinstriped, stood up to welcome him. He managed to achieve an expression that was equal parts condolence, worry, and quiet confidence that somehow all difficulty would be overcome.

"Marcus!" he said simply. He gestured to the empty place on his right-hand side. "Welcome back." Marcus walked toward him, and his extended right hand merged into the lukewarm buddy hug of old friends in tough times. He sat down on the antique Hepplewhite chair, and he felt his tiredness lift as he saw the eager faces clustered around the polished mahogany of the boardroom table.

He had asked McKinley to arrange a high-powered meeting in less than an hour. It seemed the mission all-but-impossible had been achieved in spades. Some of the people he recognized. Now, McKinley filled in the gaps. His chairman-of-the-board style was billiard-ball smooth as he made the introductions. Facts and flattery were cunningly mixed.

"Well, now that our main man has arrived, I think we can get under way. This, of course, is our very old friend, the world-famous psychiatrist, writer, and priest, Dr. Marcus Douglas. Marcus is the man with the facts here. We should defer to his enormous knowledge on every subject. However, Marcus, as you requested, I have managed to obtain the services of others, to help out as they can. First, on conference call from Boston, from the faculty of Harvard Law where he is a professor of law, we have Alan Dershowitz. From his office in West Palm Beach, Florida, the state of jurisdiction, we have the advice of esteemed criminal lawyer F. Lee Bailey. Also on call, from the neuro-psychiatric unit at Johns Hopkins University in Baltimore, we have Professor Paul McHugh. He is a friend of yours, Marcus, I think . . . and a man who can give you moral support on the psychiatric side of things . . ."

McKinley paused, aware that he had pulled a sly trick. Marcus's eyebrows arched. Paul McHugh was a top, no-nonsense psychiatrist, and an acquaintance if not a friend. It was crystal clear, however, that he was sitting in not necessarily to support Douglas, but to monitor him. He was the second opinion. Mark McKinley trusted no one, including his "old friend, the world-famous psychiatrist."

McKinley continued around the table. "The legal team here at World, you know," he said quickly. "But we are also lucky enough, at such short notice, to be able to welcome Dr. Kanders and Dr. Bronowski. They are two of the most able and esteemed American Civil Liberties Union lawyers here in New York City. I think we may find their advice particularly interesting. To supplement the skills of our own excellent PR department, I have persuaded Susan Magrino to join us. Susan is the bright, new, shining star of publicity here in the Big Apple. We will listen very carefully to what she has to say." Susan Magrino, pert and pretty in red, and flanked by two sharp-looking assistants, smiled at the room. "Other colleagues on the World board you know, of course, Marcus."

"Can I just say," said Marcus, "that we are to be joined by Bertram Applegate of Applegate, Myers, and Runne. I see he has not yet arrived. I can guarantee that his input will be of the utmost importance to anything that is decided here today."

Silence descended in a cloak of mystery. Who was Applegate? What was he?

McKinley didn't like surprises. His look of discomfort
signaled that. His stranglehold on the meeting had been
effortlessly broken. He wanted it back.

"I think we all know the bare bones of the situation. The
purpose of this meeting is to identify the threat to the interests
of World Publishers and to those of Ms. Jones, our author. The
further purpose is to come up with courses of action that will
neutralize that threat."

Marcus heard the shorthand. Tari's interests were para-
mount in *his* mind. World Publishers' interests were in the
forefront of McKinley's. He hoped the two would coincide.

"Here is the bottom line," said McKinley. "Ms. Jones has
written a very wonderful, very important book. World has a vast
investment in it. There have been suggestions that the book
has been divinely inspired. Advance sales are through the roof.
Media interest is enormous. A number one best-seller was in
the making." He paused to let the "was" sink in. "Now, Ms.
Jones is publicly diagnosed as suffering from schizophrenia by
supposedly reputable doctors. She is the subject of a committal
order to a psychiatric institution. And she has disappeared. If
this order and this diagnosis are allowed to stand, unchal-
lenged, unrepudiated, and unreversed, then World cannot
continue to publish *All for Love*. Further, World's considerable
reputation will have suffered a severe and damaging blow.
Either way, the financial consequences to World will be
enormous."

The discouraging words sailed down the shining table. They
winged their way over the lines to Boston, West Palm Beach,
and Baltimore. They arrowed into the psyche of Marcus
Douglas. Screw World and their miserable profits. What about
Tari?

"It is true," said Marcus, his voice heavy with scorn, "that for
Tarleton Jones to be misdiagnosed as a schizophrenic would
be a financial setback for World Publishers. There would,
believe it or not, be unfortunate results for Tari, too. For a
generation, we have been sickened by the abuses of Soviet
psychiatry. We have watched in horror as good and brave men

and women have been turned into vegetables because their beliefs were regarded as inconvenient to a brutal and narrow-minded elite, obsessed only with retaining its own power and prestige. With all due respect to World Publishers' financial position, I am shaken and shocked that it is not Tarleton Jones's interests that have been put first on today's agenda. If America is to become the new home of psychiatric repression on this planet, then it will have to pass over my dead body to achieve that position."

"I didn't mean for one second to suggest . . ." tried McKinley, but it was too late.

Marcus cut him off brutally. "To get past the bullshit, here is the problem. How do we get the two signatories of the Jones commitment order to revoke the document? Professor Hodges and Professor Shindler must be persuaded to change their minds. Merely to demonstrate that they were wrong in their diagnosis will not be enough, although they *were* wrong. There is a review-board procedure that can reverse commitment orders. It would, however, take months to get the case heard. Central to that process would be interviews with Tari herself. But Tari is not here, and we don't know when she will be here . . ."

He paused at the incredibly sad implications of that fact. Then anger flowed in from the edges of his mind. His razor brain was at work once more. "It is a catch-22 situation. The commitment order cannot be revoked on appeal until Tari returns. Tari, however, will not return while the commitment order is in effect."

"Can I come in here?" said Professor McHugh from Johns Hopkins. "How are you, Marcus? Marcus, may I just ask this? In a nutshell, can you let us know the basis for the commitment order?"

"Hello, Paul. Well, as you know, the basis of any commitment order is the mental state of the patient in conjunction with the 'imminent danger' test. Tari was diagnosed as suffering from schizophrenia. In my professional opinion, that diagnosis was incorrect. However, professional opinions concerning mental states can be debated. What cannot be debated is the 'imminent danger' test. Tari was never an imminent danger to herself or to others. She was never any danger at all. The professors at the medical school acted in a paternalistic and high-handed manner toward one of their students. To sign that order was malpractice."

"Marcus is right," said McHugh. "And the key word is 'imminent.' The test is clear. It is not enough that she may become a threat tomorrow, or that she was a threat yesterday. She must actually *be* a threat at the time of the signing of the order. Whether or not she is or was completely crazy is immaterial if the 'threat' criterion is not met. And there was no evidence of any threat to herself or to society?"

"Absolutely none. I recommend that a mammoth malpractice suit be brought against these two doctors to intimidate them into rescinding their order."

Dershowitz came in at this point.

"A malpractice suit would have to be brought by Tarleton Jones, and by nobody else. She is not here to bring it. And by rescinding their order, the doctors would be providing prima facie evidence of wrongful decision. Any lawyer would advise them against doing that, even as part of an out-of-court settlement. The central problem in any civil action against the doctors is that the damaged party, Ms. Jones, is not here to bring it. That would be true of any libels, slanders, breaches of professional confidences, or anything like that."

"Perhaps World could sue for damage to its professional reputation, financial loss flowing from that damage, etc.," said the head of the World legal team.

"It's arm's length," said Dershowitz. "I wouldn't go that way."

Marcus's knuckles tightened under the table. Where the hell was Applegate? That was the information this table needed. So far they were getting nowhere.

Then, quite suddenly, they were.

"May I come in at this point?" said Lee Bailey from West Palm. His voice was clear as a bell over the loudspeaker. "It may be that what we have here is a civil-rights violation. That is a serious crime ... a felony. And it's a federal offense. A criminal prosecution would not require Tari's presence in its initial stages. If the Justice Department in Washington could be persuaded that a potential violation of Tari's civil rights. had occurred, they could order a federal grand jury investigation. Neither of the Miami professors would relish being the object of a criminal investigation. There would be the threat of jail, of losing their medical licenses, of the total ruin of their careers."

"Perhaps this is our area of expertise," said Dr. Bronowski, a bespectacled lawyer from the ACLU. "First, I should say that Dr. Douglas's extremely generous donation to our organization has no effect whatsoever on our advice and attitudes. That goes without saying, but is best said, nevertheless." He allowed himself a small, tight smile. "However, this is precisely the sort of case the ACLU is interested in. A Justice Department investigation will only take place, I can assure you, if considerable political pressure is brought to bear. Without the infamous videotape, I suspect that Rodney King's civil rights would not have become an issue. As you know, the ACLU is a political organization with formidable contacts in Washington. We could be of considerable help in getting such an investigation started."

"We should not forget," said Marcus, "that we possess very impressive, extraordinarily persuasive, evidence of Tari's mental state. In particular, it shows clearly that she has never been an 'imminent danger.' We have *All for Love*. Why don't we arrange to publish extracts from it, more or less immediately? This would increase the already intense press interest, and create grass-roots pressure on Washington to take some sort of action."

"That's a very good idea," said McKinley. For a publisher, free publicity always was. "Susan?"

"The problem is time," said Susan Magrino. "But we could get something like *Newsday* to run extracts. It's current. It's news. If *Newsday* runs it, it could be on the street in a day or two. Magazines have a three-month lead time. This is a hot story. It could run and run. I mean, really . . . God, sanity, sex, a mysterious disappearance, a movie star . . . the only thing that's missing is money."

The door opened on cue. Bertram Applegate stood framed in it. If money had been missing from the plot, it looked to have arrived. The attorney beamed out great waves of plutocracy as he slid into the room. So did the people who followed him.

Marcus jumped to his feet. He had never imagined he would be so pleased to see anyone as loathsome as Bertram Applegate. Adversity made strange bedfellows.

Marcus made the introductions, but Applegate had some of his own.

"Sorry to be a little late, but I had to organize my team," he said, heading to the end of the table, opposite McKinley. "This is my partner, Benjamin Myers. My assistant, his assistant, Mr. . . . ah . . . and Mr. . . . yes, well, and my secretary, Ms. Marconi. And this is Mr. Stephen Carruthers, senior vice president of J. P. Morgan."

The thought occurred to everyone in the room simultaneously. What on God's earth was the senior vice president of J. P. Morgan, one of the oldest and most respected banks in America, doing at the World boardroom table?

"I don't want to interrupt anything," said Applegate, clearly dying to do just that. He opened a briefcase so thin that it resembled a thick piece of paper. From it, he took a single folder. He placed it on the table in front of him. They all looked at it, as they were supposed to. He smiled at Ms. Marconi. She smiled back, moistening her lips as she did so. The Applegate life was obviously well-organized.

Marcus spoke up.

"I think we should postpone the present discussion until we have heard what Mr. Applegate has to say."

There was silence. The silence deepened. It was broken by the clearing of the Applegate throat.

"I am here today," said Applegate, "to discuss Tarleton Jones and aspects of Tarleton Jones's life that will not be known to you. I am aware of the present situation, of the commitment order, of her disappearance, etc." He waved his hand in the air, dismissing them. They had ceased to be problems in the light of what he was going to say. They were about to become a giant and ridiculous irrelevance. His fat little hand expunged them from the consideration of serious minds. Marcus had to admit it was brilliantly done.

Everyone sat very still. Nobody wanted to move a muscle because of the noise it might make.

"My firm," he said, "represents the interests of Lorenzo,

count of Lonza; of his son, Antonio Lonza; and of the
companies they own. Most of you will know that name."

Billions. The richest family in the Western world. In the
silence, money was jabbering.

"Last night, at the Savoy Hotel in London, Antonio Lonza
met with Dr. Marcus Douglas. The subject of their meeting was
Tarleton Jones."

The eyes were on Marcus. All of them. They bored into him
from every side. Douglas and the billionaire's son at the Savoy
in London? Last night? One or two in the audience sneaked a
glance at their watches. Applegate picked up the folder and
dropped it again.

"My client, the young count of Lonza, was very much affected
by some of the things that Marcus Douglas told him. He was very
deeply affected in a way that is hard to describe in mere words."
He picked up the folder once again. He adjusted his glasses on
the end of his nose, opened the folder, and read one sentence.
"From this holy man it seemed to me that I was hearing the will
of God." He put the folder down carefully. When he spoke
again, he spoke slowly. "The count was so affected that he asked
Dr. Douglas to hear his confession, and Dr. Douglas did so . . .
in the American Bar at the Savoy Hotel."

From Boston to Baltimore, from Florida to Manhattan, they
waited.

"I am authorized by Antonio Lonza to say that during that
confession, he told Dr. Douglas this. Twenty-five years ago, in
Italy, he fell in love with a woman called Maria Mirabella. She
was a maid in his father's house, and a lady devoted to God. It
was the obsessive love of a young and spoiled man for a very
beautiful, very religious, and very unobtainable woman. From
a variety of sources, it is clear that Maria was a remarkable
person. There was talk of miracles surrounding her, much in
the way that there has been talk of them surrounding Tarleton
Jones. Maria constantly rejected Antonio's advances. To his
eternal shame, one evening, he took by force what he could
not otherwise have. He raped Maria Mirabella. She became
pregnant with his child. And she bore that child. That child is
Tarleton Jones. I have the count of Lonza's affidavit to that
effect before me now."

Tarleton Jones Lonza. It was different. It was not the same.

But it wasn't over. The Applegate hand was in the air to signal that. Mouths hung open. Jaws dropped.

"Maria Mirabella came to America and died giving birth to Tari, who was then adopted. Until yesterday, there had been no relationship between Tari and the Lonza family, except the relationship of blood. Some thirty years ago, however, Lorenzo Lonza set up a trust fund for his yet-to-be-born grandchildren. Each year since, that trust has received and invested one-half of the income of the entire Lonza empire."

They were getting there now. The sun was rising in some of the brighter eyes.

Applegate's face was beginning to glow. His cheeks were bathed in red. He was approaching some sort of orgasmic moment.

"But there are no grandchildren. Antonio was his father's only child, and he never married. He never recovered from his experience with Tari's mother. But the lawyers who drafted the trust deed had made provision for that eventuality. Under the terms of this trust, the sworn affidavit of Antonio Lonza that he is the father of a child is sufficient under law for that child to become the sole beneficiary of the Lonza fund on his or her twenty-fifth birthday. As I said before, such an affidavit is here on the table in front of me."

He picked it up, and held it in the air like a flag over some field of victory.

"Due to the intervention of Dr. Douglas, Tarleton Jones Lonza is the sole beneficiary of the Lonza Trust," said Applegate, as a coup de grace.

There was only one question left. Applegate peered around the table. Who would have the balls to ask it?

"How much?" said Susan Magrino simply.

"Exactly," said Applegate, as if to a star pupil. "Stephen?"

It was where J. P. Morgan had always come in.

Stephen Carruthers fished in his pocket. He pulled out what looked like an old and slightly grubby envelope.

"At the end of the last quarter, and excluding income and capital-gains taxes incurred in the last two months, approximately . . . two billion, seven hundred and fifty-five million, six hundred and sixty-six thousand, fifty dollars and thirteen cents," he said.

44

"**W**HAT WOULD you do, Rickey, if you were really, really rich?" said Tari. She lay back and allowed the sand to sift through her fingers.

"Spend my life lying here on this beach with you," said Rickey.

Tari kicked out at his leg in mock irritation.

"No, seriously."

"I am rich," said Rickey, with a laugh.

"No, but I mean megarich. You know . . . billions," said Tari.

"Thinking while you sunbathe is bad for the brain," said Rickey. "Oh, I don't know. I guess I'd buy a few houses, the most beautiful sailboat in the world, go lots of places, irritate lots of people. And I'd set up a foundation."

"You would? Set up a foundation?"

"Yeah, sure. I wouldn't want a guilt trip."

Tari sat up, digging both elbows into the floury white sand. She looked out to the sandbar. Two Bahamians were skin-diving for sponges over the reef. Their boat was bright green and very small against the dark blue of the Gulf Stream. A billion dollars to them would be without meaning. Perhaps it was to her, too, and to Rickey.

"What would you do, Tari?"

But Tari had drifted away from him. The islands in the stream were softening her mind, and a new obsession, Rickey, was making her old ones fade. She was wide-open now to a world of the senses that she had never before experienced. Her body was, at last, an equal to her mind. Lust warred with her love of God, as the present battled convincingly with her so-recent past.

What had it all been about? What had it meant? She knew she had not been crazy, but she was beginning to wonder if she had ever been holy. What had been the nature of the conviction that she was God's daughter? A delusion? Part of an illness? Or had it been merely an overvalued idea, one that had taken on a life of its own at a period of intense religious experience? She was adopted. She had no father. Was it not understandable that she had claimed God to fill the human void? Nuns were the daughters of God. Her creed talked of God, the Father. Had he not sired the world? Wasn't that what Christians believed, including the ones who had judged her mad? "Our Father, which art in Heaven." That was what Professor Hodges said when she knelt in prayer on Sundays. Did she not believe it? If so, why would she so faithfully repeat it?

Ah, yes, but people had biological fathers, too, that would be their point. Sperm, eggs, and the zygotes they formed were the real religion in the medical schools of the Western world. But in the beginning there had been nothing. Something had formed in the primordial soup, in the sea out there in which the spongers sponged. So God was at the beginning of the chain of biological science. Was it really so very ridiculous to believe that one was the daughter of God? It began to slip into perspective. An overvalued idea. You were allowed those in psychiatry. They fell short of delusions, of disease, but nonetheless they were a little hard for others to take. Those that exhibited them ended up as seers and charismatics, as saints and swamis. In their single-mindedness, they created faith in others, and they drew followers to them . . . the fainthearted, the lost, and those whose purpose and whose hope had gone. But they also created enemies among the pedestrians of life. People conspired against them because they were the foes of mediocrity and because they gave the lie to the necessity for the lives of quiet desperation that so many led. That had been her fate. It was her fate now. Although here, on the beach in Bimini, beneath the coconut palms and the casuarina trees, with the most desirable man in the world, it seemed that fate had been kind, not cruel.

"Hey, billionairess, where did you go? Come back here." Rickey's voice cut into her thoughts.

"Oh, yes. What? Oh, my spending plans." Tari had started this. She should finish it. But she didn't want to play anymore. She wanted to empty her mind, and allow the sun to bleach out the confusion. Maybe Rickey was right. Beaches and brain work together were bad for your health. "First, I'd have to go back home, and clear up the mess. I guess billions would help there. Money always seems to in America, doesn't it?"

Rickey thought so, too, but he wasn't happy with the "going home" bit. He was winning her. Minute by minute, and hour by hour, he was creeping into her heart. He could see it happen. She was filling up with him. At some crucial point, sometime soon, there would be no turning back for her. He would hold her heart. He would have her forever. But it was not yet. Still, she had other longings.

Tari paused, choosing her words. "Before, to publish *All for Love* was everything. I thought that if that was done, there wouldn't need to be anything else. The words would do the rest. People would pass it on, one to another, because it was the truth, the perfect sense that everyone tries and fails to make of life. Now, I wonder if that's enough. It needs to be sold. Everything in America does. It needs to be publicized and advertised, explained and emphasized. For it to work, for love to have a chance, everyone must know about it. So, with my billions, I would circulate my book. I'd give it away. I'd translate it into every language on the planet. There wouldn't be one remote village, one tiny town anywhere, in which people weren't exposed to it. I'd use my money to give the gift of God's word, because I believe the book is from him. It is inspired by him. It was given by him." Her voice was ringing with enthusiasm now. With every sentence, her tone gained in conviction as she painted the picture of a future in which Rickey could see no place for himself.

"And I would set up a mighty foundation and do something wonderful that the government won't do, like finding the cure for AIDS. I'd work every second to make the billions grow so that they could do more good and bring more happiness than any fortune has ever done before. And I'd get Marcus to help me . . . and . . ." Tari clapped her hands in delighted enthusiasm as she turned to him to share it.

But Rickey wasn't sharing it. One word had poleaxed him. Marcus. He was still there. The rival. The opposite. The hero of the part of Tari he couldn't touch. Douglas was the coauthor of *All for Love*. He was an integral part of this strange future about which Tari still dreamed. During the last few days, catching sailfish off Cuba, swimming amid schools of porpoises in the wide-open ocean, grilling grouper on the beach to the distant sounds of a reggae band . . . Marcus Douglas had seemed to have gone from Tari's mind. In his place, Rickey had crept into it. But, like a dormant virus, he lived on. When, eventually, they returned, who would Tari choose? Would it come to that? Would she go with the part of her heart that Rickey held—the sensual, fun-loving young girl part that was interested in babies and families and a life of excitement and joy at the high end of normality? Or would she listen to the heart half that Marcus still ruled—the Tari of immortal longings and undiluted love of humanity, who would cast aside all thought of her own happiness in exchange for a deeper, less immediate satisfaction? As he lay there beneath the burning sun, Rickey knew that sometime soon that decision would be made. He didn't know how it would be decided. And he was sure that Tari didn't either.

Tari watched the gloom of his thoughts, and she knew them, because she shared them. She was sorry for the pain they caused this man who had brought her freedom, a second chance, and so very much happiness. She rolled over on the sand toward him so that her body was next to his, and she kissed him.

"Let's go into Bimini," she said. "Let's go find some restaurant, go see the Hemingway museum, and look at some people."

He smiled at her, thankful for her warmth during his moment of doubt. "Sure we can," he said. "We need fuel. We can tie up at the Big Game Club. It'd be fun."

"Great!" said Tari. "I want to get a T-shirt. Something to prove all this isn't just a beautiful dream."

But as she spoke, she had a funny feeling that a dream was what all this was.

45

THEY WALKED hand in hand down the main
street of North Bimini, past the clapboard houses
with their peeling multicolors, past poor bars,
billiard halls, and sparse shops. Some sold cameras and things
that ships needed, but only to white people from ships. There
were smells of grilled conch, and the hot air was stained with
salt from the sea as they walked along. It was narrow, the street
and the island, and on the harbor side the masts of schooners
rose above the wooden buildings that advertised cheap rooms
for inexpensive people. Everyone smiled here, in the genteel
poverty of the little island that the Bahamas government, for
political reasons, liked to forget. There was a lightness to the
brightness and a care to the casualness that was charming and
apparent.

They stopped in a dark bar, happy to escape the frontal
force of the heat, and they sipped cold beer and watched ice
hockey from the mainland on a crackling TV.

"Somehow, you don't expect the Kings in Bimini," said
Rickey.

Tari was entranced by it all. It was so near, yet so very far away. Two short hours across the stream was Miami, and all the problems in the world. Here was a life of ease and freedom. How would the two be reconciled?

"You want CNN?" said the guy behind the bar. They were his only customers.

"Whatever," said Rickey. The L.A. ice-hockey team was not an altogether welcome intrusion.

The barman flicked the remote.

It was "Headline News." *They* were headline news. It was as simple as that. They watched transfixed. They listened in shock.

"There have been more extraordinary developments in the story of Tarleton Jones, the medical student from Miami who escaped a psychiatric committal order and is thought to be somewhere on a boat in the Caribbean with the movie actor Ricky Cage. Today it was announced that Ms. Jones, who was adopted, is in fact the grandchild of the billionaire Italian industrialist, the count of Lonza, and the daughter of his son, Antonio.

"Lawyers for the Lonza business empire announced this morning that Tarleton Jones is the sole beneficiary of a Lonza family trust valued at nearly three billion dollars. It is highly likely both that Ms. Jones is unaware of her parentage, and also of her sole interest in this vast inheritance. *Fortune* magazine has confirmed that Ms. Jones is America's richest woman, and the world's second-richest, after the queen of England.

"In supposedly unrelated developments today, the Justice Department announced in Washington that they have initiated investigations into the possible violation of Tarleton Jones's civil rights by two professors at the Florida State Medical College who issued a committal order that would have placed Ms. Jones in a psychiatric facility against her will. A spokesman for the Justice Department said that they were reacting to complaints from the American Civil Liberties Union and others, and that a prima facie case existed for referral of the case to a federal grand jury. Such a jury would consider the possibility of indicting the two Florida State Medical College professors.

"At a press conference this morning, Dr. Marcus Douglas, the celebrated psychiatrist and best-selling author, maintained that the Miami doctors were guilty of felonious malpractice in their issuing of the Jones committal order. He said, in extraordinarily outspoken terms for a doctor discussing his colleagues, that the Miami professors had been inspired in their actions by what amounted to criminal intent and by professional jealousies, and that they had acted conspiratorially, unethically, and illegally.

"Mr. Bertram Applegate, a lawyer for the Lonzas, emphasized at the same press conference the vital role of Dr. Douglas in reconciling the Lonza family with their blood relative with whom they had lost all contact. The conference ended when Dr. Douglas, who is also a Roman Catholic priest, became visibly upset and angry when a reporter asked him if he had any romantic interest in Ms. Jones. We will keep you posted on developments in what is clearly a rapidly developing story. . . ."

They looked at each other then. There were too many thoughts and not enough words. What to say first? What to think? What to feel? Tari held onto bits of it. A father. A family found. The billions that less than an hour ago they had laughed about on the beach. The billions that could save the world, but that would tear her apart from the man she loved. And Marcus. Central to it all. Good, honest Marcus, who had learned to love her, and who had become upset and angry when asked of his love. The world turned in the nowhere bar in the nowhere town on the nowhere island where she had been happier than anywhere, anytime, anyhow. A father who was not God, but a man. A father who was not a man, but a billionaire. A celibate priest who loved her. A moody, blue hero, his shoulders slumped beside her, whom she adored.

"Oh, Tari," he said, and she put out her hand to him because she knew that her news could only hurt him.

"Do you think it means I can go back?" she said in a small voice.

"We could have been happy," he said, and she saw the moisture in his eyes.

"God did this," said Tari. It had to be his plan for her. She had thought her work was over, but it was just beginning. He had tested her. Then, he had saved her. Now, he had given her the weapons to fight the war of love.

"Fuck God," said Rickey. His voice was low and explosive. He banged his fist on the flyblown bar. The film over his eyes deepened as he saw the beginnings of the pain that must come.

She touched his arm to comfort him, but already she could feel the bigness of the future settling on her shoulders.

"I have to call Miami," she said gently.

There was a phone in the corner. She reversed the charges to Marcus's clinic. In seconds, he was on the line to her.

"Oh, Tari. Oh, my God, Tari. Where are you? Are you all right?"

"I'm in the islands," she said. Already, a strange calm was descending upon her. "I just saw CNN. I just heard the news. I'm . . . I guess I'm just in shock. Is it true? Is he my father?"

"Yes, he is. Yes, it is. I didn't see the report. It's on every program. There's nothing else on the television or in the papers."

"What's he like?"

"Who?"

"My father."

"Oh, of course. Oh, I don't know. He's okay. He's . . . I mean he's . . . well, he's Italian."

She had to laugh. She was calmer than he. Yet her whole life had changed. But so, perhaps, had Marcus's.

"Does he look like me?"

"Look like you? I don't really know, Tari. I mean . . . yes, I suppose he does. Sort of upper-class Al Pacino, but where are you? I have to be there."

Their priorities were different. Or were they? Was this the very beginning of "them"? Marcus would know how to do all the things that would need to be done. But he was so serious. Even now, at this extraordinary crossroads in her life, she wanted to make fun of him.

"So I'm a billionaire bastard, not the daughter of God," she said.

"I think you can be both, Tari."

She looked around her. The bar was one of ten thousand in

the tropics. It was warm and dirty, and the fan struggled to keep the smoky air on the move. There was the click of ball against billiard ball and the muted hum of island patois as the locals served the collective solitary confinement in paradise. On the bar stool sat Rickey, talking the body language of defeat. On the wall by the telephone was the number of the "constable," for calling when the rum reached fists. It was written big in black marker so that unfocused eyes could read it.

They had said she was mad because God had talked to her; she had climbed on board a boat to Bimini; and now she was the richest woman in America. Who *was* she? Would she ever know? Was that the cross she would bear to her sometime grave? She had been adopted, then God had adopted her. If he had wanted her to be his daughter, then she *was* his daughter. Not to be able to believe that, without an immaculate conception, was a remark about her and the limits of her faith. So maybe Marcus was right. She could be both. To love another with all one's soul was to see the face of God. To love the world with a true, blind love was to be divine. She felt a chill at her back in this humid place. God was working his purpose out. There were wonders to perform.

"Can I come home?" she said.

"I think so. I think by this evening it will be over. Hodges and Shindler are under more pressure than they can take. *All for Love* has begun to run in *Newsday*. They can't keep the copies on the newsstands. The interest is incredible. Every lead writer in the States is on the case. They're unanimous. Nobody who wrote this book could be sick, could be a danger. World has advance orders pushing two million. You can't get through to them on the telephone. I can't begin to tell you what it's like here. It's the money, of course. It shouldn't be, but it is. Everyone thinks it's like a fairy tale. The public is fascinated, and furious. Righteous indignation everywhere. The politicians are desperate to get on the bandwagon. They're talking about it in Congress. If the professors don't rescind the committal, they'll get lynched or jailed, or both. The rest is just beginning."

"What is the rest, Marcus?"

"What you want it to be, Tari."

She heard what he was asking in between the lines.

"I'm here with Rickey," she said.

"I know." Again, the volumes were spoken.

"So I am but a woman," said Tari.

"If I gave up the priesthood, I would be a man," said Marcus.

She paused.

"Marcus, I'm in love with Rickey."

"Yes," he said simply. He had already bled from that wound.

"You can't desert God now. We have so much work to do for him."

"We?"

"Yes, of course. You'll help me, won't you?"

"I don't know that I can . . ."

"If you love me, and I love someone else?"

"So direct, Tari."

"You're asking me to choose."

"I can't ask that."

"But you're asking me in your fashion."

The line hummed in the silence.

"What are you going to do, Tari?"

"I don't know," she said.

46

VERONICA HODGES was funky with fear. She herself could smell it through the extra dose of Chanel No. 5 she had put on to get her through this interview. Beside her, Professor Shindler was doing no better. He looked like a rat who had been denied permission to leave the sinking ship. In their faces, up their nostrils, was the possibility, at the very best, of career ruin. At the worst was an array of fates far worse than death.

At the other end of the table, the two Justice Department lawyers and the brace of FBI agents were formidably polite. It was the sinister politeness of those who knew that they held all the cards.

"I should emphasize," said the lead attorney in his boxlike Brooks Brothers suit and Washington glasses, "that this is a preliminary part of the investigation. I advised that you have your attorneys present, because it is always better to have an attorney present." He laughed a short, braying laugh. "But I would say that, wouldn't I?" he added, to show that he was subhuman. "What I mean," he said, receiving nothing except white panic from the mice to whom he was playing cat, "is that I will not be reading any Miranda rights on this occasion."

The "this occasion" hung in the air like a mushroom cloud.

"As your attorney will have told you, it is for a grand jury to hand down any federal indictment in this case. It is for us to collect facts and to determine whether a grand jury should get to examine them. We are here to find out if there is probable cause that a violation of civil rights occurred. So we ask questions, and we hope we get answers." He paused. "And there may be some things we can say that will help you decide how best you should proceed."

Hodges heard it. So did Shindler. So did their attorney beside them. Dressed up in the jargon of the last sentence was a lifeline . . . the deal. All three leaned forward, hearts beating, underarm apocrine glands pumping on overtime.

They had seen the green shoots that might be the carrot. Now, they battened down for the stick.

"The case hinges on the 'imminent danger' issue. So let me ask you this. What was your evidence . . . notes, tape recordings, affidavits, etc. . . . for the fact that Tarleton Jones was a danger to herself or to others?"

Veronica Hodges thought she was going to faint. There was no evidence of danger. It was as simple as that. Tari had been committed because she had heard voices, had experienced a primary delusion, and maintained she was God's daughter. Therefore she had schizophrenia. Therefore she needed to be treated. When she had refused treatment, it had been forced upon her because it was in her own best interest, and she was a medical student to boot, and because she was difficult, offensive, and the other students worshiped her. Hodges and Shindler had taken a shortcut across Tarleton Jones's civil rights because, basically, they didn't believe in the rights of others. They believed instead in their rights as professors, bosses, and general autocrats of science and technology. Chickens never came home to roost for people like them, because the chickens they bullied never had billions of dollars and powerful, dangerous allies like Dr. Marcus Douglas.

Their attorney spoke. He could see that both his clients were all but beyond speech.

"My clients will rely on the well-established medical defense that they acted in good faith, and that any error of judgment that may have occurred flowed from good-faith motivation and . . ."

The Justice Department attorney cut in.

"May I just say here that we have taken a deposition from a respected psychiatrist who denies that good faith existed. That is putting it mildly. This doctor also maintains that your diagnosis was rubbish. I don't think the 'good-faith' defense is going to obviate the need for a grand jury."

"What is?" said Shindler in a small voice.

"Yes," agreed Hodges, in a smaller one.

"It is not my job to tell you what to do now," said the man from Justice with a cunning half-smile. "We are in the business of investigating whether a crime might have *occurred* . . . in the past. My point is . . . it either did, or it didn't." More stick. The professors prayed for more carrot.

"My personal opinion, however, is that to rescind the committal order at this stage, albeit after the event, might have some influence on what I and my superiors decide with regard to a referral to a grand jury."

"But if we go back on our original decision, if we change our minds about a professional diagnosis professionally made, we would look like . . ." Veronica Hodges tried to get the dread word out. But her mouth wouldn't work.

"Fools," said Shindler by her side.

"Yes," said Hodges.

The attorney's smile was now snare-drum tight.

"Better," he said, "a fool than a felon."

Veronica Hodges swallowed, but there was no saliva to lubricate the motion. Her Adam's apple bobbed like a bottle at sea.

"I am not certain, however, that a simple rescinding of the order would be enough. There would have to be an apology. The consumption of a certain amount of humble pie . . . in public. Yes, I think that's what would be required."

The stocks. In a dunce's cap. Rotten eggs. Bad vegetables. The secret of Veronica Hodges's mediocrity would be on world view at last. The truth that she had tried so hard and for so long to conceal would be revealed. It would be the ultimate humiliation, to which a jail cell might be an acceptable alternative. No, it wouldn't. America wouldn't differentiate between an inmate and an idiot. In the popular wisdom, the one would imply the other. Nobody would see her as having sacrificed herself on the altar of professional principle. She wouldn't be viewed as the woman who would go to jail rather than betray the diagnostic dictates of her mighty intellect. She would be merely another bent doctor doing time in the pen. It was unthinkable. Either way, she lost everything she cared about.

Veronica Hodges stood up. Her attorney looked startled. At the edge of the only deal in town, this was no time to walk. It was the time to sit and pray. He put out his arm to restrain her, but she shook it off.

To forestall her, the attorney spoke quickly.

"I think my clients might be able to agree to something along those lines," he said. Shindler nodded vigorously. He *knew* he was clever. To change his mind wouldn't be the end of his world. A criminal investigation would be.

But Veronica Hodges was thinking about something else. It was all unwinding. The credits were rolling at the end of her movie. She said nothing, but walked quickly to the door.

"Veronica!" said Professor Shindler. Where would his deal be without her? "Where the hell is she going?" he whispered to the attorney by his side.

The eyebrows of the man from Justice were going up. He had sensed victory. Had the buttoned-down shrink got a weak bladder? Whatever. He had a mission. Get the press off the administration's back. Turn this whole Tarleton Jones business into history. Get the doctors to tear up their committal order.

Veronica Hodges closed the door behind her. In front of her, the corridor led to the roof garden. She walked carefully along it, as if she might slide on the nonslip linoleum. Neon glowed in the windowless space, but ahead, through the glass doors, she could see the sun shining in a blue Miami sky. A junior doctor scurried past, his eyes averted. She smiled a bitter, twisted smile. She was an untouchable now. It was as if she had never been. All the struggles, all the snakes and ladders of the journey to the top of her little heap, had been washed away in the scandal that had engulfed her. She was a victim of one central fact, and a tiny part of her recognized that as she pushed through the swing doors and out onto the rooftop sixteen stories above the ground. She had risen to the top of a caring profession, and she had never learned to care. And she didn't care now. With something of a shock, she realized she had never cared less. The pointlessness of it all was strong within her as she remembered a song that she had liked a long time ago: "The evening sun shone lightly on the eyes of Lucy Jordan, as she walked up to the rooftop when the laughter grew too loud." Veronica Hodges strode through the hibiscus, past the bougainvillea and the Areca palms, until she reached the parapet. She didn't mess around. She put one foot on the edge of a flower pot. She stepped up onto the balcony. She took one deep breath, and she jumped.

47

THE SEAPLANE winged in low. Tari looked out of its window. She had never seen Miami so beautiful. The water was emerald milk. The I.M. Pei building was daggered by bright sun. The cruise ships in the cut were great white ladies full of fantasy and fun. She wiped a tear from her eye, and tried to concentrate on the loveliness as they swooped into land. Behind her was Rickey. Before her was Marcus, and her scary, brand-new world. What would her future hold? Not the simple joy of love in the islands. For sure, not that. It would be limos and private planes, meetings and endless lawyers, and the struggle to remain pure in the stinking pile of money.

She took a deep breath. She had to be strong. She couldn't live for herself. How could she love Rickey, have his babies, and become a Hollywood housewife when God needed her for his mission and the world cried out so desperately for care? Yet, she hadn't come to terms with any of it. Her mind was a jigsaw of unplaced thoughts. Sometimes bits seemed to fit. Then it all fell apart again in a mess of unreality. There were only two reference points. Rickey behind her. Marcus in front. Marcus would help her. He would know what to do, and more important, how to think. He loved her, too. And her feelings toward him were so tender because he had been kind and caring, and he had allowed her to be and to become so much. But was gratitude enough? Would like and respect be a firm enough foundation on which to build a future? What were they compared to the feelings she had for Rickey . . . the overpowering lust, the obsession, the power and all the glory of genuine physical love?

"Is your seat belt fastened, Ms. Jones?"

"Oh!" Tari fastened it, absentmindedly. The plane was skimming the water, running parallel to a boat that looked a bit like Rickey's. She felt the pang of longing. She remembered the sad silence of their parting. It had seemed better to make the break clean, for her and for him. So he had returned by sea, and she, later, by Chalks Airline. She had taken the high road, and he the low one. Yet Rickey would be in Miami before her.

Tari sighed. A chapter was over. Professor Hodges had jumped from the sixteenth floor of the hospital. Tari's heart jumped in her chest as she thought about the terrible end of the woman who had persecuted her. What horror of the soul must she have experienced. Tari had never wanted such a revenge, and she was sorry for it, but death was a passage, and God was in control. There was work to do, and little time for regrets. There was no committal order now. Half of it had died with Hodges, and Shindler had hurried to tear up the rest. Marcus had told her on the telephone of the abject and humiliating apology that Shindler had made personally to Tari in her absence. So now she was free. She was free to do all of the good of which she had dreamed. She was free to choose. She was free to deny herself the one chance she had for personal happiness.

There was a bump as the plane landed on the water. It was not unlike a tarmac touchdown landing, but the seaplane slowed faster. In no time, they were pulling up to the landing bay. Tari, tanned and tousled from the islands, disembarked. She felt shaky inside. As her foot touched America, she knew it was not the same place. Had it changed toward her? Or had she changed? One thing was for sure. She was about to find out.

She could see Marcus by the arrivals. Gaunt, bent like a strong tree that had survived many storms, he waited for her. She waved at him before disappearing into the customs shed. The procedure did not take long, and Tari was relieved that her new fame had not yet reached the immigration desk at the seaplane port. Now, she smiled as she approached Marcus. She wondered what she felt about seeing him again. They hugged without speaking, and tight in his arms once again, she knew. She felt safe and warm. She had the feeling that everything would be possible in the shadow of his oak. She stood back, and he did.

"You look magnificent," he said. His voice was heavy with sincerity.

"And you," she said, with less conviction. He looked tired. His eyes, always so deep, seemed further sunken in the face that carried the cares of the world.

"Oh, Tari. Where to begin?" he said.

She smiled. Yes, that was the question.

But already she knew where *he* wanted to begin, and end. With her. With them.

He took her bag, and they walked to the parking lot. She looked for his battered Chevy. A stretch limo was what she found.

"The new world?" she asked wryly as the driver opened the door for her.

"I wanted to have a chance to talk to you in peace before the press conference," he said, almost apologetically. "It'll be a zoo."

They sank into the cushions.

"Tell me about my mother," she said suddenly.

The car pulled out onto the causeway, and he told her, leaving out nothing. He steeled himself against her pain as he talked of Antonio Lonza's rape of Maria Mirabella.

Tari just nodded. She was shell-shocked into near indifference by the pace and magnitude of the events that were unfolding all around her. Body and mind had a safety mechanism to deal with such input overload. They suspended themselves, on hold, in a never-never numbness.

"What a wanted child I must have been," said Tari. The

frisson of self-pity poked through the cotton-candy chaos in her mind.

"You're a very wanted grown-up," said Marcus. He reached out and touched her hand in support, and in something else.

She smiled wryly at him.

"My friends in Rome found out a great deal about her. Your mother was a very special woman," he said. "When I say she was saintly, I'm not exaggerating. She had some of the same kind of feelings that you have . . . a closeness to God, the belief that her child was somehow a part of him."

She turned to him. "Marcus, those feelings I had. They've faded. I mean, in the islands, with Rickey . . ." She saw him wince. She went on. "I don't think I was ill, but I don't think I'm holy, either. I think I had an intense religious experience, and I latched onto what you could call an overvalued idea. It was somewhere in between a false belief and a true belief. Are you allowed those?"

"Tari," he said. "I'm a priest and a psychiatrist. How could I ever believe that things are either black or white? I believe you are very close to God. I think he touched you. A tiny handful of humans throughout history are chosen for that. Mere minds can't grasp it. Mere words can't explain it. I think there have been miracles around you. I believe there were miracles around your mother. It was extraordinary to hear the way that Lonza talked about her. He was a man obsessed with her memory. Your mother wasn't ill. And I know you. You're not sick. You didn't inherit disease from her. But you may have inherited the special interest of God."

"But I want to be normal," said Tari. Her voice was almost plaintive.

"Lonza is your biological father. I don't doubt that," said Marcus.

He shifted uncomfortably in the comfortable seat. Tari wanted to be normal. What did he want? Her. Two things stood between him and his objective, his priesthood and the movie star. The one was just possible to obliterate. But the other?

Tari sensed that the conversation had changed course. The sage, the mystic, the scientist had become the man who needed.

"Don't love me, Marcus."

He looked stricken. His face fell away as she spoke. *I don't love you* was what she had said. *I love Rickey* was what she meant.

She put out her hand and held his. He squeezed it and looked out of the window at the aquamarine sea to hide the tears that filled his eyes.

In silence, he composed himself.

"Have you made your decision?" he said. It was the second time he had asked her that.

She took a deep breath. "I will work with you for the glory of God. We will publish *All for Love* and we will use my money in the way it should be used. You will help me, won't you, Marcus?"

Oh yes, he would. He turned to her. The moisture was still in his eyes, with the hope. He would take second-best for now, because the future always came.

"It will be a lifetime's mission," he said. "A total commitment from both of us," he added, in case she should doubt his meaning.

"I know," she said. She knew. There would be no room for the luxury of personal love. There would be no room for Rickey. For the richest girl in America, there would be only sacrifice, and the secondhand satisfaction of duty done.

"Do we have to do this press conference now?" she said. Lord, make me good, but not yet.

He smiled at her tenderly, aware of what she had just given up. In these next days of her doubts, he would have to be the strength of her conscience.

"There are a thousand journalists at the Inter-Continental," he said. "They've waited all day for you."

"Yes, I understand," she said. She understood the words. "What do I say?"

"What's in your heart, Tari. There's no question you can't answer."

He turned toward her, because she didn't reply.

There was a reason. Tears were streaming down her cheeks.

48

BLOCK away from the Inter-Continental the excitement was tangible. There were extra cops, the traffic was more dense, and on the sidewalks, the passersby seemed energized by the mediafest-to-be. As the limo turned into the hotel driveway, the full extent of the show was apparent. The walkway was rigid with camera crews poised to catch the arrival of the brand-new billionairess with her fairy-tale rags-to-riches story. Journalists jostled, sound men fiddled with boom microphones, and everyone's eyes watched everything in case the moment might be missed. All around the hotel, on fire escapes, at back entrances, there were stakeouts. But the heavy guns were here in front, certain that no one certified sane in America would miss out on the chance to be on TV.

"Shit," said Tari.

"It would be counterproductive for them to kill us. Hang onto that," said Marcus grimly as the first shouts of recognition rose from the sidewalk. Nikon-toting kamikazes ran alongside the limo, blazing flash into its inner gloom, illuminating Tari with cluster bombs of light. The media wave on the sidewalk flowed toward the steps of the hotel's entrance, and splashed into a gauntlet of hatchet-faced anchorettes and carnivorous newshounds. The limo stopped and a wedge-shaped phalanx of hotel security men surged down the steps to break open a passage through the crowd.

"Will you take the Lonza name?" screamed a brittle blond. "Do you feel like an aristocrat?" yelled democracy's voice. "Why did they think you were crazy?" howled a front-line guardian of free speech.

Tari and Marcus were all but picked out of the limo by the security men. They were half-pulled and half-pushed onto the steps and thrust, like Japanese commuters on a train, toward the hotel's entrance. Several hard-nosed, harder-headed journalists touched Tari for luck as she floated past them. She smiled in desperation as she was blown through the entrance and into the marble mausoleum that was the Inter-Continental's lobby. The manager met them there, and the hotel publicity people, a man from the mayor's office, and a local congressman who'd "been there for a drink." There were lawyers from the Lonza trust, muttering advice and compliments, the World PR team, and there was Susan Magrino, wired for sound, and talking to what seemed like several people at once via a mouthpiece-headset combination.

"The ballroom is standing-room-only, I'm afraid," said the manager, pleased as punch. He led them there. The more privileged news teams roamed around the edges of the group. The networks were inside, and CNN, the local station with clout, and the classier foreign crews such as the BBC.

They entered the ballroom by a side entrance. A traditional green baize table was the grass beneath a black forest of microphones. The table was raised on a stage and lit by banks of light that made Tari sweat just to look at them. A howl of welcome rose from the packed ranks of journalists. Tari sat down and sipped at the glass of water with a hand that shook. Beside her, Marcus squeezed her other hand for support. Slowly, conducted by the hotel manager, the noise subsided. He gave a short speech of welcome and laid down some ground rules. Then he picked the *People* magazine journalist to ask the first question.

The bush was not beaten about.

"What does it feel like for a nobody to become the richest woman in America overnight?"

The silence of the grave descended. Pencils hovered over pads. It would be all downhill from this one on.

Tari opened her mouth. "I've never felt like a nobody until now," she said.

What? She clearly hadn't understood the question. Maybe she was weird. The shrinks had thought so not so long ago.

"What I mean," said the *People* guy in what he hoped was a kindly tone, "is that you were poor and now you are incredibly rich . . . with billions. How does that feel?"

Tari wanted to tell the truth. The truth was that it didn't feel like anything. If she had felt numb before, she now felt paralyzed. Her brain was a bag of cotton balls. She was acutely aware, however, that to say that she felt like a cotton ball was not the answer *People* and America were expecting.

"I guess you could say I'm in shock. But it's not just the money. I mean, learning about my blood family, and the problems with the doctors, and . . . and . . ."

Marcus's fingers were tight on her arm.

"But the billions," persisted the *People* man. "I mean, that is an almost *incredible* amount of money. If you won't tell us how you feel about it, could you tell us what you are going to do with it?"

Ah, that was easy.

"God will spend it," said Tari.

The murmur of shock rumbled through the hall. God spend it? Billions of dollars? She didn't mean it. She was far crazier than anyone had dared to suspect. Where were the doctors? Wasn't that Douglas by her side? Why didn't he do something?

Tari looked around in desperation. She had never dreamed it would be like this. And this was just the beginning. It was the first hour of the rest of her life. The horror broke over her, pushing through the numbness from the edges. She was suddenly drenched in it, bathed in a mental perspiration that smelled like the flesh of a rotting corpse.

"Now that you're rich, are you going to dump Rickey Cage?" yelled someone from the back.

Tari stood up. She turned to Marcus, and she said, quite simply, "I'm sorry."

She turned to her right, pushed back her chair, and half-walked, half-ran from the room.

49

RICKEY LAY on the dirty floor. The room spun around him. He looked up at the window. It was getting dark. He reached for the bottle of scotch. He put it to his lips and tried to sit up. It sloshed onto his chest, leaving a damp patch on his dirty vest. It was evening. He'd been drinking since way before daybreak. He'd sailed from Bimini in the muggy dawn, and by the time he had reached Miami, he had been loaded on cold beer. Now, he was on a different level of high, but still the pain hadn't gone away.

Around him, the paintings watched the artist. It was his soul, this room. The real Rickey lived here. The real Rickey would die here. His mind was muddled with a patchwork of ideas, sorrows, and might-have-beens. What did it add up to? The answers were as slippery and elusive as the scotch. He tried to keep the room still. He tried to focus on the painting on the easel. That was the heart of the matter. There was Tari.

It was all Tari. She'd come to him on the plane that time, light years ago, and his life had exploded into a nothingness that was everything. He smiled at the notion. Nothing being everything. Ha! Ha! But it was kinda true. He crawled to the stairs and looked down them. They were spinning like everything else, but they held the memories. Tari and him, locked in love, down there at the bottom and up here at the top where he was. He rolled over and stared at the ceiling. Getting up was going to be a problem. He was almost too drunk to stand. At least there were some things he knew.

Where was she now, this girl he loved? High up on the cash cloud. Back with her priest-shrink. Way out of his reach. He got hold of the scotch. He wrapped his teeth around the neck tight, like a dog getting a good grip on a bone. *Yeah, get away now, fucking drink. Got you.* He swallowed hard. No escape for the scotch. Married to that, for sure, if not married to Tari.

Tari! Oh, Tari. The name stuck in his heart. The knife twisted there. He wanted her. He wanted to marry her, and he'd gotten so close. He had felt her come so near to him and then, in one moment, before a flickering TV in a hellhole bar, he had lost her. He had been touched by her love. *So* strongly. It had flowed from her to him. It had lit him up. Fairy lights around his heart. He could feel the warm glow of it now, drunk on the floor. He banged his hand on the bare boards until it hurt. He twisted his head from side to side, and then he banged that, too, in the frustration and agony of the loss.

Once again, the easel picture caught his gaze. That was where it had gone wrong. That was the moment the beauty had begun to unravel. There was the problem. He lay still. He took a deep breath. Then he hauled himself into a sitting position. He got up, crouching, and stumbled sideways. But he didn't fall. Upright, he circled the room, his arms out for balance. It had to go. It all had to go. It had to be cleaned. He had to be cleaned. He was dirty and unworthy of her. He always had been. He was the star, but what was a star, a grain of sand on the beach. She was the heavens. She was heaven. The can of turpentine was against the wall. He staggered toward it. He picked it up, hooking his forefinger through the loop of metal. Now he sloshed it around. It pooled on the floor as it should. It dripped from the paintings when he threw it over those, as it should again. It was doing everything right, this fuel of destruction. No mistakes now. Not ever again.

There was a lighter over there. Always had been. He got it.

The can swung from his right hand. The Bic sat in his left one. Flame and fuel. On the one hand, this. On the other, that.

He stood in front of his masterpiece. He loved her, and he remembered her. He remembered her body, bit by glorious bit of it, and he remembered her whole. He remembered the woman who had taught him how to love. The tears came then. Wild and free, they burst from him, because somehow he knew it was some sort of end. He swung his right arm up and threw the turpentine at the painting. It ran in rivulets down the canvas. It soaked the acrylic. It pooled on Tari's face, the hard rain that would fall.

He flicked on the lighter and lit the painting. He stood back as flame flared. The heat was instant. He took a step back. Then he knelt down and he lit the floor. It ran away from him, orange tongues darting to new places, until the boards of the studio danced to the music of fire. He sobbed as he saw it. His whole life was burning. He had set himself on fire, because he couldn't have the woman he wanted.

The flames were all around him. He backed through them, wiping tears from his eyes. He retreated from the blaze toward the stairs, stumbling, off-balance. His foot caught on the top step, and he fell, grabbing the rail with his right hand and dropping the can of fuel. Down he went, into the narrow space, his limbs flailing. There was no pain, no fear. He heard the noise his body made as his nostrils flared around the smell of the flames. *Bump. Bump. Bump.* He went down to the bottom, and black clouds of smoke wafted down the stairway toward him. There he was, at the foot of the stairs, a crumpled, anesthetized heap of a former person. The noise of his fall had stopped. His arm was bent beneath him. It wouldn't work when he tried to use it as a prop to help him stand. He could feel himself slipping away from consciousness. It was the breathing that was the problem, and not being able to get up and open the door and walk out into the street. But it wasn't a problem. It was no problem. It was called dying, and everyone did it. He let himself go. He relaxed into it, but even at the end there was only sorrow.

"When you hear the wind in the trees and see the sunlight on the water . . . please believe it will be me."

50

ARI RAN down the street, scattering the cats and the drunks. The early-evening sky was already full of smoke from the burning building. She knew whose it was, even before her eyes could tell her for sure. She ran faster, kicking off her shoes, oblivious to the broken glass and the nails and the nastier things that lived on the warm asphalt. *Oh, dear God in heaven, this is the true meaning of prayer.* Her mind was focused in so tight it hurt. There was only one thing in her head. One word. One name. *Rickey. Save him, God. God, save him.* Her legs wobbled with the effort. Her lungs heaved in the battle for breath. Fifty feet, forty, less. She was almost there. But orange tongues of flame licked from the burning window. Thick black smoke belched from it. The sky was alive with sparks. The crackling fury of the fire was the soundtrack to tragedy.

She stopped at the so-well-remembered door. There was one last prayer. One last answered prayer. It was open. A dense cloud of smoke and heat billowed out at her. She looked away, coughing, as she forced herself into the darkness. *Hold your breath. Don't get dead. Shit, be useful, Tari.*

She tried to see in the gloom, but the smoke was in her eyes with the tears.

"Rickey," she screamed. "Rickey, where are you?"

Only the fire answered. It roared above her. Spears of heat lanced down the stairs, poking at her face. Then she felt something against her foot. She knelt down, below the smoke, and she found him. She crept up his body to his head, fighting back the panic in her heart. She put her hand to his neck and felt the pulse. His heart was beating. Dear God, he was alive. She took hold of both his legs and pulled. But he was caught. She pulled harder, then harder still as adrenaline pumped into her blood. At last, he moved. He was coming with her. He bumped down the final three steps, and she heard his head bang on the floor as he cleared the last one. Then, they were in the street, safe from the flames, but what damage done?

She cradled his head in her arms. His chest rose and fell.

"Oh, Rickey. Oh, Rickey, what have I done to you?" she sobbed.

He stirred in her arms. He opened his eyes and tried to focus them.

"Tari? Tari?" It was the bemused, faraway voice of a man who could trust no more, not his senses, not the world, not anything.

"Rickey. Darling, Rickey, it's me," she said.

His smile answered her. "Hello," he said.

He was out of it. She could smell the drink on his breath. He had inhaled smoke, and his arm dangled uselessly by his side. He was probably concussed from the fall, but now he said her name softly, repeating it like a caress.

"Tari. Tari. You came back."

"Yes. Yes, I did. I did, darling," she said, and the tears of relief came now because she would not leave again. She squeezed him tight to her, although it was the wrong thing to do, and she leaned her tear-stained face over his and covered him with kisses.

Round about them, the drunks circled, muttering in the twilight. A siren sounded a few blocks away. Doors in the street that God had forgotten and now remembered carried the silhouettes of broken people—too timid and too suspicious to offer the help they had never received.

"I was going to die in there," he said. His voice broke on the words. "I rescued you. You rescued me."

"Oh, Rickey." The love welled up inside Tari . . . love for a man, for a mortal, for this so very flawed and so very wonderful human in her arms.

"Will you marry me, Rickey?" she said.

"That was my line," he said, sober now in the shock of his brand-new birth.

"Will you? Will you?" Tari half-shook and half-squeezed him in her arms.

"Yes," he murmured. And their tears mingled on the South Beach street, as the fire burned, and their love flared brighter than the fire, on this, the first moment of their future together.